...ick lives in a cott... ...vale of Belvoir in Nottinghamshire with her husband and their three dogs. Her first novel, *The Wild Hunt*, won a Betty Trask Award and *To Defy a King* won the RNA's 2011 Historical Novel Prize. She was also shortlisted for the Romantic Novelists' Award in 1998 for *The Champion*, in 2001 for *Lords of the White Castle*, in 2002 for *The Winter Mantle* and in 2003 for *The Falcons of Montabard*. Her sixteenth novel, *The Scarlet Lion*, was nominated by Richard Lee, founder of the Historical Novel Society, as one of the top ten historical novels of the last decade. She often lectures at conferences and historical venues, has been consulted for television documentaries, and is a member of the Royal Historical Society.

For more details on Elizabeth Chadwick and her books, visit www.elizabethchadwick.com, follow her on Twitter, read her blogs or chat to her on Facebook.

🐦 @chadwickauthor
📘 ElizabethChadwick

THE
IRISH
PRINCESS

ELIZABETH
CHADWICK

sphere

SPHERE

First published in Great Britain in 2019 by Sphere

This paperback edition published by Sphere in 2020

1 3 5 7 9 10 8 6 4 2

A CIP catalogue record for this book is available from the British Library.

ISBN 978-0-7515-6501-0

Typeset in BT Baskerville by Palimpsest Book Production Ltd,
Falkirk, Stirlingshire
Printed and bound in Great Britain by Clays Ltd, Elcograf S.p.A.

Papers used by Sphere are from well-managed forests
and other responsible sources.

MIX
Paper from
responsible sources
FSC
www.fsc.org   FSC® C104740

Sphere
An imprint of
Little, Brown Book Group
Carmelite House
50 Victoria Embankment
London
EC4Y 0DZ

An Hachette UK Company
www.hachette.co.uk

www.littlebrown.co.uk

Great Britain

0   50   100   150 Miles

0   50   100   150   200 Kms

N

SCOTLAND

North Sea

Atlantic Ocean

IRELAND

Irish Sea

Trim ●
Dublin ●
Dunamase ●
Leinster
Kilkenny ●
Fearns ●
Waterford ●   ● Wexford

Dun Domhnail Head

WALES

Cardigan ●
Haverford ●
Hubberston ●
Pembroke ●

Goodrich ●
Tintern ●
Striguil ●
● Bristol

ENGLAND

● London

Dover ●

Southampton ●

English Channel

A Cast of Characters
(in order of appearance in the novel)

The Irish
Diarmait MacMurchada – King of Leinster
Enna – Diarmait's son, Aoife's half-brother
Domnall – Diarmait's son, Aoife's half-brother
Ainne – Aoife's nurse
Aoife – Diarmait's daughter
Maurice Regan – Diarmait's bard and interpreter
Môr – Diarmait's wife, Aoife's mother
Connor – Diarmait's son, Aoife's full brother
Lorcan, Archbishop of Dublin – Môr's brother and Aoife's uncle
Bronagh – a woman of Môr's chamber
Lugh – Diarmait's messenger
Ruari ua Connor – High King of Ireland
Deirdre – Aoife's serving maid
Tiernan ua Ruari – provincial king of Bréifne and Diarmait's
  deadly enemy. Does not appear in the novel but has a strong
  off-stage impact

The Normans
Richard de Clare – Earl of Striguil (and formerly of Pembroke)
Basilia de Clare – Richard's sister
Isabelle de Clare née Beaumont – Richard's mother
Alard – a groom/messenger
Hervey de Montmorency – Richard's maternal uncle

Rohese – Richard's mistress (existed but name unknown to history)

Matilda de Clare – Richard and Rohese's daughter

Simon – Richard's squire

Aline de Clare – Richard and Rohese's daughter

Robert FitzHarding – a wealthy Bristol merchant with his fingers in many pies

Raymond FitzWilliam (le Gros) of Carew – one of Richard's household knights and son of William FitzGerald lord of Carew, Constable of Pembroke

Henry, Abbot of Tintern Abbey – a former soldier and now a monk

Robert FitzStephen – a Cambro-Norman knight and adventurer, related to Raymond of Carew and the lord Rhys ap Gruffydd

Richard de la Roche – an adventuring knight of Flemish extraction living near Haverford, South Wales

Maurice of Prendergast – knight adventurer

Maurice FitzGerald – a Flemish Knight

Robert de Quency – Richard de Clare's standard bearer, later married to Richard's daughter Matilda

William Ferrand – a leper knight

Alice of Abergavenny – possibly did not exist, but detailed in one chronicle as a soldier's woman

Gervase – Hervey's squire

Nicolas – Richard's scribe and chaplain

Miles Cogan – knight adventurer

Philip of Prendergast – Maurice's son

Father Nicholas – a common soldiers' chaplain

Meilyr FitzHenry – knight adventurer and grandson of Henry I down an illegitimate line

Isabelle de Clare – Richard and Aoife's daughter

Hugh de Lacy – Richard's ally and rival (but not enemy) in terms of influence over Irish territory

William FitzMaurice – husband to Richard's daughter Aline

Gilbert de Clare – Richard and Aoife's son

Osbert de Horlotera, Master de Genermes, Master de Bendignes and Master le Poer – King Henry's investigative officers

The Welsh
The lord Rhys ap Gruffydd – ruler of Deheubarth, South Wales

Owen – the lord Rhys's son (existed but name unknown to history)

The Angevin Court
Henry II – King of England, Duke of Normandy, Count of Anjou and Aquitaine (in right of his wife Alienor of Aquitaine)

Empress Matilda – Henry II's mother

Rosamund de Clifford – Henry II's mistress

Princess Matilda – King Henry's daughter

Alienor of Aquitaine – Queen of England and Duchess of Aquitaine

Henry the Young King – Henry II's heir, crowned to secure the succession during his father's lifetime

John FitzJohn and William Marshal – knights and servants of the Angevin court

The Hiberno-Norse
Ragnall – leader and warrior

Asculev – leader and warrior

A Quick Word on Pronunciation

The pronunciation of Irish names and places can be problematical for readers not versed in the beautiful Irish language, so I have taken the decision, after much pondering, to render most of the names in a way that will flow smoothly for readers unfamiliar with Irish. Thus Conchobar, for example, is rendered as Connor, and Debforghaill as Derval. Aoife I have left as it is – her name should be pronounced 'Eefa'. Diarmait is pronounced 'Dear-mid'. His queen Môr is as the name suggests with the 'o' as in 'mob'. Tiernan ua Ruari should be pronounced 'Tear-nan O'Roo-ri'. Places mostly have their modern spellings and names, although modern-day Chepstow is referred to as Striguil, the name it was known as in the twelfth century when Richard was Earl of Striguil. It is pronounced with a 'g' as in 'garden' – 'Strig-eel'.

Prologue

At dawn the women came to tell Diarmait his new wife had borne a daughter.

He grunted at the news for he had been hoping for another son to grow tall and strong and join the spears in his warband – although sons, like spears, could be dangerous. He knew how to handle both, but he was always watchful, never off his guard.

The youths were eyeing him now as they sat round the fire, drinking bowls of foamy fresh milk. He sensed their relief at the birth of a girl. Môr, their stepmother, was united in lawful Christian wedlock with him, but their mothers had been hand-fasted in the old way, and their own legitimacy was tenuous.

Diarmait studied them with knowing amusement and wiped milk from his beard. His two bear cubs. Enna and Domnall. Sturdy, strong lads of fourteen and eleven who, God willing, would make fine warriors and cleave to each other as he and his own brother had not. Love your kin to their very bones, but never trust them.

He turned to the women. 'Bring me the child, I would see her.'

They curtseyed and hurried away.

'Well now.' Diarmait fixed his sons with a piercing stare, his voice harsh from a lifetime of bellowing commands and forcing others to his will. 'You have a new sister to protect. See that you do for it is your duty, even as it is your duty to bind yourself to each other and to me.'

1

'It shall be so, father, I swear it.' Enna met Diarmait's gaze squarely with his clear, light eyes, and Domnall swiftly followed his brother's lead.

'You shall so promise in church before all when she is baptised.'

'What will you name her?' Enna asked.

'I will know when I see her.' Môr had been chattering of names for weeks now, but most of it had swept clean through his ears because she changed her mind more often than he drank horns of wine at a feast.

The women returned, Môr's own former nurse Ainne cradling a bundle of blue blanket. The sounds emerging from the folds reminded Diarmait of a little crow. Babies were women's business. He had no interest except as proof of his virility, but still, the rituals must be observed and the child acknowledged. Although she had seen her mother's eyes first, he would be her imprint, and she would belong to him for life.

He received the baby from Ainne and parted the blanket with his callused forefinger to look at her and make sure she was whole and perfect. Ten fingers, ten toes. A fluffy crown of dark hair. So tiny a scrap to hold a beating heart. She continued to snuffle and squeak as he rose and carried her from the smoky hall and stood on the threshold to examine her in the light of the rising sun.

Falling suddenly silent, she gazed into his eyes and his breathing snagged, for he saw in her a fathomless wisdom that knew everything he had forgotten. She was so small and delicate, so intricate and fine. Knowing he could crush her skull with one squeeze of his fist made him feel raw and vulnerable. He found himself smiling foolishly into her solemn little face, while a glow of protective love expanded his chest.

'Well then, daughter,' he rumbled softly, 'what shall we name you?'

He watched the sun broach the horizon and hem the sky with gold. He was forty-two years old, battle-scarred, cynical, ruthless,

Palace of Fearns, Leinster, Ireland, spring 1152

but in this moment, holding his newborn daughter, he felt half that age – as though through her, he had drunk from a chalice of hope and renewal. His eyes prickled with the power of his emotions; and now he knew her name. Tenderly folding the blanket around her, he kissed her forehead. 'Aoife,' he said. 'I name you Aoife.' For it meant both radiance and beauty, and he could think of nothing more fitting.

Pembroke Castle, South Wales, November 1154

The messenger arrived at noon when everyone was eating in the great hall. Already the light was fading as low rain clouds swept in from the Irish Sea, veiling the castle in a dull grey mizzle.

Richard de Clare, Earl of Pembroke and Striguil, listened with dull resignation to his mother and his sister Basilia discussing the cost of the candles, how many were left in the stores and what they could afford to order. Most of their funds were spent on maintaining the fabric and defences of their castles. What remained had to be husbanded against an uncertain future. There had been peace for a year now, but it was fragile.

In Richard's childhood before the war, money had mattered less, but now it dominated his thoughts. He was twenty-four years old. His father had died when he was eighteen and the entire burden of an embattled earldom had landed on his shoulders, catapulting him from a youth under tutelage straight into manhood. It was like being hurled against a wall. He had picked himself up, stunned, disbelieving, but knowing there was no one else, and had set out to honour his father's memory and to survive.

He knew and trusted every man sitting at this table eating his bread, drinking his wine and keeping warm at his hearth. Their clothes, their weapons, their wages. It was his responsibility to provide and provide well. To fail would be shameful, but it was often a struggle.

He dipped his spoon into the mutton pottage – a basic staple of the season, although the cooks had added pepper and cumin to make it more appetising. His hand was halfway to his mouth when he saw his usher escorting a mud-spattered messenger towards the dais – Alard, a groom from Striguil, who often carried news.

Alard stumbled as he reached the dais and folded to his knees, white with exhaustion. 'Sire, King Stephen is dead – at Faversham of a belly gripe four days ago.'

The words stayed on the surface of Richard's mind; if he let them sink in they would have to be true and their recent stability would be torn asunder again. He did not ask Alard to repeat the news. Once was enough. Once was too much. And four days ago meant everything had changed while he dwelt here unaware, enclosed in the sea-mist at Pembroke.

He dismissed the exhausted messenger, telling him to eat and find a bed for the night, and pushed his bowl aside, his appetite destroyed.

'Dead,' his mother said with a sniff. 'He made a folly of his rule and now he cannot even end his life successfully.' She too had stopped eating, but her jaw moved from side to side, chewing on what they had just heard. 'What will this mean for us?' She turned a gimlet stare on Richard, clearly expecting him to have an answer.

He didn't have one. He hadn't bargained on this. After fifteen years of battling over the English throne with his cousin Matilda, King Stephen had made peace last year with her upstart son, Henry. It had been agreed that the crown would pass to Henry on Stephen's death. For those who had fought staunchly to uphold Stephen's rule and been rewarded for it – in his father's case with an earldom – the future was suddenly precarious. Richard suspected Henry would not be open-handed.

'I do not know, mother, save that we should prepare ourselves and husband our resources. Henry FitzEmpress has a bold reputation, but who knows what he will decide to do?' He recovered his bowl and forced himself to begin eating again to restore a semblance of normality. Henry would be king, and all they could do was stand firm and face whatever came at them.

He had met Henry FitzEmpress during the peace negotiations last year, but it had not been cordial. Henry saw him as someone to be put in his place, preferably with a foot over his neck. They were of a similar age, but Richard was slightly older and a full handspan taller; Henry had disliked having to look up at him.

'The new King is in Normandy. He will have to cross the Narrow Sea first and then come to Westminster.' Richard grimaced. He had been intending to spend Christmas at Pembroke, but this changed everything.

'You must make sure our castles are fully provisioned and garrisoned,' his mother said. 'Recruit men if you must.'

He answered her with silence. She had little idea of the harsh truths beyond their domain. She wanted to believe they were more powerful than they were and commanded their own destiny. She would belabour Richard with tales of what a great man his father had been and how Richard must live up to his reputation, but it was easier said than accomplished and his father's death had polished a reputation not always as bright in life. What also lay in the silence between them was that kings could give, and kings could take away. She was afraid, and so was he.

'We will come through this,' his uncle Hervey intervened in his rich, soothing voice, ever the peacemaker. 'We can do nothing until we know more. It is fruitful to plan, but wasteful to worry.' He picked up his spoon and deliberately attended to his mutton pottage.

Richard gave his uncle a grateful if slightly wry look. Hervey frequently peddled such wisdoms. He meant them sincerely even if they were sometimes trite or obvious, and Richard appreciated his calming influence in the household, especially where his mother was concerned. 'Yes, uncle,' he said. 'A timely reminder for us all.'

* * *

Later Richard climbed to the battlements, but the sea-mist was as thick as wool and he could barely see a handspan beyond his face. It seemed like a reflection of his future. If he put his hand into the fog, it would disappear, and if he followed it, he might disappear too.

'Richard?'

He turned at a gentle touch on his arm and faced his mistress. Two years ago, he had given Rohese refuge when her husband, a minor knight owing him service, had died in a skirmish with the Welsh. Matters had developed from there and they had become lovers. Five months ago, she had borne him a daughter, Matilda.

'You are troubled, my love.' Her breath was fine vapour twirling into the fog.

'I cannot see my way forward,' he said bleakly.

'Will it make such a big difference, having Henry FitzEmpress as king?'

'I fear so. I was hoping Stephen would live a while longer, but you should never put your trust in kings.' He leaned against the hard, grey stone and sighed. 'When I was a boy, I saw some enemy soldiers trapped in a castle ditch and slaughtered because there was no escape. Even though they meant me harm, I pitied them and I knew from that moment I never wanted to be the one in the ditch. And now I find myself scrabbling up the sides, trapped.'

She slipped her arm around his waist inside his cloak. 'Come within and I will give you hot wine and rub your feet. It is pointless standing out in the cold, and there is nothing to see until this fog has cleared.'

Making an effort, he turned to her and seeing the anxiety in her soft hazel eyes managed a smile for her sake. 'Where would I be without your wisdom and common sense?'

'Lost in the mist?' She kissed him, and he tasted the cold of her lips and the warmth of her mouth.

'You do not know how close to the truth you are,' he said and followed her down the steps through the biting grains of frozen cloud to his private chamber in the room above the hall. The central hearth sent out welcome streamers of charcoal heat and his face and hands began to tingle. A cradle stood near the fur-piled box bed, and he went to gaze at his daughter. She was awake, but content, cooing and gurgling to herself. He leaned over to chuck her under the chin and thanked God for such gifts in trying times.

2

Castle of Striguil, Welsh Marches, July 1155

Eight months later, waking in his bed at Striguil, Richard folded his hands behind his head and looked at the early sunlight spilling through the open shutters. He had ridden in from Worcester yesterday evening with bats flitting in the twilight and a sickle moon rising over the Wye. He had been exhausted, but grim determination had pushed him on. Whether he had done sufficient through the summer to win the new King's approval he did not know. Henry had seen fit once the crown was on his head to remove the earldom of Pembroke from him and the castle.

At the court gathering in Westminster, Henry had sat in his great chair, one hand cupping his chin, his gaze watchful, and unpitying as a list was read out detailing the castles and lands that were either to be razed or returned to the crown without appeal. Richard was one of many barons thus deprived, including men close to Henry, but it had not lessened the humiliation. At least he knew where he stood. Skewered on the point of a pin and made to dance at the new King's behest. He might still be lord of Striguil, Usk and Goodrich, but Pembroke, his father's pride, was lost, and Richard could not help but feel he had let him down.

His gaze landed on Rohese who was combing her hair in the embrasure, creating silky ripples through the brown waves. She looked up as he spoke her name and her face lit with a smile. Leaving her grooming, she brought him a cup of watered wine. 'You have slept a long time,' she said, joining him on the bed.

He sat up and drank slowly. 'We pushed the horses,' he said. 'We did not set out from Worcester until noon yesterday – after Mortimer surrendered. All the time we were besieging Wigmore and Bridgnorth I was thinking it could have been me had I refused to yield Pembroke. Instead I ran with the pack and brought Hugh Mortimer to bay.' His expression contorted with disgust. 'It was like drinking rich wine to have everyone's friendship and to know I was obeying the King's will, hoping he might restore my earldom, but realising in cold daylight that nothing had changed. Henry FitzEmpress is perhaps the most focused and ruthless man I have ever met.'

'Apart from yourself,' she said with a teasing smile.

He looked at her in astonishment. 'You think that of me?'

She clasped her hands at her knees. 'You focus on your desire like the centre of a target. Perhaps that is why the King wants to keep you in order. He strikes me as a man who dislikes being overshadowed.'

Richard snorted. 'How would I overshadow him? If I rebelled, he would crush me as he has crushed Mortimer. The wounds of the long war are barely scabbed over. It would take little for my enemies to turn on me and tear me to pieces.'

'Then perhaps he sees you as a personal threat. Perhaps he fears your ambition and what you would do if you still had Pembroke – what you might become. Even if you encounter setbacks, you always go forward.'

He sipped the wine and thought about her words. He often felt despair, but he never let it show in his dealings with others. A stoical façade was a means of survival, a refusal to be beaten that he gripped like a man clutching a piece of broken ship and hoping to find a safe shore before he drowned.

'When you want something, you bend all your will to obtaining it.' Changing the mood, she slanted him a provocative look and touched his thigh.

He set his empty cup aside. 'Is that so?' Turning, he cupped her breast through her chemise, feeling the firm, delicious weight under the cloth. 'Perhaps you are right. I am bending all my intention now, and I shall let nothing hinder my way.' He reached to the hem of her garment and pulled it up.

'I am always right,' she responded, laughing. 'You should know that by now.'

In the aftermath of their lovemaking Richard lazed for a while. He knew he should rise and be about his work, but he wanted to savour these moments. Rohese donned her chemise again and left the bed, returning with their thirteen-month-old daughter. Matilda gripped her mother's hand tightly and tottered along, precariously putting one foot in front of the other.

'Walking!' Richard exclaimed with delight. 'And she has grown!' He swung her into his arms and kissed her fluffy curls.

'And talking,' Rohese said proudly. 'She already says "Mama" and "horse" and "bread".'

He cuddled his daughter, enjoying the feel of her small body in his arms. He could be the pragmatic warlord, the impassive courtier and the able administrator, but when he sloughed off his armour, and his cares, the small things mattered the most, and those small things were here, in this chamber. Family, warmth, belonging. 'We are told pride is a sin,' he said, 'but I cannot see it as that when my heart is bursting and my pride is also joy.'

'What would you say if I told you I was with child again?'

He looked at her over the top of their daughter's head.

A blush tinted her cheeks. 'It was the night before you left to campaign with the King.'

A little over three months ago, then. He studied her with fresh appraisal and smiled. 'That is even more good news to fill my heart.' His daughter in one arm, he embraced her with the other. 'When I feel I have nothing, you come to me and give me everything.'

* * *

Five months later, Richard leaned on his elbow and looked down at Rohese lying beside him on the bed. They were fully clothed. She was great with child and they had not made love, but it was enough to have her beside him.

'It will not be long now the midwives say.' She pressed the tip of his nose with her forefinger and smiled. 'Wait until you have a healthy son to dandle in your arms.'

'I am looking forward to it.' He stroked her belly. She wanted so much to bear a son. He wanted it too, although God would dispose as He desired.

'I wish . . .' she said wistfully, and shook her head.

'What do you wish?'

'I will keep it to myself.' She wove her fingers through his. 'I know it cannot come true, but I can dream, and in my dream, I can have my wish.'

He suspected what that dream was, and that it could never be reality.

Beyond the door, Richard's squire Simon cleared his throat loudly. 'Sire, you are sought, your lady mother is here.'

Richard suppressed a groan. 'Tell her I shall be with her soon.' He kissed Rohese's palm. 'I have to go, we will talk later.'

He smiled at her over his shoulder as he opened the door and she blew a kiss to him on her fingers.

'It is time you found a proper wife,' his mother said as they sat by the fire. 'It is all very well having a mistress to sate your appetite, but you cannot raise a dynasty with her.'

Richard eyed his mother. Her features were angular and austere but held a trace of the golden beauty that had captivated King Henry's grandsire whose mistress she had been for a short time, albeit reluctantly in order to win favour for her brothers. His relationship with her was not close. In childhood his sustenance, love and affection had come from his nurse. But his mother always spoke her mind without falsehood or subterfuge and he respected her for it. She was immensely proud and living up to her expectations and often unrealistic standards was a burden.

'I would take Rohese to wife if I could.'

'That is impossible!' She shot him a censorious look. 'She is not of your rank. You have a duty to find a wife of your own status who will bring an illustrious name and fine lands to a marriage.'

'Where will I find such a woman?' he demanded irritably. 'The King blocks me at every turn, and the men with daughters of the rank you crave for me have no desire to pursue an alliance with a man who does not have royal favour.'

'That can be changed. I shall write to my brother at court. The King will listen to him. You must petition others to speak on your behalf. What would your father think to hear you now? He would not allow the King to treat him thus.'

She was like a dog with a bone. Abruptly Richard rose and went to the window. His father. Always his father. Always having to live up to his achievements and reputation. 'Since he died before Henry came to the throne, we will never know,' he said in a flat tone that gave no indication of the volatile emotions boiling inside him. 'I do my best, and if it is not good enough, then it is not.'

She made no reply but he could sense her displeasure.

'I take your advice and I shall put the matter in hand,' he said with controlled courtesy, 'but do not push me. I am not my father. I am my own man and I shall make my own way.'

His mother left three days later, returning to her dower lands in Essex, and Richard sighed with relief. He owed her his filial duty, and somewhere deep within a small boy craved her love and approval, but he kept that part locked away; it was better to leave the scab upon the wound than pick at it.

He was eating in the hall just before noon when Basilia came to tell him that Rohese had begun her labour and all was well.

'Tell her I send my love and hope to rejoice with her soon,' he said.

'Of course.'

His sister's practical disposition was like their mother's. She dwelt with Richard as his chatelaine, running his domestic affairs with smooth efficiency. Familiarity meant he tended to take her for granted, treating her almost as an extension of himself – an extra pair of hands and a quick brain – rather than seeing her in her own light. Given their current standing in the King's eyes, Basilia was unlikely to make a marriage and thus her position was permanent.

Having dined, Richard went to check on the chestnut colt foal belonging to his favourite brood mare. He was two months old with a fuzzy infant coat and long legs out of all proportion with his body. Richard had named him Ajax after the Greek hero and intended to train him as his next warhorse should he prove to have the mettle. Stroking the mare and rubbing the foal's inquisitive nose, he pondered the matter of bloodlines. Mares and stallions, men and women. He was content with Rohese; she made him happy and he loved her. Even if he did eventually marry to further his dynasty, which he doubted given the state of his relations with the King, it would only be lip service.

Pretending to be startled the foal took off, bucking and kicking around the paddock, galloping flat out on his spindly legs. Amused, Richard watched him for a while before returning to his chamber where he sat down to play chess with his uncle Hervey and bide his time until the child was born.

His hand was poised over a knight when the door opened and he looked up to see the midwife, her apron drenched in blood, her expression taut and grim. She did not speak, but wordlessly shook her head.

He jerked to his feet, ice flowing down his spine, and pushed Hervey away as the latter sought to grab his arm. 'Let me see her.' He headed to the door. 'I must see her.'

'Sire, you should not . . .'

Unheeding, he pushed the woman aside and ran up the stairs. The ladies cried out in alarm as he burst into the chamber but he was oblivious as he strode to the bedside. Rohese lay under a blanket but her arms were outside the covers, folded on her breast. Her eyes were closed and her lips slightly parted, as though she slept, but her flesh was the bloodless colour of death. 'Ah no,' he gasped. 'No!' Leaning over her body, he put his lips on hers. They were still warm, still soft. She could not be dead, yet the rise and fall of breath was absent, and her face a slack mask.

Hearing a snuffling sound, he turned his head towards the crib by the fire. Basilia stood beside it, her gaze fixed on him, glassy with unshed tears. 'You have a daughter.' She stooped to pick up a swaddled baby. 'We could not help her. The afterbirth came away too quickly; the midwives could not stop the bleeding. Do not blame them.'

He shook his head, too numb to think of blame, except perhaps on himself for begetting the child on her.

'There is a wet nurse in the village; I have sent for her.'

Richard nodded wordless acknowledgement, grateful for Basilia's practicality. Rohese had been so certain it was a boy. She had wanted to give him a son, and now she was dead. He took his daughter from Basilia and gazed into her puckered little face before gently kissing her brow and placing her upon her mother's silent heart. Unfolding Rohese's arms, he put them around the baby. 'A child should know the touch of its mother,' he said. 'A child should know that it is loved.'

The women sniffled and sobbed but his own eyes were dry. His emotion was bright and intense like hard sunlight. It was his responsibility to do the right thing in this moment. He turned to the women. 'I thank you for all you have done, but I would ask you to leave and give me a few moments alone with my lady.'

Basilia hesitated but then nodded, ushered everyone out and closed the door.

Richard lay down beside Rohese as he had always done when they talked of daily things. Taking her hand, he rubbed his thumb over her ring. 'I loved you like a wife,' he said. 'And I honour you like a wife. I will treasure our daughters and do my best for them.' He paused, his voice threatening to crack. 'I will go on alone but I will miss you and cherish your memory. I will teach our girls about you so they will know through me all that you were.' He raised her hand and kissed it. 'Farewell, my love. God keep you.'

Taking the baby, he left the bed and opened the door. 'Let everything be done for her to the highest standard,' he said to the waiting women. 'She was my lady and you will honour her as such.'

Basilia touched his arm. 'I am sorry. I was fond of her and I know what she was to you.'

Richard thought she did not know at all. No one did. 'I have two daughters to raise now.' He swallowed a surge of grief. 'They are her essence, and I must do my best in her stead.'

A nurse offered to take the baby from him but he shook his head, not ready to relinquish her yet; she was the living spark out of death, and while he held her, he could still feel Rohese beside him.

3

Palace of Fearns, Leinster, Ireland, autumn 1157

Diarmait laughed and swung Aoife in his arms, making her squeal. 'Ah but you are a beauty!' he growled. She wrapped her arms around his neck and hugged him as tightly as she could. 'Sure, and you cling like a little ape! Hah, shall I sell you now to this fine English merchant?'

A green silk ribbon shone in Aoife's peat-dark hair, a gift from Bristol trader Robert FitzHarding with whom Diarmait had bartered timber, marten skins and cow hides in exchange for Gascon wine and chests of weapons that would go a long way to keeping his warband content and eager for the fray.

FitzHarding's ship had been the first to arrive out of Bristol after several weeks of furious storms that had crashed in white thunder along Leinster's coastline, making any sort of landing impossible.

'How much do you want for her?' FitzHarding's shrewd eyes twinkled. His good nature was part of his success, as were his unparalleled bargaining skills. He knew exactly what his customers wanted before they realised it themselves. And those customers were the high nobility of the land. He served earls and bishops and kings. He arranged funds, he brokered loans. No common merchant this. His winter robe was of heavy scarlet cloth trimmed with sable.

'Ah, it would be a price beyond riches,' Diarmait replied. 'For she is my most precious jewel.' He kissed Aoife's cheek and set her down, his heart warm with emotion. He loved his sons but in a different way. Their destiny was to follow him as men and warriors – a visceral thing of the gut and the loins, whereas Aoife had pierced the hidden soft places inside him.

'I can see that is so,' FitzHarding said. 'Every man should be so blessed.'

Diarmait seated the merchant before the hearth with a cup of wine and summoned his interpreter and bard Maurice. Diarmait recognised the advantage of speaking other tongues, and had employed Maurice, fluent in the Norman language, to teach him and to interpret when necessary.

Diarmait refreshed the cups. 'And how is that new king of yours faring?'

'Well indeed,' FitzHarding said. 'We had the news his queen had borne him a third son as I was making ready to leave.'

'A man of mettle then.' Diarmait slanted him a grin.

Aoife leaned against his leg. Gently stroking her dark hair, he made a note that Henry had three sons who would one day marry, and why not to an Irish princess? 'I hope he will remember those who helped him when he had need.'

FitzHarding smiled blandly. 'Indeed, and I have greetings from him to you.' He handed Diarmait a letter, the attached seal hanging from a plaited red cord.

Diarmait took the parchment and with a swift slash of his knife removed both cord and seal and handed them to Aoife.

'Here, daughter,' he said, 'hold tight now, for it is proof of the King's word.'

She nodded to show she understood and smiled coyly at FitzHarding, who chuckled and winked at her.

Diarmait passed the parchment to Maurice Regan. 'Read it to me.'

The letter consisted of felicitations and greetings but was all words and no substance. 'The new King of England could benefit greatly if we were to cooperate together,' Diarmait said, running his tongue over his teeth.

'I am sure he desires to foster good relations,' FitzHarding replied smoothly.

A predator himself, Diarmait recognised other men's ambitions. Henry was also Duke of Normandy, Count of Anjou and Maine, and consort Duke of Aquitaine. Such a man had it within him to swallow the world, never mind Ireland. He thoroughly intended to question FitzHarding further after he had mellowed him with food and several horns of wine.

'How is the lady Derval these days?' FitzHarding asked with a sharp smile.

Diarmait twisted the long end of his beard around his forefinger. FitzHarding's last personal visit had taken place shortly after Diarmait had raided the lands of his enemy and rival Tiernan ua Ruari and carried off his wife, Derval, with all her goods. It had been at Derval's request because she had quarrelled with Tiernan, and Diarmait had been unable to resist the opportunity to rub his rival's pride in the dirt. 'She is well,' he said cautiously, 'although I have not seen her in a while.'

'We heard rumours you were going to make her your queen.'

Diarmait's eyes widened in feigned astonishment. 'Now why would I be doing that when I have a lovely young wife with a fertile womb?' He cast his eyes towards Môr who was sitting at her embroidery with the women. 'You should not listen to rumours, Master FitzHarding. Men always embellish stories.' The gossip did not displease him for it added a certain cachet to the incident, and what was a man if his life did not contain such tales? 'I did the honourable thing and escorted her back to her father's hall as she desired.'

'And the husband?'

'I believe they came to an arrangement.' Diarmait studied his fingernails. 'The lady returned to him, but on her own terms.' He omitted to say that a furious and humiliated Tiernan had savaged his Kildare lands while Diarmait was otherwise occupied and had stolen valuable cattle and plunder. Diarmait preferred to recount his victories not his setbacks. He still considered that abducting Derval had been worth the risk. Tiernan was forever marked as a dishonoured cuckold, to the delight of Diarmait's heart, and it bothered him not one whit that he had made an enemy for life, for one day he intended to be High King of all Ireland.

Aoife knew if she was discovered that she would be grabbed and carried off to join the women and children sitting apart from the men gathered around her father. It always happened, but it had not stopped her; some things were worth the risk and she loved to hear the strong masculine voices as they discussed matters far beyond the hall's threshold.

As the men continued to talk, she had hidden under her father's seat, curled up like a kitten, concealed by the folds of his heavy cloak draped over the back of the chair. She could see his shoes and his dark green trews and she could hear the deep rumble of his voice and the creak as he moved on the seat. There were other shoes and other legs too. Her brother Enna, whose boots were wearing out at the toe where a scuff was almost a hole. Next to her father sat his translator and bard Maurice Regan, one foot tapping the floor as though he was listening to a tune no one else could hear. .

On her father's other side sat their visitor Robert FitzHarding from Bristol, whom her father had been plying with food and wine as the autumn afternoon darkened into evening. His hose fascinated her for they were as red as blood. His shoes were red also, embellished with gold braid and matching laces at the instep. Aoife wished she had shoes like that; she would ask her father for a pair. He could do anything he wanted and she was learning all the different ways to make him focus on her instead of on her little brother Connor. He might be a boy, but he was barely out of babyhood and a nuisance, whereas she was a big girl of five years old.

She watched the feet and listened to the talk, loving the lilt and play of words. She had her father's aptitude for language and beyond her native Irish she regularly imbibed scraps of Latin and the tongue of the Normans from Maurice Regan and from the merchants who visited their court to trade.

'So,' her father said, and she heard the bear-growl of anger in his voice, 'your king would come to Ireland and devour it for himself, claiming it is for the sake of reforming our Church and correcting our heathen ways? Ah, but he would eat the world. Does he not have enough ado governing his own lands without stealing the territory of others?'

Aoife wondered what the world tasted like that someone would want to eat it.

'The Pope has given him a sealed brief to enforce Church reform in Ireland,' FitzHarding replied, 'and has sent him an emerald ring in token of that will.'

'Hah, and since when has the King of England taken such an interest?' her father demanded. 'He is devout because he wants what is here in Ireland, and that is not the religion.' He gave a harsh grunt. 'Well then, when are we to expect him?'

'He has deferred the intention for now,' FitzHarding said. 'As you say, he has other lands to administer, but I give you fair warning he will not put it from his mind.'

Her father's chair squeaked as he shifted his weight. 'I have founded abbeys at Baltinglas, and Cashiel, and I shall build here at Fearns. If the Church requires reform, we can do it ourselves. An English king has no right to meddle.' Aoife heard mutters of assent and nodded her own head too, because her father was always right.

'But what you do not need and what happens are often different things,' said FitzHarding. 'Besides, you are a man who knows how to take advantage of whatever comes his way.'

'And what advantage would that be?'

'You do not need me to tell you that should King Henry come

to Ireland, he will be generous to his allies. Their lands would come under his protection while remaining in their owners' possession, and together, campaigns might be undertaken to the great advantage of both.'

'You also do not need to tell me he would take power for himself,' her father scoffed.

'But with so many other dominions to watch over, that power would be in the hands of another. You are already beholden, even as King of Leinster to the overall High King of all Ireland. You would only be exchanging one for the other and you would be left to your own devices to rule as you chose once Henry departed to his other territories. There would also be the matter of King Henry bringing Dublin into his sphere.'

Aoife heard her father catch his breath. FitzHarding's foot had been swinging to and fro, but that stopped too.

'Well now, that is interesting,' her father said. 'You weave your spell like a bard, and I would hear more of your tales by and by. For now, it costs you nothing to tell me your king has chosen to defer his interest in Ireland. But you warn me it may yet come to pass.'

'Indeed,' FitzHarding said. 'We have interests in common and I thought you should know – friends are always given the first consideration.'

Aoife heard her father laugh the way he did when challenging someone but not yet ready to draw his sword. 'We have no snakes here, but truly, many snakes that walk on two legs greatly desire to make it their home.'

'I agree,' FitzHarding said equably, 'but it is how you deal with the matter that determines whether you survive or not. If you would rather your enemies were bitten by serpents than yourself . . .'

Aoife watched his leg begin to swing again. She disliked the talk of serpents and being bitten and she wrapped the folds of the cloak more closely around her.

'You must always be careful when keeping the company of serpents, even if they swear they will not bite you,' her father said. 'He has sons I hear, and I have a daughter. I will think on your advice.'

Aoife wondered what he meant, but her eyes were heavy and the cloak was warm. The conversation continued in a stream flowing over her head in a constant babble. Her father's rumble, FitzHarding's answers. Occasional exchanges from her brothers. Laughter, and the swinging of the red shoe, forward and back, forward and back . . .

She did not hear the serving maid asking her father where she was, nor was she aware of the increasingly frantic hunt as the search expanded from the hall and people sought in chambers and chests, and then in kennels and midden heaps and down the well.

She was woken by her father trying to tug his cloak off his chair and exclaiming at the weight rolled up in it. Down on his hands and knees, he peered beneath and she met his bright gaze. 'By Saint Bridget, child, what are you doing under there?'

She knuckled her eyes, bewildered and disorientated. He lifted the chair away and picked her up, plucking pieces of floor straw out of her hair. 'Your mother has been worried to death!' He gave her a small, rough shake to emphasise his words. Aoife hid her face against the scratchy softness of his tunic.

'You've found her,' said FitzHarding. 'Thank Christ.'

'Asleep under my chair if you please.' Diarmait chuckled and tilted up her chin. 'Well then, my little spy, what did you learn?'

Aoife ducked her head again. His skin was warmly damp and smelled of smoke. 'I don't want a serpent to bite me,' she said, her voice quavering.

Her father's chest vibrated against her body as he laughed. 'Ah well, we'll see what we can do, my little princess. I don't want a serpent to bite you either! Come, away to your mother now.'

Aoife clung to him for an instant more, but in truth she was eager to return to the women and the safety of her bed and made no protest as she was taken from his arms and fussed over and scolded.

'Let her be,' Diarmait said, his voice gruff, but gentle. 'She was not in danger. Put her to bed and let her sleep.'

While the women were busy with Aoife, he took the opportunity to look at his small son who was sleeping in his crib, his thumb in his mouth.

Aoife drank milk from her own cow-horn cup and squirmed with jealousy as she watched her father touch Connor's head in a tender benediction.

'Did FitzHarding say anything of interest?' Mór enquired.

Diarmait raised his head and shrugged. 'Only that the King of England has an eye to Ireland but lacks the time for now to do more than look at us the way a man looks at a woman's backside as she passes beyond him.' He left the crib and came to put his arm around her and kiss the back of her neck under her braid. 'But that there is scope for matchmaking and courtship in the future.'

'Is that so?'

'Indeed it is. I shall come back later and tell you all.'

Hearing the intimate note in her father's voice, seeing the way he pinched her mother's waist, high up at the side of her breast, Aoife loudly pretended to choke on her milk. Her nurse, Ainne, was immediately at her side, scolding her and patting her back. When she looked up again, her father was eyeing her with knowing amusement. 'Goodnight, my brave and precious girl,' he said, and gave her cheek a whiskery kiss. 'You be good now.'

Aoife watched him leave, and then curled up under the clean linen sheet, fists clutched under her chin.

Her mother sighed and came to stroke her hair. 'Ah my daughter,' she said, drawing the marten fur cover over Aoife's shoulder, 'what shall the world have in store for you?'

Already sinking into slumber, Aoife murmured, 'Red shoes.'

Her mother sat beside her and softly sang a lullaby, about wild seas and how no Norsemen would come while there were storms. On the final edge of consciousness, Aoife heard Ainne muttering she hoped red shoes did not mean the child would walk in blood, and her mother's sharp remonstration.

4

Palace of Fearns, Leinster, Ireland, summer 1159

Concentrating, careful not to spill a drop, Aoife presented the silver chalice of wine to her uncle Lorcan who was visiting their household. Her father had stolen the cup while raiding the Abbey of Kildare in his youth. Everyone knew the tale but no one ever told it in front of her uncle who was Abbot of Glendalough.

Lorcan's dark hair crinkled around his tonsure and his eyes were twinkly blue, surrounded by laughter lines. He was not so much God fearing as God loving, although he could be sombre and serious when the occasion demanded. He took the cup from her gravely just before the wine slopped over the rim, and although he eyed the chalice wryly, he made no comment.

'You are becoming a fine young lady, niece,' he said instead with a smile. 'How old are you now?'

Aoife lifted her chin. 'Nearly eight years old.' Always admit to more, never to less.

'It is a long time since I was that age.' He turned to Môr. 'What of you, sister? Do you remember?'

'I remember you put a mouse in my dinner once.' She widened her eyes at Aoife. 'Can you imagine your uncle doing that? And now he is an abbot?'

Aoife giggled, relieved to laugh and ease the tension that had been growing ever since her father had ridden out with his warband. She had watched the supplies of spears and weapons pile up and the men striding about, their faces taut with purpose and bravado. She did not fully understand what was happening

26

but knew something momentous was afoot. Her mother's smile had developed a fixed quality and she had prayed a lot more than usual.

To keep her uncle's attention, Aoife fetched her willow-wood harp to play to him.

'She has talent beyond her years and an exceptional voice,' Mór said proudly.

Aoife tuned the harp and sang a hymn in praise of the Virgin Mary, each note as pure and clear as glass, while her fingers wove through the strings like a breeze through grass.

'Angelic,' her uncle remarked, wiping his eyes.

'If nothing else, her voice indeed has the quality of angels,' her mother said ruefully.

Lorcan raised his brows. 'She is Diarmait's daughter. No obstacle is too great. She will set her mind to anything – sometimes it is a good thing, but not always. She will break before her determination does.'

A horn sounded outside. Her mother's hound Orca raised his head, a growl vibrating against his collar. The horn sounded again, clearer, stronger, announcing an arrival. But it was sunset, and visitors who warranted the horn would be more than just a couple of weary travellers.

'It's Daidí!' Aoife's heart leaped like a salmon up a waterfall. Abandoning her harp, she sped to the door, reaching it just as a watchman opened it from the other side.

'The King is home!' he announced at the top of his voice. 'Victorious! The King is home!'

Aoife snaked around him and raced into the courtyard. The sky was charcoal, except for a blood-red strip on the horizon, and mounted men were streaming through the gates, spears glittering in the last of the light. Aoife saw her father on his big brown stallion, his hair blowing in the wind. Tied to the horse's breast band by hair and by beard were the heads of enemy warriors. One stared at her balefully. Another had a missing ear and shreds of flesh hanging down from his torn cheekbone. The stallion's shoulders were darkly streaked with blood.

Aoife stared, transfixed and horrified, but fascinated too because her father was up on that horse above all the gore and smiling with his teeth bared. Enna and Domnall too bore trophies on their harnesses.

A horse swung towards her and their heads bobbed together, rubbing foreheads, mingling hair. The pungent stench of decaying flesh filled her lungs as she inhaled. And then her uncle Lorcan arrived, blocking the sight, sweeping her round to hide her face in his robe. 'This is no place for you,' he said grimly, and pulled her back towards the hall. She wriggled in his grip, but he held her tightly. 'Quiet, child. Your father is home and victorious. Go and make ready to receive him, like a good woman of the household.'

At the door, he handed Aoife to Ainne with a warning look. The nurse grabbed her firmly by the arm and marched her away to the women's quarters. At first Aoife struggled to escape but Ainne's grasp was strong, and although Aoife fought for form's sake, she was glad to be away from the courtyard and what she had seen even though she would still have run to her father with an open heart, braving her fear.

The chamber ladies fussed around her mother, helping her don her best gown of violet wool and threading her hair with gold ribbons.

'Why did Papa have all those heads on his harness?' Aoife asked.

'Because he has won a huge victory against his enemies,' her mother replied. 'That is what you do to your enemies. Your father is a great man, second only to the High King, and you are a princess.'

Aoife absorbed the words and wondered what would happen if her father's enemies came to find her. Would they cut off her head and hang it from a saddle? 'What will happen to the heads?'

Her mother swept her cloak around her shoulders. 'It is for your father to decide and none of our business. Come, put on your best dress to welcome him home – quickly now.'

By the time Aoife entered the hall, food had been provided for the warriors, although it was mostly stew, it being too late to prepare a feast. The casks of Rouen wine had been broached though as well as the mead. Men toasted each other with brimming horns. Her father had exchanged his armour for a scarlet tunic and a gold circlet at his brow and presided over the gathering in his great chair.

'Ah, here's my best girl, my princess!' Diarmait seized her from Ainne and, setting her on his knee, gave her a drink from his ivory horn. She took too big a gulp and spluttered, making him roar with laughter. The drink tasted of spices, so she knew it was a special occasion. Her father's tunic smelled of herbs from the clothing chest mingled with the harsh aroma of male sweat. His arms were hard and his eyes still bright from battle.

'What do you think?' he said. 'Your papa is a mighty king and we have won a great battle!' He thumped the table. 'No one shall stand against us!'

Aoife looked round the hall, beyond the cheering men, and saw the heads thrust on spears around the edge. She pressed her face into her father's tunic.

'You don't like our visitors at the feast?'

She shook her head and felt his chest rumble with amusement.

'Ah well, they will soon be gone; they are here to bear witness. Your uncle says it is ungodly and we must abide by what the Church tells us.' He flicked his gaze to Lorcan. 'I have promised I will build an abbey here in recompense and your uncle may bury the dead as he desires.' He lifted her from his knee and returned her to Ainne. 'Go now, child, and remember they cannot harm you while I am here to protect you.'

* * *

That night Aoife dreamed of the heads staring at her in bed, jaws wagging as they spoke. But how could that be when they had been cut off from their voices? She woke gasping with terror, but stifled the sound lest they heard her, for they still had their ears. She rolled over, burying her face in the mattress. Her bladder was full and she considered wetting the bed rather than leaving it, but knew after the initial hot rush her chemise would be cold and sodden and she would be punished.

Trembling, she left the warm security of her blankets and made her way to the pot where everyone pissed at night. The door was open a crack and as she squatted she stared at it, imagining what might appear round the edge from the other world. She shut her eyes tightly and gripped her hair in her fists, pulling until the pain became greater than her terror.

From her mother's chamber, she heard a fast, rhythmic grunting and soft whimpers in counterpoint. She knew her father was in there mating with her mother like the bull in the field with the cows. Sometimes he did it with the slave women too with no more thought and in less time than gulping his wine and wiping his mouth.

Leaving the pot, Aoife tip-toed into the hall, a resolute little ghost in her pale chemise. The only way to defeat her fears was to face them and to have a greater courage than their ability to scare her.

Snoring men strewed the hall, curled in their cloaks upon rough straw mattresses. Her father's chair was empty, although his horn stood on its ebony stand, glinting in the lights still burning so that men could find their way to piss.

In the deep shadows edging the hall the heads stood sentinel on their spears and she almost lost her bravery and ran back to bed. But hadn't her father cut off their heads to destroy his enemies? They could not harm her. They were only like the heads of the slaughtered pigs and cows she saw in the kitchens every day.

She approached the one closest to the light and made herself look at it. The eyes were dull glints, the skin grey, the neck edged with a ragged purple hem. A dirty blond moustache concealed the lips, and as a fly crawled near the mouth, she heard words in her head.

A sound made her whirl round with a stifled scream, but then she realised it was only one of her uncle Lorcan's servants crossing the hall towards the store room, a linen bundle tucked under his arm. Curious, eager to escape the gruesome stares of the dead, she followed him, barefoot and light as a doe.

The store-room barrels and supplies had been moved to make room for several straw mattresses occupied by wounded warriors. Her uncle Lorcan was kneeling beside one man, and as she arrived, he gently closed the spearman's eyes and anointed his forehead with the sign of the cross. Glancing up, he met her stare and immediately rose to his feet, his pale robe matted with red-brown stains.

'Child, what are you doing here?'

'I woke up,' Aoife said. 'The heads were talking to me.'

The shadows in the doorway darkened as her father arrived. He wore a loose shirt, a sheepskin cloak thrown over it, and his legs were bare. 'What did they say?' he demanded, picking her up. Lorcan made a sound and Diarmait quelled him with a look. 'What did they say, my precious girl?'

He smelled of wine and sweat, of bedclothes and her mother. 'That they were going to eat me.'

'Well, and how would they do that without stomachs?' he asked, chuckling.

'But they have teeth, and tongues. They said they will wait for you, and all you have will burn.'

'Hah,' he said harshly. 'Then they will wait for eternity.'

Despite his bold words she felt him shudder. He turned with her in his arms to face the room. 'These are my brave warriors, wounded in battle. They could not come to the feast but they shall be toasted at my board when they are recovered and I shall honour them and bury with grief those who die. There is always a price to pay, daughter, remember that, but if you are willing to pay, then it is worth the sacrifice and never to be regretted.'

Aoife wondered if consequences were the same as paying a price, and what one might receive in return.

5

Castle of Striguil, Welsh Marches, summer 1164

From across the room, Richard watched his daughters at their needlework and was tenderly proud of their diligence even while a pang tugged his heart. He wished Rohese could be with him and share this moment.

He still visited the mound of her grave at St Mary's in the town grown over with grass, and he spoke of her often to their daughters.

He joined them, feeling that in lieu of their mother he should offer them praise, even if it was not a man's place to do so and he was not qualified to pass comment on stitches. Basilia cared for them but she was not a parent, nor especially maternal, even though she was kind to her nieces.

Aline had sewn a tiny fox into the corner of her work with accomplished skill.

'I was hearing that the fox had got into the hen coop again,' he said. 'Perhaps if you trap him in your canvas it will be a charm to make him go away before we have no hens left.'

Aline wrinkled her nose at him. 'You have hair like a fox, Papa,' she said. 'I thought of you when I was sewing.'

'And white teeth,' Matilda added, not to be outdone.

Richard bared them at her. 'And shall I eat you both like a pair of chickens?'

'If you are a fox, then we are foxes too,' Matilda replied with inarguable logic.

Richard chuckled. 'There you have me.'

Watching them sew, his wistful longing for Rohese dissolved into something gentler and time-faded. In the years since her loss he had continued to serve the King with stoical diligence but with little to show in terms of reward. Henry still kept him at arm's length – indifferent in general but with undertones of suspicion. He refused to entrust him with a senior command in the constant struggle against the Welsh and although he had relatives in high position at court, Richard was never summoned to witness charters. He courted patience and told himself he was biding his time, but often thought he was wasting it. He was not part of the golden clique and he was never going to infiltrate that area around the King. He had castles and lands. He had the duties of a lord, but it was like eating bread without salt.

Simon, his squire, poked his head around the chamber door. 'Sire, Raymond FitzWilliam of Carew has arrived.'

Richard acknowledged the message and rose to his feet.

Basilia looked up from her own sewing. 'His father's the King's constable at Pembroke, isn't he?'

'Yes,' Richard said, 'but I have no quarrel with William of Carew. His son will be a useful addition to the household. I was impressed by his potential when I saw him on campaign last year and that is why I offered to take him on. New blood keeps us fresh.'

Raymond FitzWilliam of Carew had earned the sobriquet Raymond le Gros because of his stoutness, but his bulk owed more to solid muscle than to fat. Richard, tall and wiry, looked as lithe as a squire against the young knight's massive frame. Raymond's size was further emphasised by his heavy mail shirt, worn not because he was taking precautions against attack, but to display the excellent state of his equipment to advantage. The squire, two men at arms and three bowmen who had accompanied him were spruced up too. The tack was clean, the horses and remounts glossy and well shod. A tan hound of middling size with a curly tail and a large white badge of hair across his chest sat attentively at his side.

'Welcome.' Richard clasped his hand. 'I have been expecting you. You come well presented.'

'Knowing your reputation, it would be an insult to show myself otherwise, sire,' Raymond replied. His curly hair was so fair as to be almost flaxen; his short beard a slightly darker shade of wiry gold. He had a high, straight nose, thin as a blade, and granite-grey eyes.

Richard smiled. 'A man's reputation is as important as the armour upon his back and the sword at his hip.'

'Indeed, sire.'

'You can stow your weapons in the armoury. They will be safe there. My grooms will see to your horses.'

Richard took his new knight to the armoury, the dog trotting beside them, and pushed the door wide on a room stacked with bundles of spears, helms, hauberks and shields. There were casks of iron bars for horseshoes. Bow staves of ash and yew. Barrels of arrows and bolts. The component parts of siege engines, marked for quick assembly. 'Much has been here since the war between King Stephen and the Empress,' Richard said, wandering between the stacks. Their finances had gone into keeping their castles in good repair, ready for siege and sortie. Before leaving Pembroke, he had swept the armoury bare. Every last sheaf of arrows, every bowstring and horseshoe nail had come to Striguil. He still had a stockpile but had sold plenty to Robert FitzHarding. The latter had taken the weapons gladly and offered to buy more. 'There is a lucrative market for such goods in Ireland.'

Raymond said, 'Unless a man is at war, he can only use so many spears and arrows. A stockpile is prudent but a surplus must bring profits.'

Richard nodded his approval. Here was someone who could think inside what he saw rather than just observing the surface. 'We receive regular commissions from FitzHarding in Bristol to supply Ireland. Spears mostly, and axes. Their princes and petty kings are constantly warring with each other and battling for the high ground.' He halted before two hooks in the wall supporting a magnificent bow of Spanish yew.

'Sire, is that . . . ?'

Richard smiled. 'My father's bow?' He lifted the weapon down. An elongated carved stag ran along the top curve and the notches resembled dogs with open mouths. Richard took a waxed string from a shelf and bracing the bow against his leg, strung it and tested the tension. Grabbing a fistful of arrows from a barrel and tucking them in his belt, he went outside to a grassy area in front of the great hall where a wooden pole had been set in the ground with a compact ball of straw shaped like a head. 'My father could use this bow tirelessly,' he said. 'He trained every day and he would strike the head every time. He said it kept him anchored in the world when our lives were spinning in the wind.'

'And you, sire?' Raymond asked.

Richard flashed him a savage grin. 'You think I need anchoring to the world?'

Raymond flushed. 'I wondered how much you practised, I meant no insult.'

Sometimes the ambiguous questions were the pertinent ones, Richard thought. 'My feet are firmly anchored, messire, but it does not mean I lack ambition.' He ran his hand along the bow stave until he came to the mid-arch of the deer's spine. 'The bow must be used often to keep its shape. So that it remembers my hand and who I am, and thus I remember also.' Facing the target, positioning his feet, he nocked an arrow, drew his arm back in a straight line and loosed in a fluid, relaxed motion. The arrow punched the centre of the 'head' between the eyes. With barely a hesitation he planted the second and third arrows beside the first.

His squire hurried to retrieve the shafts and had to tug with all his might to draw them free. Richard presented the bow to Raymond. 'See what you can do.'

Raymond wiped his hands on his tunic and pulled the bowstring back to his ear. A look of surprise crossed his face as he encountered the resistance, and Richard's lips curved in a knowing smile.

The lad handed an arrow to Raymond. The young knight positioned his arm and made a credible effort to keep it straight and his aim true. The first shot bounced off the pole, as did the second. The third lodged in the top of the head in the area of the temple.

'A good effort.' Richard clapped Raymond's shoulder. 'The skill lies in the strength of the hand and the stance. All must be smooth and relaxed, and your eye must focus on the point and guide it to the heart of your target.'

Raymond's eyes brightened at the words, absorbing wisdom, acknowledging the challenge. 'Indeed, sire. I hope to learn and prove worthy.'

Richard shot again several times, his aim unerring. Raymond shot too with increased success and although unable to match Richard's precision, he was determined rather than daunted.

Leaving the armoury, Richard took him to the hall and the young man gazed round, assessing everything with a soldier's eye, looking for weak spots, estimating booty.

Basilia entered, talking to the steward, indicating where extra trestles were to be set out for the midday meal.

'Sister.' Richard beckoned her over. 'This is Raymond FitzWilliam of Carew who will be joining our household. Messire, this is my honoured sister and chatelaine, the lady Basilia.'

Basilia inclined her head. 'You are welcome, messire,' she said with impersonal courtesy. Her glance swept over him and down to the dog at his heels and she raised an eyebrow.

'Thank you, my lady.' Raymond bowed. 'This is Badge.'

Hearing his name, the dog wagged his tail and looked up at his master.

'He is welcome too,' she responded. 'Providing he knows his place and his manners.'

'I can assure you we both do.'

'Then all is well.'

Their eyes met in brief, mutual assessment before Basilia excused herself and returned to her business.

'My sister cares for my domestic chamber and has duties elsewhere in the household,' Richard said. 'She consults with me and orders our provisions and supplies.' He gave Raymond a pointed look. 'I will elaborate on what she said to you. I expect you to extend civility to every woman under this roof. All receive my protection whether family or servants. Let your men know this. There are ladies who will launder their clothes and provide other services at their discretion – my guards will tell you who they are.'

'I will make sure it is known, sire.'

'Good, then we know where we stand. Simon will show you to your sleeping quarters and we shall talk more later.'

The following day Robert FitzHarding arrived from Bristol with supplies for the castle and loaded up for the return journey with fleeces from the recent sheep-shearing.

Richard sat with the merchant in the shade of the wall overlooking the moorings at the foot of the rock watching the last of the barrels being winched up the cliff side. FitzHarding was perspiring freely in the airless heat and had removed his hat to wipe his glistening forehead. Richard had known him since childhood and the merchant had barely changed in thirty years, save that his once thick brown hair was now white and sparse. He was well past sixty with competent sons, but still kept a keen eye on business, and occasionally travelled with the cargo in person to talk to his customers. He was affable, hard and shrewd.

'How is the trade with Ireland these days?' Richard enquired.

FitzHarding shrugged. 'Relatively calm, but it will not remain thus. The Irish lords are forever quarrelling. So many small kings and each one wants more than he has and they are all inter-related or else tied by foster kinship. They make alliances and swear on them for ever – and "for ever" lasts as long as it takes to draw an axe from a belt or hurl a spear. Speaking of which, I will take as many spears as you can make and whatever else you have. Diarmait of Leinster has asked me.'

'I have heard the Irish do not use bits on their bridles and ride without stirrups?' Richard said curiously.

FitzHarding leaned back and folded his arms. 'Aye, and it is a sight to behold for they can turn their horses on a penny and be in and out in a flash.'

'But could they withstand a Norman charge in full mail with lances?'

FitzHarding shook his head. 'Many of their warriors come to the fray in nothing but leather jerkins and bare-legged, but do not underestimate them. They are swift and fierce and even if they do break and run, they will return and fight another day, or they will come upon you at night. They will spill your brains with an axe or wind your entrails round a spear before cutting off your head. The tales they tell around the fire of their heroes are but exaggerations of the truth. No, they could not withstand such a charge, but never think for a moment that you have won, for in that moment you are dead.'

The nape of Richard's neck tingled for FitzHarding's expression was sombre. 'Does the King still plan to go to Ireland?'

The elderly merchant rubbed his chin. 'You have to imagine he has a shelf for his plans and there are numerous rolls of them stacked to the ceiling. He never throws any away and he never forgets. Even if some gather dust, he still knows where they are; he is merely biding his time.'

6

Palace of Fearns, Leinster, Ireland, summer 1166

Aoife sat upright on a stool while her mother stood behind her with a comb. 'They say if you wash your hair in the water of a certain well in Armagh, it never turns grey,' Môr said as she worked on her daughter's tresses, 'but no one ever seems to find it. That is a pity since I have grey in mine now, but yours is like dark water under the stars.'

Aoife preened, proud of her hair – thick and glossy, and almost long enough to sit upon.

Môr expertly created six plaits, twining them with red silk ribbons and weighting them with crystal beads. 'You are swiftly becoming a woman. Soon enough you will marry and have sons and daughters of your own.'

Aoife's first bleed had happened six months before at winter's end. Her breasts had started to bud and her hips to curve. The women often talked to her of marriage but she had no wish to leave her family, especially her father, and she had seen no man she wanted, even the handsomest and bravest in his warband. Her blood might stir with feelings that made her hot and unsettled, but she would recall the rutting she had observed in dark corners and remember the heavy grunts from her parents' great bed, and it made her want to run away. She knew she must wed as her father dictated, but she would deal with it when the time came, and that time was not now.

'Daidí needs that well too,' she said to distract her mother, 'because all of his hair is grey.'

'And no surprise,' Môr said, and compressed her lips.

Hearing the worry in her mother's voice, Aoife shivered. Her father was away on campaign, defending their territory. MacGloghlan the High King of Ireland had died during a recent skirmish and his rival Ruari ua Connor was making a bid to claim the position for himself. To that end he was busy either annexing or destroying all of MacGloghlan's supporters, including her father who fell into the latter category. Diarmait had appealed to the families sworn to defend him, but few had answered his summons for help. No one had come to him at Fearns and he had ridden out to gather support in person.

Aoife could taste the fear in the air. 'He will be all right,' she said fiercely, almost angrily, to her mother. At the back of her mind lurked the image of the heads on spears standing around their hall. She still dreamed of them, and sometimes they belonged to her own family. Once she had seen her own head spiked there and had woken with blood between her thighs and a cold full moon streaming through the open shutters onto her bed.

The braiding finished, Aoife fetched her harp and sat to play while the other women took up their sewing and weaving. Her twelve-year-old brother Connor was rolling about with his adolescent hound pup, tickling the dog's pale tummy, laughing at his ungainly antics. Supposedly he was the heir because he was the only son born in lawful wedlock, but it remained to be seen how much influence the Church truly had when the time came to decide. Aoife loved him, but she was resentful, for she was the firstborn of that lawful marriage and but for her gender would have been her father's heir.

Joining her voice to the resonance of the harp she sang of heroes – warriors with jewelled armour and shields bossed in silver, and one named Rochad with auburn hair and a white-toothed smile who led a great force of invincible spearmen.

Pausing between songs, she heard the hoofbeats. Her mother raised her head, her needle poised between stitches. Orca started to bark. Aoife left her harp and flew to open the door in time to see her father arrive at a gallop. Even before his sweating stallion had slewed to a stop, he had dismounted, stumbling as he landed. Behind him the rest of the warband milled into the courtyard and Aoife saw the riderless horses, the gaps in the ranks, and the bloody wounds, although Domnall and Enna were at her father's side, whole but grim.

Others ran out behind her; Bronagh, a woman from her mother's chamber, saw her son's mount on a leading rein and began to scream and tear her hair. Diarmait took a single stride forward and felled her with a resounding blow. 'Silence, woman! There is no time for your bawling. Too many have fallen in battle and Ruari ua Connor is upon us. We must leave!'

He yelled orders and the troops dismounted and scattered to do his bidding. Bronagh lay where she had fallen. Sick with fear, Aoife made no effort to help her because it would show weakness and disobedience to her father. Instead, she hurried into the hall, to the high table, filled his horn to the brim with wine and brought it out to him.

He snatched it from her and downed the contents in a few swift gulps and wiped his mouth and dripping beard. 'You're a good girl, Aoife.'

His praise steadied her. 'What do you want me to do?'

'Go to your mother. Gather together everything of value and bring it to the courtyard. Hurry, we have no time.'

He turned from her as Domnall arrived with a spade and a crowbar and they entered the hall and began breaking up the hard-packed earth around one of the supporting pillars. Enna and Maurice Regan were doing the same at the fire, prising up the hearth stones. Seeing them wildly digging, seeing everyone packing and in frantic motion, Aoife realised that this was real and they were in dire trouble.

Bronagh had risen to her knees, blood dripping from her split lip onto her gown. Aoife dragged her to her feet and pulled her into the hall, intent on her father's bidding. 'Quickly,' she said. 'You can mourn later.'

At the hearth, she met Enna's stunned blue gaze. A narrow cut striped his cheek and blood caked his fingernails. 'We were caught and slaughtered like rats,' he said roughly. 'Abandoned by our so-called allies – they will not stand against Ruari ua Connor and Tiernan ua Ruari. And now they are coming to Fearns.'

She swallowed. 'Where will we go?'

'The abbey, to the protection of the Church.'

Aoife tugged Bronagh to Môr's chamber and handed her to Ainne. On the surface she was determined and pragmatic. Her father had given her a task and she would perform it to the best of her ability. But inside she was terrified; inside she was just like Bronagh.

Her mother was sorting through a chest but paused to give Aoife a hard embrace. 'Oh, my daughter,' she said. Hearing the fear in her voice, Aoife pushed herself out of Môr's arms. 'Daidí says we have to gather all the valuables together and bring them to the courtyard.' Practicality was her anchor. Being active meant not being helpless. It meant not having to think that her father had failed and could not protect them.

She used the cover from her bed to bundle up her clothes, calling upon the other women to do the same. Looking dazed, her mother turned back to the chest and stuffed its contents into a sheet. Aoife grabbed the box containing her jewels and combs. She emptied the textile cupboards of the precious cloths and linens, forcing herself to be swift but not frantic.

Back and forth to the baggage animals she ran, packing the bigger items in panniers but keeping her jewel box in her own satchel because she trusted no one. She saddled her dun pony, her fingers nimble, a frown of concentration on her face. Amid the stomach-churning fear and the effort to remain calm, she was aware of a dark thread of exhilaration, a stirring response to a battle where her back was to the wall but she was facing her enemies with a dagger in her hand to cut out their hearts.

Connor arrived to saddle his mount. He was white-faced and swallowing. 'What if they take us away and turn us into slaves?'

Aoife tossed her head. 'They won't do that, Daidí won't allow them to.'

'But what if he can't stop them? What if they kill him?'

Terror burned up inside Aoife again and she swallowed sour bile. Her father often related the story of how the Norse had murdered his own father when he was just five years old and had buried him with a dog to show their contempt. 'They won't,' she said defiantly. 'We shall survive. Don't be a baby.'

Connor flashed her a furious look, hating her to belittle him. 'You know nothing,' he scoffed. 'You're just a girl.'

Before she could answer, he had leaped across his pony's back and smacked its rump, sending it skittering out of the stable. Aoife shouted an insult in his wake and turned to put her harp behind the saddle in its leather bag.

Returning to the hall, she found her father piling straw, powdered wood and flammable fungus shreds against the pillars where he had dug out their treasure. His face was streaked with blood and soil and his hands were filthy. He looked like an old madman.

'Daidí?' She dared to touch his arm.

Wild-eyed, he shook her off. His other hand gripped a torch soaked in pine pitch and he leaned to the fire pit and kindled a flame. 'I may have to bow my head to Ruari ua Connor, but I will burn this hall to the ground before I let him set foot inside it,' he said hoarsely. 'If I cannot sit in my great chair and pass judgement on men and feast my warriors, no man shall. I give Fearns to the ashes.' He squeezed his eyes tightly shut for an instant and when he opened them again, his lashes were wet. 'Go, my precious girl, this is no place for you, but I swear on this hearth I now destroy that I will rebuild anew, watered by the blood of my foes. I shall trample them all and they shall pay. I swear this by God's holy mother and the crone of the Morrighan.'

Aoife clenched her fists and remained rooted to the spot although he had told her to leave. He thrust the torch into the kindling, and as the smoke swirled and the flames licked, he drew his sleeve across his eyes. 'A blessing on this house, and a curse on anyone who stands on this ground lest they be of my own flesh and blood,' he swore. He took the precious ceramic oil lamps Robert FitzHarding had brought from Bristol and smashed them on the floor. Aoife watched the flames lick lasciviously up a timber support and embrace the carved, coiled snake at the apex with tongues of fire, giving the serpent a semblance of life even as it was devoured. Her eyes stung and she started to cough. Her own father was destroying her home; her security, her existence for fourteen years. She felt shock and terror; she felt anger on the edge of rage, and still that awful sense of exhilaration flickered through her veins.

Her father drew her from the hall to their waiting mounts, and above their heads, flying above the smoke, Aoife saw the three crows of the Morrighan, lady of war, taker of men. She shivered, feeling the weight of destiny close around them. Grabbing her pony's reins, she leaped across his back, lithe as a youth and full of defiance. Her father mounted his sweating stallion and she saw tears rolling down his face into his matted beard. He had said their enemies would pay for what they had done, and she vowed it too, but turned her own grief inwards, like cutting herself with a knife.

All that night the palace burned, a red glow against the sky visible from the abbey, and the stench of smoke was thick on the wind. The ordinary folk had fled their homes and taken refuge either in the abbey precincts or further out in the countryside. The church was crammed with people praying to the Virgin, begging for her help and mercy in their hour of need, their pleas mingled with the wails of the bereaved and the groans of the wounded.

The women alternated between prayer and tending to the battle-savaged men. Aoife worked stoically beside her mother, protecting herself behind a hard façade and showing nothing to the world. The men had gone into a huddle to discuss the situation, but she wasn't allowed near them and she was too big to hide under a chair these days.

The sun moved in the sky from dawn to noon without a sign of the High King and his men, but they knew he would come and the waiting was dread. Towards late afternoon, Aoife and the other women climbed the abbey's high stone tower and sat in the top chamber by the window to keep watch.

Her uncle Lorcan joined them briefly from his ministrations and had a swift smile and reassurance for Aoife. 'There now, child. You are safe here. I will not let anything happen to you.'

These days her uncle was the Archbishop of Dublin and possessed a forceful spiritual power and political presence, but he still had a twinkle in his eye for her. A safe boat on stormy seas. 'I am not worried,' she said, lifting her chin. It wasn't true.

'So how are we to emerge from this bind?' her mother demanded. 'Where do we go from here?'

'When the High King arrives, acknowledge him as such, and submit to his will.' Lorcan took her hands in his. 'Honour him and give tribute and then he will be soothed. It is important you do this, sister. You know how to comport yourself. Your husband, if he has any wit about him, will act as he must for the good of all.'

Môr clasped her hands together. 'But will it be enough?'

'I am the Archbishop of Dublin.' Lorcan drew himself up. 'The new High King desires my cooperation and goodwill and that means I can intercede from a position of strength. Trust in God and all will be well.'

Her expression still full of anxiety, Môr gave him a bulging leather sack containing many of their treasures including the silver chalice from Kildare. 'I am giving you custody of our wealth,' she said. 'I ask you to keep it safe for us. The chalice is yours.'

He hesitated, and then, setting his lips, took the bag. 'It shall be done.'

Aoife's spark of indignation at her mother's bestowal of their treasure only lasted a moment as she realised the wisdom of the deed. Like a squirrel preparing for winter that had to bury nuts in many places to avoid starvation.

Lorcan departed to conceal the sack, his expression one of distaste. Aoife went to look out of the window. To the west she could see the embers glowing against the encroaching sunset and smell the smoke. The fire had devoured all the timber, leaving their home a smouldering skeleton of cracked stones.

Detecting a movement, she narrowed her eyes and realised there were men advancing on the abbey, black as insects in the dying light. Her stomach lurched. 'He's here,' she said, her breath short with tension. 'The High King is here.'

Her mother was instantly beside her, craning to see. The insects came on like ants pouring from a nest, swarming until they were at the abbey gates, and then spread out and began pitching a camp at the perimeter, their long shadows encroaching on the abbey buildings.

Her mother whirled from the window, pulling Aoife with her. 'Quickly. Put on your best gown and comb your hair. To be treated as royalty, we must comport ourselves as such.' Her mother's demeanour was decisive, albeit that her eyes were wild like those of a deer run hard by the hunters.

Aoife hastened to don her best red gown. She fastened her cloak with a gold hound clasp and smoothed her braids.

Môr nodded approval. 'To honour this family – to save this family – you and Connor must be its credit, but do not seek to draw attention to yourselves either. Listen to your uncle Lorcan and let him guide us.' Going to Connor, she tenderly stroked his fair hair before drawing everyone together to kneel and pray to the Virgin Mary for protection and succour.

To Aoife the prayer seemed endless. Pain struck up through her knees, and a gnat bite on her ankle itched intolerably. She forced herself not to unclasp her hands and scratch it. She had no awareness of being bathed in the comfort of a holy presence; all was ordinary and very frightening.

A fist banged on the door and she jumped, suppressing a scream. Her mother rose from her knees and, commanding Ainne to open it, stood straight and regal, with Aoife and Connor behind her.

A warrior stood on the threshold, a red cloak pinned at his shoulder over his short mail shirt. 'Madam, you and your children are summoned to come before the High King,' he said.

Môr gave a cool nod of assent. 'Then we shall do as we are bidden.'

He stepped aside but they had to edge past him, knowing he would follow on behind them. Aoife thought it was like being herded with no means of escape from the slaughter pen.

The stairs were dark for the last of the sun had set in the west. The church, however, blazed with the light of a hundred candles and the nave was crowded with their own people, and the warriors and lords of Ruari ua Connor. Grim-faced men, smelling of sweat and battle, but standing in formal array. A path lay through the middle to the altar steps where the High King sat in the Abbot's chair. Aoife saw the glint of gold on his brow and the fur lining to his heavy cloak. Her father knelt before him, his head bowed in submission, and to Aoife, accustomed to seeing her father all powerful, the shock was like a stone dropping into her stomach. Domnall and Enna were on their knees too, their necks bent.

The High King beckoned them forward and Aoife dropped her gaze and clasped her hands together, making a conscious effort not to clench them into fists. Her mother came into her own now, for she had learned from a young age how to please highborn men and how to serve them while retaining her dignity. She advanced gracefully to the foot of Ruari's chair and made an elegant curtsey, her eyes downcast. Aoife followed her example and stared at the ground because nowhere else was safe. A sidelong glance at Connor showed him in similar pose on their mother's other side.

'We throw ourselves upon your mercy, sire,' Môr said quietly, 'and we acknowledge your greatness.'

Ruari ua Connor stroked his silver beard. 'I am no ogre to women and children,' he replied. He had uneven teeth, crowding his mouth and a solid, rotund belly. 'You are renowned as a refined lady who does not deserve what has been set upon you by others.' He cast a disparaging glance at Diarmait as though he was a slug he was about to squash. 'I do not blame you, or your offspring.'

'You are gracious, sire.'

'Indeed, I am when graciously treated in return.' Rising from the chair, he took Môr's hands between his own and kissed her cheeks before directing her to one side. He swept a sharp glance over Aoife and Connor. Imitating her mother's example, Aoife displayed a meek air that masked anger, defiance and fear. Obeisance performed, she hid behind her mother and waited.

Ruari returned his focus to her father and brothers. 'Thank God's mercy for your life and the land you hold,' he said. 'You will renounce all claims to the kingship and if you rise against me, I will destroy you. I will have hostages from you, including your son Enna. Should you go back on your word, I will blot the sun from his sight, as you yourself have done to so many, and I will bury you with a dog as was done to your father, that I promise!'

Aoife stifled a gasp, her gaze flying to Enna, who was staring grimly at the candles on the high altar. The thought of someone holding Enna down and putting out his beautiful blue eyes was unbearable. The mention of the dog was an unforgiveable and humiliating insult.

'I think we have an understanding,' Ruari said curtly, and her father nodded stiffly in submission, his throat muscles like rock. 'Then I will have your oath on the cross of Christ and before God.'

Her father stood up and placed his hand upon the altar. 'I do so swear by all that is holy that I will keep the peace and never raise my sword or any weapon against Ruari ua Connor, High King of Ireland, Amen.'

'So be it,' Ruari said. 'I call on all to witness your sacred oath.'

King Ruari left after that, his cloak bannering behind him and his warriors tailing his path. Enna and three other male hostages were jostled among them, without time for farewells. The only backward look Enna gave was to Diarmait – steady, knowing, bleak. Aoife could see the anger vibrating through her father like the battle rage of Cúchulainn whose tales were so often sung in the hall at night. One hand still on the altar, he clenched his other into a white-knuckled fist. 'Bury me with a dog, would he?' He spat on the floor and ground the spittle underfoot. 'I vow on my father's bones, I will not rest until my enemies are dirt under my boots, and that is my true word, not an oath taken under duress.' He stamped down the altar steps and glared at her uncle Lorcan, daring him to speak.

Lorcan said nothing, but stood tall and upright, his cheeks sucked in, hollowing his face.

Diarmait shouldered his way through his men, his eyes hot with violence.

Aoife started towards him but was stopped by her mother's grip on her arm. 'No,' Môr said, 'let him go. He is a wounded bear, and you would not enter the cave of such a one.'

Aoife briefly tried to pull away, but yielded without too much fight, for her mother was right, and she was grateful to have a reason not to go. But she felt guilty too, and afraid, for if her father crumbled, who would protect them? Her uncle Lorcan was an archbishop, but he had not prevented their enemies from entering the abbey and had stood by while her father was humiliated and her brother taken hostage. What kind of strength was that?

King Ruari departed at dawn, the imprints of his army's camp fires ringing the church like Satan's hoofprints. Aoife watched him ride away from the tower window. She did not know where her father had spent the night but he had not slept for he was bleary-eyed and grey-faced over his dish of bread and cheese. The morning light exposed lines where none had dwelt before, and his beard was matted and tangled. The wildness in him was subdued now. She could still sense the danger; but she was his daughter and she would face him steadfastly.

She followed him when he returned to the smouldering palace and stood amid the stones and rubble. Some blackened timbers were still recognisable but much of it was hot ash drifting in the wind. She gazed at the ruins of her home, feeling numb, but beneath that numbness her heart quivered with grief. Where she had slept, curled up and secure, was nothing but an outline on the ground.

'I chose to do this rather than let an enemy enter my home,' her father said and, stooping, took a fistful of hot ash and trickled it into an open leather pouch in his other hand. 'I will carry this with me until the day I build a new and better palace here, when I am restored to my power.'

'You will be king here again,' Aoife said with fierce loyalty. 'And no one will dare to gainsay you.' The words were an oath. She wanted them to be a true foretelling. She wanted to bind the wounds inflicted and heal them, but the wanting itself was so intense it hurt. Just how they were to rebuild was beyond her understanding. Her father had few allies beyond his immediate warband and household. His ability to hold his own, let alone fight back, had been stripped away. Without resources, without allies, and with Enna a hostage, he was isolated and vulnerable.

He gave her a preoccupied smile. 'You are a good girl, Aoife,' he said, and gently touched her hair. 'I still have you.'

She swallowed her tears and, looking up, gave him her brightest and best smile.

Two days later Aoife was sitting with her family, eating bread and fish in the lower room of the tower they had made their lodging, when one of her father's scouts arrived at the abbey at a breakneck gallop and threw himself at Diarmait's feet, panting for breath. 'My lord, there are men on the road – Tiernan ua Ruari and the men of Dublin. The High King has left the way open for them – they will be upon us before sunset.'

Aoife stared at the young warrior in shock. She had been raised on the story of how her father had stolen the wife of Tiernan ua Ruari and knew he was her father's deadliest enemy because of it even though she had never seen him. He would show no mercy.

Her father shook himself like an animal trying to rid itself of gnats. 'We have no choice but to leave and fight another day. I would gladly meet him face to face, but we are too few to stand against him and he will slaughter us all.' Already he was rising to his feet.

'But where can we go?' Domnall had risen too, his hand on his sword hilt. 'Our backs are to the wall.'

'No, lad, our backs are to the sea,' Diarmait said. 'We must turn and face it, for on the other side we can hire men who are not bound by Irish ties.'

'You will buy mercenaries?' Domnall's eyes widened.

'Why not? There are hard men for hire in Wales and England. King Henry owes me his goodwill from the days when he lacked a throne. Now he may repay his debt and help me in my turn.'

'He also wants Ireland,' Domnall pointed out.

'What if he does? He is like a fine silver fish that can be tickled into a net if we handle him carefully.'

'More like one to devour us.'

'If he comes of his own accord, he will devour everyone anyway. Better to be his ally that we may also devour others. Henry will help us if we approach him in the right way and both of us shall benefit.'

'But if you ask, there is no going back.'

'You think there is any coming back from this if we do not seek help?' Diarmait struck the table with his fist. 'Outside help is the only way to fight back. We must be away from here before Tiernan arrives; there is no time. Gather everything together – make haste.'

Once more Aoife raced to pack her mount and helped to transfer their goods onto carts and packhorses. If Tiernan arrived and discovered them still here, they would be dragged out of the abbey and slaughtered, her uncle's status as an archbishop notwithstanding. She wondered what it would be like to die – to have her throat cut because her father could not protect her. And then she stopped thinking at all, unable to deal with the images filling her mind.

In the haste to pack the carts, a hen had been trampled underfoot and was flapping about in the dust with a broken wing. Aoife stared at it, sickened by its plight which seemed to reflect their own, and what a waste too. She seized the bird, and in a practised move wrung its neck. And then she took her knife and cut off its head and poured the blood onto the ground in a red necklace around her feet. 'We will return,' she said. 'I swear I shall serve my family all the days of my life even unto my own death.' She wiped the soles of her shoes in the blood to complete the oath and tossed the dead hen into one of the carts; it could be put in a stew, and nothing must be wasted in their current perilous state.

* * *

Her fists gripped in her cloak, Aoife faced the cold sea breeze and watched the waves chopping the water under the laden ships moored at the end of the jetty. Her mother and Connor were already aboard, but she had lingered to stand a few last moments on her home soil.

It had taken two days of hard travelling to reach the small coastal inlet of St Kearns on the Bannow estuary, and throughout the ride she had been waiting for a shout behind them and the sharp glint of Tiernan's spears, but the only thing at their backs had been a horizon of exile, and ahead of them the salt smell of the sea waiting to bear them to England.

She loosed her braid to unbind the life force and the wind snagged the roots of her hair which became a physical manifestation of her tangled emotions, beating about her face. Seagulls wheeled above the ship's madder-red sail and the tang of the ocean was sharp in her nostrils. The sailors said the night would be clear and they would steer to England by the stars. Aoife had travelled on the rivers of Leinster by boat sometimes and had even sailed the coastline on inshore fishing craft, but she had never ventured out to sea. However, she was resolute and they had no alternative. Their vessel was a solid craft that plied its trade between Bristol and Ireland; the shipmaster was a friend of FitzHarding's who was being well paid to carry them to succour and safety.

'Are you ready, daughter?' Her father laid a hand on her shoulder.

'Yes, Daidí. I am not afraid.' She spoke staunchly to prove to herself that she wasn't.

She felt the heavy pressure of his hand squeezing her shoulder in reassurance. 'I know you are not. You have courage – how could you not being mine?'

His words warmed and steadied her. It was them against the world and she would do anything for him. Anything.

7

Bristol, England, summer 1166

Aoife stood behind her father, ready to fill his cup. She guarded the task jealously for if she made herself part of the background, she often overheard privileged information just as she had done hiding under his chair as a little girl.

Robert FitzHarding had arranged to lodge their wider entourage at the Abbey of St Augustine of which he was patron but had offered her father and his household the hospitality of his own fine hall.

FitzHarding sat beside her father, a genial expression on his rotund features. His eyes, however, were calculating and shrewd. He had been magnanimous in every way, but Aoife had not taken him at face value. She knew he would be wondering how much wealth they had salvaged as they fled, and what he could gain from them. He was a merchant prince, wealthy enough to loan money to the King of England, who had granted him lands and a barony. She had tried not to be impressed by the luxury and comfort of his home with its rich hangings, colourful furniture and exquisite tableware but knew she could grow to love such a life.

'So,' said FitzHarding, setting his cup down on the board and facing her father. 'The King is occupied with business across the Narrow Sea and unlikely to return to England until next year and you cannot afford to wait that long. You should seek him out and speak face to face; letters and messengers are not enough.'

'Cross the sea again?' Her father frowned.

FitzHarding nodded emphatically. 'The King has more business to conduct than he has time in the day. A personal supplication will carry more weight than a letter that might go astray or be ignored by a clerk. He will give audience to a fellow king who has helped him in the past when he himself was an exile.'

Her father folded his arms, considering.

'Go and pay your respects. Let him know that you wish for aid but avoid saying you have been overthrown.'

Her father bristled. 'I have not been overthrown.'

'Indeed not,' FitzHarding soothed, 'but you require help from allies to pacify turbulent factions. Emphasise how grateful you will be for his help. Take your family with you, for they will be an asset.' He looked meaningfully at Aoife.

'I need further guidance.' Diarmait turned to her. 'Aoife, bring the oracle.'

She set the jug down and from one of their baggage chests brought a shallow brass bowl and a small cloth bag containing resin and wood shavings.

FitzHarding cupped his chin and watched with interest as she placed the bowl in front of her father. 'Divination? I knew a monk who used to scry into a bowl of water. He claimed to see all manner of things, but I have never had any success with such dealings.'

Diarmait placed a few lumps of resin and wood shavings into the centre of the brass dish. 'Interpretation is all,' he said, glancing sharply at FitzHarding, 'but you have your own ways of seeing I think.' He opened his belt pouch, pinched some ashes from the bag he had filled at Fearns and sprinkled them over the resin and shavings. 'Now we shall see.' Taking a candle from one of the stands, he lit the shavings, invoking Jesus Christ and the Virgin Mary. As a thin line of smoke started to twist upward, he blew gently upon it. 'With my breath,' he said, 'how so shall I move?'

Everyone watched the coil of smoke. Diarmait studied the

shape and direction of the twist with narrowed eyes. Aoife loved to see her father read the smoke. She had asked him how he knew and he had replied that as he watched the pattern of the twirls the answer would come into his heart. She had tried to do this herself, but she was never certain that the feeling was right.

After a moment, her father nodded to FitzHarding. 'It seems a fair wind is at our back. We shall do as you say and go to King Henry.'

FitzHarding beamed. 'I am glad your foretelling accords with my own instinct. I can provide you with a ship and guides to take you to his court wherever he should be. I have letters for the King and goods he has ordered which he will be glad to receive.' He opened his hands, age-mottled but firm and strong. 'I shall miss your company, but doubtless you will return this way.' He ordered the servants to broach some special sweet wine of Cyprus and pour it into cups of green glass that he had imported with the wine.

'We are in your debt,' Diarmait said.

'Ah, let us have no talk of debt among friends. Rather of mutual favour and interests.'

Sipping from the dainty cup, Aoife tasted warm, complex gold on her tongue. Anxiety and excitement churned her belly. Once again, their lives were being uprooted. They were going to cross another sea to visit the King of England who would give them men and the wherewithal to regain their homeland – but at what price?

FitzHarding called for music and dancing, and for a while it was like old times at Fearns and Aoife was happy to see a smile on her father's face and a glint in his eye. Domnall danced with her, spinning her round and lifting her effortlessly over his shoulder. 'Who knows, little sister,' he teased as he set her back down, 'we might find a rich Norman husband for you at court!'

Her eyes widened for the thought had not entered her head

and she was immediately alarmed. To leave her family, to have some stranger lay hands on her as a marital right – never!

Her father, close enough to hear, wagged his forefinger. 'Now, now, none of that, Domnall. Do not tease your sister.'

'I wasn't teasing,' Domnall replied. 'If we have to offer rewards, we should count all our treasures, including our most precious. Think what an asset Aoife could be. Look at her. She is a tempting marriage prize for sure.'

Diarmait gave his son a hard look. Aoife tensed, ready to fight, envisaging her clenched fist connecting with Domnall's jaw.

'But I would not give my greatest treasure away, now would I?' Diarmait picked Aoife up as Domnall had done and swung her round. 'She is not for leaving my side, are you, girl?'

'No!' Aoife flashed a resentful glare at her brother. 'Never!'

Her father laughed and gave her one of his enormous bear hugs, but when he let her go and she stepped back to restore the breath he had squeezed from her lungs, she saw him exchanging a thoughtful second glance with Domnall, and her anxiety heightened.

8

Bristol, England, summer 1166

Robert FitzHarding handed Richard de Clare a cup of wine and both men sat down companionably before the merchant's fire. An attendant moved around the room, lighting candles and closing the shutters, while another set out an informal light meal of bread, cheese and dried fruit at a side table.

Richard was in Bristol buying cloth and had been looking at some napped Flemish wool that had recently arrived in FitzHarding's warehouse. Basilia and his daughters had accompanied him for Basilia had the task of choosing fabric to make into gowns and cloaks for herself and the girls, and also to buy cloth for the annual clothing allowance of Striguil's knights and retainers. FitzHarding had driven a hard bargain, but so had Richard, and both men were satisfied that a fair price had been agreed.

'So, my lord,' FitzHarding said, 'how is life at Striguil?'

Richard contemplated his wine. 'The same as usual. We have to contend with raids from the Welsh and be vigilant, especially now the lord Rhys sits in Ceredigion.' He nodded towards the bulky fair-haired young man sitting with a group of knights at another table. 'Raymond performs an excellent task of patrolling our perimeters and our walls and our diligence keeps us safe. Lord Rhys knows how far to test the boundaries.' He raised his cup. 'I admit I pity Ceredigion's former constable. I would free FitzStephen if I could, but the lord Rhys will never do so until he kneels to him.'

FitzHarding grunted. 'I doubt that will happen.'

'So do I,' Richard said wryly. Prince Rhys of Deheubarth had seized the castle at Ceredigion from its Norman overlords and had fettered its constable, Robert FitzStephen, in the dungeon. The men being cousins, the lord Rhys had spared FitzStephen's life but would only free him if he agreed to renounce his fealty to King Henry and swore never to fight for him again in Wales. FitzStephen had refused, and so remained a prisoner. Richard thought Robert FitzStephen a loyal, tenacious terrier and fine military tactician, but stubborn to the point of stupidity. 'I do not have the resources to challenge the lord Rhys on FitzStephen's behalf, and the King shows no inclination to intervene, so there is nothing to be done.'

'He should rethink his stance, although his loyalty to the King is commendable.'

Richard said nothing. His own continuing loyalty to Henry went unremarked and unrewarded. He kept his men sharp and his fortresses alert and well stocked, but sometimes he felt as if he was dissolving into greyness. He wondered what his father would say about his situation, and beyond that his distant ancestors who were also the ancestors of William the Bastard, a man who had seized England in his mailed fist and carved himself a kingdom and a dynasty. Richard shared in part the same lineage as his king, and while Henry ruled an empire, Richard had no role and no heirs.

A soft giggle came from the table where Basilia and his daughters were sitting with FitzHarding's womenfolk. Richard smiled to see how much his girls were enjoying the company and conversation.

'If you had been here last week, I could have introduced you to my Irish guests,' FitzHarding said. 'Diarmait of Leinster is the man who buys your weaponry.'

'I am sorry to have missed him,' Richard responded with genuine regret. 'Was there a particular purpose for his visit?'

FitzHarding stroked his moustache. 'Indeed yes. He is momentarily a man in exile. His enemies have unseated him and he has been forced to flee with his family.'

Richard was dismayed, the Irish lord was a regular customer, but he waited, intrigued by the glint in FitzHarding's eye. Perhaps the victors in Ireland would be good customers too. 'I am sorry to hear that. You said "momentarily"?'

'He intends to return and overthrow his rivals. I know him well – he will not stop until he has achieved his goal or else died in the attempt.'

'And you have offered to help him?'

FitzHarding pressed his fingertips together. 'Let us say I have directed him. He is quite capable of helping himself. He is ruthless, savage and clever – anyone who underestimates him is a fool. I sent him and his family to seek aid of the King. He has a young and very beautiful unwed daughter among his assets – and I mean beautiful.' He gave Richard a meaningful look.

'You believe the King will render that aid?'

'Who can say? But if I were a wagering man . . .'

'Which you are when the odds are in your favour,' Richard said, grinning.

FitzHarding conceded the point with a chuckle. '. . . I hazard the King will be most interested. He may not have time to deal with the matter himself, but he might find it to his advantage to permit MacMurchada to recruit among the Welsh and the lords of the Marches. Men who might be better employed across the Hibernian Sea rather than causing trouble at home. Moreover, men who might, if they succeed, carve out lands that will then fall to Henry's rule. Succeed or fail, there is no loss to him. For more than ten years he has wanted to gain a foothold in Ireland, and in Diarmait of Leinster he has his chance.'

Richard frowned. 'Why are you telling me this?'

'MacMurchada will gain the King's permission to recruit – Henry will not refuse. You have supplied Diarmait with arms and weaponry and are an earl of high standing with an eye to new horizons because the old ones are not fruitful. You are ideally placed to provide Diarmait of Leinster with support and make a profit into the bargain. You will have to spend in order to accumulate, but MacMurchada is not without resources and Ireland is there to be exploited. A man might carve a kingdom for himself . . .'

'Or for others.'

'Who would spend little time there because of their other concerns.'

Richard pursed his lips. 'What would you gain from this?'

FitzHarding smiled. 'I am a man of business and I have to make a profit, but I have my loyalties and friendships as we all do. I help the Irish by finding them a way to return home and defeat their enemies, and that in turn is of advantage to the King who desires Ireland but has little time to devote to it. I put opportunity in your hands and say, "Do what you will." There are three fine ports in Ireland, controlled by the Norse. Closer ties and controls between Dublin and Bristol would not go amiss. There are many opportunities to be explored. My question to you is this: when Diarmait MacMurchada returns to me, shall I send him to Striguil to discuss matters of mutual interest? Provision of men and materials perhaps?'

Richard realised the savour had returned to his day and the grey horizon had suddenly lifted to show a narrow band of gold. He had still to digest the information but he felt a visceral sympathy with a man determined not to be deprived of his land and his heritage. 'Certainly, you may send him to me,' he said, 'and I shall see what he has to say.'

9

Aoife stared in wonder at the golden autumn light washing the decorated arches over the palace doorway. If this was King Henry's temporary home on his way elsewhere, then what a great man he must be. Fearns was almost a hovel by comparison.

A group of youths emerged through the doors, talking among themselves, dressed in bright colours, long hair shining, and walked past the newly arrived Irish party as if they were of no consequence. Aoife stepped aside for them, and immediately felt at a disadvantage for having done so, for she was a princess and they should have deferred to her. They had been many weeks on the road, always being told that the King was a stage further on; finding him had been like chasing a fox through a labyrinth. Finally, they had caught up with him at Saumur, the autumn sun setting westwards behind them, turning the Loire to gold and gilding the white tuffeau stone of town, church and castle.

More folk emerged, and then a man wearing a tunic of good brown wool, who introduced himself as one of the King's ushers and enquired their purpose. Maurice Regan, her father's interpreter, stepped forward and gave the man greetings and the necessary details in fluent French, presenting him with the letters of recommendation from Robert FitzHarding. The usher glanced at FitzHarding's seal. 'I will see that the King receives these immediately,' he said. 'In the meantime, please refresh yourselves.' He instructed a squire to escort them to a building beyond the palace and up some stairs to a small but pleasantly appointed chamber with a fire burning at a central hearth. Other servants arrived and set up a trestle table, placing on it a basket of bread and a slab of cold salt beef from which they could carve slices with their knives.

Her father and brothers attacked the food eagerly. Aoife was too tense to do more than nibble but she drank a cup of the pale Angevin wine for courage and wondered at the largesse provided to visitors even before they had been summoned to the King. Warm rose water and towels arrived for washing hands and feet. Aoife changed her dusty travelling gown for her best one, dismayed to find it crumpled and slightly torn at the top of the sleeve. She had grown in the weeks since she had last worn the garment and found it tight across her bosom, and the hem was slightly short. But before the sewing basket could come out, the usher returned to escort them to the King, and Aoife had to make do with covering the damage with her cloak.

The great hall at Saumur was draped with rich textile hangings and the walls were plastered and brightly painted with hunting scenes. Aoife could feel the curious stares fixed upon their party as they followed the usher to a canopied dais at the far end of the room where the King sat upon a gilded chair with brass statues of leopards placed to right and left. Henry resembled a compact auburn lion and Aoife could feel the weight of authority and power emanating from him.

As they neared the dais, his gaze fixed on them and for an instant concentrated on Aoife. Although awed by the surroundings, she returned his look with pride, determined to show the King of England that they were royalty too. His wide mouth curled with amusement and he stroked his beard in a grooming gesture.

The family knelt at the foot of the dais to make their obeisance and Aoife admired the decorated floor tiles with their patterns of hares and running stags.

'Welcome.' Henry gestured for them to rise. 'I hear you have travelled far.' He was holding the letters of recommendation from Robert FitzHarding. Aoife thought his voice not unlike her father's; it had the same smoky roughness.

'Indeed, sire, across turbulent seas and travelling many roads to find you to ask for your help in defeating our enemies.' Her father understood more French than he spoke, and replied in Irish, which Maurice translated.

Henry continued to stroke his beard and again Aoife felt his eyes on her, assessing, devouring. 'I understand you find yourself in difficulties and you do not have the resources to deal with them alone.'

Aoife felt a stab of unease, for Henry's demeanour was not as supportive as FitzHarding had led them to believe it would be. She was aware of the courtiers watching from the sides, listening with avid attention.

'Leinster has belonged to my family time out of mind,' her father said, standing erect and strong. 'Ruari ua Connor and Tiernan ua Ruari have no right to drive me out. As I recall, sire, you fought for your own lands even when all seemed hopeless, and you sought succour from other men – including myself.'

'That is true,' Henry acknowledged. 'I have always been on good terms with you and I recognise your help and goodwill in times past. I certainly wish to continue those good relations, more especially should you be lord of your own lands.'

'I am lord of my own lands,' her father said firmly, 'and eager with your help to return to them.'

Henry rested the letter on his knee under his fist. 'As a good friend and neighbour, I am willing to support you of course, but for the moment I have other matters requiring my attention. Nevertheless, you have my leave to seek support in my realms and recruit men to assist your cause. You shall have letters of sanction. If my vassals are willing to please me, they will be willing to please you also. Master FitzHarding speaks well of your intentions and he is a shrewd judge of men. You have my goodwill and the freedom to recruit men in my dominions.'

Aoife saw the disappointment flicker across her father's face. 'Sire, you are generous,' he said. 'But I had hoped you might provide me with men or lend me the wherewithal to hire them.'

Henry tapped his fingers against the letters. 'Return to Master FitzHarding and he will deal with both matters for you. He is experienced in such transactions. If you do regain your lands, I may be able to send you reinforcements and assistance to strengthen your defences. But the first risk is rightly yours.'

Aoife set her jaw. Henry was saying they could attempt to regain their lands at their own expense, and if they succeeded, he would help them in return for concessions as yet unspecified. A dangerous bargain indeed.

'I shall have the letters ready for you shortly, and in the meantime, you shall be my honoured guests and sit at my table.' Henry's tone was affable but dismissive.

Aoife and her family were ushered from the room and shown to a larger chamber than before with provision of mattresses, linen sheets and blankets.

Her father was not as angry and agitated as Aoife had expected him to be; rather he was thoughtful, as though studying a board of gaming pieces. 'Ah but he is a great king, and a sly one,' he said with reluctant admiration. 'He has the measure of us all – but perhaps also I have his.' He touched the side of his nose.

'So, what do we do?' Domnall demanded.

'We take his letters and we accept his offer; there is no other way forward for us and he knows it. But perhaps it is not such a bad thing.'

'For us to do the work and him to come and take everything away?' Domnall's eyes were bright with indignation. 'I think not!'

'Did your mother birth me a son without brains?' Diarmait growled. 'We cannot go home without help. If he demands a reward for that help, he is entitled to do so. Look at all he has, at all he owns and the resources he commands. Better to swear an oath to him than to Ruari ua Connor. Better to be his representative and go our own way. Everyone wants something, remember that. Nothing comes without a price. What we have will suffice for now, and we have always known how to bargain and move the goods around on the stall and renegotiate. King Henry is a survivor, but so am I, and I have lived more years than he has.' He raised a warning forefinger. 'Be on your best behaviour. Smile and agree with him until we have those letters in our hands.'

A chamberlain arrived with a serving woman in tow, bearing fresh clothes for Diarmait and his family as gifts from Henry. Domnall was prepared to be insulted. 'Does he think our own not good enough?' he said roughly in Irish.

Diarmait made a swift chopping gesture with his forearm. 'Do not be an idiot, boy. It's a sign of high esteem. Wear your own cloak over the top if it troubles you.'

Aoife fell on the gown provided for her with a cry of delight. The deep, dusky pink cloth was embellished with gold wool embroidery. A braid belt with a rock crystal buckle matched the colour of the gown. Enchanted, Aoife donned the garment and danced around the room, swirling the full skirt high and low, thinking that Henry could give them as many presents as he wanted!

Her father, who had just been praising and defending Henry's largesse and had willingly donned the red-brown tunic intended for himself, scowled as he watched her dance. 'You be careful, my girl,' he warned. 'Stop showing yourself off like that. Men will take it as an invitation to be familiar. Your virtue and chastity are more valuable than gold – especially now!'

'Daidí!' Mortified, Aoife flung to face him, her cheeks burning.

Her mother caught her sleeve. 'Your father is right. Everything comes at a price and the cost of that gown shall not be your chastity.'

'But it's a gift from the King!' Aoife protested indignantly. 'He gives gifts to other people too – to everyone in this room!'

'He doesn't want to bed any of us though,' Domnall said, smirking, and received a cuff from their father.

'Enough of that talk,' Diarmait growled. 'Aoife, you're to be careful and it behoves all of us to keep watch. You are not to be alone with him.'

'But I have to smile and be nice to him – you said . . .'

Her father drew a deep breath and she waited for a tirade, but instead he exhaled on a hard sigh. 'I know what I said but that was before I saw you in that gown. You are a beauty and you will attract attention, and not only from the King. I want you to stay within reach of me or your brothers at all times.' He squinted in the way he did when considering subterfuge. 'But still, we must keep the King on good terms. We do not want to attract his anger. Smile at him but hold to your honour, and we shall stay close at hand. I am trusting you, Aoife. Your reputation and your family's future are at stake here. Do you understand, my girl?'

A surge of excitement threaded with fear shivered through her body. She had always enjoyed attention, and the beautiful dress made her feel desirable and womanly. Her duty was to capture a king but not let herself be captured – a marvellous, terrifying game. 'Yes, Daidí,' she said. 'I understand.'

Dinner had been eaten earlier that day and the evening meal was informal. The tables were arranged with dishes of bread and cheese, spiced eggs, smoked meats and small dainties. Henry presided at the high table under a fabric canopy with his eleven-year-old heir and namesake at his side. He sent choice morsels to his Irish guests, including small spiced wafers, and a little dish of apples and honey that Aoife thought was sublime.

She was strongly aware of Henry's scrutiny. Even when ostensibly not looking at her, she still felt his presence. The moments she did catch his gaze, she stared directly back at him, telling him that she knew his intent and was not intimidated by it. She felt flattered and excited to be playing with fire, knowing her father and brothers would provide a barrier if the heat grew too intense. She could test her female power while retaining a safe refuge. It was all very delicious.

Musicians played throughout the meal and the skill of Henry's Welsh harper brought tears to Aoife's eyes and made her long for home.

'My daughter plays the harp and sings too,' Diarmait told Henry. 'She has a rare skill.'

'Then we would dearly enjoy hearing her,' Henry said, gesturing with an open hand.

Aoife blushed, but eagerly fetched her harp to play for the company. She had expected her father to engineer just such a moment to show the King what a jewel she was but in a laudable and honourable way.

She played and sang for him, her voice as pure and clear as a new dawn, her fingers weaving a story through the harp strings, and she was in her element, her skill holding everyone in thrall. Her reward as she plucked the last sweet, icy note from the harp was her father's shining pride and the look of surprise and naked hunger on Henry's face.

'Your daughter has a rare skill indeed,' Henry said, his expression avid.

'And she is all the more precious to her family because of it,' Diarmait replied with a crafty smile.

Henry left his chair and came around the table to Aoife. 'That was beautiful,' he said. 'You have a great talent, my dear. I shall send you a gift in gratitude for the pleasure you have given to all of us – do you understand me?'

'Yes, sire, I speak more French than you do Irish,' Aoife replied, mischievously. 'I am glad to win your approval, and I thank you for the beautiful gown.'

'It is nothing,' he said with a wave of his hand. 'A fine setting for a rare jewel.' He looked her up and down, his gaze lingering on her breasts for just a moment too long. He took her hand and raised it to his lips, and Aoife felt the tip of his tongue on her skin. 'Will you sing for us again?'

'If that is your wish, sire,' she said.

'Yes, it is.' He returned to his seat and sat down, his eyes never leaving her face.

Aoife performed two more songs, and throughout Henry gazed with predatory hunger and she returned his stare, acknowledging him but refusing to be prey. She wondered what the gift might be. Another gown? Jewels? Money?

Later, after the entertainment, the courtiers gathered to talk and play dice. Aoife spoke to Morgan, Henry's Welsh harpist, and they shared some lore of harp and song. Henry, his son at his side, was talking to her father and Domnall and she assumed from the serious looks on their faces that they were discussing business. Various courtiers glanced her way, their knowing smirks telling her exactly what they had construed from the exchanges. Her father and Domnall had been right in their assessment of Henry's intentions.

She turned to depart with her mother and Connor, leaving the men to their wine and talk, but Henry hastily broke off his conversation to bid goodnight. 'And especially thank you for giving us the pleasure of hearing your voice,' he said to Aoife, taking her hand again. 'I trust to hear it again soon.'

'Indeed, sire, I hope so,' Aoife replied sweetly. She removed her hand from his and went deliberately to her father and stood on tip-toe to kiss his cheek. He hugged her, whispering in her ear, 'Well done, precious girl, well done indeed.'

A warm feeling of success in her heart, she took her leave and swayed her hips just a little, knowing Henry would be watching her.

'You have a beautiful daughter,' Henry said softly to Diarmait. 'Much could be made of her future.'

'Indeed.' Diarmait smiled at Henry with a hard twinkle in his eyes. 'I often give thought to Aoife's future. I am as proud of her as you must be of your own daughters and I must do what is best for her and for Leinster.'

Henry gave him a considering look filled with grudging respect for a worthy opponent. 'Yes,' he said. 'Of course, you must.'

By morning their letters of safe conduct and permissions to recruit were ready and they prepared to return to Bristol. Henry presented Aoife with an exquisite goblet of Tyrian glass decorated with blue swirls. 'So that you may drink to moisten your voice before you sing, and remember your first visit to court,' he said. 'I hope to hear you play again on another occasion.'

The words were gracious and Henry's behaviour impeccable, but still with a predatory nuance. Aoife curtseyed. 'It is a beautiful gift, and it will be my pleasure, sire,' she said, and once more met his gaze steadily before withdrawing firmly behind her mother and brothers.

As they rode away, Aoife pondered her experience at Henry's court and the wheels of power that turned beyond Ireland. The dominance and charisma of the man whose every gesture and command was as a spoke of a wheel sent outward from the hub to the rim intrigued her. Nothing moved save by his will. What it would be to possess such power, or to control it. It was on a different scale to her father's authority. She understood now why it was better to be Henry's ally than his enemy. Her eyes had been opened and she was hungry for more.

10

Bristol, England, February 1167

Aoife sat over her harp, polishing the wood with a soft cloth. Outside it was bitterly cold with snow in the wind, but the hearth fire was warm and the shutters latched against the draught. Connor and Domnall were engaged in a fierce battle of chess by the fire, a game they had taken to playing ever since returning from King Henry's court where it was extremely popular. Her mother was repairing a tear in Connor's hose and her father was sitting over a jug of wine with Robert FitzHarding, considering Henry's reply and how they should progress.

'You should visit Richard de Clare, Earl of Striguil, as soon as you may,' FitzHarding said. 'I spoke of you to him when I saw him in the autumn and he expressed an interest.'

Her father grunted. 'Why should I go to him in particular, and why should you have told him about me?'

FitzHarding poured fresh wine into Diarmait's cup. 'His concerns match well with your own. His father fought for King Stephen in the war for the succession and when he died, his son followed suit. As a result, although there is peace now, de Clare is not within the King's favoured circle.'

'And that is a reason to recommend him? I hardly think looking to King Henry's enemies will further my cause and keep his goodwill.'

FitzHarding shook his head. 'I did not say he was his enemy, just not one of the favoured, and since the King will not advance him at court, he has no way forward from that source and is therefore more likely to commit to an undertaking in Ireland – providing the rewards are sufficient for his services. I have always had profitable business dealings with him. Many of your weapons come from his stores and their quality speaks for the man.'

Her father frowned, and Aoife did too, unconsciously mirroring his expression.

'He is still on the young side of his prime, but he has experience. His men are loyal to the bone and trained warriors. Moreover, he has useful contacts with others you might want to recruit. I believe you will find him amenable to your approach.' FitzHarding stroked his white moustaches. 'De Clare is unwed. The King has not seen fit to grant him permission to do so. He does not want him gaining power through a marriage alliance. But of course, were he to match with an Irish heiress . . .' He let the point hang while he replenished Diarmait's cup. 'He is personable enough, and perhaps through a woman's eyes he might be considered handsome. My own womenfolk certainly think so.'

Aoife's stomach lurched. Her father and her brothers were eyeing her with speculation. She looked down, biting her lower lip while she took a moment to think. Clearly FitzHarding believed this Richard de Clare would be a vital lynchpin to her father's campaign and it was not in FitzHarding's interests to misdirect them. She knew he wanted this as much as they did because of the ports, especially Dublin. The suggestion of a marriage alliance made her queasy, but she would agree if it meant they would regain their land. If this Richard de Clare was as strong a warrior and as handsome as FitzHarding intimated, then it might be bearable. If she did not like him, she could be rid of him once they reached Ireland. There were always knives in the dark.

Domnall's expression was eager. 'It would be the kind of sweetener we could offer without giving too much away. Aoife is beautiful; who would not want her for a bride? It would be safer for her in England too.'

Aoife glared at him. Marriage was one thing, leaving her family quite another and she had no intention of being eased away from her influence with their father. 'I have more value than you know!' she said haughtily to Domnall. 'I will decide for myself whether this is a marriage worth having. It has to be for the good of all, and not just because you want to give me to some Norman stranger we have yet to meet!'

Domnall laughed and pretended to cower away from her ire.

Diarmait's complexion reddened. 'This cannot be decided on the moment and we must bargain with guile.' He fixed Domnall with a stern gaze. 'A daughter can only be given once in marriage and a family must be very sure before they set such a thing in motion. Never, never trust anyone on the hearsay of others, even if you value that person's words. Let us see the measure of de Clare for ourselves and judge him accordingly.'

'You will find him as I say,' FitzHarding said calmly, 'but you are wise not to take my word for it, and I respect you for it. You are right that no marriage – indeed no enterprise – should ever be entered into without great consideration.'

Diarmait hunched his broad shoulders inside his furs and glowered at Domnall. 'We will have no more talk about your sister for now. It is my duty as a father to bestow my daughter as I see fit, and not for her brothers to interfere – understood?'

Domnall nodded stiffly and looked down.

'If it should come to it, and this man prove worthy, I shall take all things into consideration. Aoife is our most valuable asset, and I shall not let her go lightly. He looked round the gathering, taking everyone into his stare. 'All of you shall do as I say. We shall go and see this Earl of Striguil and find out what manner of man he is for ourselves and decide how to proceed from there.'

11

'We need to prepare for visitors.' Richard leaned against the wall watching Basilia inspect the bolts of linen fabric that had arrived to make shirts for the knights at Easter. Three seamstresses were already busy at work sitting in the light from the window where a cool spring breeze was wafting through the open shutters.

She looked up from the cloth and he received a jolt because she looked exactly like their mother, but thirty years younger. Her features were framed by a plain white wimple, not so much as a strand of hair on show. Her eyes reflected the deep blue of her gown and might have softened her appearance had they not been filled with wariness verging on disapproval.

'Visitors?' she repeated. 'Who?'

'Robert FitzHarding has asked me to receive Diarmait MacMurchada, King of Leinster, and his family. I agreed to do so and now he sends word they will soon be on their way.'

Basilia gave a piece of linen to one of the seamstresses. 'How many and for how long?'

He could see her already mentally counting what they had in the stores. Her pride was her duty to provide whatever the circumstances. 'FitzHarding says about thirty people – some are remaining in Bristol. We must make provision for Diarmait's wife and daughter, and their women. There is Diarmait himself, a grown son, and another aged twelve and their interpreter, although I am told they understand our language and speak it to a degree. The rest are men of his affinity. I do not know how long they will stay. It could be a week, it might be two. It depends on the negotiations.'

'That is no small drain on our supplies and resources.'

'I am asking a great deal of you, but I know you can manage, and if all goes well, it will be worthwhile.'

She gave him a hard stare. 'Just what are they coming here to negotiate?'

'FitzHarding says MacMurchada wishes to hire soldiers to fight in Ireland and has King Henry's permission to recruit from his dominions. I suppose the King thinks it better for men to fight in Ireland than at home where they will be a nuisance to him.'

'And what does he want from you?'

'That remains to be seen, but I suspect he is seeking men, weapons and expertise. I have useful contacts with the Welsh, the Marcher lords and their affinities. At the least he will be looking for advice and assistance.'

'And at the most?'

Richard felt pinned by his sister's sharp perception. 'Collaboration. Alliance.' Before she could speak he added, 'It is an opportunity, and opportunities these days are few and far between. I will hear what he has to say, and I will make my own decisions from there. All we need do for now is offer hospitality and a courteous welcome. You have leave to make the necessary arrangements.'

'It will cost money to buy in provisions.'

'Whatever you need you shall have it. FitzHarding is sending some supplies on the ship with them – raisin wine and spices and flour for bread.'

'For which he is doubtless charging us to his own profit.'

'The wine is a gift and so are the spices.'

'So, he must be expecting a lucrative return on whatever investment he is making.'

Richard shrugged. 'I think we may all hope for that, otherwise what would be the point? You'll put it in hand then?' He clasped his hands together in a beseeching gesture and widened his eyes and was rewarded with a smile of sorts.

'You need not think you can get around me with one of your looks,' Basilia sniffed. 'I will do it for duty and for family honour and obligation.'

'You might enjoy their company.'

'Like everything else that remains to be seen.'

He kissed her cheek and left, knowing she would come round. He was fond of his sister, but their relationship had its frictions. She preferred a life of seemly, settled routine; a safe world over which she had control; where she knew exactly where the next meal was coming from and what it would be. Her attitude had its advantages, but Richard felt as if his own life was being stifled. A safe harbour and daily bucolic routine had much to commend it, but without different fare it became a monotonous table indeed. The Irish were a new prospect and his interest was piqued.

Aoife packed the dusky pink court gown Henry had given to her and a new one of green wool with red sleeve linings that was a gift from Robert FitzHarding. She had clothes now that were fit for her status and she was intent on making an impression. Her stomach was tight with fear and excitement when she thought of the visit to Striguil. Her role in the proceedings had been brought to the fore with the possibility of her marriage having been added to the assets at her father's disposal when bargaining for aid.

FitzHarding had painted a highly attractive portrait of Richard de Clare, but words could be vehicles for evasions and lies, for exaggeration and misdirection. If FitzHarding spoke the truth, then de Clare was a paragon. The merchant seemed to think he was their best opportunity, with others paling in comparison. They would have to be on their mettle to secure his services. If it meant marriage she was steeled to it, but the fear and the fight still coursed through her veins.

Servants came to take their baggage to the ship. FitzHarding was lending them the *Maria*, to take them across the Severn and up the Wye to Striguil.

'Are there any ladies at Striguil?' Aoife asked. The thought had been preying on her mind. She kept imagining a warriors' camp, for the talk between her father and Domnall was of armies and weapons and soldiers. Where would she sleep in such a place, and would there be somewhere to take refuge?

FitzHarding's weathered features creased into a smile and his eyes twinkled. 'I see we have been talking too much of military matters. Yes, indeed, there are ladies at Striguil and you will be comfortable there, and well looked after. The Earl has a sister, the lady Basilia, who keeps his household, and a seemly gracious lady she is. There are serving ladies of gentle birth. The Earl's mother dwells on her dower lands, but sometimes visits, and the Earl has two daughters, Aline and Matilda.'

Aoife stiffened. 'He has been married before?'

FitzHarding shook his head. 'No. He and the girls' mother did not go before a priest for she was not of his rank, and the King would not permit him to marry anyway, but the lady was no whore. She died many years ago and he has taken responsibility for the girls and raised them in his household. Matilda is close to your own age, Aline a little younger.'

She wondered if de Clare's womenfolk had any influence over him as she had over her own father. At least the domestic arrangements at Striguil would provide her with some security.

Her father arrived to escort them to the wharf and the waiting ship. He wore the red-brown tunic and a fur-lined cloak King Henry had given him, and FitzHarding's barber had trimmed his hair and beard so that he better resembled a regal warlord than his usual Norse pirate straight off a raiding boat. Her brothers too had been spruced up, their rough edges smoothed to reflect

Norman aristocratic sensibilities. Her father gave her a strong hug. 'There's my brave girl,' he said. 'We'll be home at Fearns before you know it.'

'You promise you won't leave me behind among strangers?' She curled her fingers in the soft fur lining his cloak. 'Even if you do make a marriage agreement?'

His chest rumbled with laughter. 'Of course, I promise. Why would I leave you behind? Should it come to an agreement, and your marriage be a part of it, he shall only have you if he comes to Ireland and makes good on his word. Otherwise I might as well be casting my greatest treasure into the midden. You are the bait in the trap, my girl, but you are not to be eaten.'

'Will it come to an agreement do you think?' She bit her lip.

He shrugged. 'Whoever I employ will expect to be rewarded. Perhaps I will have to bind such a man with family ties, but we shall see. Do not worry about it.'

'I am not worried,' Aoife said staunchly. 'And if it is the only way I will do it – for you.'

He rewarded her with a big smile. 'My beautiful girl.' He hugged her again. 'I am in no haste to bargain you away, never think that.'

His words settled her down. She would go forward with confidence, and make sure everyone knew how much she was worth, especially this Richard de Clare.

Bats flitted overhead in the spring twilight as Aoife and her family arrived at Striguil. They disembarked at the wharf in front of the castle and stepped out onto the causeway leading up to the gates. The sky was clear in the west but it had rained earlier, and the ground was damp underfoot. Aoife lifted her gown above the mud and fought her anxiety. She wanted to arrive in royal state, not like a draggled refugee.

The Severn had been in spring spate and they had had to time the tide out of Bristol. Joining the Wye, they had meandered up the estuary in a series of snaking brown curves and Aoife had been watching Striguil approach for some time, losing sight of the castle, regaining it. Built upon the cliff face, the fortress reared like a geometrical extension of the rock with occasional window arches and narrow viewing slits. It was imposing rather than welcoming, but certainly looked secure.

At the timber gatehouse fronting the fortress, two soldiers stood guard, spears at the ready. Aoife sensed her father's tension as he gripped his staff and her own stomach clenched with fear.

'I am Diarmait MacMurchada, King of Leinster,' her father announced, his voice loud, and harsh, sounding almost angry because of his unease. 'I come as an invited guest and I come on business with your lord, the Earl of Striguil.'

A man stepped forward through the entrance, tall and as broad as a door, fair-haired with eyes the colour of flints. Unlike the guards he wore no armour, although a sword adorned his hip, hanging from a belt punched with silver decorations. He bowed deeply to Diarmait, and at a gesture the soldiers knelt too. 'Welcome,' he said. 'My lord is expecting you and all is prepared. I am Raymond FitzWilliam of Carew, a knight of his household. I will conduct you to him.'

Her father flexed his shoulders and settled himself at this appropriate show of respect, and Aoife's anxiety diminished a little.

Beyond the gatehouse reared a high stone wall and through another door, also guarded by soldiers, she saw the towering rectangular Norman keep they had seen from the river. Not as great or refined as the King's palace at Saumur, it had its own kind of solid majesty, grounded and definite.

The entrance to the castle was above ground level with steps leading to a doorway decorated with a patterned arch of zig-zags and painted chevrons. A man stepped from the darkness of the arch and came down the steps to greet them. Tall and well proportioned, he moved with confident grace. His tunic was grey, topped by a cloak of a darker, charcoal hue, lined with squirrel fur, creating a strong but subtle contrast. His hair was the same rich auburn as the squirrel pelts.

'Welcome to Striguil, sire.' He bowed his head in courtesy and extended his hand to clasp her father's. 'I trust you have journeyed well?' His voice was light, but the words were clearly spoken and his smile showed a flash of white teeth. He sent a brief glance in her direction, as he encompassed everyone in his greeting.

'Well enough, my lord,' her father answered in accented French. 'But glad to arrive. You have a fine castle.' His gaze roved the walls.

'It serves its purpose well,' de Clare replied, still smiling. 'Will you come within?'

Diarmait presented Aoife's mother and her brothers to de Clare, and then spread his arm in a flourish. 'And this is my daughter, Aoife.'

Aoife swallowed and held her ground as she had held it before King Henry. De Clare's eyes were clear with a glassy mingling of sea-colours, utterly striking against the dark contrast of his pupils. His stare was as intense as Henry's had been but assessing rather than predatory.

'My lady, you are indeed welcome,' he said, speaking slowly and clearly to help her understand him. 'Word of your great beauty has carried before you, and it is not exaggerated.'

Aoife's face burned and she briefly looked away, uncertain of his courtliness, but then she forced her gaze back to his. 'You are kind, sire.' Her reply was in keeping with his comment, but she was too flustered to know what else to say.

'I hope always to be so to ladies,' he replied, with a smile. 'This is my sister, Basilia, and she shall take you to refresh yourselves after your journey.'

Aoife turned her attention to the woman who had joined Richard on the steps. She was tall too, and elegant, with patrician features severely framed by a pristine white wimple. She reminded

Aoife of a cathedral statue in a niche or even a nun. 'Come,' Basilia said, extending her hand, 'you must be tired and cold. I know what the wind on the river is like.'

Aoife was not sure about leaving her father, but he was already clapping Richard on the back as if they were old drinking cronies and allowing himself to be led away into masculine camaraderie. Glancing over his shoulder at Aoife, he gave her a swift, almost piratical wink that did not settle her anxiety one little bit.

The lady Basilia brought them to a large room behind the hall, furnished with carved benches and tables. A fire glowed in the hearth and the sides of the room were lined with arched alcoves with benches, the de Clare chevrons decorating both cushions and the alcove interiors. The walls were whitewashed, making the room light and airy. An embroidery frame stood by one of the benches and beside it a large basket of brightly coloured wool.

'In daylight, you can see the river from the windows,' Basilia said. 'It is a pleasant place to look out and sew, especially in summer. But it is a strong defensive position too. This keep is the safest on all the border.' She directed her guests to the long benches before the fire. Maids arrived with bowls of warm rose water to wash the visitors' feet. Basilia herself saw to the washing of Môr's feet and Aoife's. 'I have arranged beds in the next chamber,' she said, indicating a doorway as she worked. 'We have sheets of good Irish linen that have been stored in lavender, so I hope you will feel at home and sleep well in them.'

The serving women brought wine and small spiced wafers drizzled with honey and sprinkled with nuts. Aoife had never tasted anything so delicious and had to restrain herself from devouring the entire platter. The wine warmed her stomach, reviving her. Gazing round the room, she imagined herself as lady of Striguil, dispensing largesse and welcoming strangers, the household keys at her belt. The lord's wife, with all this at her command. She would be able to help her father; instead of being his dependant, she would be a great lady with access to all these resources.

Until now she had not truly realised what being the wife of a Norman lord meant, but now her eyes were open. She would not want to live among strangers – she would need her own people with her – but from thinking of Striguil as a forbidding fortress, she was now considering it as a possible comfortable home. Richard de Clare was the key to everything, and she shivered, partly with fear, partly with excitement at the enormity of change she was contemplating.

'Are you cold?' Basilia asked with concern.

Finding a polite smile, Aoife shook her head. 'I was just wondering . . . I need to . . . it has been a long journey.'

'Ah.' Basilia indicated a low doorway.

Aoife thanked her, rose and went into the room, closing the door behind her, and attended to the business of emptying her bladder. A basket of soft moss stood ready at the side of the hole and she wiped herself and cast the moss down the shaft. And then she put her face in her hands, her shoulders shaking. She would not show weakness in front of others. Her façade was the adult, dignified lady and princess of her people, and for her father's sake she must carry this through and own the role as if she was solid to the core. But no matter the toughness of her outer shell, inside there stood a small, scared and desperate child, her face streaked with tears and soot as she walked away from her burning home.

Richard settled his Irish visitors in the great hall before the fire while the servants set up trestle tables, adorning them with fine napery. He introduced his senior knights and retainers. Diarmait and his entourage reminded him of the entertainers and players who had visited Striguil when he was a child. The sort who wore outlandish clothes and danced on sword points and would steal the money out of your purse while looking you straight in the eyes. But even while you dared not take your attention off them for an instant, they made the room vibrant and alive.

Diarmait MacMurchada in his furs, with his beard combed down over his chest and his thick iron-grey hair, was a bear of a man, exaggerated and imposing. Domnall was a lighter version of his sire, and the youngster was a handsome lad on the verge of adolescence, fair-haired and freckled. Diarmait's daughter, although still very young, was an eye-catching beauty; FitzHarding had not lied, and Richard had already identified her role in Diarmait's strategy.

Diarmait held out his hands to the fire. 'You see us clad in our travelling clothes,' he said with a shrewd glance at Richard as if reading his mind. 'I assure you we have better in our baggage and we are not some ragged company who has thrown ourselves in your path.'

Richard gestured with an open hand and smiled. 'It matters not to me. I welcome you as you are.'

A squire arrived with wine and cups and Richard set about serving his guests personally as a mark of honour.

Diarmait drank and smacked his lips. 'Good.'

'Raisin wine of Cyprus,' Richard said. 'I confess to a fondness.'

His uncle Hervey de Montmorency handed round cinnamon wafers, hot from the irons, served in napkins to prevent the eaters from burning their fingers.

'You have a fine castle here,' Diarmait said as Richard sat down across from him, 'and fine fare.' He chewed and swallowed and accepted another wafer, blowing on it first before he took a bite. 'Master FitzHarding told us you were a man of taste and standing. I greatly admire the quality of the weapons that come from your workshops.'

'I hope to continue in that vein with any bargains we may strike in future,' Richard said, toasting Diarmait. His guests were here to discuss matters of mutual interest but it was still like a session of weapons practice. Circling each other, testing for weakness, seeking an opening. 'I know some of what brings you to these shores, but perhaps you will tell us all a little more.' He gestured to his men.

Diarmait finished his second wafer, took a swallow of wine and rested his cup on his thigh. 'Let us say it has been necessary to be away from our lands for a little while because of sore rebellion and contention. To deal with it, I am recruiting men of sound military ability.'

'That much we had heard, sire.' Richard was interested in how carefully Diarmait was choosing his words.

'There is a long-standing feud between myself and other Irish lords – the reasons do not matter for now, although surely I will tell you in time. You must know of such things from your own experience, and how fickle fate can be.'

'Indeed,' Richard agreed, not without sympathy.

'They came upon us in treachery and had I not acted swiftly we would have been murdered in our beds even down to the last child.' Diarmait's eyes sparked with angry pain. 'I burned down my own palace rather than have those traitors step foot inside it, and I brought my family across the sea to safety. I still have resources and my enemies will not stay united for long. They will quarrel with each other soon enough and bury their axes in each other's skulls. I have loyal clansmen in Leinster awaiting my return, and there will be rich rewards for all true men when I take back what is mine. All we need are the necessary trained warriors to finish this for good – and that includes seizing the ports.'

Richard was intrigued and a little amused by Diarmait's combination of fierce bluster and sincerity. Now was not the time to discuss those rewards, but their presence on the table was tantalising. 'Do you have a time by which you hope to return?'

Diarmait shrugged. 'That depends on how quickly I can recruit the right men. Tomorrow if it were possible, although I know it will take longer than that. When we return, we shall not spare our enemies the blade.' The bluster was gone and Richard saw the steel in Diarmait's expression. 'I will pay the price, whatever I must, to have dominion.'

'We should talk terms,' Richard said. 'Not tonight, when you have so recently arrived, but tomorrow perhaps.'

Diarmait gave a short nod. 'Aye, tomorrow,' he agreed. 'First thing.'

The main meal was usually eaten around noon, but to honour their guests, the cooks at Striguil had prepared a beef stew spiced with cinnamon and pepper and baked a fresh batch of bread.

Refreshed, the women joined the men in the hall. Aoife sat demurely beside her mother. She had changed her travelling gown for the green wool trimmed with red, and green jewels shone in her hair. Again, her beauty struck Richard – that dark hair somewhere between black and brown, the alabaster skin and flecked green eyes. But there was something more elusive about her too. Perhaps an awareness of how different she was to the Norman women of his acquaintance. She had an air of constrained wildness that reminded him of a hawk with bound wings. The way she met his gaze with flashing challenge although she was barely a woman intrigued him. He supposed she had experienced the hard face of warfare, including the burning of her home, and her father's entourage seemed to be no place for gentle manners. She was bait in the trap; he knew that much.

'You keep a generous and orderly table, my lord,' Diarmait said as they ate. He leaned towards Richard's uncle Hervey. 'Is it always thus or is this a performance for the guests?' He smiled broadly to show that he was jesting. Or was he?

Richard had been watching Diarmait's eyes sweep over his men, had seen the shrewd evaluation going on behind the affable façade. And behind the smile was a pertinent if crudely phrased question, the answer to which, as a buyer, Diarmait had every right to know. Richard sent Hervey an amused look.

'I have lived in this household for more than a score of years and the standard has never changed, save perhaps to improve,' Hervey said, folding his arms in a comfortable manner. 'You will not find better trained, better equipped or better fed knights among any of your travels. My nephew attracts the best to his banner precisely because of the way he maintains his household – he is generous, but do not mistake generosity for softness. No man shirks his duties and we train hard. The Marches are no place for anyone who cannot stand his ground.'

'Neither is Ireland,' Diarmait said, clearly impressed, but striving not to seem too eager.

'I put my resources into things that matter,' Richard said. 'My father taught me to care for my retainers, as I am sure you care for yours. That way we remain strong and fight back to back until the last man standing.' He looked Diarmait in the eyes. 'We do not desert our friends. We trust each other absolutely and my men know I will never let them down. While I have it, they will always have meat in their bellies and wine in their cups, even if I must go without.'

'But it comes at a cost.'

'Everything comes at a cost, as you know. If something is worth having, it is worth paying for, but you should always be sure it is worth owning and know when the price goes beyond the value you have set on your desire.'

Diarmait ran his tongue around his teeth. 'Then we are of a kind, and we can do business together. But as you say, that is for another day.' He took a fistful of raisins from a dish in the centre of the table and began eating them one by one.

Richard judged it the right time to call for entertainment and summoned Hervey to sing for them in his powerful, melodic voice. A second song followed with a rousing chorus that everyone could join in, and the men linked arms and swayed at the tables. Diarmait's sons rose to demonstrate some dances of their country, their steps swift and dextrous. Diarmait's bard Maurice narrated an Irish tale in translation of the great warrior hero Cúchulainn and his feats of strength.

And then, Diarmait rose to his feet, called for silence and raised his cup. 'My hosts and fellow kinsmen!' he announced in heavily accented French. 'Today is an auspicious meeting of new friends and allies! To show our appreciation for the friendship and hospitality we have received, my beloved daughter Aoife shall play and sing for you and never, I guarantee, will you have heard such music before!'

Richard raised his cup courteously to Aoife, who was blushing at her father's declaration. He was curious, but cautious, and not fooled for one moment. The bait had just been attached to the hook.

The girl murmured to an attendant, who disappeared, returning moments later with a leather case containing her harp. She removed the instrument and brought it to the bench that her father's bard had recently vacated. Richard admired the way the green gown flowed over her body, and now she was in the open he saw that the sides were fastened with crimson laces, hinting at that suppressed wild side of her. Her shoes peeped out from beneath the full hem of the gown, Irish shoes with delicate criss-cross ties, and they too were red. She stroked the gleaming curve of the harp's spine as she would a beloved child.

Silence fell, save for the crackle of the fire, and everyone watched Aoife.

Her fingers undulated through the harp strings, delicate and sure. A slight flush still brightened her face, but she was radiant now, rather than embarrassed. Richard closed his eyes and let the liquid music ripple over him. When she sang, her ice-pure voice raised the hair on his nape and along his arms. The notes soared and he soared with them, absorbing the magic as the shivers ran down his spine.

The final note resonated and faded and the hall was once more silent, this time because her audience was both captive and

Stanway Library
Renewals/Enquiries: 0345 603 7628
Visit us online: libraries.essex.gov.uk

Customer ID: ********9476

Items that you have borrowed

Title: The Irish princess
ID: 30130301980727
Due: 02 April 2022

Total items: 1
Account balance: £0.00
Borrowed: 3
Overdue: 1
Hold requests: 0
Ready for collection: 0
12/03/2022 10:35

Items that you already have on loan

Title:
ID: 30130303565251 8/1/2022 11:09
ESTSTW b £6.55 Time to say goodbye

Title: Time to say goodbye
ID: 30130303565251
Due: 29 January 2022

Thank you for using Essex Libraries

Essex **Library** Services

Stanway Library
Renewals/Enquiries 0345 603 7628
Visit us online: libraries.essex.gov.uk

Customer ID: **********9476

Items that you have borrowed

Title: The Irish princess
ID   30130300136727
Due: 02 April 2022

Total items: 1
Account balance: £0.00
Borrowed: 3
Overdue: 1
Hold requests: 0
Ready for collection: 0
12/03/2022 10:35

Items that you already have on loan

Title:
ID: 30130300355251 8/1/2022,11:09
         ESTSTW b £6.55 Time to say goodbye

Title: Time to say goodbye
ID: 30130300355251
Due: 29 January 2022

Thank you for using Essex Libraries

dumb. With an effort, Richard opened his eyes and swallowed. He didn't want to come back from the place she had taken him; he wanted to hold the beauty for ever, but it was as fleeting as a flash of sunlight over a leaping salmon in the Wye. Standing, he raised his cup to her. 'My lady, you have honoured us deeply with your voice and your playing. Truly you have a gift from God, and I thank you for sharing it with us. Never have I been so moved by a single moment of music.'

Her blush returned more fiercely than before. Her eyes in the evening firelight were as dark as the green jewels in her hair. She curtseyed in acknowledgement and the tension broke as Richard set down his cup to applaud and the rest of the gathering followed his lead with calls for more.

Diarmait leaped over the trestle to embrace her, giving her smacking kisses on both cheeks. He swept her up and swung her round, to cheers and laughter, and sat beside her on the bench. 'Sing the one about the swans you always sang to me when you were a little girl,' he encouraged, and then spoke in Irish: 'Pretend it is just for me, precious girl, and no one else.'

Aoife put her harp aside, took a breath and sang unaccompanied, her voice clean and soaring. Richard was utterly besotted by the sound and did not even have to understand the words for images to fill his head. He had never experienced such a channelling of purity, and it expanded his own being. If this girl was wild, she was also innocent and elemental, and in this moment he wanted her and her magic for himself for ever. Diarmait looked at him over Aoife's head. Their eyes met in perfect understanding and Diarmait smiled and did not have to say that now Richard knew the value of the prize and that it was worth any price.

Aoife finished her song to more rapturous applause and the women prepared to retire and leave the men to their drinking and bonding.

'I hope you will sing again for us during your stay,' Richard said to Aoife. 'You have a truly remarkable voice.'

'Thank you, sire,' she murmured. 'If it be your pleasure, I shall be glad.'

With the women gone, Richard felt almost bereft. The experience of hearing Aoife sing still resonated within him but he was starting to rationalise his initial reaction. He wanted her as he wanted a rare and valuable object, but he did not know her personally, nor if he could live with her day to day as his wife. Any bargain he struck with Diarmait had to be advantageous for himself and his dynasty. Marriage to Aoife would elevate his status beyond that of Diarmait's hired fist and would vouchsafe his power, but a wife could be either a helpmate or a shackle. She could season a stew or poison it, and need was always more important than want.

12

Castle of Striguil, Welsh Marches, spring 1167

In the morning, Richard took his Irish guest to see the armoury. Diarmait remained affable and circumspect and Richard was patient, recognising the game. At some stage they would come to the point, but for now they continued to gauge each other's strengths and weaknesses.

He showed Diarmait the barrels of arrows, the spears, the mail shirts and coifs, the shields bearing the de Clare chevrons. Everything tidy, organised, cared for. He unsheathed a sword and made a few practice cuts before handing it to Diarmait.

'A fine hilt and blade,' Diarmait said. 'Good balance.' With the sudden speed of a striking snake, he flashed the side of the blade within inches of Richard's throat. 'Very fine indeed.' He grinned at Richard's recoil, relishing the ripple of shock it had caused in the Norman contingent. Richard hastily recalibrated his notions concerning Diarmait. He had not seen that move coming, nor expected so much speed from a man fast approaching his sixtieth year.

'I can see I must stay on my mettle and take nothing for granted,' Richard said with a short laugh. 'Keep the sword if you will, sire.' He gestured round the space, including his hearth knights in the sweep of his arm. 'What do you think all this is worth to you?'

Diarmait tugged his beard and screwed up his face and eventually named a cautious price. Richard nodded. 'That could be a basis for negotiation. What if I told you I was looking for more than twice that amount.'

Diarmait narrowed his eyes. 'I would say you take me for a fool.'

'Come.' Richard crossed the room and opened a second door leading through to another chamber filled with more weaponry, with pieces of siege equipment, rope, barrels of nails, and bars of iron for horseshoes. Two men were engaged in cleaning the equipment, and beyond that was a workshop and forge under an awning where a smith was fashioning arrow heads.

Diarmait gazed around, thrusting out his jaw. He walked further into the room, touching and examining. 'We might be able to reach an agreement,' he said cautiously.

'Then perhaps you will tell me more of your purpose now you have seen our measure.'

Diarmait examined a spear. 'I am hoping you will help us to regain Leinster from its usurpers. If you choose to come, then you shall be a friend for life, and I shall personally treat you like a son.'

Diarmait's response did not give Richard much more information than last night, but the final part of the sentence was telling. 'Then we must see what can be done. We should sit down and talk seriously about it in friendship and alliance.'

Diarmait smiled. 'I am ready when you are.'

They returned to the first room and Diarmait stopped at the bow on the wall. 'Now that is a fine thing.'

Richard lifted it down and handed it to him. 'I will give you any number of swords and axes,' he said. 'You may have my men and my expertise, but not this.'

'Ah, I do not shoot the bow,' Diarmait said with a smile. 'I would rather feel my enemy's blood running down my wrist than deal with him at arrow's length. But I would gladly see you shoot it.'

The men repaired to the practice ground and Diarmait watched Richard's demonstration with a keen eye. 'You have skill,' he said, and tested the draw of the bow before Richard returned it to the armoury. 'And you are stronger than you look.' A new respect gleamed in his eyes.

'Appearances are often deceptive,' Richard replied. 'A man should be honourable to his allies, but it is no bad thing to take an enemy by surprise.'

Diarmait bared his teeth in laughter and slapped Richard's shoulder. 'A man after my own heart!'

Standing at the window in the ladies' chamber, Aoife listened to male shouts drifting up from somewhere below, and the clunk of shields battering against each other.

'The men are training,' Basilia said, looking up from her sewing frame.

Aoife had picked up a needle to help because it was the accepted social thing to do, but sewing was not her favourite pastime and she had abandoned it at the first sounds of combat through the open window.

'Do they train often?' Môr asked. She sat beside Basilia, plying her own needle with dexterity.

'Most days,' Basilia replied. 'Dwelling on the Welsh border, we have to stay on our mettle.'

'I would like to go down and see them,' Aoife said, adding, 'if it is possible.' She gave Basilia a smile and a shy look to enhance her request. 'I would like to see your knights in training. Perhaps the men would like an audience to admire their skill?'

Basilia carefully set her needle in the fabric. 'Why not? It is a fine day, and I do not believe my brother would object.' She pushed the frame aside and called for their cloaks, donning hers sedately and adjusting the edges to make them level. Aoife had to stop herself from flinging on her own and running down the stairs. Instead she made a studied effort to match Basilia's decorum.

The bracing spring breeze flapped the ladies' veils against their faces. The sky was a vivid deep blue and the clouds as white as packed snow.

On a grassy area between the outer and inner walls the men were at weapons practice, and Aoife's breath shortened at the sight of Richard de Clare sparring with his uncle Hervey de Montmorency. She had often watched her brothers and was accustomed to seeing daring, speed and dexterity, but Richard had a way of changing his move at the last moment without signalling, or of coming in at an unexpected angle, that was controlled and fluid – an intricate dance where he changed the steps at will and never false-footed. She watched, a strange feeling in the pit of her belly. In the hall and in his pleasantries to her family, he had seemed urbane and ordinary with little indication that he possessed such forceful grace. Now he was dominant and determined to win, but every risk was calculated.

His men were highly trained; indeed, they were formidable, and they were holding back. Imagining what they would be like when unleashed in battle made her swallow. Her father had to have these soldiers and more like them because no one in Ireland would be able to stand against them. Picturing what they would do to Tiernan ua Ruari gave her a fierce burn of anticipatory vengeance.

The men broke off to drink watered wine and rest. Richard was breathing hard but not overtaxed. His face was flushed and his hair dark chestnut at the tips with sweat as he moved among his knights, slapping shoulders, laughing, offering advice and discussing tactics. He glanced briefly over to the women and smiled at Aoife. Her cheeks burning, she returned his stare then dropped her gaze.

Her father stepped forward. 'Now it is our turn!' he declared, clearly attempting to conceal how impressed he had been. He gestured to Domnall and his men and they came together to demonstrate their own skills with shield and spear and axe. Again there were quicksilver movements, the dexterity of men trained in their art. Aoife noted how Richard watched it all closely, particularly the axe play. She was proud of the way their warriors performed, but she saw their wildness, their laxer discipline, and they did not have the armour that Richard's men wore like a second skin. To strike at the Normans would be like hitting a solid wall. And that was even before it came to the matter of their cavalry, of which she had heard fearsome things. These people were deadly and it made her restless, excited and more than a little afraid.

When the men had finished, they repaired to the armoury, talking between themselves, clapping each other on the back. Her father looked over his shoulder to give her a meaningful grin and a wink.

Back in the women's chambers, Aoife could not settle; the sight of the sewing made her want to run and scream. She needed to talk to her father, not be cooped in here with female company and needlework of which Richard's sister seemed terribly fond. If she became lady of Striguil, Aoife vowed she would not spend her time sewing. There were servants for that. She drifted into a reverie, imagining the keys of the household at her belt.

A short while later, Richard arrived. He had removed his mail and wore an indoor robe of soft blue wool girded with a red leather belt. Aoife imagined him walking into a room where she had the power of being his wife and she put every iota of that imagination into the look she sent him. *I will have you. You are mine.* And saw an answering gleam in his eyes.

Richard bowed to the women. 'I trust you enjoyed the entertainment, ladies.'

'Indeed, my lord, we did,' Môr replied. 'It was most instructive.'

'And you, demoiselle?' He turned to Aoife.

'As my mother says, it was indeed. I hope for your part you found our Irish warrior skills instructive too.'

His lips twitched. 'Certainly, and I have been given much to think about.' He turned to Basilia. 'A quick word if you will, sister.'

Basilia set her sewing aside and went further into the room

with him, out of earshot. Aoife watched them and felt a tug of envy. It could be her in that position in future. She could be his confidante and adviser. His gaze flicked to her and she busied herself sorting threads while her mind worked at its own needlecraft, stitching a narrative in her imagination and embellishing it to her desire.

'I need you to check the stores again,' Richard said to Basilia. 'We shall be expecting more visitors.'

'More?' Her lips tightened with surprise and displeasure, but she kept her voice pitched low. 'How many?'

'I have written to men who might be interested in fighting for King Diarmait. We need to make provision for those who choose to answer in person rather than by letter.'

Basilia gave an annoyed sigh. 'You have been so keen to husband our resources in the past, yet you are spending them most profligately now, and to what gain?'

'What would you do if you were in my situation, sister?' Richard said, irritated with her. 'Would you sit here and stultify, or would you take action that was available to you? I have to consider my future and that of our family. I am no longer Earl of Pembroke as our father was. That title has been stripped away through no fault of our own. We cannot afford to sit on our haunches. I am not acting rashly even if you think I am – I have waited too long for this to be a rash act.'

'But it is still a great risk.'

'Yes, but that is different to being rash. I have to know the risks in order to go beyond them. I am playing to win. Diarmait MacMurchada needs men to help him retake his birth right, but I am not about to be a mere hireling. If I go to his aid, I will command an army and I will make my mark, not for coin, but for land and family. This is not about a few piddling provisions of meat and wine and beds for the night. It is about reclaiming the power we have been denied, and reclaiming it many-fold. That is what is to be gained and I will not have you scowling at me and calling me to task. Do you understand?' He swallowed his anger, realising that although their voices were low, their visitors would still be aware that an altercation was taking place. 'Once we have negotiated the details, our Irish guests will be leaving to talk with the lord Rhys in Ceredigion. I have promised to escort them there. You will not have to abide a full keep for long. This is our best opportunity to move forward and I intend to seize it in both hands.'

She had flushed as he castigated her, but now withdrew into icy composure. 'You have made things very clear,' she said stiffly. 'But let me ask you – what will the King say when he hears of your plans?'

'Since Robert FitzHarding sent the Irish first to the King and then to me, he is a common link between us and Henry agreed to let Diarmait of Leinster recruit throughout his dominions. I shall seek Henry's permission and be careful with him, but I hope he will see the benefit to all parties. If he wants Ireland, I am his means, and I need this enterprise to succeed.' To conciliate, he gave her a peck on the cheek.

She sighed. 'I will check the stores and tell you later.'

'Thank you, I am grateful.'

'I hope you are,' she said, turning on her heel.

Richard went to the door, bowing again to the women, and in particular to Aoife, who did not meet his look beyond a swift glance.

Going to the stables, he ordered his groom to saddle up Ajax. His uncle Hervey was talking to a couple of squires nearby and Richard beckoned to him. 'Ride with me,' he said.

The big chestnut pricked his ears and nickered at Richard, already questing for the morsel of bread and honey concealed in Richard's hand. Smiling, Richard held out his palm, allowing the stallion to whiffle up the treat with his soft muzzle. The preliminaries observed, he gathered the reins and swung into the saddle. Hervey joined him on his dun and the men rode out of Striguil side by side.

Hervey's face wore its customary expression of good humour and he was content to ride in silence and wait for Richard to broach whatever was troubling him. Richard took the road to his great uncle's Cistercian foundation at Tintern, a little over five miles from Striguil. He would bring the Irish here if all went well, but for now he wished to visit alone. As they rode, he glanced at the grazing sheep, the pasture and the thick woodland with its timber and forage. He was fortunate to have this, yet he longed for something more. A challenge, a purpose.

'What do you think of our Irish guests?' he asked.

His uncle's eyes creased with a smile. 'They are entertaining for certain,' he said, 'and they have stirred us out of our usual routines.'

'Indeed.' Richard's smile was rueful.

'They want you to coordinate a force to cross the Irish Sea and retake their land – that is the gist of it.'

'Yes, and now I must decide whether I want the task and balance what I shall ask in payment against what it might cost.'

'I think you have already decided to agree,' Hervey said. 'I have not seen you so restless or so engaged for many a day.'

'It's a risk, uncle, and I am potentially endangering all of this for something I have yet to attain.'

'Yes,' Hervey agreed, 'you are. And for people you have but recently met and do not know – people in exile with very different customs and ways, and whose only coin might be promises. Better the bird in the hand perhaps.'

It was why he had brought Hervey with him. His uncle always gave him the truth and voiced the doubts that others would not speak. 'But the bird in the hand is a sorry plucked thing. Our ancestors came from Normandy with King William and they took the same risks. If I do not do this, I shall be letting them down. What do I have to show for my time as custodian of our family name? I have already heard it said that my ancestors are more illustrious than their current scion.'

'You know that is not the truth,' Hervey said gently.

'It is what the world sees as the truth, and thus it stands in the eyes of men,' Richard countered bitterly. 'What it comes down to is that I can either stagnate here or take my chance.'

'Then you have your answer, and you do not need me.'

'But I do, uncle, because you ask me the questions that matter. I like the Irish king. I might not trust him, but I like him. He has great courage and enterprise.'

'And his daughter?' Hervey asked with a smile.

Richard ran his tongue over his teeth. 'His daughter,' he repeated, and Aoife's stare filled his mind; those green eyes, minutely flecked with gold and all that challenge and innocence. 'If I do agree to fight in Ireland, there must be binding ties – family ties. As MacMurchada's son-in-law, I would be embedded in his dynasty and any children born of the match would be his potential heirs.'

'The girl would be entitled to a third of your lands in dower,' Hervey pointed out.

'As would any wife, and I am unlikely to have one with Henry's blessing.' He glanced at Hervey. 'I would have fine warrior sons of that stock, and beautiful daughters.'

Hervey nodded judiciously. 'That is true.'

'Did you hear her voice?' Briefly Richard closed his eyes, remembering the soaring purity.

'Yes,' Hervey replied quietly. 'She has a gift from God.'

Silence lingered between them for a while and then Richard said, 'It would be a fresh start – clean ground. But first I must obtain as much as possible from Diarmait. I need to anchor his promises in a marriage with his daughter, while giving as little as possible away for my own part. If I am to take this risk, it has to be right, or else it is nothing.'

He drew rein as they came in sight of the abbey's grey stone walls with their backdrop of forest clad in new-leaf green. Ewes with lambs at foot grazed the fields of the water meadow. A monk leaned on his shepherd's crook to watch them pass and summoned his dogs to heel.

'You need the King's consent to go to Ireland,' Hervey said. 'The lord of Leinster has permission to recruit mercenaries, but Henry may not see it in his interests to let you go.'

Richard grimaced. 'That is a dilemma. I need to make it as attractive and palatable as I can.' It would be no simple task for he and Henry would begin from a position of mistrust, not neutrality.

Abbot Henry of Tintern was a dedicated Cistercian with a robust physique and an attitude that anything could be achieved if the will was there and centred in the love of God. The latter emotion would occasionally overwhelm him and bring him to tears at the altar, but he was no mystic or aesthete. In the years before he took up his calling he had been a mercenary soldier who had freely indulged in rapine, thievery and plunder. He brought pragmatic skills to his position and a compassionate knowledge of the frailty of his fellow man. He and Richard had always dealt very well with each other.

'Doughty fighters the Irish,' he said when told of their visitors. 'I have crossed the Hibernian Sea a time or two and faced their axes and spears. I never served Diarmait MacMurchada, but he has a fearsome reputation.' He looked at Richard from under heavy silver brows. 'Bound for Ireland, then, are you?'

'Perhaps,' Richard replied. 'It depends on many things.'

'Then I shall pray for you.' The Abbot signed his breast with the cross.

In the church founded by his great uncle Walter, Richard knelt to his own prayers, asking God for His support and for the strength, wisdom and fortitude to carry his plan through. He had been undecided when he set out to Tintern, but as he prayed, his purpose firmed into determination. He envisioned himself as a hawk with the wind ruffling his feathers and the Hibernian

Sea stretching out before him in layers of white-capped waves and furrows. His destiny was to cross that sea, and behind his closed eyes he saw that he could fly higher than any opposition and whatever happened be more than he was now.

His prayers finished, he and Hervey dined with the Abbot in his quarters on sweet mutton that had been slaughtered to make parchment of its hide.

'Diarmait of Leinster,' said the Abbot, made loquacious by the wine he was serving his guests and drinking copiously himself. 'A cunning and sly old badger, but he has had to be to survive. In Ireland there are many kings. In England they would be of the rank of earl and they answer to a high king, although more often than not that answer is rebellion against his authority.' He gave Richard and Hervey a wry look. 'The man with the strongest sword, the tightest kinship ties and the greatest influence holds the title until he is toppled. In seeking your aid, MacMurchada has just raised the stakes.'

Richard looked at his distorted reflection in the side of his silver cup. Did he want to be a part of that gamble? He had his reservations, but still his blood sang at the thought.

'It is a rich land, Ireland,' Abbot Henry continued. 'The Irish count their wealth in cattle and grain, and the jewels they wear. The grass of Leinster is lush and green.'

'And the Norsemen controlling the ports?'

The Abbot wiped wine from his lips and, leaning back, folded his arms. 'They bring wealth to the land with their weapons and their textiles, and the sale of slaves. Sometimes they acknowledge the Irish kings and sometimes they war against them depending on the advantage they see to themselves. MacMurchada has taken tribute and allegiance from Dublin when high on Fortune's wheel, and been turned upon and savaged when his rule has been brought low. The tale is well known of how he was a small boy when they buried his father with the corpse of a dog. If you ask me what drives the man, then I would give you that deed as his compass.' He opened his hand towards Richard. 'I wish you God's luck with the Irish of Leinster. You are young and vigorous enough to be quickened by the adventure.' His smile was self-deprecating. 'I am glad that I broke my spear over my knee many years ago, and that today I heed a different song, because otherwise I might be tempted.'

As dusk fell, the company gathered again in Striguil's hall to eat chicken flavoured with mint and sage, the juices soaked up by fresh white bread. Aoife sang again for the company and her voice sent shivers through Richard's bones and the shivers turned to fire. Knowing Diarmait was watching closely, he retained an impassive façade and praised the performance as would a courteous host rather than a man enthralled. He noticed the way Aoife bit her lip and the swift glance she shot her father and it made him even more determined not to be manipulated, especially after what he had been told by Abbot Henry this afternoon.

The women retired and Richard bowed them chivalrously from the hall and sent for fresh jugs of wine accompanied by dishes of nuts and dried fruits. Then he gathered his inner council of knights and his Irish guests and settled at a table near the fire.

Diarmait took it upon himself to pour the wine and handed Richard a brimming goblet. 'So,' he said with one eye bright, the other half squinting, 'you have shown us you have the power to strike and now you want to know if it is worth striking.'

'Indeed.' Richard took a swallow of wine and waited.

Diarmait hunched his shoulders. 'I can tell you that the more you try to nail my enemies down, the harder they retaliate. We must strike decisively and with full resources. Only then shall we succeed. But if you can help me to do so, then the land is full of rich grazing, cattle and timber. Grain is plentiful. We shall all be wealthy indeed.' He raised his cup to his men, who saluted in return and banged their fists on the board in unison.

'And what will be our recompense for this?' Richard asked.

'How will we benefit from these Irish lands?' He indicated his own men. 'I take it you are including all of us when you say "we"?'

Diarmait gave him a crafty look. 'Of course. You will be richly rewarded for your part.'

Richard set his cup down. 'We must reach a point where we become more specific about those rewards. General promises may grease the wheels, but they do not of themselves start the cart rolling.'

Diarmait rubbed his palm over his beard. 'Aye,' he said, 'let us then show the hound the hare, why not?' He called for Maurice Regan and taking a scroll from his hand, spread a parchment map of Irish towns and territories on the table and named sums and estates that would be given to Richard and his men if they agreed to come.

Richard noted that much of the territory on offer was not Diarmait's but under the influence of either the Norse or his rival kings. 'It is no easy undertaking and would require reconnaissance before any major campaign was conducted or even decided upon,' he said. 'I cannot commit unless it is worth my while.'

Diarmait threw a handful of cracked nutshells into the fire. 'What more could I give you without beggaring myself?'

They locked eyes. 'You have brought your daughter with you,' Richard said, 'and you have been at pains to extol her virtues and present her as your rarest jewel. You are not now going to tell me she is not part of your strategy. What of her marriage?'

Diarmait scratched his jaw. 'Ah, her marriage.' Although his eyes twinkled, his gaze was hard.

'It is very simple,' Richard said. 'Without you offering her in marriage to me, nothing will happen; it is not negotiable.' In his peripheral vision he was aware of raised eyebrows among his men, although his uncle was nodding sagely. Raymond le Gros had pricked up his ears.

Diarmait said nothing.

'You would not have brought her to Striguil unless you intended to make her part of your plans,' Richard continued, his gaze as hard as Diarmait's. 'You could have left her in Bristol and no harm would have come to her. A marriage would guarantee my security and standing when I set foot in Ireland. It is one thing to fight for money, and another to have family ties. There is no point in me risking my all without that bond. It must be a full commitment. I am unlikely to find a suitable wife this side of the Irish Sea and my line will fail. I desire legitimate offspring, and I would have your daughter bear them; I see her mettle and I see the future our children would have.'

Diarmait dropped his gaze to his fingers and moved his thumb upon them as if counting. 'Aoife is very precious to me,' he said. 'There is no other like her and I shall sorely miss her when she goes to another man.' He paused, drawing the moment out, and Richard endured the silence, refusing to let it unsettle him.

'If you should take her in marriage,' Diarmait said eventually, 'I want her to remain close at hand with me. She shall still have her family.'

Richard nodded his assent, but thought that when it came the time, he would decide what was right for his own household, although he would not intentionally estrange father from daughter. Influence flowed in both directions. 'You are agreeing then?' he said. 'Let us be clear on this.'

Diarmait pursed his lips. 'In principle, yes.'

'In principle?'

'On the condition that it will only be binding when you personally set foot on Irish soil. If you are to wed my daughter, the marriage must take place before all of my people and on my land. Only when you arrive shall we have a wedding. And that too is where our negotiation begins and ends.'

Richard had suspected Diarmait would make that stipulation. He would have to go to Ireland to fight anyway. His insistence on the marriage and Diarmait's requirement that it take place in Ireland were just two ends of a circle waiting to clasp. After a suitable pause, he said, 'I think we have an agreement – pending permission from King Henry. Once I have it, I shall come. In the meantime, I shall start planning a campaign and obtaining soldiers and supplies. When I set foot in Ireland and achieve what you desire, I shall become your son-in-law.'

Diarmait nodded brusquely. 'Aye, we have an accord.' He extended his hand and Richard clasped it. Feeling the strength of Diarmait's callused palm and fingers, he acknowledged both the challenge and the affinity.

Aoife strolled through Striguil's garden carrying a basket and using a small set of shears to snip early dog roses from a tumbling hedge to make the scented hair lotion for which Basilia had promised her the recipe. Basilia herself was sitting on a bench sewing with Môr, but Aoife preferred to pick flowers. She watched the bees burrowing into the heart of the blossoms and inhaled the fresh, delicate perfume. The sun was warm on her spine and she should have felt at peace, but she was tense and unsettled. The men had spent all last night in detailed political discussion but she had no idea how the negotiations were progressing and whether they were any closer to an agreement. She had not spoken to her father this morning and he was again busy in council. She hated this waiting and was queasy with apprehension. What if Richard de Clare declined the offer and they came away with nothing? Their entire future depended on this. They were exiles, at the mercy of strangers who would only become friends and allies because they had something to gain.

She snipped another rose, and feeling a sensation of being watched, turned around, recoiling with a gasp for Richard was standing behind her and she had not heard his footfall. He had recently washed, for the ends of his hair were damp and a faint aroma of olive soap emanated from him. He smiled at her and she clutched the basket of roses like a shield.

'I wondered where I might find you.' Gently he prised the basket out of her arms and having set it down at their feet, took her hands in his. 'I wanted to tell you myself. Your father has granted me your hand in marriage, provisional on my coming to Ireland and supplying him with the men to retake your family's lands. You have given me reason to hope that this is agreeable to you also.'

Aoife swallowed and managed a nod. She was close to tears as all the suppressed emotion welled to the surface. Through blurred eyes she saw the concern on his face. 'I am sorry,' she said in a choked voice. 'It has been a difficult time for my family. I . . . I am glad you and my father have reached an agreement, and his wish is mine.' She tried to look at him but could not sustain the contact. She should be overwhelmed with joy at their success, but she wanted to run away because instead of a concept it was real and he was real and her hand was trapped in his lean fingers. This man would be her husband. He would share her bed and be intimate with her in the way her father was intimate with her mother. She would go from being a cherished and protected daughter to focusing her life on Richard de Clare's needs and demands. Suddenly those chatelaine's keys she had been coveting were an object of anxiety not desire.

'Look at me, Aoife.'

She forced herself to raise her head and prayed for her mother and Basilia to rescue her.

'You must not be afraid of me,' he said softly. 'I will not harm you. You will be honoured and protected in my household, and you shall have every privilege of a wife.'

'I am not afraid,' she said, although she had never been more frightened in her life.

'I am pleased to hear it – fear is no basis for trust and harmony between husband and wife. Come,' he said, 'let us walk awhile and you shall become accustomed to my company. Your mother and my sister are nearby – there is no cause for alarm. I only wish to speak to you.' He released her hand but then tucked her arm within his and walked with her along the garden path with the roses opening into blossom along the surrounding walls.

Aoife was conscious of every step she took. Looking down, she watched her shoes peep out from and withdraw under her skirts. The brush of her gown against his legs was almost too intimate.

'I am sure your father will tell you more,' he said. 'But I am pleased we have reached an accord.'

'But you will not be my husband until you come to Ireland?'

'That is the agreement, and I have every intention of honouring it.'

'How soon will that be?' She wondered how much leeway she had.

'As soon as can be arranged, and I have urgent reason to bring it to fruition now, but even so it will not be until next year.' He stopped and faced her. 'I know this is strange and new and we barely know each other, but in time it will become familiar, and it will be good, I promise you.'

He leaned in towards her and she ducked out from under his embrace. 'I have never held hands with a man before in any sort of intimacy,' she said, her voice tight with panic. 'I need to . . . you will excuse me.' She gathered her skirts and fled from him, her heels flashing as she ran. This was what she had worked for. They had their agreement and they could set about regaining all they had lost and wreak vengeance on their enemies, but now it was real and the potential consequences to herself were overwhelming.

Her mother looked up from her sewing, and Basilia half rose to her feet, but Aoife sped past the women out of the garden, fleeing towards safety. On reaching the bower, she slammed the door and leaned against it, eyes closed, heart hammering against her ribs.

Richard stared at the space where she had been standing,

puffed out his breath and raked his hands through his hair. He realised anew how young she was. Her tough façade was just that – a façade. He was dealing with a girl little older than his daughters. As she had said as she snatched her hand from his, she had had no contact with men. An upbringing amid violence and warfare, unprotected from its sights, might have made her aware of the world in many ways, but it had not prepared her for a personal daily relationship. He had to tread the most delicate path of his life and he had to succeed; he could not afford strife.

Taking the basket of roses, he returned it to Basilia and Môr who were staring in the direction Aoife had run.

'I did nothing,' Richard said as they regarded him with accusing eyes. 'I told her that her father and I had reached an agreement over Leinster and that our marriage would seal it.'

'She knows her duty to her family,' Môr replied. 'She is overcome, that is all. The matter has been much on her mind. I am pleased you and my husband are in accord.'

'As am I, madam.' Richard bowed to her – his future mother by marriage. She was a pleasant enough lady, but he did not know her, and she was another he would have to cultivate.

'I shall go and talk to her,' Môr said, and excused herself.

Basilia looked at Richard narrow-eyed. 'So, it is done,' she said. 'You have committed yourself to helping this Irish lord.'

'You knew it was my intention.' Basilia pressed her lips together, and Richard sighed and rubbed the back of his neck. 'It will be worth it, I promise you.'

'I wonder how you will manage with her as your chatelaine,' she said with a sniff. 'Do you think she can count stores and order supplies and run a great household? I tell you now, I will not be her servant.'

'No one said you would be,' he said curtly. 'Even if there is an agreement to wed it will not happen yet. I have to obtain the King's permission to go to Ireland and that means travelling to

Normandy. I have to organise warriors and weapons, ships and supplies, so it will not be until next spring at the earliest. I am sure Aoife will be capable of performing her duties when the time comes. She may be young and out of her depth for the moment, but she is not foolish and I can see already that she has a quick mind and the ability to learn. You will not be her servant, I promise you, but you will be kind to her and I will have harmony in my household.'

'Let us hope you are not like the fool wishing for the moon and trying to rake it out of a pool then,' she snapped.

He gave her a hard look. 'I can only do my best and expect the best from others.'

Colour flooded her cheeks. 'I have never given you less than my best, and even now you shall have it. But I will hold you to all you say. I shall be kind to the girl, indeed I feel sorry for her, but she is a wild thing, Richard. Have a care lest she rip out not only your heart but your entrails and then hands your cadaver to her father.'

'I think I am wise enough not to let that happen. Sometimes a little faith from you would be welcome.'

Her flush deepened but she did not apologise. 'What happens now? Are our guests remaining, or do they leave?'

'They will leave as soon as they have met and spoken to the men I have summoned. I want Robert FitzStephen for the task, so that means taking the Irish to Ceredigion to speak to the lord Rhys. After that I must go to the King and then to Master FitzHarding in Bristol to arrange finances.'

'"Arrange finances"? You mean go into debt?'

'I mean making sure I have the wherewithal to carry this through.'

She fell silent, although her misgiving and resentment were palpable. He knew it stemmed from her own need for security and her desire for order. But sometimes that order had to be disturbed to avoid stagnation.

'We will talk again later,' he said, and for form's sake kissed her cheek before leaving the garden.

Aoife looked at the ring on her finger and slowly turned it round, watching the ruby and sapphire gems gleam in the light. On several occasions she had tried it on in the relative privacy of the bower, but other than the night Richard had presented it to her in the great hall, she had not worn it on display. For the moment she had threaded it on a cord around her neck, and every now and again she touched its hard shape lying against her skin beneath her chemise.

It was not a betrothal ring; her father had been very clear in his announcement. He had called for silence, raised his drinking horn and proclaimed that he and Richard had struck a bargain. When Richard set foot in Ireland, he would become a lord of Ireland and would have Aoife's hand in marriage. The binding part was the setting foot on Irish soil. Until then it was an understanding and not a formal betrothal. The ring was a token of the promise to marry on those terms.

Several assemblies had already taken place and more were planned. Richard had made it known he was recruiting and the scribes had been toiling from dawn until dusk while messengers rode out with satchels full of letters to Richard's vassals, neighbours and acquaintances, informing them of the proposed expedition.

'Are you ready?' Môr asked from the doorway.

The last of their baggage had been loaded on the packhorses and the room was empty of their belongings, the bedclothes stripped for washing and airing.

Aoife tucked the ring away inside her gown and, fastening her cloak, followed her mother to the courtyard where the horses were saddled and waiting.

Her father was talking to Richard who wore a mail shirt of dark rings hemmed with a dagged pattern of bronze links. Last night she had watched him dancing at their farewell feast. The light from the fire had shone down one side of him leaving the other in shadow and had made his movements flickering and fast and blazed his hair with ruby glints. The effect had fascinated her and she had been unable to take her eyes from him. Her father had seen that look and winked at her, knowingly, making her blush. He was delighted with the outcome of their visit. He had his deal, and on terms he was prepared to pay.

'You have a little time yet,' he had said to her, chucking her under the chin. 'Do you think I would let anything bad happen to you?'

She had mutely shaken her head, pushing aside the memory of Fearns burning to the ground. He had given her a hug and she had inhaled the musty fur smell of his cloak.

'Whatever happens, you still belong to me. I made you and you are flesh of my flesh. The Norman is a fine catch, but you shall rule him, girl, just as surely as you are mine.'

The thought of ruling Richard de Clare set her on edge. She liked to imagine having that power, but making it happen was a different prospect, especially when he watched her with those piercing sea-coloured eyes. He was looking at her now and she made herself stare defiantly back, her chin raised. His lips twitched. Turning to a groom, he took the bridle of a fine tawny palfrey with silver bells jingling on the breast band and led it over to her.

'This is Melin,' he said. 'She is yours as a gift whether matters come to fruition or not. You need a good riding horse. She is bred from my own stable and fit to bear a princess.'

Aoife's cheeks burned. 'She is beautiful,' she said. 'Thank you.'

'Then she is like her new mistress,' Richard responded gallantly. 'Take care of her and she will take care of you.'

He returned the reins to the waiting groom and cupped his hands to boost Aoife into the saddle. The intimacy of setting her foot in his linked palms and pressing down into them sent a jolt through her body, reminding her that one day he would have the right to much greater familiarity than this.

Richard went to his own bright sorrel and she watched him leap astride without assistance. The stallion pranced and he reined him back, before touching him lightly with his heel to make him dance. The sight stirred her blood and it was an effort to tear her eyes away.

Riding out of Striguil, they took the road westwards towards Wales. Aoife glanced back at the castle, the sturdy grey stones picked out against the bright blue sky and sailing white clouds. A perfect day for a journey, and although excited to be setting out, she felt a wisp of regret to be leaving.

She rode with her mother and their women, two by two along the road, rutted with the iron marks of cart wheels, and dipped here and there with sky-mirrored puddles. Their escort was heavily armed, the sun sparkling on lances, and mail. Richard's squire bore his banner of six red chevrons on a yellow background, the silks rippling in the light breeze. Everyone was well armed and Aoife was not afraid. No one was going to attack such a force. This was about displaying strength to the people through whose lands they passed, and indeed a most fitting entourage for royalty. She held her head high, feeling adult and important and determined to rise to the occasion.

After a while Richard trotted back through the line to converse with their group. He spoke of the countryside and pointed out familiar landmarks along the way. A tree that had been struck by lightning last year, an ancient boundary stone rising out of the wayside grass. Aoife listened to his voice, so different to her father's deep rumble. Richard's was lighter and urbane but pleasant. Eventually he saluted the women and rode to rejoin her father. She studied his straight spine and the way he moved in alignment with the horse.

'I was concerned when your father mooted this marriage,' her mother said. 'But I believe he has chosen well for you.'

112

Aoife played with a strand of Melin's flaxen mane. 'He has yet to prove himself,' she said, feeling defensive. 'What are words without deeds?'

'Well, he seems to be setting those in motion.' Her mother gave her a shrewd look. 'You have time to grow used to the idea and become a woman.' She leaned across their horses to touch Aoife's sleeve. 'Ah, you are still so young and you have so much to learn.'

They rode on in silence. Aoife watched the red kites sailing high in the blue and drew in lungfuls of the bright spring air. The sun was warm on her head and she could hear Richard and her father laughing together. She thought she had learned everything she needed to know a long time ago – indeed, too much.

13

Cardigan Castle, Wales, early summer 1167

Curtseying, Aoife made her obeisance to Rhys ap Gruffydd, prince of Deheubarth, conquering lord of Ceredigion. In front of her, Richard and her father knelt with heads bowed. The lord Rhys sat in his great chair upon the dais, a gold circlet binding his crisp, dark hair. He had agreed to grant them an audience and his eyes were bright with curiosity as he studied his guests.

'You are welcome in my hall, let all know this,' he declared in a clear, firm voice and rose to bestow the kiss of peace on his guests. 'Come, you will take some mead.' He directed them to benches at the foot of his chair, and reseated himself in the higher, dominant position.

Two retainers arrived bearing cups and jugs and efficiently served the visitors and the prince. Aoife sipped from her cup. The Welsh mead was excellent although not as good as the mead at home, but still, the powerful tang of honey took her back to the hall at Fearns and warmed her stomach with golden flames.

'Any hall that serves fine mead makes me feel welcome,' her father said, smacking his lips. 'You are a man after my own heart. We must have much in common that we can explore together.'

Rhys smiled back, although his gaze was as sharp and cold as obsidian, especially when it flicked to Richard. 'Indeed. I understand that this is more than just a social visit to drink good mead and keep fine company. You have been to the court of the English king, and more recently have been a guest at Striguil. I hear you are in need of practical assistance.'

'That is so, my lord,' Diarmait replied. 'I am recruiting warriors to return to Ireland with me and restore to me what has been stolen.'

Rhys contemplated his drink. 'King Henry gave you leave to recruit men throughout his lands, but the ground on which you now stand does not belong to him, or any *sais.*' He shot another cold glance at Richard as he spoke the Welsh word for a foreigner 'I am not sure I should give you the same permission to recruit Welshmen to this venture of yours.'

'Then perhaps I can persuade you otherwise.' Diarmait flourished his arm so that his gold bracelets flashed on his wrists. 'I am willing to pay for their services.'

Rhys tugged thoughtfully on his moustaches. Behind his chair, a raven-haired youth watched Diarmait with hungry eyes.

'Sire, may I speak?' Richard said.

Rhys gestured with an open hand and a sardonic expression. 'By all means.'

'Any men recruited outside your territories for Ireland will no longer be a threat to your borders, so it is to your advantage. Keeping your own men around you will give you more resources to expand your territories, but also more mouths to feed, and outlay you might not recoup.'

'You state the obvious, my lord,' Rhys said in a bored voice. 'I hope you have more in your budget than this.'

'Forgive me, sire, for summarising. It might be an opportunity to be rid of a certain prisoner you are keeping in your dungeon. Robert FitzStephen is a thorn in your side and it would solve your dilemma were he to swear himself to King Diarmait and fight for him in Leinster.'

'My cousin constantly tells me he is perfectly happy in his chains and refuses to give up his oath to fight for King Henry,' Rhys said with bright-eyed scorn.

'But in Ireland he is no longer a problem for you and he is out of your territory. King Diarmait can use a man of his mettle and it will not concern him that FitzStephen's first oath is to Henry. It is a great waste to keep him locked up and a stain on his honour.'

'Do not talk of honour to me, Norman,' Rhys scoffed.

'I strive to be honourable and I am here today in good faith,' Richard replied with dogged patience. 'The King of Leinster could use your illustrious cousin and do you a service at the same time.'

Rhys leaned forward in his chair. 'And you, my lord? Are you also to go to Ireland? You will only do me a service if that service suits you.'

'Sire, the King of Leinster has entrusted me with the task of raising sufficient troops and Robert FitzStephen is a strong fighter. I would be glad to see him breathe fresh air again and having such a man to help organise the expedition would be of great benefit. A service that is good for all is surely worth pursuing.'

Rhys pondered before turning to an attendant and instructing him to bring FitzStephen to the hall. 'I warn you, he has been three years in chains,' he said to his guests. 'He said he would rather go fettered than yield to me and I have abided by his wish.'

Moments later two guards entered the hall dragging a man between them. From what she had heard, Aoife was expecting FitzStephen to be a ragged bundle of bones but the prisoner blinking in the light from the hall windows was in reasonable condition considering some of her father's prisoners she had seen. His hair and beard were unkempt but had been choppily cut. He smelled stale as he was pulled past her, but it wasn't an awful stink and his clothes, although rumpled and threadbare, were not yet rags. Fetters clanked on his ankles as he moved and his wrists bore red chafe marks and scabby sores. He was pale and hollow-cheeked, but defiance gleamed from his dark eyes as they flicked around the gathering, resting on Richard briefly before fixing on Rhys.

'Am I the entertainment for your guests tonight?' He turned with a sardonic bow. 'My apologies for my appearance. I would have better arrayed myself if I had known, but my cousin clearly felt that a surprise would provide better amusement.'

'Your tongue has grown no less foolish for three years in a dungeon,' Rhys growled. 'But I have a proposition for you.'

'If it is like all your other propositions the answer is no. I will never deny the fealty I owe to my king and I shall never surrender to you whether you are my kin or not!'

Aoife admired FitzStephen's fire and she could tell her father was impressed; he would have done exactly the same. Richard, she noticed, was straight-faced but with a spark in his eyes.

Rhys sighed. 'I have never known a man so willing to cut off his nose to spite his face, but against my better judgement I have brought you from your ignominious hole to offer you a way out of your predicament if you are not too stubborn to listen.' A gesture brought a stool for the prisoner to sit upon, and a cup of mead was thrust into his hand.

'You must indeed be desperate,' FitzStephen said with a savage grin. He scrutinised the gathering again, giving Aoife a look of frank admiration which she returned with her best steely glare. 'What is this proposition then?'

'Ireland,' Richard said. 'This is Diarmait, King of Leinster, and he seeks men willing to fight for him to regain his lands. There is no need to forswear your oath to King Henry. If you go to Ireland, it will remain intact.'

FitzStephen narrowed his eyes. 'What has this to do with you, de Clare?'

Richard shrugged. 'We have known each other a long time and often enjoyed a drink together. I am pained to think of you rotting away in a dungeon because of an oath you refuse to break. The King of Leinster wants me to organise an expedition to Ireland to reclaim his lands and recruit the best men for the task – men who have either burned their bridges or who have good reason to look to other horizons, and who recognise an opportunity when it arises. From Hubberston it is a day's sail in good weather.'

FitzStephen drank his mead and his chains rattled. 'What would be in it for me,' he asked, 'beyond being rid of these jewels?'

'Reward aplenty,' Diarmait intervened. 'There is land for the taking. I shall have what is mine and pay you in good silver, but you may take what you want from my enemies with my goodwill. You shall have riches beyond your dreams if you will fight for me.'

FitzStephen rubbed his badly trimmed beard. 'I do not know you, my lord,' he said. 'And you do not know my dreams.'

'That is true, but we play the dice we throw,' Diarmait replied. 'The Earl of Striguil speaks highly of you and his word is good enough for me. If you will declare for me and come to Ireland and fight, I will enrich you, I swear. The lord Rhys will release you and be glad he no longer has to hold his cousin in a dungeon. Indeed, sire,' he added, grinning at Rhys, 'I shall be doing you a great service.'

The lord Rhys snorted with sour amusement. 'It seems a fine bargain to me. I am sick of keeping this stubborn fool alive. Take him and have done.'

FitzStephen set his jaw, one fist clenched on his knee.

'Oh, for God's sake, man, have the grace to agree!' Richard snapped. 'Do you want to end your life in a dungeon? You have a chance to be free without abandoning your oath to King Henry. There will be no more opportunities like this.'

FitzStephen grimaced. 'If this is my only way out I accept and offer my services,' he said, adding belligerently, 'but I will not bow the knee to any man save King Henry.'

Rhys curled his lip. 'Take him. The sooner he is gone the better – I will seize the opportunity, even if he is reluctant.' He beckoned to the guard. 'Unlock his fetters and give him clean raiment.'

*　　*　　*

The next day the party left Ceredigion and rode into South Wales. Although Richard was no longer Earl of Pembroke, he still had lands and manors in the county and as they journeyed he continued to introduce potential soldiers to Diarmait, to recruit promises of aid, and take stock of resources.

The newly released Robert FitzStephen travelled with them, clad in the robes he had once worn as Constable of Ceredigion, although they hung on him like baggy sails. He was quiet initially and had enough ado staying on his horse after three years cooped in a dungeon. He had a persistent cough, but as they rode his condition improved, and as he spoke to Diarmait, the latter started to look on him a little less like a horse trader promised a thoroughbred and sold a nag. Also riding with them was Rhys's son Owen, the youth who had been eagerly watching from behind his father's chair. He had managed to plead his way into accompanying the party and Diarmait had welcomed him with indulgent amusement.

Reaching Haverford, they picked up the baron Richard de la Roche, a knight of Flemish origins keen to test his mettle in Ireland, and with him several knights and serjeants from the locality. That evening the men gathered around the fire in the castle's great hall and Aoife played her harp as they sat over their plans.

'When will you be ready to sail?' Diarmait hunched his shoulders and thrust his head towards Richard like a hungry bird of prey. 'By spring next year?'

Richard rubbed his chin. 'It might be possible but will depend on the King's reply and on finances. I know you are eager, as am I, but thorough planning is the key to success.'

'I have survived near sixty winters and more hardship and violence than you will ever know,' Diarmait said impatiently. 'Plans are all very well. You need to know how many and how long and how far, but sometimes you have to fly with the direction of the wind.' He pointed to the window. 'From this place I can smell Leinster. Ireland is a day's sail in good weather. I am of a mind to go there and rejoin my kin.'

'Is that wise?'

Diarmait rose and paced to the window. 'I have already been gone too long. I cannot kick my heels in Bristol for another winter, spending my resources on standing still. I have enough warriors to bring home with me even without an army and I need to judge the lie of the land for myself. You take your risks, my lord, and I will take mine.'

Richard opened his hands. 'It is your choice, sire, but I cannot say for sure when I will be ready, although I shall make as much haste as I can.'

'Then do so. I shall take a shipload of your men to show my supporters what is coming to them in greater numbers.'

'I agree that we must have preliminary reconnaissance,' Richard said with a thoughtful frown.

'I will go,' de la Roche volunteered. 'I can as easily spend the winter in Ireland as here and report back to you.'

Richard knew de la Roche for an intelligent, pragmatic warrior, keen on the shine of silver, but never shirking the task. 'Very well,' he said. 'Take thirty men and a ship and accompany King Diarmait.'

Aoife stood on the beach at Hubberston watching the ships being loaded with supplies. Men toiled in the summer sun, stripped to shirts and braies, their legs bare. A festive air inhabited the preparations with shouts and whistles, jests and bursts of horseplay amid the industry. They were going home, and whatever waited on the other side of the sea, it was still Ireland and a cause for joy, even if seasoned with anxiety.

Richard detached from a group of men talking on the beach and plodded towards her across the sandy shingle, his blue travelling cloak flapping like a pair of wings. Her stomach tightened with anxiety.

'I must leave if I am to have the best of the day for riding,' he said as he reached her.

'I wish you Godspeed, my lord.' She took refuge in standard formality.

'And I you. I will send messages and keep your father informed. I wish I could sail with you now but I have much to do first.'

She nodded wordlessly.

'I will miss you,' he said. 'I will miss your singing and your quickness at chess. I will miss your light feet in the dance and your fierceness.'

She twisted her hands together awkwardly. 'I do not know if I will miss you,' she replied, 'but I suppose I shall find out.'

His lips twitched with amusement, but then he sobered. 'I will come for you, I promise, as I have promised your father.'

'A promise is nothing until it is kept, and I have learned not to anticipate on word alone.'

'That is true. Trust no one, Aoife.' He took her hands in his. Her father's hands were meaty paws, scarred and hefty, but Richard's were thin and strong. He leaned towards her and she drew back in alarm, thinking he was going to kiss her mouth, but he lightly saluted her cheek instead. 'You are safe,' he said with a rueful smile. 'I shall not claim your lips until I have a husband's right – until you are mine, and I am yours.' He looked at her and his eyes were the colour of a folded wave tumbling to shore. 'All in good time.'

She watched him walk away and her stomach continued to churn as though she was in mid-voyage. She raised one hand to her cheek, the two kisses pressing together.

Richard too was unsettled as he left Aoife. He would indeed miss her but his own emotions were caught up in the pursuit of ambition. She intrigued and exasperated him, she had insinuated herself under his skin, but she was a fledgling. The land meant more to him than she did. However, since she was the key to that land, he had to tread delicately.

He went to speak to the men loading the ships and sought out de la Roche for a few final words. 'It is in your hands for now,' he said. 'Guard King Diarmait and be my eyes and ears. I shall anticipate your report in due course.'

'Sire, you can trust me and my men to give a good accounting.'

'I know. The weather is set fair for a swift crossing. God be with you.'

He clasped de la Roche's shoulder and then made his way over to Diarmait who was sitting on a post, drinking wine with Domnall and watching the loading. Diarmait handed his cup to his son and rose to engulf Richard in one of his huge embraces.

'May the wind carry you swiftly and safely to your shores,' Richard said.

'Do not leave it too long until you join us,' Diarmait replied. 'Your welcome is assured and I would not want to give to another man what I have sworn to you.'

'And I would not want to think either of us has sworn a pact with a man who does not keep his word,' Richard answered.

He bowed to Diarmait and turned to his waiting troop. As he gained the saddle, he took a last look at the ships and the glitter of the sun on the sea, and then reined about, taking the road back to Striguil and preparations for the spring.

14

Fearns, Leinster, Ireland, summer/autumn 1167

One late afternoon in August, Aoife wandered the ruins of the palace at Fearns, touching the stones, her gown brushing the weeds straggling through the cracks. The scars of the fire were still evident but had been softened by trellises of greenery. They had returned to Fearns on landing, and her father had summoned his supporters who had been lying low. He had paraded the mailed warriors he had brought from England and Wales. De la Roche and his men had given an impressive demonstration of their weapon skills while her father delivered a rousing speech about this being a mere foretaste of what was to come.

The Norman tents were pitched beyond the abbey's perimeter in the same place that Ruari ua Connor had camped on the day he came to take her father's pride. The soldiers spent most of their time training and wearing their armour to impress their skills upon their Irish hosts and to emphasise how formidable they were. News of her father's return had sped to the settlements and various lords had arrived to see this wondrous fighting force for themselves. Some had been sufficiently impressed to swear oaths to her father, but others had gone sneaking with tales to High King Ruari and Tiernan ua Ruari. Her father said they must take the risk. To make a stew, you had to light a fire under the cauldron.

Amid all her father's boasting and exhortation, he had not mentioned his agreement to wed her to Richard de Clare, but she understood his circumspection. He might speak passionately about seizing their enemy's lands but he was silent about what it would mean closer to home. Aoife was content with his reticence. While the marriage remained a distant notion, she was free to breathe her own air, and because of the deal with de Clare, her father was not seeking to match her with other suitors – at least not for the moment. She had precious time, and it was a gift beyond gold.

She wandered to the charred foundations that approximated to her mother's chamber and envisaged herself curled up in bed, secure beneath her covers – insofar as she had ever truly been secure in her life. A new hall of timber and withies was being built close to the old one, but would not be ready until late autumn, so for now they dwelt at the abbey and their plans continued apace.

Scuffing her toe in the black dust, she was dragged from her thoughts by the arrival of the young Welsh prince Owen ap Rhys, eighteen years old and as handsome as a hawk. She had little interest in him for he was a boy in search of adventure and she had seen the bloody reality of that side of life.

'What are you doing?' He looked at her askance.

'Remembering when this was my father's palace with a fine hall and stables, and dwellings for many warriors,' she said. 'This was my childhood home.'

'I am sorry,' he said with a shrug.

'So am I, but what use is that?'

'You can make it better next time.'

She shook her head and looked at the skeleton of the new hall rising against the sky. Next time would not be the same. The feeling of empty longing was a hunger in her belly.

'I will gladly fight for your father and protect you.' He puffed out his chest with bravado. 'I know what it's like in war.'

She gave him a long-suffering look for he did not know at all. Beyond him, she saw Connor hurrying towards them and was glad of the interruption.

'Visitors,' Connor said. 'Uncle Lorcan is here and asking for you.' He flicked Owen a suspicious look since Owen was older and granted more privileges among the warriors.

Aoife's heart lit up. Without a second thought for the Welsh youth, she picked up her skirts and dashed towards the abbey.

Her uncle was standing by the abbey door, and a smile lit his face when he saw her hurrying towards him. Reaching him, Aoife dropped to her knees and kissed the sapphire archbishop's ring on his finger.

'Little Aoife! When did you become so tall and grown up?' Setting aside the dignity of his status, and ignoring the looks from his attendants, Lorcan raised her up and pulled her into his arms for a hug.

Aoife laughed and squeezed him in return. 'When you weren't looking!' she said. She had been walking on quicksand and now here was a solid path that would not fail her.

'I am pleased to see you home, although I am not so sure about your escort.' He glanced in the direction of the Norman tents.

'They will help my father take back our land,' she replied, tossing her hair.

Her uncle shook his head. 'Wolves are always wolves, remember that.'

'But at least they are our wolves.'

'Are they?'

She did not answer and walked beside him to join her father at the edge of the Norman camp.

Fresh supplies had arrived from Richard – barrels of herrings, bushels of oats, chests of weapons. Richard's messenger informed them that Richard was on his way to King Henry and all was progressing well. Her father slapped Lorcan's shoulder with familiarity and introduced him to de la Roche who was taking an inventory of the supplies.

'There is more where this came from,' Diarmait told Lorcan, 'and when it arrives, Ruari and Tiernan shall rue the day they ever pushed me to seek aid across the sea.'

Lorcan frowned and his fist tightened around his crosier.

'You have not seen the like of these warriors before and neither have my enemies,' Diarmait added gleefully. 'They will not know what has hit them.'

They had been speaking French, but now Lorcan switched to Irish. 'And just how are you going to pay them?'

Diarmait glowered at him. 'If a man is not on top of his enemies, he might as well be dead. I would rather employ such as these than bend my neck to Ruari and Tiernan. Let them feel my hand, not I theirs.'

'I hope you know what you are doing.'

'I know exactly what I am doing,' Diarmait said with hard confidence. 'This is not a whim but considered strategy and it is about survival.'

Later that day, Lorcan dined at Diarmait's table on tender beef stew washed down with a pale wine from Rouen. De la Roche was present too and Diarmait regaled Lorcan with exaggerated tales of his visits to kings, nobles and adventurers across the Hibernian Sea. Aoife ate her stew and listened to her father and de la Roche paint Richard in glowing colours as they spoke of his network of contacts. Her uncle paid close attention, his shoulders hunched and his lips tight with disapproval.

De la Roche said, 'When he arrives and marries your daughter, he will care diligently for the lands you give him.'

Lorcan put down his spoon and stared at the knight. 'What is this?'

Aoife bit her lip and looked at her father.

'Ah well.' Diarmait picked at a blob of wax on the cloth. 'Nothing has been decided yet.'

'What do you mean "nothing has been decided"?' Suffused with anger, Lorcan drew himself up. 'What have you done?' He turned to de la Roche. 'Tell me what you meant by saying he will marry Aoife.'

De la Roche cleared his throat. 'I may have spoken out of turn, but the Earl of Striguil is to wed the lady when he arrives in Leinster with his knights and soldiers. So it was agreed.'

Lorcan turned to Diarmait, eyes glittering with fury. 'Without consideration of her family? Without consulting the Church? You have promised my niece to one of these men? And you cannot tell me yourself?'

'Oh, put your mitre in your mouth,' Diarmait snapped. 'I know what is best for my own daughter and my people.'

'For yourself you mean! I have defended you to others. I have been ready to stand at your side against your enemies, but if I were not in holy orders I would strike you down for this!'

'You know nothing,' Diarmait retorted, breathing heavily. 'Leave the decisions of state to me and stay out of my business, priest.'

'This *is* my business,' Lorcan snapped. 'Aoife is my niece, and I will not have her sold to buy swords!'

'And I will not have you meddling with my decisions.'

Lorcan jerked to his feet. 'There are times when you are nothing but a beast of low cunning and a defiler of your crown. You disgust me. May God be willing to forgive you, for I do not.' He glared round the assembled men, seized his crosier and stormed out.

In the silence following his departure, Aoife felt as though a stone had lodged in her stomach. Her father shrugged and laughed but beyond the bravado she could sense his trepidation. Her uncle was an archbishop, influential and charismatic. If he deserted them, their situation could become perilous, especially as they were sheltering in an ecclesiastical sanctuary.

'Pay no heed,' Diarmait said roughly to the Normans. 'I will talk him round. His heart rules his mind but he will come to understand.' He bade attendants go around with the flagons again and raised his drinking horn in toast. 'Aoife, play for us, girl!'

She fetched her harp and tried to feel staunch towards her father, but she harboured sympathy for Lorcan too. He had a maternal uncle's right to negotiate a niece's marriage on behalf of the family; he was bound to be dismayed at this flouting of the rules. She also understood his anxiety about her marrying a Norman, but her father was right. He had not been there and he did not comprehend the necessity. And he had not met Richard de Clare.

Aoife was making curd cheese when her uncle came to her mother's quarters next day. Twisting the bulging linen cloth, she was squeezing the last of the whey from the curds into a bowl as he arrived. No one had seen him since he had stalked out of the feast. He had shut himself away to pray and made himself unavailable to any but his immediate servants.

This morning he came alone, dressed in a plain habit of dark wool, a skull cap covering his tonsure. Môr rose from her sewing and offered him a cup of mead, which he declined in preference for water. Aoife brought him a dish of the new cheese, sprinkled with salt and finely chopped sage.

He smiled as he took the bowl, and she was relieved that he seemed to be in a better humour this morning. He tasted the cheese curd and made an appreciative sound. 'No one makes this as well as you, niece.'

'Of course not,' she said, returning his smile.

'Now' – he turned to Môr – 'what happened when you were in England, sister? What is all this from Diarmait about betrothing Aoife to one of their warriors? From what I have seen so far, they are not men I would desire as kin. If he has sold Aoife to a mercenary in a mail shirt, I shall excommunicate him.'

Môr lightly touched his arm. 'Now, do not fret. It is not like that. Richard de Clare is a great lord in his own land with fine castles and monasteries. He is a godly man too – perhaps more so than Diarmait.'

Lorcan raised his brows. 'Why should he want to come here if he has all of this at home? Why involve himself with us, and what is the nature of this promise?'

'His family supported King Stephen in the war for the English crown. So now King Henry watches him closely. Like Diarmait he is constrained. But he still has resources and he is willing to help us.'

'In exchange for what?' Lorcan was not smiling now. 'With just what kind of felon has my brother-in-law made his pact?'

'He's not a felon.' Aoife spoke up defensively. 'He was courteous and treated us as his guests. He will take back our land.'

Lorcan's face twisted in disgust. 'For a promise of marriage in return. He serves himself. Take is the right word.'

Môr said, 'The marriage will only happen when he comes to Ireland and if he succeeds. If he does not fulfil those terms, then Aoife will remain unwed.'

'It should never have been allowed to happen,' Lorcan said grimly.

'I consented of my own free will,' Aoife told him. 'I go into this knowingly and for Leinster.'

'His castles are efficiently run,' Môr said. 'His sister is his chatelaine and a fine and gracious lady. As I have said, he reveres the Church. Should Aoife marry him, she will be entitled to a third of his own lands as her dower, and that is a great consideration. It is a good strategy, Lorcan.'

He pressed his lips together.

'I understand your anger at not being consulted, but my husband has my support in this matter and Aoife, as she says, has willingly consented.'

Lorcan grimaced, but eventually heaved a deep sigh. 'I will take your word, sister, but it is still a gamble and with your own daughter.' He turned to Aoife. 'Child, you must come to me if you are in any doubt at all and I will defend you. And for now, you are truly willing?'

'Yes,' Aoife said firmly. 'I swear on the Bible.'

'Very well, I will take your word for it, but I shall not apologise to your father. I am resigned to what he has arranged, but I am far from content.'

He started to eat again but stopped as Connor came flying into the chamber, his blue eyes wide and scared. 'The High King and Tiernan ua Ruari are here!' he cried.

Mór gasped and put her hand to her mouth.

'Stay here,' Lorcan said, and hurried out.

Her stomach somersaulting with fear, Aoife looked around. Their gold and jewels were still packed ready for a hasty retreat. They could flee if they had to at a moment's notice.

Her mother's face was white. 'We should have stayed in Bristol.'

Unable to remain still, Aoife leaped to her feet and ran after her uncle, ignoring her mother's cry. Her father was swiftly assembling his small band of Irish warriors and the Normans were saddling up their horses and checking their weapons.

'I will never retreat from my homeland again.' Diarmait bared his teeth at Domnall as they made rapid preparations. 'They will not push me into the sea again, I swear.'

'Daidí . . .'

He swung round, and she saw the grim determination in his eyes. 'Hold fast, precious girl,' he said. 'I trust to your courage and your blood. Pray for us.' He gave her a rough kiss and set her to one side, his focus on his warriors.

Watching the men ride away, Aoife pressed her hand to her mouth, and felt a sick burning in her stomach. It was all very well for him to say hold fast, but at least he was being active. If he died, it would be in battle, whereas the non-combatants were trapped, their fate in the hands of others – therein lay the true terror. Without the men, the women and children were as cattle to the slaughter. She could not rely on anyone, even her father; all she had was herself, and it hurt.

15

Rouen, August 1167

Escorted up the great hall by an usher, Richard was brought to King Henry's throne, each step reminding him of occasions he had done this before only to face the hostility and rejection of the man watching him with judgemental eyes. He had planned meticulously, but his body was tight with anxiety, for Henry had already kept him waiting for three days.

The King had put on girth around his middle but still exuded an air of charismatic vigour. He leaned forward, his gaze fixed on Richard, his right fist clenched around his rod of office. To one side clerks were busy at lecterns, copying out writs on strips of parchment. Courtiers and officials were witnessing the deeds and dealing with the correspondence. A few men stood around Henry as advisers, although none with whom Richard was especially familiar or friendly.

Richard knelt at Henry's feet and, bowing his head, fixed his gaze on a painted golden leopard positioned to the right of the throne. Drawing a breath, he inhaled the smell of incense from the resin smoking in a bronze bowl near Henry's elbow. 'Sire, I bring you my allegiance and loyalty and I trust my service has pleased you so far. I present you with this gift in token of my esteem.'

An usher stepped forward and gave Henry a sword scabbarded in rose-coloured leather with ornate fittings. Richard had not been permitted to come armed into Henry's presence, not even with a gift.

Blank-faced, Henry received the sword and removed it from the scabbard to examine the mirror-bright blade. 'Exquisite,' he said and, sheathing it, handed it to the usher. His eyes were alert with curiosity. 'You have clearly prospered enough to afford such a gift, but I have not summoned you, even if I am pleased to see you. You are here because you want something from me, so let us have it out in the open.'

Richard heard the challenge and the hard amusement in Henry's voice. What he really wanted he could not have – Pembroke and the restoration of his right to call himself its earl. He drew a deep breath. 'Sire, I wish to do my duty by you and I wish to extend your influence in Ireland. Diarmait MacMurchada, King of Leinster, has asked for my help, and I have said I will give it to him, pending your permission and goodwill to let me cross the Hibernian Sea.'

'Is that so?'

Richard saw surprise and speculation in Henry's gaze before he schooled it to neutrality. 'He approached me on Robert FitzHarding's advice and I agreed to help him provisional on your consent. I also accompanied King Diarmait to Ceredigion and secured the release of Robert FitzStephen from Prince Rhys.' Richard told Henry what had happened thus far, carefully omitting the detail of the marriage agreement which was testing the ground a little too far. 'I have had my scribe write down the pertinent details.' He presented Henry with a bundle of parchment.

Without dropping his gaze from Richard's, Henry received the package and handed it to a clerk. 'I shall study and consider further,' he said. 'You are welcome to stay at court and eat at my board while you await my answer.' A wave of his hand indicated that Richard was dismissed.

Richard had been expecting such a response; Henry always left matters dangling to allow his supplicant to worry and sweat. Concealing a stab of impatience, he bowed and backed from

Henry's presence. At least he had not been denied or banished, and that kept his hopes alive.

For the next week Richard kicked his heels at court, outwardly patient, inwardly seething. He knew that pushing Henry would only cause him to further procrastinate, so he reined in his exasperation and played the waiting game with as much insouciance as he could muster.

Henry's mother, the dowager Empress Matilda, was at court and he had to pay his obligatory respects. She was unwell with stiff hips and a wheezy cough and even in this warmer weather she wore several layers of clothing and sat beside the fire. His family had fought against this haughty, indomitable woman during the long years of civil war. Her name had been vilified in his father's household. She had caused fifteen years of misery through her refusal to acknowledge that the throne belonged to her cousin Stephen. She was the reason he had lost Pembroke and bitterness welled up in him although he strove to swallow it down and not dwell on the past.

'De Clare,' she said harshly. 'You and your father caused me much vexation.'

Her eyes were a faded milky blue and her face was heavily lined with pain, but she was still as sharp as a nail. A ring with a stone resembling a melted pearl almost covered the lower knuckle of her right index finger. Her gown was stiff with jewels, further stating her magnificence. An old woman decked out in a glittering carapace that enhanced rather than disguised her frailty, but even in failing old age, Richard knew how much influence she had with her son.

'Madam, we all made choices; the war wounded everyone and we still dwell with the scars. I honour you and respect you, as I honour the King.'

She gave him a disbelieving look. 'I doubt that.'

'I understand your caution, but we have been at peace for

fourteen years and my only desire is to serve and to be given due recognition for that service.'

'You are here because you are seeking to go to Ireland,' she said sharply and pointed to a stool near her feet. 'Sit.'

Richard did so, trying to fold his long legs into a comfortable position and not to feel as though she was ordering him around like a dog. 'Indeed, madam, for which I need the King's permission.'

Her gnarled right hand clenched around the jet handle of her walking stick. 'And why should he give it to you?'

'I have proven myself a loyal vassal. I have served the King and paid my dues in good faith. Since I cannot change what has gone before, I must strive to enhance the future.'

She made a contemptuous sound. 'And your striving involves becoming entangled with the Irish?'

'They sought my help, madam. Robert FitzHarding sent them specifically to me and when King Diarmait told me what he required, it seemed a fine opportunity. That is why I am here, seeking the King's permission.'

Her hand continued to work on the top of her stick. 'Ireland belongs to my son, sanctioned by the Pope,' she said. 'Whatever is done there is for him to decide, no one else.'

'Indeed, madam, I understand,' Richard said diplomatically.

'I hope so, for he shall brook nothing else. You may go, and I shall speak with him.'

Richard stood up, trying not to trip over the stool, and flourished her a deep bow before making his escape. He felt as though he had been ground to dust inside a hand quern. He was not certain that her having words with Henry would be of benefit. She was as likely to persuade him to decline as to give permission.

From the royal residence, Richard visited the cathedral and knelt to beseech God for a good outcome to his request. He was worried Henry would seize on his plan and send someone else instead, or destabilise him with Diarmait, both of which Henry was very capable of doing. He knew full well the King would be hostile to the proposed marriage alliance. Wedding Diarmait of Leinster's daughter was a step far beyond organising mercenaries to go and fight there. He tried to rationalise the concealment by telling himself that until he arrived in Ireland nothing was certain but knew it was a duplicitous excuse.

Henry summoned Richard again the next morning, not to the hall this time, but to his personal chamber. At the back of the room the royal bed made a statement from the shadows with its ornate cover of red and gold damask. A very young woman with floaty golden-brown hair sat on it feeding a small dog from a dish of meat scraps. The usual collection of scribes and courtiers populated the room and their swift toing and froing made the space almost as busy as a town street on market day.

Wearing a loose woollen robe over his shirt, Henry had not yet donned his belt or his jewels but was pacing the room with his customary restlessness. 'Ah,' he said on seeing Richard, and fixed him with a bright glance. 'I have been thinking on the matter you set before me the other day.'

'Sire.' Richard rose from his bow.

'Indeed, you are ambitious. My mother says not to trust you – she thinks you will stab me in the back.'

Richard knew what he would like to do to the Empress but retained his composure. 'Sire, I do not know what gave her that impression. I would be a fool to do such a thing.'

'And yet you would go to Ireland?'

'Is that so foolish, sire?'

Henry raised one eyebrow, clearly waiting for a better answer.

'I have sworn fealty to you, sire, and I hold to it. As a young man I pledged my oath to King Stephen as my father had done, and I held to my loyalty while he lived. It is the same with my loyalty to you. I do not break my promises.' He put all of his will into the look he gave Henry, thinking it ironic that Henry would frequently swear one thing and do another as it suited him.

Henry's expression was inscrutable. He gestured to the table. 'Bread and wine,' he said. 'You are welcome to break your fast.'

Richard was not hungry and he knew the royal wine by its dreadful reputation, but he sat down and applied himself in order to be agreeable. Henry perched one haunch on the edge of the table and tore a crust off a loaf.

'I think your plan has merit,' he said between rotations of his jaw, 'and I am willing to give you my permission on one condition.'

Richard forced himself to swallow; it wouldn't do to choke to death on good news. His instinct was to yell with joy and agree to anything Henry said, but he contained himself for who knew what Henry had cooked up for him.

'My mother and I agree on two things,' Henry said, sucking honey off his thumb. 'We need to know you are capable of going into unfamiliar territory and fulfilling a task among people not your own. You can do this as a warrior, but I need to know how good an envoy you are.'

Richard wondered what Henry thought he had been doing when organising the Irish and arranging for FitzStephen's release from Ceredigion's dungeon. 'I am confident that I am, sire.'

'Good, because I have a mission for you, and if you do it well, it will be to your credit.' Henry took a swallow of wine to wash down his bread. 'I am entrusting you with the safety of my daughter Matilda when she goes to her marriage with Henry of Saxony. I require you to join the entourage accompanying her to her new husband.'

Astonished, Richard lost his courtly mask and his jaw dropped for he had not bargained on anything like this.

'The Earl of Arundel will be going too, and others. It is important my daughter has a full dignity of noble lords from her own lands. You have daughters of your own, as does Arundel – you are both accustomed to girls of that age.'

Richard put down his bread. 'As you wish, sire,' he said woodenly. 'I shall gladly serve you and the lady Matilda, as you see fit.' He acknowledged to himself that Henry's strategy was faultless, and a masterly example of procrastination. He was sending Richard out of sight but keeping him fettered by means of a diplomatic embassy, and with plenty of others to observe his behaviour and report back. So near and yet so far.

'Do this for me and do it well and I shall sanction your voyage to Ireland,' Henry said. Leaving the table, he wandered over to the young woman and chucked her under the chin. 'But do not come to me demanding funds and support. Let us be clear that aiding Diarmait MacMurchada is your project as is the financial risk.'

'Yes, sire,' Richard said tautly.

Henry left his young mistress, walked towards the window and pulled a sheet of parchment from a pile on a trestle. Opened out, it proved to be a crude map of Ireland. 'I want you to mark on this what you think you will acquire on your campaign and then send to me how much land is accrued to my kingdom.' He gave Richard a hard look. 'Do you understand?'

'Yes, sire, perfectly.' Henry was saying that any land conquered belonged to him, but Richard decided he would cross that bridge when he came to it. The prize was having Henry's consent. This mission Henry had foisted on him meant he would be delayed and would have to think of a way to keep faith with Diarmait, but if Henry thought it a deterrent, he was very wrong.

Dismissed, Richard left Henry's chamber, folding the map down inside his tunic. It was a shackle, but it was also authority and mandate. He had his permission. Now to roll the dice.

Richard set about preparing to escort eleven-year-old Princess Matilda to her wedding in Germany. She was a pretty child with fine golden-brown hair, delicate features, and a lively but sweet disposition, the latter a surprise to Richard given the powerful personalities of her parents. Richard had little to do with her save to ensure that her travel arrangements were comfortable, safe and in good order. He was pleasant but circumspect with his fellow barons, and behind a bland, genial façade his plans and dreams lay with Ireland.

He warmed to Queen Alienor who possessed a lively, flirtatious wit, her smiling rapport a contrast to the frigid disapproval he had received from Henry's mother. Alienor used charm to win loyalty rather than demanding it with a frozen face. Her sons Richard and Geoffrey were handfuls, especially Richard, a strong, wiry lad of ten years with fiery hair, and a personality to match; a boy full of vigour and intelligence with an endless curiosity, especially about military things. Showing him how to tie various knots in a rope, Richard de Clare was envious of Henry and even a little angry. *I could have had a son like you by now*, he thought bitterly.

'I am so pleased you are accompanying my daughter,' Alienor said. 'It is rare to see a man who has time for children.'

'It is a great blessing to have heirs, madam,' he replied. 'I have two daughters – their mother is dead and we were not married – but one day I hope to have a wife and a son to inherit, God willing.'

'I shall pray so too, my lord,' she said, and touched his sleeve.

He recognised the courtly platitude, but at the same time if he could win the Queen's sympathy, she might be an advocate for him at court. Only a foolish man underestimated the power of women.

In the rainy dusk, waiting to embark at Southampton, he retired to his lodging to deal with correspondence and eat a light meal of bread and cheese. He was organising his finances with the FitzHarding family in Bristol and sorting out what he could afford to sell to raise funds for ships and men for Ireland. How much he could borrow too, and that made him frown as he studied the parchments scattered in front of him.

His brooding was interrupted by a knock on the door and his uncle Hervey announced the arrival of Richard de la Roche. Rain dripped from the latter's cloak and his boots were saturated. A pungent aroma of horse wafted from his garments. Pushing his work to one side, Richard bade his squire take de la Roche's cloak and bring him dry clothes. Another servant was sent for food and drink.

'Mistress Basilia told me you were in Southampton, sire,' de la Roche said as he sat heavily on the bench before the hearth, removed his sodden boots and peeled off his inner socks to expose white, wrinkled feet.

'Did she also tell you why?'

'Yes, sire.' De la Roche gave him a wary, slightly sympathetic look.

Richard sighed. 'Since you are here in person, I take it the news from Ireland is complicated.' He wondered pessimistically if it had all ended before it had begun. Perhaps he would not need to borrow money after all. He passed his own wine to de la Roche, who took a grateful drink.

'You might say that. I have a letter for you from King Diarmait.' De la Roche produced a damp leather satchel that had been partially protected by his cloak and removed a sealed document.

The servant and squire returned, and while de la Roche changed into dry clothes and filled his stomach, Richard read the letter. Mostly it consisted of reassurances and defiant language couched in the flowery style of Maurice Regan, Diarmait's translator. The last lines exhorted Richard to come as soon as he could.

Richard looked at de la Roche, who was fiddling crumbs out of his beard. 'Tell me yourself,' he said. 'Tell me what you consider important.'

De la Roche belched. 'Fearns is a burned-out ruin, sire, but we camped in the abbey grounds next door and we did well enough. King Diarmait's vassals flocked to him, but soon enough so did his enemies. Their high king Ruari ua Connor came down on us and he had King Diarmait's sworn enemy Tiernan ua Ruari with him.'

'Go on,' Richard said, remaining impassive although he was anticipating the worst.

'They said they had come to negotiate, and that was indeed how it began. We took no part but stood guard in our armour. The High King disliked our presence and so did Tiernan. Some of his warriors decided to prove that thirty Normans were no match for them and tried to end negotiations by attacking us.' A sour smile curved his lips. 'We cut them down like scything wheat in a field and for all that King Diarmait says that the Irish can stand hard, they fled like hares.'

Richard raised his brows.

'We knew better than to give chase, so we stood firm. They came at us again in greater numbers and again we cut them down. Many of Diarmait's Irish died, but we were the mailed core and our archers earned their pay more than twice over.' De la Roche shook his head. 'The Welsh lad, Prince Rhys's son, took a spear in the chest. It's grim news for his father but the lad had his death written on him from the beginning. He threw himself into the fray with senseless bravado and paid for it. After that the High King stopped the slaughter and pulled back and we returned to negotiating.'

'Go on,' Richard said, folding his arms.

'He is a hard man, King Ruari, and no fool,' said de la Roche. 'Tiernan ua Ruari precipitated the attack, but he was a dog on the High King's leash. In the end, Diarmait had to yield because he was outnumbered and was forced to give hostages including young Connor. He had to pay a hundred ounces of gold to Tiernan ua Ruari in recompense for stealing his wife and he was made to send us home – which is why I am here. We could all have been killed, but instead we have returned, alive but with flat purses.'

A fresh burst of rain pelted against the shutters and de la Roche sloshed more wine into his cup.

'But Diarmait could afford to pay a hundred ounces of gold to his enemies even if he did not pay his soldiers,' Hervey noted astutely.

De la Roche grunted. 'It has beggared him though – it was a large portion out of his resources.'

Richard grimaced, for it meant the onus of the expense would be on him, although knowing Diarmait's cunning he probably still had secret reserves concealed here and there. The content of this letter was not one of defeat. 'Sending you home does not appear to mean he has given up.'

'No,' agreed de la Roche. 'He desires more men to mount a full campaign. He wants the high kingship for himself now. All that Ruari ua Connor has done by this action is stick his foot in an ants' nest.'

'But it seems to me that Diarmait has a great deal of ambition and few resources,' Richard said wryly.

De la Roche rested his cup on his thigh. 'Are you having second thoughts, sire?'

Richard rubbed his chin. 'It is always wise to have second thoughts. I understand enough of Diarmait MacMurchada to know he will not yield when his back is to the wall; he will keep on coming. What of the Irish warriors you faced? Tell me more.'

'They are not well armed, sire. They have ferocious skill with their spears and axes, but their bows are not as good as ours and discipline is lax. If we have men and supplies in sufficient quantity, we can vanquish them. As you say, there is no lack in King Diarmait. His defeat has only made him more determined to seek victory, but he needs an armoured backbone.'

Richard nodded. 'I will think on matters,' he said, 'and we shall see what to do in the spring when I return from this mission.'

16

Fearns, Leinster, Ireland, late spring 1168

Aoife groped around under the hen and shooed her from the nest. The indignant bird squawked and after a quick peck ran out to join the other poultry, feathers ruffling. Three damp warm eggs gleamed like chalk in the straw. At least the birds were laying again as the days lengthened away from winter's cold. Food had been scarce at times but they had managed. Only part of the hollow feeling in her belly was hunger, the other part was a sense of diminishment. Her place in the world felt smaller these days and insecure.

Aoife cooked two of the eggs over the fire pit in the living chamber, added salt and herbs and brought them to her father. He was suffering from a heavy cold and had taken to his bed, coughing and red-eyed. She hated to see him so ill and draggled.

'The sun is warm today, Daidí,' she said. 'You should sit outside for a while. It will make you feel better.'

'What would make me feel better is having an army at my back and the wherewithal to grind our enemies underfoot,' he retorted in a thick voice. 'I would be a king and not a beggar. I swear I will carve my name on the bones of my enemies. Whatever happens I shall live long enough to do that.'

'Of course you will, Daidí.'

She sat with him as he ate. His nose was blocked and he chewed with his mouth open, but she was relieved to see him devouring the food fast with a powerful appetite.

'It is time we had news from across the sea,' he said, wiping his lips on his sleeve. 'The ships were supposed to arrive with the first swallows but we have heard nothing. De la Roche was supposed to tell de Clare and the others to come as swiftly as they could and that my oath to be rid of foreign mercenaries meant nothing.'

'Perhaps they did not mean their oaths to you either,' she said. 'Perhaps de la Roche's report made them change their minds.'

He gave her a keen look. 'Is that what you think, my girl?'

'I do not know, but when no word comes on the trading ships out of Bristol, what does it suggest?' She thought of Richard's sincerity as he bade her farewell. Had it been mere platitude?

Her father coughed harshly. 'Word will come. I can bide my time and we can heal our wounds a while longer. The grass is lush and the cows are calving. When I am well, we shall be ready.'

'Yes, Daidí.'

She stayed for a while, combing his hair and beard and playing her harp for him, and when he fell asleep, she went outside. Recent graves were becoming green mounds in the abbey burial ground. Men who had died in the fighting last year, including Owen ap Rhys of Ceredigion – a handsome, foolish youth cut down like an ear of wheat. One spear thrust through the heart and he was no more. So many of their men killed and Connor taken hostage. She had been terrified for him, furious and tearful as he was taken away in the High King's retinue with the hundred ounces of gold her father had been forced to pay to Tiernan ua Ruari. Now they only had crumbs with which to lure the Norman soldiers to fight.

She pulled out Richard's ring on its cord and held it on her palm to watch the jewels gleam in the sunlight, and to remember the moment he had given it to her in the hall at Striguil. At times she was tempted to fling it into the sea, but whether to summon him or let him go, she was unsure. Perhaps to forget him.

Returning to the hall, it was as if her handling of the ring had released some trapped energy for one of Richard's messengers had arrived. Her father had left his bed and was sitting by the fire in the hall, wrapped in his cloak.

'Is there news?' she asked with trepidation.

'Not the news we might have wished for, but not the worst,' Diarmait replied. 'King Henry sent de Clare on a mission to escort his daughter to her marriage in Germany. He has now returned and has the King's permission to campaign, but he has been delayed at court.'

Aoife's heart sank. 'So he won't be here this year? Not even in late summer?'

Her father shook his head. 'No matter. We will endure and grow stronger, but we shall do it quietly. De Clare is sending his uncle to liaise with us and the Bristol trading ships will keep us informed and supplied.'

'And what if they do not come again next year and the year after and the year after?' she demanded, hands on hips.

'They will come,' Diarmait said, and wiped his dripping nose. 'A good huntsman always bides his time.'

Her father had spoken as if he were the huntsman, but Aoife wondered. Perhaps the Normans were the hunters and they were the prey. And perhaps King Henry was the greatest huntsman of all.

FitzHarding poured wine into cups for himself, his son and Richard. 'So, the King has given you leave to go to Ireland.'

'Yes.' Richard fondled the silky ears of the pewter-grey hound lying at his feet. 'Although it will not be this year. The autumn storms will soon be upon us and the weather no good for a campaign. It will have to be next spring.' As Henry had well known. The mission to escort the princess to Germany and see her safely married had lasted until February. He had reported back to Henry in March, but the King had not freed him for

144

another two and a half months. By the time he had arrived back in the Marches, all hope of organising a crossing this year had been over. He had written to Diarmait, keeping him informed, and Hervey was preparing to go to Ireland to smooth the waters, but Richard was deeply frustrated by the King's prevarication. If not for Henry, he could have been there now instead of kicking his heels in Bristol with the FitzHardings, about to enter into debt. 'I need to speak with you about Ireland,' he said.

FitzHarding opened his hand, encouraging him to continue.

'I need ships, men and equipment and they cost money I do not have, although if all goes well, I shall be wealthy in due course.' His mouth twisted with distaste even while he tried to be pragmatic. 'I have some land to sell, if you could help me find a buyer.' Land that should belong to his heirs if he had them. Land that should be bringing him an income for years to come, but with which he was gambling in the hope of greater gain. 'I would not ask this of you were it not important. And I may need ready money above and beyond that.' He felt sick, but at least the words were out. He had toyed with the notion of sending one of his clerks to broker the request, but he had known FitzHarding too long for that and it had to be in person to have the best impact.

The merchant nodded sympathetically. 'We can do that for you,' he said, looking at his son. 'We can assist you with the ships for a good price since your success will benefit our trade. I can advance you some funds and I can put your factors in touch with others who will be able to help you. Josce of Gloucester is a good man for all he is a Jew. He will give you a good rate if your request comes through me.'

Richard tightened his lips but nodded agreement for he had no choice. 'That would be useful. It will set my mind at rest and help me continue with my plans.'

'I know it is hard for you, and times have been difficult,' FitzHarding said, 'but I would not be doing this unless I thought you had a chance. You are a risk worth taking.' He directed a servant to refill Richard's cup. 'Like me, you do your business face to face, and I will go a long way for a customer I trust.'

Richard gave a humourless smile. 'Since you were responsible for mooting the idea in the first place, I hoped you would.' He raised his cup in toast. 'To new horizons.'

Walking from the abbey to the dairy, Aoife drew a deep breath of the late September air. Cobwebs spangled the wattle fences and hedges and the dew sparkled on the grass like drops of rock crystal.

A fruitful harvest had been gathered and the lush grass had made the cows sleek and fat and produced plentiful butter and cheese for the winter months. In the dairy the women were busy with the morning's milk, putting it in dishes to settle the cream ready for skimming. Aoife inspected the cheeses, unwrapping one from its linen binding to reveal a hard-golden wheel like a small sun. She cut a narrow slice from the side and taking a nibble found it sweet and good, tasting of rich summer grazing. Closing her eyes to savour it, she appreciated the cheese more keenly because she had overseen the making herself. She ordered the women to cut a larger wedge from the wheel and wrapped it in a cloth to take to her father.

He was in good spirits because Hervey de Montmorency had arrived with a letter from Richard de Clare bearing news that preparations for a spring campaign were going forward. Hervey had brought a shipload of food and wine and more weapons including fine mail shirts for her father and Domnall. For her there had been a braid belt stitched with garnets and pearls. She had hidden it away in her coffer because it unsettled her. She was not Richard de Clare's until he set foot in Ireland and without his presence, words and gifts were nothing. She had matured since the visit to Striguil. Thinking of him still gave her a frisson, but less intense these days; indeed, she was even a little disappointed.

She found her father sitting by the fire staring into the flames, his lips tight and his body hunched. When she joined him he neither acknowledged her nor gave the appearance of knowing she was there.

'I have brought you some cheese, Daidí,' she said. 'Will you taste it?'

He ignored her outstretched hand. 'Enna is coming home,' he said in a dull voice.

She gazed at him in worried surprise, trying to make sense of why he was so disgruntled and cross. 'When?' She set the cheese aside.

'Later today.' Another silence. His eyes were dark and angry.

'Then we must make more food and prepare a room.'

Her father grunted. 'Make his favourite stew and do not stint on the ingredients.'

'Of course not, Daidí . . . but . . .'

He gave a stiff nod and, rising to his feet, turned his shoulder on her and went to talk to Domnall. She frowned after him and then made herself busy chivvying the servants to begin the stew before seeking out her mother to ask where they should make sleeping space for Enna.

She found her in the church on her knees counting her prayer beads and signing her breast. Aoife knelt down beside her. 'Enna is coming home,' she said, feeling queasy, for something was definitely wrong.

Môr stopped counting. 'Yes,' she said. 'A messenger arrived while you were busy in the dairy.' Turning, she gripped Aoife's hand in hers. 'It is . . . I do not know how to tell you this . . . The men of Ossory have blinded him.'

'No, that's not true!' The words were a flimsy barrier and did not withstand the impact of the news. 'Why would they do that?'

'Who knows?' Môr said, bitterly. 'Because the harvest has been good and we have been recovering. Because the ships from Wales continue to come and your father's enemies see them. Because your father has done the same in his turn. Because they do not want your father to have an heir.' Her mother pressed her lips together. Unspoken between them lay the knowledge that if this had happened to Enna, what might they do to Connor? It was a dire warning of intent.

'No.' Aoife shook her head again. 'It isn't true!' She wouldn't let it be true. Enna's beautiful blue eyes. She snatched her hand out of her mother's grasp. 'I promised Daidí I would make Enna's favourite stew. I have to go and do it before he arrives.'

'Aoife . . .'

'No!'

Leaving her mother still on her knees, Aoife stumbled back to the hall and began preparing food, chopping the roots and the good beef, dismissing the serving women and rejecting all help. She kept telling herself it couldn't be true and every time her mind veered towards the news, she closed it off and made it a blank while she wielded the knife.

She was stirring the cauldron when Enna arrived, brought into the hall by her father and a monk from the abbey, the latter talking to him gently, guiding his faltering feet. A white bandage was bound around his head, covering his eyes, and the sight broke through the barrier of Aoife's denial. Abandoning the spoon, she fled to the women's chamber at the top of the tower and hid under the bedclothes as she had done as a little girl. She did not want her own eyes to see Enna like that and be forced to confront reality. She curled up and sobbed, and then felt wretchedly guilty because she had tears to shed.

Her mother came to find her and, sitting on her pillow, folded a small ivory cross into her hand for comfort and took her in her arms.

'Why does God do this?' Aoife railed. 'It would be better if there was no God!'

Môr made a shocked sound. 'Hush, hush, child. It is not God who has done this, but man. Let God be your succour.'

148

Her mother's attempts at comfort did nothing to assuage Aoife's grief, nor her shame for being so distraught when Enna had the worst of it. 'I do not want to see Enna like this,' she said, her voice cracking. 'I cannot bear it, so how can he? I want him as he was, and that can never be!'

'No, it cannot.'

Eventually Aoife sat up and wiped her face on the cloth her mother gave to her. She felt sick but she had to be brave for Enna's sake. How much more bravery would he need? Her own was nothing by comparison.

She descended the sleeping loft stairs one rung at a time, feeling with her feet and counting, knowing this would be her brother's lot until the end of his life.

Enna was sitting by the fire and Aoife had to swallow hard because the sight of the bandaging around his eyes made her want to retch. The linen was thickly layered and clean with no blood or other stains in evidence, but that made it no better. She forced herself to sit beside him and put her arms around his body. 'Enna, it is Aoife,' she said. 'I am so sorry this has happened to you.'

He turned to her voice and felt her face with his hand. 'Aoife,' he said, and swallowed. 'I thought never to see you again.' They both realised what he had said and a shudder rippled through him and into her. 'And so I shan't.'

'I cannot accept this has happened to you,' she whispered.

'I cannot accept it either, yet I must.'

Aoife drew away to pour him a drink and gave it to him, folding the fingers of his right hand around the cup. 'Why?' she said in a breaking voice. 'In the name of God, why?'

Her father was sitting on the other side of the fire, his eyes glittering like coals. 'I will tell you why,' he said harshly. 'Because they fear what we will become even against all odds if they do not squash us now. They have destroyed the sight of my child, my heir. They have taken my wealth, my land, and my sons.

They may say they have given me what I deserve. Well then, I shall return their own just deserts with interest.'

Enna said in an exhausted voice, 'They know you were communicating with the Normans and building up supplies.'

'It is no more than trade,' Diarmait growled, but he turned his head aside.

Hervey de Montmorency was also sitting by the fire, tight-lipped and grim. He kept his own eyes on Enna and they were filled with pity and compassion.

Enna said quietly, bitterly, 'No, my father. I know you and what you have done and are doing. I lay no blame at your door. You have been backed into this corner and you have no choice but to fight. I would have done the same. I always knew the game might end badly for me. Even if I do not accept it, I own it.' His hand trembled and mead slopped over the side of the cup. 'But what use am I now at your hearth? What use am I to anyone, even to myself, when the only place I am able to have sight is in my dreams?'

Aoife almost choked striving not to cry, and gripped his other hand, noting the abrasions crusting his wrist where they had bound him while they blinded him.

Diarmait jerked to his feet, his own eyes bright with tears. 'There will be a reckoning for this, I swear on the cross of Christ. All of us shall be avenged.' He strode from the room, but they all heard the roar of anguish and grief trailing behind him like a lost soul. Aoife shivered, feeling the sound in her bones, but Enna said nothing.

That night Enna developed a raging fever. Aoife sat at his bedside and nursed him. No longer silent, he raved and sobbed in anguish. When she touched him, he thought she was coming to put out his eyes and it took her a long time to calm him, especially when the monks from St Mary's infirmary tried to give him a draught to make him sleep. It was men who had blinded him and he clung to Aoife, screaming and begging for mercy.

When at last he fell into a restless slumber, Aoife briefly left his bedside and sought her father, finding him huddled in a corner, his face in his hands, body silently shaking. She bit her lips, knowing it would be like approaching a wounded bear, but still she went to him and touched his shoulder. Eventually he raised his hand to hers and took it, squeezing her fingers so hard she stifled a gasp.

'They want to break me, precious girl,' he said, tears running down his cheeks, 'but I will endure. I will destroy all of them, whatever the cost. This I swear on the bones of my father and the dog they buried with him. I will have revenge for this.'

Aoife shivered. Nothing would ever compensate for this. Enna was sightless for the rest of his days and they would all have to live with the guilt and the burden.

A cold autumn wind blew through the Marches. The last of the leaves fluttered like tattered golden rags on the oaks and elms of the Wye valley forests. Striguil's pigs had been fattening on the coppery beechmast carpeting the forest floor and it would soon be slaughter time. In his chamber, Richard stared out over the river, brown and pocked with rain under a dull sky. A day to stay by the fire, mending, planning, marking time.

Turning from the window, he regarded Hervey who had recently returned from Ireland and was leaning against the wall, cup in hand, as he addressed the gathered men in the chamber. Raymond le Gros, Robert FitzStephen, and his half-brother Maurice FitzGerald. Hervey had been telling them about Enna.

'Men do terrible things to gain and keep power,' Richard said. 'MacMurchada is no innocent himself.'

'They said it was a warning – that they knew about his communications with us and he must cease them forthwith.' A shudder ran through Hervey's elegant frame. 'I thought the young man would die – perhaps better if he had. He was out of his wits with high fever for several days. Indeed, when the fever cooled, he remained stupefied. He just sits by the fire now and sometimes has surges of temper like a wild animal. His sister cared for him when he was very sick, but he is in the hands of the monks now.'

Raymond le Gros folded his arms across his broad chest. 'I do not understand why this is any of our concern.'

Hervey shot him an irritated look. 'It tells us the High King and his allies are determined to keep Diarmait pinned down. It also tells us they fear him. They have blinded his most promising son. Enna will never rule, and his youngest heir, the legitimate one, is also a hostage, and that adds to the pressure. He has been warned what could happen.'

Robert FitzStephen was tight-lipped and silent having recently been a prisoner himself. He had spent the previous winter recovering and putting on flesh while gaining distance from the experience.

'It will not stop him,' Hervey continued. 'MacMurchada knows the risks and he will still take them. I have never seen a man with such a fire for vengeance. He will burn down the world in order to have it.'

Richard gnawed his thumb knuckle. Hervey's assessment was sobering and unsettling. Ireland was the edge of the world in more ways than one and Diarmait was an unpredictable force of nature. More than once he had considered dropping the enterprise. It was like trying to remove bread from a very hot oven with too short a paddle.

'Of course,' Raymond said, 'this could all work to our advantage.'

Richard eyed him keenly. 'In what way?'

'If the most promising son can no longer lead, and the youngest is a hostage, Domnall is the only contender, but he is a follower not a ruler from what I saw at Striguil. That leaves the daughter. If you wed her, your heirs will have a claim to the throne of Leinster. Even if you do not sit there yourself, your offspring have every opportunity to do so.'

A jolt shot through Richard's heart. The notion had long dwelt at the back of his mind but he had kept it there because his dreams were practical ones. 'Mayhap,' he said, 'but we must tackle the immediate situation and decide how far to risk. Everyone has interests to protect, not just the Irish. We have to ask what this is worth to us and what we can do with the resources we possess. Ireland will still be there in the spring and we can do nothing until then.' He looked at Hervey. 'Uncle, I want you to return to Diarmait with messages of goodwill and continue to cultivate him. I will not burn bridges, but neither do I wish to risk all.' He looked round at the other men. 'Do any of you have anything to say?'

'I am bound to go for I have sworn my oath and I have more to lose by remaining,' said FitzStephen. 'There is nothing for me here save a return to the lord Rhys's dungeon. I will willingly cross the sea if I have the necessary funds.'

'I will go with you,' said Maurice FitzGerald. He gave a twisted smile. 'We can share the spoils.'

'You have my goodwill and help to do so,' Richard said. 'But venture carefully and make no rash plans. The Irish are unpredictable and fierce. We may have better armour and discipline, but do not underestimate their skill. Beware too the Norsemen of the ports. Wexford, Waterford and Dublin are all hostile and are not easy meat. Do not bite off more than you can chew.'

'Only enough to feed us,' FitzStephen said, and, smiling, raised his cup. 'To new horizons – may they never end.'

'Aunt Basilia, do you think Papa will go to Ireland?' Matilda asked.

'I cannot say, my dear,' Basilia replied.

She was sitting in the great hall with her nieces, slightly apart from the men who had been enthusiastically discussing the matter of FitzStephen's expedition for several hours. Basilia glanced at her brother. The firelight reflected in his hair as he sat fondling the head of a hound and listening to what the others had to say, occasionally interrupting to make a point or direct the conversation. She knew that look of old. He was absorbing all the ideas and information and filtering them to blend with his own and formulate strategies.

'But really, do you think he will?' Matilda persisted, toying with her bread. 'They have been talking all day.'

Basilia shook her head. 'You know your father. He takes time to make up his mind. We will know when we know.' *When he decides to tell us*, she thought bitterly.

'If he does go, will we have to go too?' Aline asked.

Basilia compressed her lips. The last thing she wanted to do was cross the Irish Sea and disrupt her life of comfortable routine. She was mistress of the household, the lady of Striguil, but it would not pertain in Ireland, especially if Richard married that hoyden wild Irish girl. What sort of example would she set to his daughters? Diarmait MacMurchada had made her shudder with his leering glances and sly smiles and sidelong hints that she might do for one of his nobles. She would rather throw herself off Striguil's cliffs than do that. She dreaded to think of the fate of the girls too. 'Again, I do not know. We must wait and see.'

'I wish we had been here when the Irish were visiting and that we could have seen them,' Matilda said wistfully. 'If Papa is to wed the Irish princess, she will become our stepmother. It would have been good to meet her.'

Basilia, to the contrary, was more than pleased they had been staying with their grandmother and not been subject to their guests. 'It remains to be seen if there is a wedding,' she said curtly. 'Never mind that for now.' She put her sewing aside, relieved to see the men were finally breaking off from their discussion. Richard called for food and wine to be brought and for musicians to play while they ate.

After the meal came socialising, singing and dancing. Richard, whatever his cares and business, kept a hall where his retainers had time for leisure and entertainment. He believed it enhanced the cohesion and kept the ties tight. Basilia had decided it was why Richard liked the Irish. He thrived on their boisterous camaraderie and sense of belonging, whereas during their stay she had felt like a cat in a hall full of dogs.

The girls were eager to dance, their faces bright with pleasure. Aline was graceful and willowy like Richard but with her mother's rich brown hair. Matilda's braids were fairer with a hint of auburn, and her eyes were Richard's blue, and joyful. Richard beckoned Basilia into the dance too and she rose to perform her duty as lady of the castle. He smiled at her in passing before they moved on and then she partnered their uncle Hervey who was light on his feet with a twinkle in his eyes. Then Robert FitzStephen, handsome, but with hard hands that dug into her waist as the circle rotated, and finally Raymond le Gros. He stood head and shoulders above her and his breadth blotted out the other dancers. His life force was so vigorous she could almost taste it and his touch made her shiver. A pragmatic soldier when on duty, he was convivial when relaxing in the hall. With the women he was most proper and never overstepped the boundaries, but sometimes she would catch his eye on her, and when they were close like this, his masculinity disturbed her equilibrium. It was like having a tame lion, but rightly fearing its teeth. He bowed and moved on.

Duty done, she escaped to the benches at the side of the room with relief.

17

Fearns, Leinster, Ireland, spring 1169

It had been a bad night for Enna. He had thrashed on his bed beset by wild and vivid dreams. 'I cannot bear this,' he told Aoife when she sat with him in the morning to help him eat bread and milk. 'To only see in my dreams and my thoughts while my world is a void. I might as well be dead for all the use I am to anyone.'

'Hush, you must not say that.'

He turned his head away. 'I can say what I wish. I still have my voice. They did not cut that out of me.'

She bit her lip. There had been so many similar barren conversations since his return. Enna had entered a shadow world where no one could reach him. Blindness had robbed him of himself, and she had lost her brother. She still visited him every day, but her father had given up. She knew he felt guilty about what had happened and could not bear to look upon the consequences of his actions. He too had become bitter and difficult to live with.

'I won't leave you,' she said, 'I will never leave you. You are dear to me. Come outside into the sunshine and sit a while. To please me, just for me.'

At first, he refused, but she gently cajoled him out of the small chamber where he dwelt in the monks' care, and outside to a sunlit bench. She spoke of inconsequential things, small daily routines, picking her words carefully, for if she described things she had seen he grew upset because his world was in darkness.

Suddenly he lifted his bandaged face to the sky. 'The swallows have returned.'

His hearing had grown sharper to compensate for his blindness but now she heard it too, and then she saw them. Birds darting and swooping on the wing with their familiar plumage of blue, white and cut-throat red. Soon all the barns and buildings would be hectic with their nests. 'Yes,' she said. 'They have.'

'Then the Normans will be here soon. They said they would come with the swallows.'

In her mind's eye she saw the ships crossing the sea and wondered if Enna was seeing them too.

'I gave my sight for them,' he said. 'They must come.'

She squeezed his hand. 'They will, I promise.'

Enna screwed up his face. 'I have learned not to have faith in promises, sister.'

Three weeks later the swallows had built their nests and laid their eggs but no ships came from across the water. Diarmait had sent lookouts to the coast but they returned without news. Enna fell into a bleak mood and refused to talk to anyone, and Diarmait, after the latest negative report from his scouts, boiled over into fury.

'Why are they not here?' he raged. 'I have made pacts and given my word to them. Are they all faithless dogs?' He glared at Domnall as if he was to blame for the empty sea. 'Where are they?'

Domnall prudently said nothing. Hearing the fury and frustration in her father's voice, Aoife kept her head down over her harp.

Diarmait banged his fist on the table. 'Richard de Clare might as well not exist. All his fine promises are worth a bag of wind. I am finished with him. I will find someone who does know how to fight and how to follow through on his word.' Aoife made a soft sound and his eyes flashed to her, wild and bloodshot. 'You can count that door closed, my girl. I refuse to waste any more of my time.'

Aoife drew into herself. There was no arguing with her father when he was lashing out in drink-fuelled rage. She was dismayed at his words, but she understood his raw frustration for she felt it herself like a stone in her stomach. Why had Richard not come? Had they not done a good enough job of securing him to their cause? Was she to blame? There must be a reason, and if he truly had chosen to abandon them, then where else could they turn?

In the morning her father's head was clearer, even if aching, and he convened his men to decide what to do about the empty sea. Choosing her moment carefully, Aoife filled his drinking horn and set a platter of bread and beef in front of him.

'Daidí, why don't you write to Richard again and ask him why he is not here himself?' she suggested.

He waved her away. 'Why should I? There are plenty of ambitious men in South Wales other than de Clare.'

'Perhaps there are reasons why he cannot come,' Aoife said.

Her father lifted an eyebrow. 'Good reasons or bad, daughter, I will wait no longer.'

Maurice Regan said, 'Send an open letter, sire, and see who answers the call. I will take it for you, and I will go again to Striguil while announcing your offer in every stronghold along the way. The word will spread. It will not be cutting off de Clare, but at the same time it will widen the net.'

Diarmait eyed Regan, one eye half shut in thought. 'Yes,' he said. 'I cannot sit here another year doing nothing. We have to act. Fetch your pen and parchment.'

'Daidí . . .' Aoife said.

Diarmait's gazed flicked to her. 'What?'

'You . . . you will not offer me in marriage to other men?'

His expression hardened. 'You are not hand-fasted to Richard

158

de Clare. The agreement was that you would be his if he came to Ireland, which he seems not to want to do. Whoever comes bringing me troops and weapons and defeats my enemies shall have that same consideration.'

Aoife's heart was banging in her chest. 'But I have to consent, that is our law.'

'Yes, that is our law, my girl, and if you cleave to your family and your father, you will do as you are bidden. This is for all of us, not just you. If Richard de Clare comes as he has promised, you shall have him. If he does not, then prepare yourself for a different binding.'

Aoife said nothing; her protests would fall on deaf ears, and she did not want to further harden her father's heart. She had steeled herself to accept Richard de Clare and she hated the uncertainty of everything being tossed in the air like a handful of soothsayer's knuckle bones.

She approached Maurice Regan next day as he was preparing to leave and gave him a small cloth pouch. 'When you visit Striguil, I want you to return this ring to Richard de Clare,' she said. 'Tell him I give it back to him; I will not hold on to false hope. But if that hope should be true against all the odds, then let him bring it back to me soon.'

Maurice Regan's expression held shrewd approval as he stowed the pouch in his purse. 'I shall do so, mistress.' He looked her directly in the eyes. 'He will come.'

'You believe it?'

'I trust to my eloquence to bring him,' he said with a smile. 'He will not want to lose this prize, but he has to be reminded what a prize it is – and your token will assist his focus.'

She watched him walk off and then, biting her lip, returned to her duties.

If anyone wishes to have land or money, horses, equipment, gold or silver, I will give him very generous payments. If anyone wants land or pasture, I will enfeoff him generously. I will also give him plenty of livestock and a rich fief.

Richard read the words written on the parchment then raised his eyes to Maurice Regan, who was sitting by the fireside in the great hall at Striguil.

'My lord says that the swallows have arrived twice in Leinster since you agreed to come and he has looked for you in vain. All he needs to complete his plans are the men and equipment you promised him in good faith. Since you have failed him, he has extended his offer to others too. I have proclaimed this letter throughout South Wales.'

Richard maintained a neutral expression despite his inner dismay. 'He has the King's permission to recruit where he will,' he said. 'I have not reneged on my promise. I had indeed hoped to come last year but the King kept me at court and did not grant me his leave until too late in the season. Since then I have been working on the matter.'

'Then you should send my lord assurances and fix a time when you will come for he is sick of waiting and his mood is dark. I have come to you again because I believe you are still willing to help us, but my lord's patience is ended.' He gestured at the parchment in Richard's hand. 'I am bidden to say to any lords who agree to this that his daughter's hand in marriage is available.' He produced Aoife's ring and gave it to Richard. 'The lady bids you keep this until you are able to return it to her in person.'

Richard tipped the circlet onto his palm and looked at the jewels winking in the firelight, and his mind filled with the image of the wild girl with a voice like a pure curl of sea spray.

'If you are coming, my lord, we need more than words. That is the beginning and end of the matter.'

Richard closed his fist over the ring and with a sigh leaned back in his chair. 'It takes time to prepare such things. Your lord promises horses and arms, gold and lands. But what does he truly have? We heard he had to pay his enemies a hundred ounces of gold in recompense for a past grievance. We hear that his son has had his eyes put out.' He raised his hand as Maurice opened his mouth to protest. 'I am sorry for what has happened and I know what it is to have others put obstacles in the path of hopes and ambitions for I battle the same difficulties every day. You come with offers, but no practical means of payment, and that means anyone who ventures to Ireland to take up King Diarmait's proposals must do so at his own expense.'

'Sire, you knew that when you made your agreements with my king.'

'That was before he had to pay Tiernan ua Ruari,' Richard retorted. 'However, I remain committed. I can send you three ships, sixty men in mail and three hundred archers. They will return with you to your lord now as a token of goodwill. The rest must wait on my finances. King Diarmait must understand this. I have resources, but they are not infinite and promises of future reward do not of themselves build ships and equip men. That takes time.' He opened his hand towards Maurice. 'You may wave this letter from here to Normandy and the Brabant, but all you will get is a rabble of individual adventurers lacking cohesion – no different to the Irish fighting the Irish. There is no one to coordinate this except me – or no one willing. Seek far and wide, but you will discover the truth of what I say.'

Maurice eyed him shrewdly. 'And do you have that wherewithal, sire? Forgive me for being blunt, but I am representing my lord.'

'When I was at the King's beck and call last year, the tidings out of Ireland were not encouraging for a full campaign. My men were sent home because your lord promised the High King he would revoke our invitation. He blows hot and cold, so what am I to believe? Trust is a sword that cuts both ways, messire Regan.' He put Aoife's ring in his belt purse and reached to his wine. 'I am still willing to come to Ireland, and those ships and men I mentioned are ready to embark. If they succeed, and your lord holds steady to his intent, more will come with next year's swallows and that is my solemn oath – and I shall come with them.'

Maurice frowned and Richard remained steady, challenging him to speak one word on the matter of solemn oaths.

'My ships will be ready to sail within a fortnight and the seigneur de Montmorency will sail with the troops and report to King Diarmait from me as he did before.'

'Then you give me good news,' Maurice said, although without smiling, 'of which I hope to hear more.'

'And so you shall. But come now, let us eat first and talk of other things.'

When Maurice retired, Richard stood in his chamber, hands braced on a trestle, eyes tightly shut and head bent. He felt as though he had been ground through a mill, but talking to Diarmait's bard had centred his thoughts. Reading Diarmait's letter he had been filled with a possessive anger, a determination to fight. He had not realised how much it meant until the moment of knowing he might lose it. Removing Aoife's ring from his purse, he looked at it again on the palm of his hand. This was the promise returned, and no one was going to take it from him. He would step over the edge and make the full commitment.

18

Fearns, Leinster, Ireland, summer 1169

Aoife was making cheese from the creamy milk of the lush summer grass. As she hung the curds to drain she sang softly to herself, not as a conscious thing but born of a primal need to comfort the scared child hiding deep inside her. Keeping busy helped too. While she was concentrating on her work and singing, she was safe.

Eventually, a row of dripping bags hung over buckets in the dairy and having left instructions for the maids she stepped outside, wiping her hands, and saw Maurice Regan dismounting from a blowing horse.

'Where is your father?' he demanded as Aoife hurried towards him.

'At the stables,' she replied, and even on her last word he was running in that direction. She sped after him, her heart thumping, because if he had returned in such haste then the news must be momentous.

Her father was observing a new foal that had been born to his favourite mare just a few hours earlier. Another filly to add to the breeding herd. Watching her suckle strongly from her dam, he was in a good mood.

'My king.' Maurice Regan bent his knee.

Diarmait turned and raised his brows. 'Well?' he demanded.

'Sire, three shiploads of warriors have arrived from Wales. Sixty knights and three hundred archers at Bannow under Robert FitzStephen and Maurice FitzGerald. They're waiting for you.'

'Three ships?' Diarmait narrowed his eyes.

'And more to come, sire. I have spoken to Richard de Clare. His uncle has travelled with us to speak further with you.'

Diarmait's brows drew together in a deep frown. 'And de Clare himself?'

'He will come,' Regan added, 'but has to raise more money. He provides this for now and it will be enough to turn the tide, I believe. They are not rabble but well-equipped fighting men.' Regan looked round to where Aoife was hanging on his words and gave her a brief nod.

Aoife watched her father assemble every man in Fearns to ride out to meet the Norman ships. Invigorated, he strode about issuing orders, but still found time to stop in front of her and give her a hard look. 'You were right to tell me to wait on de Clare, my girl, but I hope you did not do it from any foolish notions of love or loyalty.'

Aoife shook her head. 'No, Daidí, my loyalty is to you.'

'That's my daughter. Always put your family first, never strangers. De Clare is not out of the woods yet.'

The atmosphere changed when the men had gone. The only males remaining were lads younger than fifteen, or grey-beards with their warrior days long behind them. Women, children and monks. The noises of daily life continued – the clucking of the poultry, the grunts of the pigs rootling in the yard, a broom sweeping over the ground, and the cries of children playing with straws in a muddy puddle. But for all the domestic sounds, the place bore the silence of insecurity. If their enemies came, the barricades were flimsy and the weapons useless. Aoife had her knife and she could grab a spear, but it was no protection. She imagined ways of escaping. Her golden mare was in the stable, but her people would look to her for leadership, and besides, she could not leave Enna. Her father and the Normans would be victorious; for their own survival they had to be.

She sought out Enna and discovered him curled up on his bed, his hand across his empty eyes.

'Enna,' she said softly, putting her hand on his shoulder.

He jerked at her touch and rolled away from her. 'I should be riding with them,' he said miserably. 'I should be leading a warband at our father's shoulder.'

'Yes, I know. It's not fair.' She stroked his hair and he grasped her hand.

'Be careful, Aoife. Never drop your guard and never trust anyone, and that includes our father. He will dig your heart out of your chest for his own ends. If all goes wrong, then run. Do not think of me. I am a burden and you have your life.'

'No . . .' The pressure of tears made her temples ache.

'I mean it . . . promise me, Aoife.' He gripped her hand tightly. 'Say it.'

'Yes, I promise.' She snatched her hand away. 'It won't come to that. Daidí will win.'

'But if he doesn't . . .'

'If he doesn't then we are all dead anyway, but for you, I promise.' She got up and walked away, rubbing her wrist and swallowing hard.

Several days passed without news. The weather grew warmer, turning the grass thick and lush. Aoife continued to make cheese, and churn butter, keeping herself busy. Her mother did the same, retreating into her sewing, making shirts for Diarmait and embroidering them with intricate stitches.

Aoife was combing her hair in her chamber when her father's messenger Lugh arrived, his horse staggering with exhaustion. Aoife hastily bundled her hair into a kerchief and ran to him, followed by her mother, her sewing still in her hand.

'We have the victory!' he cried. 'Wexford is ours! The King says to prepare a feast. He will be here tonight with the Normans!'

Aoife could barely comprehend what Lugh was saying. Wexford

was one of the bastions of the Norse settlers who had dwelt for so long in opposition to her father with disgruntled truces at best. Wexford had fallen?

'Praise be to God!' Her mother crossed herself and embraced Aoife fervently.

Servants were sent running to the cauldrons to prepare food for an army and the hall of timber and withies that had been built on the site of the charred palace was quickly made ready. Embers were raked along the full length of the fire pit running down the hall and cauldrons were set to bubbling. Chickens were slaughtered and plucked. The kitchen servants set about making stews, breads and porridges while others brought cheeses from the dairy and crocks of honey from the stores.

Aoife helped Enna dress and brought him to the fire. She kissed his cheek and murmured assurances – the warriors were coming home; all was well and their enemies had suffered a great defeat.

'No defeat can be too great,' Enna said. 'I would blot them out as they have blotted my sight if I could.'

Her father's return was a tide surging into Fearns. A glittering forest of spears and armour surrounded him as he moved through the throng, laughing, fierce-eyed and red-cheeked. She heard the swift lilt of Welsh voices, mingled with Flemish French, and Irish.

There were wounded, but not a great number, and but a single cartload of dead men. Aoife watched them being borne into the church on boards and the monks going within to attend them. A Norman soldier struggled off the back of another cart bearing the wounded. He staggered a few paces like a complete drunk and then fell to his knees, vomiting. She recognised Robert FitzStephen, the man who had been freed from his fetters at Ceredigion. Two soldiers took him in hand and carried him off between them to the infirmary.

Once more the Normans pitched their tents but this time their greater numbers turned their camp into a small town.

Aoife hurried to the hall to ensure that everyone had something to drink and a sleeping space. Her father was busy, and she would tackle him later when his ebullience had died down, but she took a horn of mead to Domnall.

'What sort of victory?' she asked him.

'We marched on Wexford.' Her half-brother's dark eyes sparkled. 'They shut their gates against us and when the Normans attacked they fought them off and killed several, but the Normans weren't deterred.' Respect flickered on his face and something akin to awe. 'They constructed siege ladders and hoardings – worked through the night to do it and were ready to fight at dawn. And then they ran up those ladders in their mail and pinned down the Norse on the battlements. They would have overrun Wexford had not our father stepped in and called on the citizens to surrender or be killed.' He took a swallow from the horn and shook his head. 'Never have I seen such warriors. They are like the sea. Even if the tide goes out, it comes in again, and again, and again. The Norse accepted the terms rather than face death, although it was all as one to the Normans. Daidí demanded their allegiance and their help to march on Tiernan. They had to accept Robert FitzStephen as their new lord and swear loyalty to him in King Henry's name. Our father gave the land between Wexford and Waterford to Hervey de Montmorency to hold for Richard de Clare as he had sworn.'

'I have just seen Robert FitzStephen being carried into the infirmary,' she said.

Domnall snorted. 'He was knocked witless on the first assault – ran out leading his men and took a stone on the helmet. His men dragged him back and had to get a smith to prise the helm off his head so severe was the dint. He's been vomiting and drowsy ever since, but he'll survive. I tell you, these Normans are . . .' He grimaced, seeking the words. 'I would say mad, but it is a cold madness. I never want them as enemies.' He returned the horn to her and went off to talk to his men, pausing at the hearth to lay a hand on Enna's shoulder and speak to him.

Aoife was heading towards the women's quarters to find her mother when Hervey de Montmorency intercepted her. From a distance she had seen him arrive wearing his armour, but now he was clad in a tunic of soft red wool with a white shirt beneath and looked as elegant as a cat.

'I am bidden to tell you from my lord and nephew that he holds you in esteem and although delayed, he remains eager to come to Ireland to fulfil his oath. He thanks you for the return of his ring and he understands why you sent it back to him but hopes to place it on your finger himself when he arrives.' He held her gaze with sincerity.

'I shall await that moment,' she replied with mature dignity, giving nothing away. The words were like water. Without a cup to hold them, they spilled on the ground and drained away to no purpose. Richard had sent men, but not himself.

Her mother was being dried by her maids after bathing and indicated that Aoife should use the tub too before the water was discarded. Môr's hair fell to her waist in fair-brown waves and another woman began working with a comb to smooth it out. A few silver strands twinkled amid the golden brown, and her belly was softly curved. She had borne no more children since Connor, although had suffered two miscarriages. Her face was calm, but Aoife recognised the mask donned as part of her preparations for the night duty with Diarmait. Môr never spoke of it save to say that a wife must do her duty and perform God's will but Aoife had been educated by observation to know more than enough about what it entailed.

Aoife undressed, pinned up her hair and stepped into the tub. A serving woman added a jugful of fresh warm water. She looked down at her own pale body. In the last year her breasts had become firmly rounded, her waist narrow, her hips curved, with a crisp dark triangle at the juncture of her thighs. She had grown taller too and the beautiful court gowns no longer fitted her. She had reluctantly put them away in a chest, although sometimes she still took them out to admire, and to remember the king who had given them to her. Her body was a woman's, fully blossomed. What would it be like if Richard did come and she had to bed with him? Open herself as her mother did for her father? To have a man inside her body and herself trapped and vulnerable? The thought frightened her and in turn that fear made her want to fight. Being made powerless was her greatest fear.

That night, her father came to her mother, fuelled with drink and the triumph of his success. Lying in the outer chamber with the other women, Aoife listened to the sounds. The grunts of each forceful thrust and her mother's stifled whimpers. At least it was soon over. A long groan from her father and the bedclothes stopped moving. Then almost immediately the reverberation of loud snores. Aoife shuddered. If such was duty, she would never grow accustomed to it when she married.

She dreamed of heads again, a mountain of them, and her father contemplating them like a glutton at a feast.

19

Tintern Abbey, Welsh Marches, winter 1169

Lantern light haloed a curtain of snowflakes as Richard emerged from the abbey with Basilia, his daughters and his knights. The sky had been patchy blue when they set out that morning to visit, but was now a lowering grey tinged with ivory, warning of a heavy fall. Already the ground was carpeted.

The grooms brought the horses out from shelter, removing blankets from their saddles. Raymond le Gros helped Basilia to mount her brown gelding while a groom held the bridle. The snow had made the horse skittish and he tossed his head up and down and stamped his hooves. The groom gripped the reins and patted his neck. 'Steady,' he said. 'Steady, lad.'

Richard saw his daughters settled on their palfreys, mounted his own horse and turned towards Striguil.

Although the castle was less than five miles away, the snowfall increased as they rode, becoming thick, wet flakes, driven into their faces by a bitter wind. Suddenly, out of the feather storm, a roebuck burst across their path in a brown blur and an instant later three lean grey wolves lunged out of the snow in hard pursuit. The horses plunged and skittered, and Basilia's gelding reared, throwing her and bolting. Richard's constable Robert de Quency managed to grab the gelding's reins and pull it in tight to his own less excitable mount. Raymond le Gros hastily swung down from his big grey and knelt beside Basilia while the others drew their swords to protect the group, although by now both wolves and deer had vanished into the curtain of snowfall.

Basilia sat up, white-faced. A few spots of bright blood stained the snow where she had cut her hand on a stone as she landed, but otherwise she was unharmed and striving not to make a scene in front of everyone, especially the wide-eyed girls.

'My lady . . .' Raymond helped her to her feet.

She had twisted her ankle in the fall and she gasped when she put her weight on it and was both embarrassed and glad of Raymond's strength steadying her. 'I am all right,' she said shakily, 'nothing is broken – except my pride.'

The gelding was led forward but the saddle had slipped and the animal was still stamping and kicking.

'My lady, you cannot ride him, not in these conditions and after your fall,' Raymond said with concern. 'I will take you up on Gris; he is strong enough to carry us both.'

Basilia nodded, teeth chattering, too shaken to disagree.

Raymond looked to Richard, who had dismounted and was looking at his sister in concern. 'With your permission, my lord.'

Richard gestured assent and Raymond mounted the big grey, removed his glove and reached down. Basilia gripped his hand and let him pull her up, Richard boosting her from behind before turning to remount his own horse.

'My lady, if it is not impertinent for me to suggest such a thing, put your hands under my cloak and hold on to my belt,' Raymond said over his shoulder. 'I would not want you to take another fall, and besides, you will be warmer that way.'

She hesitated and then did as he asked. Since they were not at war with the Welsh, he was not wearing his mail, but a padded tunic for warmth with his sword belt over the top. She gripped the leather and felt his solid body, and although she was cold, her cheeks blazed with heat. He clicked his tongue to the horse and they set out again through the whirling whiteness. Her cut hand ached with icy pain.

'Wolves will be prowling around the sheep pens,' Richard said with a worried frown. 'I will send a message to the abbey and we'll hold a hunt as soon as the weather lifts.' He grimaced. 'You clear them out but sooner or later they return.' He looked across at Basilia. 'Are you sure you are all right?'

'Yes, it was nothing.' She did not want a fuss made or to be singled out. 'I will be all right once we reach Striguil.'

They made their way home, covering the three remaining miles in close formation. Everyone was on edge knowing wolves were once more in the vicinity. Basilia could see little in front of her because of Raymond's solid body, padded by winter garments and covered in his heavy blue cloak. To either side curtains of snow draped the land in thick white swathes, and although she was surrounded by company she was also alone, gripping the belt of this great bulwark of a man and trying with all her might to distance herself from him.

At Striguil, the guards swiftly opened the gate. 'Sire, Maurice of Prendergast and the seigneur de Montmorency are here – they are in the hall awaiting you,' the young soldier on duty announced, his lips chapped with cold.

Richard acknowledged the news as he dismounted. Raymond had already helped Basilia from his horse and she was gingerly testing her ankle.

'If you have guests I need to see to arrangements,' she said.

Richard shook his head. 'You can issue orders from your chamber and others can deal with it. The girls are fully capable. Raymond will bear you there.'

The knight inclined his head. 'By your leave, madam.' Picking her up as if she weighed no more than a snow feather, he bore her away to the domestic chamber. Basilia compressed her lips and endured. When he settled her on the bench in front of the hearth, she thanked him woodenly. He bowed, his expression straight, his breathing barely affected despite having carried her up two sets of stairs over his shoulder.

'I am glad to be of service, my lady.' He fixed her with his direct grey stare. 'I hope your ankle soon mends. I'll send the steward, shall I?'

He went out, and Basilia exhaled a shaky sigh of relief and tried not to think of the embarrassment of being carried up the stairs like a sack of grain. Her hand and ankle were throbbing but she had no time for her injuries now; not with duties to perform.

Once changed into dry garments, Richard joined the men in the hall. His uncle Hervey and Maurice of Prendergast, a Flemish knight who had accompanied FitzStephen and his half brother, were standing by the fire. Hervey strode to greet him with an embrace, Prendergast with a bow and a hand clasp, his hazel eyes wary. Richard had already noted that Prendergast had brought his core troop with him and that their horses were warmly stabled, eating Striguil's hay supplies.

'You are fortunate to be here,' Richard said. 'You might have been stranded by the snow.'

'We arrived as it started,' Hervey replied. 'You might have been stranded yourself.'

'We would have turned back to Tintern.' He told them about the wolves as they settled by the fire to drink hot wine, and once they were comfortable, he returned to business. 'I take it you have news.'

'Yes,' Hervey said. 'Diarmait is over-wintering at Fearns and the other Irish lords have retreated to their hearths. There will be no warfare until the spring so we thought it an opportune moment to come and tell you what is happening.'

Richard stroked the hound that came to flop at his feet and glanced up as Raymond arrived to join them. 'Why are your men here too?' he demanded of Prendergast.

'Sire, it is not a simple story.' Prendergast flicked a glance at Hervey.

'But I have time to listen,' Richard assured him. 'I am not going anywhere for the rest of the day.'

Prendergast squared his shoulder and related the details concerning the battle for Wexford and FitzStephen's head injury, from which he had now made a full recovery. Then they had engaged in another pitched battle against the men of Ossory. 'We were outnumbered, but we hid fifty archers in the bushes and feigned a flight. When the Ossory men chased us, we loosed our arrows on them and after that we were able to split them up and cut them down.'

'Led by Maurice,' Hervey said. 'He fought with great daring and courage.'

Richard raised his brows, for the statement was one of Hervey's typical softeners to mitigate unwelcome news.

Prendergast flushed. 'We took several hostages, and many more were killed or injured . . .' He paused to take a drink.

'Go on,' Richard said.

Hervey took up the story. 'King Diarmait was a man possessed after the victory. He . . . He offered silver for every head of an Ossory warrior presented to him, the way we would offer silver for the pelt of a wolf.' Hervey swallowed, and the hair rose on Richard's nape. Hervey and Maurice were battle-hardened veterans and this hesitancy was disturbing. Hervey looked round, checking no one else was in earshot. 'He had the heads brought to him and piled up before his chair.'

Maurice of Prendergast muttered under his breath and palmed his face.

'Then he selected the head of someone he recognised on the pile. He picked it up by the ears . . . and God help us all, my lord . . . he tore off the nose and the lips with his own teeth and spat them to the floor for the dogs to eat and said thus would he serve all of his enemies and they should fear the name of MacMurchada throughout the land for he was coming for them and for their children because they had blinded his son.'

A log shifted on the fire and a burst of sparks stitched the smoke. Nothing was said for a long time.

Eventually Maurice cleared his throat. 'Even when the battle rage had gone from him, he considered his actions justified and he encouraged people to spread the tale abroad.'

'Sometimes peace is bought at the cost of brutality,' Raymond observed pragmatically.

'Yes,' Prendergast said, 'but he was settling old scores, not buying peace. Peace does not matter to him, only that he should rule and trample his enemies. That is the only way he will have peace. We have become the tail of a mad dog.'

'And is that why I am seeing you here at Striguil and not in Ireland?' Richard raised his brows again.

Prendergast pushed his hands through his receding hair. 'In truth, after what I witnessed with that pile of heads, my stomach quailed and I am no puking squire. I stayed with him until we had driven off the men of Ossory, but while others were offered land and wealth, all he gave us was silver and I thought it insufficient recompense.'

'You would have received lands in due course,' Hervey said shortly.

Maurice shrugged. 'Still not enough for what we were expected to do. I told King Diarmait I was returning to Wales and he denied me safe passage and demanded that I stay and fight.' His eyes flashed with indignation. 'When I agree to serve, I do so with full honour and a whole heart, but I shall not be taken for a fool or have my will snatched from me. He refused to give me land, and he was preventing me from leaving. He backed me into a corner, so I offered my sword elsewhere to show him how easily the tables could turn. Indirectly it served the others well because Diarmait swiftly realised he could not take us for granted.'

'You fought Diarmait?' Richard strove to keep his voice and temper level.

Prendergast gave another shrug. 'A few skirmishes and raids, but no full battles, and not with Diarmait himself. Our new employers did not want to reward us either. We managed to commandeer a ship in Waterford and sailed home. Now I am here to make my report. I have served the men of Ossory; I have served MacMurchada and have amassed much knowledge.'

'And your question now is, what is that knowledge worth to me?'

'Sire, I would willingly serve under your banner,' Prendergast said, 'but not MacMurchada's. Never again.'

Richard met the shrewd hazel eyes. 'And for me for a consideration?'

'When you go to Ireland, you will receive land and you will grant some to your followers as reward for service. You will have the right to bestow it as you choose.'

Richard nodded. 'I will hear more of your story by and by,' he said, 'but you will spend the winter at your own expense for I cannot feed you and your men in the slack season. Return to me in the spring and we shall talk more. For now, be welcome here until after the snow.'

Once Prendergast had departed, Richard turned to Hervey. 'Is it going to be a problem?' he asked. 'Will men be deserting me when I need them?'

Hervey pursed his lips. 'Not when you arrive,' he said. 'There is rivalry for land and most of it has to be won by the sword before it can be claimed. MacMurchada may be half mad but he's shrewd and very careful how he parcels it out. I would say he has been taught a lesson. Prendergast was justified in what he did and MacMurchada now knows we are not his dogs to be unleashed when he chooses and then kicked back into the kennel. We have to stand our ground.' He gave Richard a wry look. 'If you are to become his son by marriage, you will need to pick your way with cunning and skill. His daughter is one of the keys to success, for she has influence with him. She entreated him earlier this year not to discard you.'

Richard was diverted by the thought and a little touched and taken aback. 'Did she?'

'She has grown up since she was at Striguil,' Hervey said. 'You will find her a changed and very interesting young woman.'

Richard smiled, intrigued and amused. 'What makes you say that?'

'She is close to her father, as you know, and she accepts him for what he is.' Hervey grimaced. 'Dear God, she was present when he did that terrible thing and she did not flinch, which was more than many of the grown men could manage, myself included. She is not afraid of him and he permits her to stay when he is in counsel and other women are dismissed, including her mother. She sits with her harp on her knee as an excuse for being there and she hears everything that is said. Looking at her you would think she was just Diarmait's beautiful daughter, present as an adornment, but you would be very wrong. She reports to him, she has opinions, and he listens. They talk between themselves when the councils are over. She will serve his wine or wash his feet or play chess and she will tell him her opinions and what she thinks he should do. To an extent she can wrap him around her finger. On the great decisions he is set and strong and nothing will change him, but he values her advice. She knows how to reason, and how to cajole, and has all the information at her fingertips.' He gave Richard a rueful look. 'One day she will be a formidable woman, and difficult to deal with unless you can control her – you will not do it easily even now. I am not sure I envy you, nephew.'

Richard smiled. 'I am suitably warned, uncle. I had already observed some of those things when she was at Striguil, but I still hope she will play her harp one day, not at the behest of her father, but for me alone.'

The snow continued to fall in heavy swathes across the Marches, but that night, surrounded by fire and candle light, the evening was convivial. Basilia, recovered from her fall, came to the hall, and so did Richard's daughters Matilda and Aline – pretty girls of fifteen and fourteen with sleek hair and clear complexions. Richard had seen Robert de Quency casting surreptitious glances at Matilda, although he was behaving very properly towards her. Matilda was returning those glances too. He decided to have a word with Basilia about keeping a benign eye, but he was not overly perturbed and it might even be a good match. It could wait until the Irish matter was settled, and if he needed to keep Rob closer, it was a good bribe. And Aline the same. There were several knights who were decent candidates for her hand in marriage, but for now she was a useful asset, and he could still enjoy her presence in the household.

The winter retreated and the days gradually lengthened. The snow melted and spring green budded the hawthorn and furred the willows with soft grey cat paws. The wolves were hunted out of the vicinity and the first lambs were born in the Cistercian flocks at Tintern. Richard felt his own sap rising with the stirring of the spring. His heart was full, his body elastic with anticipation.

Hervey returned to Ireland and Richard pored over parchments with his captains, detailing ships, soldiers and supplies. He did not want to gather them too soon because of the cost involved. He needed to have everything in place but with flexibility and room for manoeuvre.

One morning at the end of April, he looked up from his plans as Raymond ushered a knight into his presence. The man was in his early middle years with grey-flecked hair, brown eyes and a sallow complexion.

'Sire, this is Messire William Ferrand. He wants to join us to fight in Ireland,' Raymond said, an odd note in his voice.

'I heard you were recruiting, my lord,' Ferrand said gruffly.

'I am,' Richard said, 'but I will call the muster at Haverford and I am not paying troops yet.'

'Sire, I have my own horse and armour and resources,' Ferrand replied. 'I do not wish for land in Ireland, or riches. Only the wherewithal to keep body and soul together and feed my mount and my servant for the time remaining to me on this earth.'

Richard gave him a questioning look.

'I am a leper, sire,' Ferrand said. 'I know my eventual end and I would rather die before that happens. Let me fight for you. You will not see me retreat in battle and I will serve you faithfully, I swear, and keep myself separate from other men.'

Richard looked him up and down. Ferrand was tall and straight and robust. 'You show no signs of the illness.'

'I have marks on my legs. I know the signs for I saw the disease in Outremer when I went on pilgrimage and brought more back with me than water from the River Jordan. But I am still strong and fit and can wield a sword and spear.'

Richard pondered briefly and then nodded. 'You are welcome to join my ranks. You may build a shelter against the castle wall and I will provide food for you. We shall find you room on the first ship to sail for Ireland's shores.'

'Thank you, sire; I will serve you well.' Ferrand bowed and left.

'He came to the gate,' Raymond said. 'His equipment was good. He has a strong horse and looks after his weapons. He will be a good man to have in the ranks, and providing he does not mingle with the men, they will not object. If his leprosy was visited upon him because of his sins . . .' Raymond shrugged. 'Well then, we are all sinners.'

'No doubt,' Richard said, and then, alerted by Raymond's bow, looked round to see Basilia coming towards them, a letter in her hand, seals dangling.

'A messenger has come from the King,' she said, expression tense.

Richard took the parchment as gingerly as if he were handling a snake. Letters from the King were never good news and he was well aware of Henry's ambivalence about letting him go to Ireland. 'Is the messenger still here?'

'Only to refresh himself and his horse. He is not expecting a reply.'

Richard removed the seal and opened the letter. As he read, his chest tightened and he clenched his jaw.

'What does he want?'

Richard's mouth twisted. 'I am summoned to court.'

'What, now? But why?'

'Not now, but in June. Henry is going to crown his eldest son and all the vassals in chief are summoned to Westminster. I have to attend; anything else would be treason.' He thrust the parchment at Basilia and took several strides across the room. In his imagination he saw himself upending the table at which he had been working and kicking over the bench, but he clenched his fists, breathing hard, holding the violence inside. 'Dear God in heaven, am I fated never to cross to Ireland?'

'Sire . . .' Raymond said, and then stopped.

'He will not prevent me. I have gone too far in this; the wheels are in motion.'

'But you have to attend the coronation,' Basilia said with dismay. 'If you do not—'

'Yes, I know! And once at court, I will have to obtain his permission to leave all over again. I shall also have to find the price of a coronation gift for the boy.' The thought of having to pay for the privilege of being foiled in his intent made Richard grind his teeth. He swung round to Raymond. 'You will have to go to Ireland and take command in my absence. Hervey is already there and FitzStephen and the men who have wintered in Leinster. Take one ship and establish a bridgehead and I will join you with the rest as soon as I can. Tell Diarmait I am coming. I shall go to Westminster because I must and when I return I shall sail immediately – whatever happens.' He snatched his cloak off the peg on the wall. 'I am going out for a ride. No, leave me,' he said as Raymond started to follow. 'I will talk to you later when I am less sick and angry.'

Basilia looked down at the letter in her hand and then at Raymond who was watching her with his intent grey stare.

'As my lord says, we are too far down that path to turn back now.'

'Yes,' she said bitterly. 'Indeed, we are, and it is my brother's decision, as in all things.' She pressed her lips together, sealing off her resentment. Raymond's loyalty was to Richard, not to her, and Raymond too would be seeking land and power across the Hibernian Sea. He had everything to gain from going there, while she had everything to lose. Her comfortable, familiar home.

'I should check on the squires,' he said. 'I left them polishing armour and if I stay away too long they will slack on the job.' He bowed to her and departed.

Basilia looked down at the letter from Henry, its edge crumpled from Richard's anger. Putting it on the table, she weighed it down with the whetstone that Richard used to sharpen his knife.

Raymond crossed the grass, walking with a strong, measured tread towards the squires sitting outside the armour beside a pile of helms. The fledged soldiers were at weapons practice on the training ground nearby. A group of women stood by the well, watching the men and gossiping. Alice, a soldiers' whore from Abergavenny, was laughing more loudly than the rest, the sound almost a cackle. She sparkled like a hard gem with a crack in the stone. She was often drunk and abrasive, with opinions she thought everyone should hear. But she had a certain feral glamour. Raymond sometimes had indecent visions of taking her up against a wall, especially when he himself had drunk too much, although the thought always sickened him at the same time.

The sort of woman he wanted was in the room he had just left. One of dignity, high morals and common sense who even in dire circumstances would stay serene and unruffled. Like cold, clear water drunk from a fresh spring. But Basilia de Clare was as far beyond his reach as the stars for he was a landless knight, a second son, and Richard was protective of his sister's standing and welfare and showed no inclination to find her a husband.

Sometimes, again when in his cups, Raymond had wondered what it would be like to kiss her, to enter her body – draw her far beyond that serene, reasoned realm she inhabited and face her with what she had never known or experienced. Thinking about it always aroused him to hardness and he strove to lock it away, because it was dishonourable and a temptation of the Devil. Richard had taken him in and nurtured his career. If he realised for one moment the thoughts he harboured about Basilia, he would have him castrated. But still, the images occasionally escaped their confines and had their way with him.

Alice's man broke off from his practice to take a breather at the well. He was laughing at a jest one of the others had made about the length of a spear. Shouting that his spear was long enough for all purposes, he took Alice by the arm, swung her round and smacked her rump. Laughing, she gave him a drink of water from a dipper before sharing a watery kiss with him and squeezing his groin. And then, with a lightning move, she snatched the spear out of his hand and jabbed at him with the blunt end. Grinning, he feinted to disarm her, but she nimbly danced out of his way and licked her lips. Amused despite himself, Raymond chuckled and stopped to watch their horseplay. 'You be careful with that spear,' he called. 'We don't want any accidents before we sail!'

Alice winked at him. 'Oh, there'll be no accidents, my lord,' she replied cheekily. 'You can't take chances with a man's spear, eh?' She handed the weapon back to her man and swept a deep curtsey to Raymond who shook his head and, laughing, turned away.

Three weeks later, Raymond and Richard stood on the shore at Hubberston, waiting for the tide. Raymond had ten knights under his command and seventy mostly Welsh archers. There were also several Flemings and a dozen Norman and English serjeants as well as a few women to do the laundry and see to the fires. One of the latter laughed raucously, out-shrilling the seagulls riding the air above the two galleys drawn up on the shoreline.

'I hope she doesn't fall overboard on the way,' Richard said, meaning the opposite as he watched the woman carry a large cauldron on board with an ease at odds with her willowy figure.

Raymond looked wry. 'Alice works hard and she is strong. She can haul water and chop wood as well as any of the men. It's a trade, one for the other.'

Richard grimaced, not sure that such a trade was good value. 'I am trusting you to establish an advance camp for a full landing. Once I return from Westminster, I will join you with the main army.'

'Yes, sire. I will not let you down.'

'Send word to Hervey as soon as you arrive and stay with our accord when it comes to Diarmait. Do not let him talk rings around you, and do not agree to anything different from our plan. But speak fairly to him also.'

'I shall, sire.'

The men clasped hands and Raymond went down to the ship to join the men, Badge nosing his heels. Alice was still shrieking.

Richard stayed to watch the ships cast off and sail away into the mouth of the estuary, becoming smaller and smaller, like children's toys and then insects. The way the wind was blowing, they would reach Ireland within a day and be beyond his reach whatever happened. He had put a huge amount of trust in Raymond and this small but select band of men and only hoped they were up to the task and his judgement sound.

20

Fearns, Leinster, Ireland, early summer 1170

Aoife brought a cup of milk to Enna who had been laid low with a fever, and found Hervey de Montmorency sitting with him, reading aloud from a book. 'One of our battle tales,' Hervey said, moving aside to let Aoife sit down beside her brother and give him the cup. 'It is called "The Song of Roland" and tells the tale of great heroes who defend a mountain pass against the Saracen enemy.'

'Yes,' Aoife said. 'I know of it.'

'You do?' Hervey asked with surprise.

Aoife gave him a superior smile. 'We know many songs, not just our own. Maurice Regan has recited "The Roland" to us before.' She pointed to the book. 'Is that yours?'

Hervey shook his head. 'It belongs to Richard, and before that to his father, but he let me borrow it and will reclaim it when he arrives.'

She studied the creamy vellum pages with their red capitals. 'Does the Earl read often?'

'Indeed, he does,' Hervey replied. 'He says it is through the stories that we come to recognise and know ourselves.'

'I used to read,' Enna said, 'and I used to write. Now I can only listen. Men will make great deeds of our strife in song, and of how we avenged ourselves on our foes. The bards will spin our blood into ink and our bones into parchment for the entertainment of others.'

'That is indeed a fine line for a bard,' Hervey said. 'Homer was blind.'

Enna bared his teeth in a humourless grin. 'Was he Irish too?'

'Greek,' Hervey said, 'but stories are the same the world over. You have a fine voice.'

Enna turned his head away.

'I will sit with Enna now,' Aoife said. 'Thank you for reading to him.'

Hervey stood up and bowed. 'My lady . . . it was my pleasure too.' He touched Enna's sleeve. 'I will come again.'

Aoife liked Hervey who treated her with deference. She might be her father's darling and sit beside him in counsel, but he could order her about or slap her at his will, whereas Hervey was polite and considerate and she felt safe with him. Some of the other Normans eyed her as if she was a tasty morsel they would snap up were she not protected by her father's power, but Hervey was always correct and kind. He was gentle to Enna too. A good man.

As Hervey reached the door, his squire Gervase arrived in a rush, brown eyes wide, and behind him came Richard's messenger, Alard. 'Sire, Raymond le Gros has landed at Dun Domhnall and is fortifying the headland ready for the Earl's arrival. He bids you come to him now with as many men as you can muster.'

Enna sat up on his elbows and Aoife gasped.

'Have you a letter?' Hervey demanded.

The messenger handed a parchment to Hervey who swiftly broke the seal and read, his brows knitting. 'Richard will be here in a few weeks' time,' he said to Aoife. 'The King has summoned him to court again – to the coronation of his eldest at Westminster. All must attend to swear their loyalty. He will come from there as soon as he can.'

'So once again the swallows arrive without him,' Aoife said, her anticipation tinged with disappointment, for it was more of the same.

'But he will be here before they leave, I promise you,' Hervey said, and left the room, his bedside manner subsumed by a soldier's urgency.

'More stories,' Enna said, leaning back and covering his eyes with his bent arm, 'but I will not be the one making them.'

'Hush now,' Aoife said, chewing her lips. 'Hush now, my brother, go to sleep.'

'How long before Richard arrives?' Hervey asked Raymond as he dropped the tent flap behind him.

Raymond shrugged and sat down on his camp bed. He was dismayed that his message to Fearns had not brought Diarmait rushing to his side with his full army. Instead just Hervey had arrived with his own small conroi. Diarmait, it appeared, was elsewhere on campaign. Raymond considered Hervey a man of smooth words and soft mettle. He was his rival for Richard's attention and resources being, like himself, a landless man, but as Richard's uncle, he stood in line for preferential treatment.

'As the messenger told you,' Raymond said shortly. 'As soon as he is free of the court and can complete preparations. In the meantime, we must work with what we have.' He dug his fingers through his hair, feeling it stiff with sea salt. 'These defences must be fortified. We do not have enough men to protect the entire peninsula; we'll have to dig earthworks. I have sent out foragers to bring in cattle so we will have meat and milk, and we have fresh water. We can dig in and hold out until King Diarmait arrives.'

'As soon as I received news of your landing I sent for him, but it will depend where he is found and how swiftly he can turn around,' Hervey said. 'News will have reached the Norse in Waterford by now and they are only half as far away as Fearns. I came at full pace, but so will they.'

'Then pray to God King Diarmait arrives soon,' Raymond said grimly, 'because there is no help from the sea. Do not take off your armour.'

Hervey gave him a hard look. 'I don't intend to.'

Raymond returned his look and said nothing, reminding himself that they were allies.

Raymond's troops continued building up the earthworks, labouring by lantern light when it grew too dark to see. Raymond's nape prickled, the way it did when a thunderstorm was imminent. Badge whined and followed at his heels while Raymond prowled along the defence line, observing the toil. He strained his ears, listening for sounds of approach and praying that if they came, it would be Diarmait and not the enemy.

Some soldiers were taking a respite sat around a fire laughing and cracking jests to relieve the tension. Raymond noticed the woman from Abergavenny hunched over a bowl of stew, chewing and swallowing vigorously like a man, her knees spread wide apart, the cloth of her gown dipping between them. Her man was sharpening his sword on a whetstone and the sound, although not loud, grated along Raymond's bones.

Behind him the shush of the sea washed against the inlet back and forth, inkily glittering, and the wind battered his ears like the noise of a banner fluttering on a stave. He continued to walk the double line of sentries, checking for alertness. Although tall and heavy-set, Raymond was light on his feet and he was almost upon one particular man before the soldier whirled, spear at the ready, shield braced.

'Too late,' Raymond snapped. 'If I were an enemy I'd have slit your throat by now. And then I would go on and kill every last one of your comrades. This is not a drill at Striguil, this is your life or your death, and mine and every other man's in the camp. If I can surprise you in stealth, then be assured that they will.'

'Sire, I did not expect—'

'No one does,' Raymond said brusquely. 'Stay vigilant.'

He walked the perimeter again, checking every post, returning to the first man, who this time was swift off the mark. Raymond gave him a satisfied nod. On his way to his tent, he noticed that

Alice and her lover were lying under a cloak now and he was ploughing her vigorously. Well, that was what some men did on the edge of a perilous situation. Like salmon leaping the river to spawn or mayflies whirling above a pond for a single afternoon. Desperate to leave a part of themselves in the world.

Reaching his own fire, he helped himself to a ladle of hot broth from the cauldron bubbling over it. Sitting to eat, he considered what reward he should demand for services rendered if he lived. 'Earl Richard will owe me more than just pay when he comes across the sea,' he told Badge, who was sharing his supper.

Hervey's tent was pitched beside his with lantern light illuminating Richard's red and gold chevron banner as it waved in the sea breeze. The flap was laced up and Raymond experienced a flicker of resentment that Hervey should be sleeping while he was prowling the night, keeping vigil and worrying. But then Hervey was a lightweight, getting by on his charm, on his connection to Richard, and on his ability to wheedle his way into people's good graces. Hervey could obviously talk, but could he fight?

Resisting the urge to check the sentry lines again, Raymond left the fire and retired, telling his squire to wake him just before first light. He stretched out on his pallet and Badge curled up beside him, nose to tail. The Irish considered it an insult that Diarmait's father had been buried with a dog, but Raymond thought it not so bad in the great scheme of things.

At dawn Raymond tested the sentries again. The sky was still dark with a single streak of burning orange on the eastern skyline over the sea. The men were alert and he did not catch anyone out, but the pressure in his skull was a dull throb. Returning to his tent, he found Hervey awake and eating a bowl of pottage. He raised his brows to greet Raymond who grunted a reply and, ladling a bowlful for himself, threw a crust to Badge.

He had barely begun eating when a young scout dashed up

to them. 'The Waterford men are sighted, sire!' he reported. 'Th-thousands of them!'

Raymond put his bowl aside and turned to his squire. 'Get the cattle inside the palisade,' he said. 'Tell the captains to do it now. Go!' He struck the boy on the shoulder and turning to Hervey, bared his teeth. 'They have come to drive us into the sea, my lord. How hard can you stand?'

'As hard as I must.' Hervey set his bowl aside and stood up.

'I hope so. Get your knights and serjeants mounted up. We have to put on a show of strength and make them hesitate. They know our reputation and no one wants to be first to die. Besides, I doubt they know our precise numbers.'

Hervey made no attempt to protest Raymond's peremptory orders although he was the senior man in the camp and representing de Clare. Having a dog, one did not need to bark oneself, and Raymond's idea was common sense.

The cattle were swiftly driven into a withy enclosure, and their restless bellowing drowned out the noise of the sea below the cliffs. Raymond had his big grey brought forward and swung into the saddle, and Hervey joined him on his bay.

Riding out to meet the men of Waterford, Raymond heard their weapons beating on shields – a sound like a collective heartbeat. The young scout had exaggerated the numbers, but there were still more than a thousand of them facing their own band of little over a hundred men. Diarmait's Irish enemies and the Norse and Irish settlers of Waterford with their sharp, bright axes and their bitter hearts had come to drive the invaders into the sea. This was what had been prickling Raymond's nape. Unlike the fighting in Wales where men were spared if they could pay their way out in silver, this was a field of kill or be killed and they were outnumbered ten to one.

'I doubt diplomacy is going to be of much use,' Hervey noted drily. 'Even if every man here was a hero in the mould of Roland, we cannot fight this many.'

Raymond scowled at the obvious remark. 'We have to split them up and destroy them piecemeal – exploit the ground to our best advantage and utilise the archers.' He gave the signal to fall back now they knew what they were facing. Hervey led the retreat. Raymond drew his sword and rode rear-guard, the leper knight William Ferrand riding stirrup to stirrup. 'You said you wished to die in battle,' Raymond said, a savage grin masking gut-churning fear, 'now's your chance.'

Their enemy realised what was happening and a ferocious yell rippled from their ranks followed by a collective roar, as the warriors charged after their retreating prey. The mounted Normans spurred into a canter and the foot soldiers ran for their lives. The front ranks reached the enclosure and piled through the entrance with Raymond and William the last through, the Irish burning their heels. As they strove to force shut the barricade across the entrance, the first Norseman pushed through, swinging his axe. Raymond cut him down with a single back swipe and Ferrand dealt with the next one. The entrance was a narrow gap like a fish trap, and it was easy to kill at the interface. Raymond and Ferrand held their ground, while Hervey bawled a command to the archers to shoot their arrows into the ranks of Norse and Irish beleaguering the defences.

The deadly hail was returned by the smaller flights of Irish archers and although the men inside the compound had protection from their mail and shields, the arrows struck the cows causing mayhem. The animals went wild, kicking and panicking, bleeding and falling with feathered shafts quivering in their flesh. White-eyed, they hurled themselves against the withy fences penning them in and the wood started to buckle.

'Let them go!' Raymond roared. 'Let them do our work for us! Drive them out and smash them open! Do it, do it now!'

Hervey bellowed orders, his cultured voice straining at the seams. Ferrand and Raymond pulled back and under a continuing hail of arrows the cattle surged out of the gateway, rumps barging, horns swinging. Raymond turned his stallion in a tight arc and, as the last beast thundered out of the compound, signalled their hornsmen to blare the attack.

The cattle acted like the first hard sweep of a cavalry charge and tore through the Irish ranks into the Norse behind, scattering them, destroying cohesion and creating mayhem. The mounted Norman warriors followed through, striking with sword and club, using their horses to trample and ram. Under Raymond they were disciplined and methodical, fighting as one body, and although they sustained their own casualties, they visited catastrophic damage on their attackers. One soldier went down under a Norse axe and fell, bleeding from a terrible wound at his shoulder. Another two were killed, but Raymond filled the breach, hacking with his sword, yelling at the men to hold together. Hervey was doing the same, precise and light but dangerous. No blow or energy was wasted.

The Irish were too lightly armed to bear the Norman assault and despite their numbers were losing so heavily that panic set in and, breaking, they fled the field. The Waterford Norse also took to their heels, although many laid down their arms and surrendered rather than be speared or trampled in retreat.

The nearest cattle were rounded up and returned to the compound. The Norse prisoners were relieved of their weapons and made to sit down near the cliffs under heavy guard.

'That was well done,' Hervey gasped to Raymond, shoulders heaving, mouth wide to fill his lungs. He had removed his helm and arming cap and his hair was dark with sweat. 'I thought we were done for.'

Raymond shook his head, feeling suddenly as weak as a kitten. The enormity hit him as he looked at the captives and the dead. A hundred and twenty men had just faced down ten times that number and with barely any casualties to their own side. In the thick of battle he had been cool-headed, knowing precisely what to do. Now his gut was churning and he needed a drink, but he couldn't lose himself because it wasn't over yet. Indeed, it had barely begun.

Hervey crossed himself. 'If we are alive it is by a miracle.'

'It is God's will,' Raymond said, baring his teeth. 'And God helps those who help themselves.'

The soldiers were moving among the dead beyond the compound, looting the bodies for anything of use or value, taking weapons, coins, clothing. Always before the crows arrived to a battlefield came the human scavengers.

A sudden terrible keening sound rising to a jagged wail made Raymond and Hervey turn, hands to scabbards. Alice of Abergavenny was leaning over her lover, her hands red to the wrists with his blood as she howled like a she-wolf.

'Her man's one of those we lost,' Hervey said. 'Axe in the shoulder.'

Raymond grimaced. 'It would have to be. Christ, send someone to shut her up before she disturbs the men.'

At Hervey's instruction two soldiers approached her but she lashed out, threatening them with the dead man's sword, and eventually they had to tie her to a tent post away from everyone else and gag her mouth.

Hervey eyed the prisoners. 'What are we going to do about them? There are nearly as many as there are of us. How are we to guard them?'

Raymond curled his lip. 'Why ask me? You are my lord's uncle and his representative at court. You say what is to be done.'

Hervey bit his thumbnail. 'Some will be worth their weight in silver and diplomacy as hostages. We should find out.'

'But that weight is a millstone round our necks. We have to feed them from our supplies. If they unite and rush us, they will cause grave damage. Our only choice is to send them to God over the side of that cliff. They would do it to us in a heartbeat. Do you think for one moment any of them would have granted us mercy?'

Hervey shook his head. 'I know what they would have done very well. But perhaps we should wait for Diarmait and let him give the order.'

'It is not Diarmait who is in this situation,' Raymond countered. 'I say he would give the order himself if he was here – he has done far worse to his enemies. With so few of us, we cannot take the risk and it benefits us at this stage to be known as ruthless conquerors.'

Hervey jutted his jaw.

'We must.'

Hervey gave a brusque nod. 'Make it clean,' he said grimly.

Raymond went to give the order and ten of the captives were dragged to the edge of the cliff beyond sight of their companions. These were men in their prime who would be difficult to contain if they rebelled en masse, and even the older ones without the musculature were still battle-hardened and wise. Raymond knew he was doing the right thing; Hervey was too squeamish.

He suddenly noticed Alice of Abergavenny, freed from her post, advancing on him, her expression as wild as a storm.

'Let me dispatch them,' she said, breathing hard. Her gown was stained with her man's blood, her fingers red under the nails. 'Grant me this boon. Give me an axe to avenge, my lord.'

Raymond stared at her in revulsion but an idea was growing rapidly. If he was going to drive the point home by executing these men, then what better way than to let this grief-mad woman strike the first blow? 'Find me a sharpened axe,' he commanded his squire. 'Not too heavy, but let the blade be capable of severing both a hair and a head. And find it from among the enemy weapons.'

The youth hurried away on his errand, returning with a fine axe, the edge gleaming with blue fire and the polished haft carved with interlacing. Raymond took it from him and swung it in his hand, feeling the perfect balance, before handing it to Alice. 'The men are yours,' he said. 'Do as you will.'

Alice took the weapon, her eyes glittering with madness. She lifted the hem of her gown at the mid-section and dragged it up, tucking it through her belt like a fishwife. And then she rolled up her sleeves and approached the warriors, all roped together, ankles and hands.

She circled them, licking her teeth, and then, uttering a scream that rose from a growl to a high-pitched ululation, swung the axe as she did when chopping wood. Blood spurted and the first man crumpled, beheaded save for a flap of skin which a second blow severed. Raymond made himself watch as she dealt with the prisoners one after another, ignoring their screams and pleas. She was a brutal instrument, messy but effective for she was physically strong and her blows were goaded by battle frenzy as she put every ounce of her being into the deed. It was sustained fury; indeed, it was insanity.

'Dear God,' Hervey said, swallowing his gorge.

'I doubt God has anything to do with this,' Raymond answered with a shudder.

When she had killed all ten, taking several blows by the end to achieve her purpose, she stood panting, looking round for more, not yet sated.

'Enough.' Raymond snapped an order to a serjeant: 'Take her and have her cleaned up and securely confined, but do not harm her.' He could not have her rampaging round the camp; she was too volatile for that.

A red-handed Morrighan, she had to be approached by Raymond's mercenaries with spears and shields for she refused to relinquish her axe and whirled it wildly around. It took three of them to disarm her and pull her away kicking and screaming, still frantic with energy. Swallowing sick distaste, Raymond had the bodies brought to the edge of the cliff and pitched over into the breaking waves where the tide would take them and wash them out to sea. Let these warriors, descendants of sea-reavers, find their graves in the ocean.

Sixty men remained to be dispatched. Raymond steeled himself and took his turn for he would not shirk anything he asked the others to do, and if there was to be blood on their hands, let it be on all. Hervey joined him and made a clean, swift job even though he was more lightly built than Raymond. And then he threw down his axe, walked away to his tent and dropped the flap.

Raymond saw to the camp. He made sure it was adequately guarded and every man at his post. Alice sat under guard, rocking back and forth, humming to herself. The blood had been sluiced from her body with buckets of water and a clean blanket was wrapped around her shoulders but he could still see her very clearly in his mind's eye, dancing in blood and whirling that axe.

He walked away on his own to patrol the perimeter. The sea boomed against the rocks and he imagined the bodies washing to and fro in the swell, each one a mother's son. He pressed the heels of his hands against his eyes and longed to blot it all out in the comfort of drink, but he could not do so while he was in charge of the men and the camp. Hervey had abdicated responsibility and left him to it, the whoreson. When all this was over he would claim a great reward in payment for today. What he had accomplished was worth lands, a castle and a chatelaine to look after them at the very least.

21

Palace of Westminster, London, late June 1170

Richard knelt to King Henry and to his son the recently anointed Young King, a golden-haired youth, fifteen years old, tall and blue-eyed. Watching the Bishop of London set the crown upon the youth's head, Richard had felt envious of Henry's good fortune in his heir and was anxious to be gone. If he was to have a son like this to embellish his own bloodline, he needed to be about the task of begetting him. He had still not mentioned the proposed match with Aoife to Henry; he had kept it well hidden for he knew Henry would disapprove. Besides, it was not a fait accompli until he set foot on Irish soil as a victor; for now, it was not even a betrothal.

He rose at Henry's gesture and made his petition. 'By your leave, sire, my preparations to go to Ireland are complete, and I ask your permission to bid you a loyal farewell and be on my way.'

Henry leaned forward on his gilded chair. One of the pearls cuffing his sleeve had started to come undone and dangled by a thread. The Young King regarded him with a half smile, reminding him of an icon, his own clothes immaculate and his boots stamped with small golden lions.

'You have my permission to leave, but on certain understandings,' Henry said. 'Whatever lands you conquer in Ireland, you will do me homage for them and know it is by my permission you hold them. You have the map I gave you.'

'Yes, sire,' Richard said. 'I understand.'

He was backed into a corner, for any protest would risk Henry denying him permission to sail. He had no choice but to agree, to render lip service until he was free.

'I hear you have gone into debt with the Jews,' Henry added. 'Remember that I own the Jews and therefore their bonds. Do not overreach yourself, my lord.'

'I do not intend to, sire.'

'Then go with my goodwill,' Henry said. 'I shall expect a report in due course.'

Richard bowed from Henry's presence and made his escape. Icy sweat clammed his armpits but he was euphoric, like a prisoner shown an open cell door, for now he could get on with the task and prepare to sail and join his bridgehead in Ireland.

Sitting at the high table, Aoife studied the woman who had entered her father's hall under the escort of three soldiers, one either side and another close behind. She had heard many tales these last few days about Alice of Abergavenny and how she had hacked off the heads of numerous Waterford Norse warriors with an axe while in a state of enraged grief for the death of her lover. Astonished and fascinated by the stories, Aoife had wanted to see the woman for herself. The account of how a hundred men had staved off several thousand was nourishing the bards and had bolstered her father's determination. He was contemplating challenging for the high kingship itself as soon as Richard arrived and was busy planning an attack on Waterford. News had already arrived by trading ship that Richard had left Westminster and was making final preparations to sail.

Alice of Abergavenny wore a gown the colour of dried blood. A man's belt of plain brown leather girded her waist and an empty dagger sheath hung at her hip, because no one came armed into the royal presence. Her dark gaze lurched around the chamber, taking everything in, never settling. The soldiers who were ostensibly providing a guard of honour stood ready to grab her at the first untoward move.

Alice curtseyed in proper fashion to Aoife, although she was still taking fierce note of everyone in the room.

'Please,' Aoife said. 'Be welcome, you are among friends. Come and sit.'

She indicated a place at her side and bade servants give the woman bread and a portion of beef. Alice immediately attacked the food like a hungry wolf.

'I heard what you did,' Aoife said. 'I am sorry you have lost your husband.'

Alice looked at her, bright-eyed. 'Sorrow will not bring him back,' she said harshly. 'No one knows what it is like until it happens to them. I am the walking dead.' She attended to her food, tearing at it hungrily. 'Who will care for me now?'

'Have you no relatives?'

'No one who would want to call me daughter, and he who named me wife is with God,' she replied through a mouthful. Another diner reached for some bread in the basket in front of her and she shot out her hand to grip his. 'That is mine,' she warned, eyes flashing. She grabbed the bread and stuffed it down the front of her gown.

Aoife experienced a mingling of pity, disgust and astonishment. The woman was plainly unbalanced. But she was disturbed to recognise some of herself in the way Alice stared around, tense and wild-eyed, ready to fight to survive in every moment.

Aoife stood up, terminating the encounter. 'Please, finish your meal and be welcome to take what you cannot eat. I will personally make sure you do not starve.' Retiring from the table to the women's chamber, Aoife grimaced and brushed down her skirts. She resolved to ask her uncle Lorcan to find Alice a place in a nunnery for the creature was clearly out of her wits. She had learned her lesson. Bold deeds were far better sung than experienced.

* * *

Richard read the letter a second time and then picked up Basilia and spun her around.

Laughing but annoyed, she pummelled his shoulders. 'Put me down, you fool!'

'Fool am I?' he gave her a white grin. 'Henry has given me permission to go to Ireland. Have you read this news?'

'Not yet. The messenger rode in not long before you did and I was busy preparing for your arrival.'

He waved the letter. 'Raymond has won a great victory against a massively superior force of Norse and Irish. Like slicing a knife through soft butter, he says.'

She took the letter and read it, her colour heightening.

'Our men have fared better than we could have hoped – only a few auxiliary troops killed. God was with them.' And that meant God was with him too, in spite of Henry. 'It is going to be a new life in Ireland. Make ready. I want to leave Striguil within the fortnight.'

She stared at him. 'I am to come with you?'

'Of course! I am not going to leave you here with the garrison, and it is not safe for you to stay in England as the sister of the Earl of Striguil. You are my heir until I beget a child in wedlock. Besides, I need you with me to organise and delegate the household.'

'I am flattered, but you will have a wife for that surely.'

'An Irish wife and still very young. I do not expect you to encroach on her territory, but you will have an important role to play in the English part of the domicile. You cannot stay here.'

She was not yet ready to yield. 'What of your daughters? Are they to come too? What if all does not go as you expect? One victory does not vouchsafe stability. Will you take Matilda and Aline into a war?'

'I shall send them to my mother until I deem it safe for them to come. It does not matter so much for them since they are not my direct heirs.'

'You are asking a great deal,' she said, frowning at him.

'Yes, I am, but the rewards will be great too, and I know you will adapt. I have every faith in you.' He took her by the shoulders. 'Basilia, I need you.'

She resisted him for a moment, but eventually sighed and capitulated, then pushed him away. 'The end of the week gives me very little time.'

'But you will manage, you always do.'

She gave him an irritated scowl. 'Do not take me for granted, Richard, I warn you, or one day you will find your trusty workhorse has left the stable.'

He did not answer, letting her have the last word, knowing she would come round. She always did.

'Will you be gone for a long time in Ireland, Papa?' Matilda asked. She was sixteen years old, an accomplished young lady with wavy auburn-fair hair and Richard's blue eyes. Just now they were filled with anxiety. She and Aline were sitting either side of him on a bench in the bower while he told them of his plans. Aline leaned against him, her arm wrapped around his, holding him fiercely.

'I do not know about a long time,' Richard said, 'but more than a few weeks.'

'But when will we see you again? You are coming back?' Matilda's eyes swam with tears.

He pinched her cheek. 'Of course I am, but it is as likely that you and your sister will come to Ireland to live with me. As soon as it is safe I will either send for you or come myself to bring you over.'

'Will you be in danger there?' Aline asked anxiously.

Richard shook his head. 'No, but things will be unsettled for a while. Your aunt Basilia is going to help manage the household, but you and your sister will be better settled with your grandmother until I come for you.'

'You will have a new wife by then,' Matilda said anxiously.

'Yes, I will, but she will welcome you.' He spoke with more optimism than knowledge. He had no idea how Aoife would react to his daughters but hoped it would be positively since she was of a similar age, like an older sister. 'I shall miss you both, but it won't be for long and I shall write and send you gifts. You are my girls, and you are my beautiful young women, and I am proud of you.'

Henry regarded with suppressed amusement the Irish messengers kneeling at his feet, heads bowed, clothes dusty from from long days on the road in search of the king, who had moved from Westminster, to Portsmouth, to Barfleur, Argentan and then Vendome. They were agitated and clearly unaccustomed to the urbane protocol of the Angevin court. Henry had learned of the magnificent victory of Richard de Clare's knight Raymond le Gros. He had been pleased and even a little proud in a vicarious way, for it was all to his personal benefit in the long run. These Irish messengers who had arrived hard on the heels of that news were naturally protesting about the savagery of the Normans and how illegal it all was. Henry had made sympathetic noises without the slightest intention of doing anything about their plight. Indeed, he was rather enjoying their discomfiture until their spokesman said in heavily accented French, 'Richard de Clare is going to set himself up as king in Ireland. Once he's married to MacMurchada's daughter there will be no stopping him.'

The accent was so thick that Henry did not understand at first and told him to repeat what he had said. When he heard the words for a second time, a wave of fury burst over him. 'What do you mean?' he said brusquely. 'Explain yourself.'

The Irish delegation exchanged glances. 'I thought you knew, sire,' said their spokesman. 'In exchange for his aid, MacMurchada has promised de Clare the hand of his daughter Aoife in marriage.

He has sworn to make him his heir. Unless he is checked, you shall have a rival king stabbing your back.'

Henry shuddered with rage at such bald evidence of treachery. De Clare had said one thing to his face, smooth as a snake, while plotting betrayal. He had even been considering finding the man a decent heiress to wed, but not any longer.

'Has de Clare sailed?' he demanded.

'No, sire, but the lanes of South Wales were full of soldiers and carts and supplies when we passed through. He must be shipping at least a thousand men!'

Henry clenched his fists. 'Leave me!' He jerked his head in dismissal. 'I will deal with the matter.'

When they had bowed from his presence, Henry sprang from his chair and paced the room in agitation as if the floor under his feet was red hot. 'Summon him back,' he commanded a clerk. 'I want Richard de Clare on his knees in front of me to answer for this calumny! Get to him before he sails for, by God, I will not be played for a fool.' He kicked a stool out of his way. 'King of Ireland? Hah! I will crown him with shackles. And as for MacMurchada and that hoyden daughter of his . . . let them dwell with the pigs in the sty for that is where they belong!'

Richard clicked his tongue to Ajax, encouraging him up the wide gangplank and onto the deck of the waiting galley. The stallion baulked, ears flickering, but when offered a morsel of his favourite bread and honey and encouraged by pats and neck rubs, he trusted Richard sufficiently to follow him on deck and join two other warhorses already tethered there. Richard secured the big chestnut and stayed a moment, soothing him, before handing him to his groom. The next time he sat astride the stallion would be in Ireland and he would be leading his men to war.

He returned to shore to oversee the loading. The fulfilment of his planning; the fruition of all the expenditure and hard work. God grant it was worth it. He would sail at sunset and arrive with the dawn. The weather was set fair with few clouds and a steady, strong breeze.

Simon his squire approached, leading a royal messenger whom Richard recognised as one of Henry's fast riders, Thomas Gobyon. His mount was lathered, with nostril linings flared red, and sides heaving. A groom took the bridle and led the horse away to rub it down and Gobyon handed a sealed parchment to Richard with a bow.

'Sire, I am instructed by the King to tell you to open this immediately and read it in my presence,' he said.

Richard's belly lurched for he knew without breaking the seal that it was another obstacle in his path. 'I hear your instruction, but the tide is ready for sailing and I do not have the leisure to read this now. You may come with me if you wish and I will look at it during the crossing.'

Gobyon gave him a steady look. 'Sire, I cannot do that, for I am to return immediately to the King, and he expects you to accompany me. I counsel you to read the letter now.'

'I have told you, I will read it when I have the leisure. Inform the King I shall reply to him in due course and that I remain his loyal vassal and servant. You have done your duty and you are in no position to force me to return – although I am in a position to put you aboard one of these ships and bring you with me. Do I make myself clear?'

'Yes, sire, you do, but the King will be greatly displeased.'

'Tell him I shall make my submission to him as soon as I am able. In the meantime, you are welcome to food and drink and fodder for your horse.'

Gobyon could do nothing but capitulate, as Richard well knew. His horse was exhausted and a replacement could not be procured this side of Haverford.

Richard left the man plodding towards the hamlet and went to look at the sea washing the estuary where the tide was rolling towards the turn.

Basilia joined him, the stiffening breeze flapping the ends of her firmly pinned veil. 'Was that a royal messenger I just saw?'

'Yes,' he said. 'I am summoned back to court.'

She stared at him with dismay. 'What are you going to do?'

'What does it look like?'

'You cannot defy the King!'

He shrugged. 'I will go to him later, but I am not leaving this enterprise now.'

'But—'

'Whatever I do I am caught on the tines of the Devil's pitchfork,' he said impatiently. 'Do you not understand? If I obey the summons I lose my chance in Ireland and impoverish myself with the Jews. If I defy Henry, at least I have the chance to gain a fortune, carved with my own hand. This is the destiny I have chosen for myself, for better or worse. Go, board the ship. The tide is turning.'

'Richard—'

'There is no point arguing. Do as I say.'

She gave him an exasperated look but turned towards the ships, although he heard her muttering under her breath about ruination. Following her, he bade the master cast off as soon as he was ready.

Richard's small fleet sailed down the wide, brown estuary, bound for the open span of the Irish Sea. The low sun kindled a path across the water, and as they struck the first harder waves of the ocean, a school of porpoises raced the ships, sleek grey backs curving the waves and speeding under them like shadows. Bright salt spray plumed the galley's bows. The wind at his back was like a hand pushing him towards his destiny and he took it as a portent before drawing a deep breath and opening Henry's letter.

As he read, his lips tightened, for Henry had indeed summoned him to court and was forbidding him to go to Ireland, on pain of forfeiture of his lands in England, Wales and Normandy. He had also strictly forbidden him to marry. Richard curled his lip. For better or worse he had embarked and this was the only future he had. If Henry was coming after him, at least he had a head start. He had to make this a different game of chess – one he could win.

Taking the parchment to the ship's side, he held it aloft and released it, watching it fly away on the wind, racing him towards Ireland.

22

Fearns, Leinster, Ireland, late August 1170

Aoife's young maid Deirdre dipped the tines of the comb in rose water before running it through her mistress's hair. Aoife's rich peat-dark tresses were tinged with glints of ruby in the morning light streaming through the hall doors. The men had ridden away to Waterford prepared for war, invigorated by the news that Richard de Clare was finally on his way. He had sent a small galley ahead with the news the day before he sailed and Aoife imagined that each stroke of the walrus ivory comb through her hair was the beat of an oar through the water, bearing him towards her on the incoming tide. Usually the hair grooming would soothe her, but Deirdre's ministrations had the opposite effect today, because this was a preparation anticipating her marriage. If Waterford fell and Richard survived, then they would be wed.

Deirdre was plaiting her hair when a messenger arrived with the news she had been anticipating and dreading. 'The ships have landed,' he announced. 'The Earl of Striguil has come and the household is bidden to leave Fearns and join the King outside Waterford.'

Aoife jumped up from her stool and went to the window, feeling nauseous. In the background her mother was telling the messenger that the baggage was ready. They had a few last things to finish and would be on their way.

Abruptly Aoife turned from the window and fled the chamber, uncaring that her hair was only half braided, wanting only to escape. She ran until she was out of breath and eventually threw herself down, lungs bursting, on a grassy bank overlooking a herd of her father's grazing cattle, their hides glossy in the late summer abundance. Their teeth tore at the lush grass and their udders swung, heavy with milk, while the cowherd leaned on his stave and watched them, his dog panting at his feet.

Aoife buried her face against her upraised knees. She barely remembered what Richard de Clare looked like beyond a distant memory of rich auburn hair and piercing sea-coloured eyes. She felt hollow and scared and feared she might go mad like that pitiful woman who had cut off all the heads. She plucked a daisy from the grass and stripped the petals one after another. 'Please make him go away,' she whispered, and then: 'Please make him stay.' A second flower followed, and a third. Go. Stay. Go. Stay. All the while knowing she had no choice.

Her mother came to find her and sat down on the bank at her side. 'It will be all right,' she soothed, kissing Aoife's brow. 'You are a princess, not a dairy maid; you should not be sitting watching cows in a field; you have a greater destiny. You are your father's daughter. Come now, walk in pride as he would wish.'

For an instant, Aoife felt an enormous flash of resentment towards her mother, but it was part of her wider anxiety. Standing up, she brushed the destroyed daisies from her gown, scattering the petals at her feet. Without a word she returned to the hall, her head carried high. Her stomach was churning but her mother's words had recalled her to her duty. Her father had promised, and so had she.

'When Waterford is ours we shall hold a wedding,' Diarmait said to Richard as they advanced on the town from their camp a short distance from the walls. 'I have sent to Fearns, and my daughter is coming. You will find her more beautiful than ever and grown to perform all the duties of a wife.' His hand described a woman's figure in the air lest Richard be in any doubt of his meaning.

Richard winced at the forthright statement and the gleam in Diarmait's eyes. He would never be so coarse about his own daughters.

Diarmait grinned and slapped his shoulder, mistaking Richard's expression. 'Ah, you'll manage very well with her. You're a man of the world!'

'I am sure I will,' Richard replied in a constricted voice, 'but first we must take the town.'

'Yes,' Diarmait replied, still with a twinkle, but darker now. 'Like taking a maidenhead. You've got to break open the door and spill the blood before you can release your seed.'

Richard winced again. Diarmait turned away to speak to one of his advisers and Richard attended to his own men. Raymond had been quiet and reticent since Richard's arrival, although he had given him a full report on the battle at Dun Domhnall. So had Hervey. Richard had heard about the death of the seventy Waterford prisoners from both men. The friction between them was obvious, although both had been circumspect. Richard assumed Raymond's taciturn behaviour was because he had bitten off as much as he could chew, and for the moment was coming to terms with his experiences.

The walls of Waterford rose before them, standing on a steep bank with a substantial ditch in front and protected by great stone towers at the North East corner and down to the riverside. The battlements bristled with a forest of spears, and occasional arrows sailed high in the air and plummeted down short of the advancing army. Despite losing many of their best warriors at Dun Domhnall, hundreds more waited behind those walls.

Richard sent Robert de Quency and de la Roche to erect his standard on the roof of the largest house in the suburbs. People had fled into the town at Diarmait's approach and the empty houses and workshops were convenient cover from which to establish a camp and plan strategy.

Richard and Raymond discussed the best place to set the ladders against the formidable walls.

'I suggest here, and here.' Raymond moved a couple of stones on the diagram they had made using items to hand, one of them a goblet holding Richard's wine. 'It will not be easy.'

'No fiercer than you faced earlier,' Richard said. 'Yes, I agree. Let us try at least.'

From the walls the Norse and Irish warriors bellowed threats and insults. Stones hurtled over the walls from slings, together with clods of dung and excrement and, to insult Diarmait, a maggot-ridden dead dog.

Richard donned his helmet and drew his sword. 'Go,' he said to Raymond. 'Let us test their mettle.'

William Ferrand, determined to die in battle, commanded the first assault with three ladders thudding home against the town wall. The stones and missiles became a hailstorm barrage as the defenders strove to force the attackers off and cast the ladders into the ditch. One of Richard's archers brought down a warrior holding a chunk of millstone over the battlements but even as the arrow struck him in the chest, the stone plunged down, striking soldiers off the top of the ladder and hurling them into the ditch below, breaking bones and crushing flesh. A fair-haired giant wielding a grapnel hook dislodged an end ladder and it toppled sideways and smashed into the ditch with its burden of men, bruising and maiming. Using his bow, Richard shot several warriors off the battlements, but the Waterford Norse remained relatively secure behind their walls and jeered at their attackers.

Raymond, who had been urging the men onward, now sounded the retreat on his horn as a second ladder crashed into the ditch. The shouting from the walls increased, victorious in pitch, taunting, filled with exultation.

Shoulders heaving, lips bared, Raymond glared up at the

howling Norse as his men dragged the dead and wounded from the broken ladders. Very much alive amid the carnage, William Ferrand was swearing and sucking at a cut on the back of his hand.

'Sons of whores, they will not live to see the sunset!' Diarmait growled.

Richard refused to let his doubts show; their choice was stark. This was do or die for him as it was for those men yelling on Waterford's walls. 'Again,' he said, 'go again!'

Once more ladders thudded against the walls and again they were repulsed with more casualties on their own side than on the Waterford one. The excrement and stones continued to pummel the besiegers and the insults grew more vociferous and triumphal.

'We have to find a way in,' Richard said grimly. 'Check the walls for signs of weakness – anything.'

He and Raymond walked along the perimeter wall, keeping out of arrow range, their kite shields protecting their bodies. Others were sent in the opposite direction, to seek out even the smallest chink in the defences.

Raymond and Richard came to a crowd of dwellings where several lean-tos were constructed against the town walls.

'Look, sire.' Raymond pointed to one building more substantial than the others, a proper little house with a beam inserted into the wall to take its weight. 'We might be able to cut through the support and bring the stones away with it.'

'Do it,' Richard ordered. 'Bring the archers; get your men in there.'

Raymond's archers, veterans of Dun Domhnall, were swift to the scene and under a supporting blizzard of arrows Raymond led a contingent into the house and set about hacking the dwelling away from the town wall by chopping through the beam attaching it. The Waterford citizens attacked from above but the relentless arrow shot kept them pinned down. Richard raised ladders either side and further along the walls to draw the defenders' attention and keep their focus off the men furiously hacking at the beam. Raymond emerged from the dwelling coughing, covered in dust and cobwebs, and shouted for ropes to be hooked to the front of the house and hitched to a pair of destriers. As the animals were whipped forward, the ropes pulled taut and the last of the beam was hacked through by a flurry of axe blows, the house tore away with a rumble, bringing down a section of wall in a bounce of stones and rubble, opening a breach for the soldiers to clamber through and no one to stop them. In hand-to-hand fighting, the Irish and Norse citizens of Waterford were no match for the mailed mercenaries pouring into the town.

Drawing his sword, Richard scrambled over the rubble into the gap and roared the men forward. The red chevrons of de Clare surged into Waterford like a burst river, tributaries flooding into the streets, sweeping all before them. People fled before the onslaught, and if they were caught, they were cut down. The soldiers were under strict orders. No stopping to loot until the town was theirs. Every fighting man was to be killed and none taken for ransom. Richard closed his mind to clemency. He banished compassion, and concentrated on the beautiful, deadly dance of the sword. His awareness was cold; he did not burn with battle frenzy like some men. He had to know how the fight was progressing and press it one way or another and adjust. Always solid at the centre. Raymond was doing the same, urging his men on, keeping them tight and focused, encouraging their ferocity but directing it with control.

The last of the Norse took refuge in a wharf-side fortified tower with their leader Ragnall and an Irish lord and his son. They barricaded themselves in the top chamber with the Normans sweeping around the base of the tower in a blood-stained tide. The latter rammed down the door, destroyed the barricades and dragged the men outside to finish the deed.

Diarmait raised his hand and called a halt before this last

small knot of resistance was destroyed. He dismounted heavily from his powerful brown stallion. Suffering from an ulcerated leg he had taken no part in the fighting, leaving Domnall to represent him, but he had been commanding and directing in the background. Limping forward, he gazed at the handful of men on their knees and his eyes shone with triumph.

'What is your will?' Richard asked, gazing dispassionately at their captives.

'Well now.' Diarmait tugged his beard. 'If they were to beg for mercy and pay tribute, I might be open to consideration in the light of their utter defeat.'

Ragnall, Diarmait's age with thinning flaxen hair and ice-blue eyes, spat on the ground at their feet. 'I would rather take my chance with death than kneel to a faithless, ill-bred dog turd such as you,' he snarled in Irish.

Diarmait gestured to Domnall who wordlessly put an axe in his hand. Diarmait gripped the haft and stepped forward. 'Then take your chance,' he said, and brought the axe round and down in a single bright blow. Ragnall's neck was powerful and corded, but Diarmait still severed it from his body in a single strike. Blood spattered; the head rolled, and the blue eyes stared at eternity. Splashed with Ragnall's blood, Diarmait turned to the remaining men. 'You have your choice,' he said. 'Accept my rule or face the same death as him. It is all one to me.'

No one else chose Ragnall's way out and all bowed their heads and submitted. Diarmait gave a single brusque nod. 'So be it. You will remain as guests under my protection until I have concluded my business. For your own safety, I counsel you not to go beyond the ring of my bodyguard.' He nudged Ragnall's head with his boot, dipping his toe in the Norseman's blood. 'Throw this in the river,' he said, his lip curling, 'and let the fish feed upon his eyes.' Then he looked at Richard.

Richard met Diarmait's stare impassively. To show even a blink of weakness would be disastrous. He was reminded of the time

Diarmait had turned the sword on him at Striguil. 'So,' he said, 'it is done and Waterford is taken. We know our arrangements.'

Diarmait's lips parted in a fierce smile. 'Aye, and so we do. I did not know if you were up to the mark, but you have proven your mettle today. If you are ready to test it in the marriage bed, I shall bring my daughter to you – and let us feast!'

23

Waterford, southern Ireland, September 1170

Aoife smoothed her hand down her wedding gown. The fine red wool set off her dark hair and green eyes to perfection. The side laces of gold cord pulled the gown tightly to her body, emphasising her narrow waist and the swell of her hips. Her veil was white silk secured by a band embroidered with garnets and pearls. Her hair, loose under her veil, was a dark river and fell to a line just below the belt of garnet and pearls Richard had sent to her.

Diarmait, who had been waiting on her final preparation, set his hands on her shoulders and turned her to face him. 'Sure, and you are more beautiful than a sunrise in May. You will be a good girl for me now, won't you?'

'Yes, Daidí.' She was determined to be resolute even if she was terrified. In a few hours she would be a wife and duty-bound to her husband and her old life would be gone like smoke in the wind.

'Remember where you came from. Remember that your loyalty is with your family, and to the head of your family first of all. Do not let me down in this.'

She flashed him an indignant look. 'I will never let you down – you know that. Have I not proved it to you time after time?' Including this marriage.

'Aye, you have. That's my brave girl. But tend that fire of yours and quench it down when you stand before Richard de Clare. We want him eating out of our hands, not striking us aside.' He pinched her cheek. 'Let's have you smiling for him. I have found you a fine man. Enjoy his body and do not waste him, my child – you know what I mean.' Aoife's cheeks burned and he laughed softly. 'Ah, you are my daughter, you will manage very well indeed, I think. Come, your bridegroom might have been tardy in his own arrival, but we shall not keep him waiting. Give me a kiss and we'll go.'

She put her arms around her father's neck and, pecking his bristly cheek, gripped him tightly for a moment against all the change that was coming.

Even before they entered Waterford, Aoife could smell the stench of burning, of blood, of rotting flesh, and she almost gagged. At her side her mother whispered under her breath and made the sign of the cross. Her father rode with his head up, a gold circlet crowning his brow, securing his long grey hair.

As they rode through the gates into the town, their own people lined the route, cheering loudly. There were men in full armour too – Normans, waving the de Clare chevron banner – but to Aoife it was like entering through the gates of hell. Riding with the dignity of a princess and inside trembling with fear.

At the cathedral of the Holy Trinity the bells were tolling to ring out the marriage and a crowd had gathered to witness the union of Murchada and Clare. Diarmait helped his daughter to dismount and tucked her arm inside his while her women processed behind, assisting her with her skirt, shaking out the train.

Walking in slow procession towards the arched cathedral entrance, Aoife saw Richard waiting, surrounded by a half circle of his senior men. He wore a tunic of dark blue wool and his red cloak was edged with gold braid. Basilia was present too, dressed in rose-coloured silk. Aoife's stomach was churning so hard she thought she would be sick.

Clad in his archbishop's robes, her uncle Lorcan stood at Richard's side, ready to perform the marriage in the sight of all on the cathedral steps. His expression was set and firm, but he had a smile for her even if he was less than enthusiastic. Clearly he had quelled his misgivings sufficiently to preside over the ceremony.

Richard took her hand at Lorcan's instruction and his fingers were steady and dry. Hers were clammy with fear.

'Are you ready?' he asked.

She nodded, and lowered her head to gaze at her feet. 'I am ready,' she replied.

'And willing?'

'Yes.'

'Will you look at me?'

She raised her gaze to his and met the piercing sea-blue and made herself hold it with her own. 'Yes,' she said again. 'I honour the pledge that was made.'

He nodded, seemingly satisfied. 'Good,' he said. 'You look beautiful.'

He vowed in a loud, firm voice to honour her with lands in dower and to do all to fulfil his role of husband in the sight of God. Reciprocating, she promised to fulfil her role as a wife the same, although her words were a tight whisper.

Raymond le Gros brought forward Richard's shield, scratched and scarred from battle, and presented it on one knee. A gold coin glittered upon the red chevrons and beside it, the ring she had returned to him. Taking the coin, Richard pressed it into her right hand. 'With this gold I endow you,' he said, 'and with this ring, I wed you.' He slipped the ring onto the heart finger of her left hand. She shivered for the act and the words bound them as one until sundered by death. He tipped her chin and kissed her, but without pressure, and the imprint of his lips on hers was like a seal upon a document. A murmur undulated through the crowd.

The formal act of binding complete, his hand upon hers, they followed the sway of her uncle's gilded robes and entered the church to celebrate mass. The atmosphere within was holy and serene, and if earlier Aoife had felt as though she had ridden through the gates of hell, now she entered the kingdom of heaven. The sun streamed into the church, illuminating her and Richard in alternating shafts of shadow and light. The nave was a setting for a jewel and she and Richard were twin gems in a golden circle. She an Irish princess and he a conquering hero as in the tales of Cúchulainn. His hair glowed like russet fire and his step was steady and firm, as she matched herself to the rhythm.

On reaching the altar steps, Lorcan turned, and they knelt side by side, ready for the mass to solemnise their union.

The marriage feast was held outside with numerous tents pitched for the guests and the soldiers. As dusk fell and the stars pricked the fabric of the evening sky, torches were lit and Diarmait called upon Aoife to sing. She took her harp, knowing with a spark of pleasure that she was the centre of attention. Her father was smiling proudly and Richard's gaze was fixed on her with avid hunger. Leaning over the harp, she plucked liquid notes from the strings and sang in a pure, clear voice, the high notes exquisitely, balanced between pain and joy. The words wove into the night and entrapped her audience. She looked at Richard, and now his eyes were closed the better to listen and the ecstatic expression on his face sent a pang through her because it was of the soul. His mute accolade encouraged her to pour more of herself into the song, turning the physical into the spiritual. When she finished, a long silence followed the final resonance, and then an enormous ripple of applause. People cuffed away their tears and raised their cups in toast.

Richard welcomed her back to his side and his cheeks were wet. 'I have longed to hear you again ever since Striguil,' he said hoarsely. 'Truly you have the voice and fingers of an angel.'

Aoife smiled at the compliment, basking in the adulation.

Then Richard took his turn to perform for the guests. He

made a jest of it, wanting to know why they should want base metal when they had just been treated to pure gold. Nevertheless, he stood forth and performed a song with a rousing chorus for everyone to sing and then he danced between a pair of crossed swords to display how nimble he was.

More dancing followed, and he and Aoife partnered each other. She had danced with him at Striguil and knew the moves – back to back and front to front. He lifted her up and set her to one side, his hands on her waist and her hands over his, and she matched him step for step while the guests clapped to the movement of their feet in unison. Aoife began to laugh and her hair bounced on her shoulders. She saw the flash of his smile, the spark in his eyes, and her breath grew short.

Diarmait, his face shiny with drink and enjoyment, directed a servant to pour mead into his drinking horn. 'A toast!' he roared. 'A toast to my beautiful daughter and to my new son-in-law! May their marriage be long and fruitful and blessed with many sons and daughters! May the land prosper and cattle and women grow fat!' He patted his belly, his expression alight with mischief. Men thumped the table with their fists, and Aoife blushed. 'May they dwell in peace and harmony! May the sword stay in the scabbard and the axe on the wall, but should warfare come, may the blade be swift and sharp across the necks of our foes! None of us would be here, celebrating in this town, were it not for our Norman allies and my new son-in-law and his bold warriors who have shed their blood with ours to win back our kingdom! I raise my horn to Richard de Clare, and I name him my kin, my son, and my heir!' He dragged Richard to his side amid wild cheers from most people and a few sidelong looks from others who were surprised, wary, or even resentful. Domnall, who might have been expected to be chosen as heir, however, hugged Richard like a brother and pledged Richard from Diarmait's horn.

Enna was led forward to add his own endorsement to his father's. He hugged Aoife, clinging to her hard, for he was well on the way to being maudlin drunk. 'I cannot weep for you, sister, so I will wish you joy,' he said. 'May you have all the pleasures in life that shall never be mine. You have brought me vengeance as your wedding gift and it is worth jewels to me.'

Richard understood why Enna had spoken with such bitter sentiment and kissed him on both cheeks. 'May you be at peace,' he said, and taking the horn Diarmait presented to him, raised it on high to all. 'King Diarmait has done me great honour in bestowing his daughter Aoife to be my wife. I acknowledge my debt to all here gathered to celebrate our union, and I will strive to do right by all of you, and to provide the protection and support of my sword to honour my word.'

There were more rousing cheers, more toasts and speeches. Richard turned to Aoife during a lull. 'I meant what I said.' He took her hand. 'Your household has accepted me, and I am yours, as you are now mine. I swear I will protect you and keep you safe for as long as I have breath in my body.'

His words sent a jolt through her, unsettling but not unpleasant. This was the man whose strength and support had returned her father to glory and wreaked vengeance on their enemies. 'I am glad,' she said. Even if everything should suddenly fail in Ireland, he still had castles and lands in England where she could be safe, and now she was his wife, she was entitled to a third of them.

'Are you?'

'Yes,' she said. 'You have fulfilled your oath to my father.'

Diarmait's horn went twice more around the room, lifted time and again in toast to the bride and groom. Unsteady on his feet, Diarmait propped the returned horn on its stand and turned to Richard. 'I think it is about time,' he said, suppressing a belch.

Aoife had been enjoying the adulation, sitting at Richard's side being the centre of attention. It had been like existing inside one of the stories she sang; but now the song had finished and reality was intruding. All the gilding began to dissolve for now came the ordeal of the bedchamber that she had so often heard her mother endure as her father claimed his part of their bargain.

Aoife paused on the threshold of the bedchamber and stared at the bed in the middle of the room, dressed with sheets of fine white linen and an embroidered red coverlet. Above the bed a chained ceramic lamp cast a glow onto the covers. Incense smoked in a brazier, giving off a resinous spicy scent. An embroidered hanging covered the window and underneath on a small trestle table stood a flagon of wine and a platter of small sweetmeats and tarts.

Her mother took her by the shoulders and kissed her forehead. 'There now,' she said. 'All women must pass through this rite when they marry – it is God's holy law. Take pride in your duty, daughter. It will soon be done.'

Aoife barely heard her words. The event was upon her, and since she could not flee, she must find the courage to endure. She stood as rigid as a statue as the women removed her beautiful dress and undergown, leaving her naked and shivering.

Ainne brought her a chemise of sun-bleached white linen. It had been washed and twist-dried so that the copious amount of material fell in crinkled pleats to the floor. Delicate white embroidery spiralled at the neck and the garment's volume was like a tent, concealing her figure, for which she was grateful.

A loud knock on the door caused her to jump and turn round, her heart hammering so hard she thought it might beat from her body.

Ainne went to lift the latch and, curtseying, admitted the men in procession led by Lorcan bearing a cross, followed by acolytes, one carrying a silver bowl filled with water. Her father came next, with Richard beside him. Richard too wore a full white chemise from throat to feet. Then the wedding guests, Norman and Irish together. Richard met Aoife's wide gaze and gave her a reassuring smile which she could not return. Had there not been so many people blocking the doorway, she would have fled.

Richard was escorted to the bed and placed in it, and the ladies brought Aoife to the other side and tucked her in. The guests gathered as witnesses were like a group of villagers watching their prize bull and cow brought to the breeding pen, she thought. She was powerless to stop this and knew no one would take her part; she was expected to do her duty. Even her uncle Lorcan was exhorting them to be fruitful and multiply while flicking her and Richard with water from the silver bowl. She dug her nails into her palms as he uttered the final amen and began ushering people from the room.

Her mother kissed her cheek and wished her well. In the doorway, her father paused to look at her over his shoulder, and she was surprised to catch a sparkle of moisture in his eyes, and a look of loss. But then after tonight nothing would be the same again.

The latch dropped with a loud clatter, and even before the sound had vibrated to silence Aoife had sprung from the bed and was halfway to the door, where she stopped and faced Richard, panting with fear, for she had nowhere to run.

He was staring at her in astonishment. Then he too left the bed and advanced on her, halting as she took a step back, and then another. 'You need not be afraid of me,' he said. 'I will not hurt you, I swear I will not.' He held out his right hand, as if coaxing an animal.

Aoife remained rooted to the spot, eyes wide, for there was plenty of which to be afraid.

'You are my wife and my helpmate, and if we are to succeed together, Norman and Irish, we must be of one accord.' He came up to her and lightly touched her cheek with his fingertips. 'Your singing today,' he said. 'I have never heard anything so exquisite or seen such beauty – it was the sweetest pain. You are a treasure, my Aoife, more precious than gold.'

'My Aoife'. She was his, but she was not sure he was 'her' Richard. He was a stranger, a man, and they had been left in this room to do what women and men did when they were married. She knew the expectations being harboured on the other side of that door.

'Come,' he said, 'we must have trust in each other. I know it has to be earned, but will you trust me now?'

She caught her lower lip in her teeth and gave a tiny nod. His hand moved from her cheek and he gently freed her lip with his thumb, then cupped the back of her neck and kissed her eyelids, her cheeks, the tip of her nose, his touch feather-soft. 'You are my wife and under my protection. I was raised to be gentle to women, and courteous. It is in my interest as well as yours to make our life together pleasant. If you look on me with fear and loathing after tonight, I will have failed, and I am not a man who likes to fail.'

'I am not afraid.' Aoife jutted her chin.

'No?' He gave a wry smile. 'Well, that is a good thing.' He continued to kiss her while delicately unfastening the ties on her chemise and pushing it down over her shoulders.

Aoife shuddered as the garment pooled at her feet and she stood before him naked.

'You are very beautiful,' he said softly.

'It would not matter if I was a hag,' she responded with a hint of defiance.

He chuckled. 'No, it would not, but even so . . .'

He stroked her hair away from her face and kissed her gently again, before setting his hand on her waist, skin to skin. Aoife gasped at the touch, but it was not unpleasant. His fingers were warm and steady. She closed her eyes and hid her face in his chest while he stroked her hair and murmured assurances. A sensation of heavy tension settled in her pelvis, a sort of warm ache. She was still frightened, but accompanying that fear were curiosity and arousal.

He paused to remove his own voluminous chemise and drew her against him again. She could smell the herbs in which he had bathed as a ritual before the marriage. The tang of male skin. The hot column of flesh against her belly. Knowing what the resolution of this courtship entailed, she was disturbed, but excited too in a way she had never experienced or expected.

He traced her cheekbone with his forefinger. 'Only you can do this for me, Aoife,' he said. 'No one else. You are the one.'

The words made her shiver, for they put her on a pedestal, and their inference suddenly made her aware of her own power. He took her hand and kissed the ring he had set upon it, and leading her to the bed, laid her down. She shivered as she felt the cold linen sheet under her spine.

'It is like a song,' he said, 'but of the body, and told in touch. Let me sing it for you, and let you sing it back to me.'

Aoife stared up into the soft glow from the lamp, one arm raised above her head, feeling languorous surprise. The duty of the marriage bed had been very different to her expectations and she was trying to assimilate what she knew and measure it against what she had experienced without succeeding. It had been gentle and tender; a close and intimate thing. She had mostly kept her eyes shut while it was happening, but opening them now and again she had seen glimpses of his body moving over hers. She had felt him within her, but the pain had been bearable and accompanied by pleasurable pressure. No heavy battering thrusts and grunts of effort, but something kinder and considerate. Not so much a song as a twining dance of limbs.

He turned towards her. The light from the chain lamp glinted on his hair, sparking the russet with gold. 'You and I,' he said with a smile, 'we must come to know each other and go forward together, but this is not such a bad start, is it?'

'No, my lord.' She touched his hair. 'It . . . it is not what I thought it would be.'

He dipped his head to nip her collarbone. 'Then how did you think it would be?'

She bit her lip, not wanting to voice her fears because they might still happen. For something to be true it had to occur more than once. She was uncomfortable at being made so vulnerable, and still a little disbelieving. What was the difference between a man who was tender and one who was weak? She was not even sure if it had been a true mating for it had not been as brutal as she had expected. 'Different,' she said, and buried her face in his chest, inhaling his scent. 'You kept your word, you did not hurt me.'

He stroked her hair. 'I would never do that. Women in my household are honoured, I told you. I hope you will grow used to it and take pleasure in the duty, because then you have the best of everything when duty is also a delight.'

He held her for a while longer and eventually his breathing grew slow and deep and he dropped into slumber. She eased stealthily out of his embrace and left the bed to wander the chamber, touching things, vividly aware of her surroundings, as if they were imbued with new texture and meaning. The wall hangings, the carving on the chests, the pattern on the goblets. At the narrow window, she gazed out into the star-studded darkness, trying to make sense of a world that had utterly changed in a moment. She could hear people still singing and carousing, but that was what happened when men came straight out of war and into celebration. They were still wild and the energy had to run its course. There would be some sore heads in the morning.

She sat on the chest by the window and, folding her knees towards her chin, rocked herself and thought about her past. About all the things she had believed about men and women that now might not be true, and if they were not true, then what other layers of falsehood had she imbibed? How did she go forward when the ground at her back was not solid?

At length she rose and returned to bed. Sitting down against the curve of his spine she leaned over him and dared to kiss his cheek. Richard stirred and sleepily turned towards her. 'What are you doing, dearling? Come back to bed. It is very late and tomorrow will be busy.'

Dearling. An English word; she would ask him what it meant.

She climbed between the covers and curled against him. He put his arm across her and went back to sleep. Aoife closed her own eyes, but did not settle immediately, for she was still assimilating this new reality and not sure she could believe in it.

Aoife woke at dawn and for an instant wondered where she was. Seeing the sleeping man beside her gave her a jolt of anxiety. When he woke up he might want to mate with her again and she was still trying to deal with the first time and sort out her feelings about it. She could not just dress and leave; she was a wife now and she was not ready to face the world beyond that door.

To give herself some distance and control, she donned her clothes, combed and braided her hair, and sat down by the narrow window to watch the world. Fishing boats and merchant craft sent their reflections into the river. A woman with a basket of fish was talking to two soldiers and someone else was walking a pair of spotted hounds on a leash. All those people had at some time done the same as she and Richard last night. It was a fact of life, like the weather.

'Up again?' Richard said, and yawned. 'Come back to bed.'

She gave a start and turned to look at him. 'But I am dressed. The sun is up and people are about.'

'We are newly married,' he answered with a lazy smile. 'They will expect a little tardiness. Come.'

He drew back the covers and left the bed. Her gaze flicked to his groin. He was not erect but there was imminent potential for it to happen and a glint in his eye suggesting it would. She swallowed, her mouth dry.

'There is nothing to be afraid of. I am not going to harm you,' he repeated. 'You are my wife and I bid you fair honour. It is God's rightful law and right to do.'

Aoife nodded, but bit her lip, on the edge of tears.

He gave her a baffled look and then sighed. 'Very well. Have the morning with your women and do what you need to do. I know this is new and unsettling for you – I shall not bother you further – for now.' He dropped his hands, turned away, dressed with swift efficiency and left the room.

When he had gone, Aoife went to the bed and stripped the covers to look at the smears of blood on the sheet – enough to show she had been a virgin and was one no longer. It had hurt very little, but there was a deeper pain for what she had lost. She had new responsibilities and obligations that made her vulnerable. She did not know her new husband and was certainly not ready to trust him whatever he said.

Cheers, shouts and raised cups greeted Richard's appearance in the hall. He was urged to eat heartily to keep up his strength and replenish his reserves. Richard accepted the goblet presented to him by Robert de Quency and returned the salutations with a broad smile. 'I am not about to comment,' he said. 'I shall leave it to your imaginations, which doubtless are running riot.'

He sat down to dine on bread and cheese. A part of his mind dealt with business and food, while another part pondered the challenge that was Aoife. He had tried to be gentle and patient. Last night's coming together had been a success in the act as far as he knew. Her whimpers had not been of pain and afterwards she had embraced and kissed him. Learned men and physicians said a woman would not conceive unless her body experienced the pleasure crisis that released her seed, and he had tried to bring her to that moment. He was not certain he had succeeded, but she had been soft and pliant in his arms afterwards and had embraced him of her own accord.

This morning, however, she had been all defensive again and he was unsure how to deal with her. She was his wife in full law and he would not have her dictating to him, but he had to keep her happy to foster a good relationship with his new Irish relatives and to beget the heir he desperately needed. She needed time, and the problem was that he had no time.

Diarmait arrived, rumpled and limping heavily. He eased down into his chair with a wince, but swiftly concealed his discomfort behind a broad grin, clapping Richard heftily on the shoulder. 'I trust you slept well.'

'Very well indeed, sire, and so did your daughter.'

'I am pleased to hear it – I knew you would treat her well,' Diarmait said gruffly, then waved the subject away. 'It is not of Aoife I wish to speak. Now the marriage is accomplished we have other urgent matters to discuss. We have control of Wexford and Waterford and it is time to move on Dublin. Then we shall control the ports and the Norse will no longer hold dominion over my seaboard.'

Richard had known this was coming but had not expected Diarmait to address the matter so immediately.

'I will send out scouts this morning,' Diarmait continued. 'The men need a few more days' rest before we start out – although none for you!' He laughed again but rubbed his leg.

'You are in pain, sire?'

'No more than a sore that's slow to mend. Môr is treating it with honey and salve. It won't hold me back. As soon as the scouts return from Dublin we can be on our way.'

The women came to Aoife's chamber that morning bringing sewing and chatter. Ainne stripped the sheets and the ladies bore witness to the bloody proof of consummation and the bride's virginity. Aoife held herself proudly as they examined the evidence. She was as good as any woman present and now had more knowledge than some, Basilia among them – and that was satisfying. She ate her morning bread and cheese with a hearty appetite, and was conscious of the women's sidelong glances, assessing her every action and movement.

'Are you well?' Môr asked, her eyes filled with concern.

'Why should I not be? It was no hardship,' Aoife replied with a shrug, making it clear the subject was closed, while at the same time giving her mother a superior, triumphant look.

At noon they joined the men in the hall for a formal meal and Aoife took her place at Richard's side, wearing a gown of saffron-gold trimmed with green, and jewels woven through her braids.

Richard greeted her with a smile and a warm kiss on the lips and then banged the haft of his knife on the table to command everyone's attention. 'Yesterday I married the daughter of Diarmait, King of Leinster, before you all. And last night . . .' He turned to look at his wife and smile, and the room erupted into rousing cheers and whistles. Aoife felt her cheeks burn. She waited for him to say something jocular and outrageous, but he called for silence and continued: 'And last night my wife performed her duty as befits the daughter of an Irish king. I declare myself well content with the bargain we have struck and I wish to honour my bride with a gift.' He beckoned, and his scribe and chaplain, Nicolas, stepped forward bearing a cushion covered by a rectangle of purple silk cloth. Richard took it and, going down on one knee, presented it to Aoife.

Fire-red with embarrassment she accepted it from him, put it on the table and lifted the cloth. Under the silk was an ivory-hilted knife in a decorated sheath, with a piece of parchment wrapped around the scabbard. The latter detailed her rights to lands in England complete with herds and flocks, and a water mill.

'These are for you alone, no other,' he said. 'To do with as you please and to dispose of as you will.' Taking her hands, he kissed them, his lips touching her wedding ring.

Tears welled in her eyes and she experienced a tender pain in her heart, like a flower opening to the sunlight. She removed one hand from his but only to touch his head and feel his hair under her hand, assuring her of reality.

Diarmait loudly cleared his throat and looked at both of them with speculation and a narrowing of his dark eyes. 'You have such a fine silver tongue, I could almost mistake you for an Irishman,' he said, whacking a hefty hand down on Richard's shoulder.

'A compliment I treasure, sire,' Richard replied, 'coming as it does from a master of the art.'

Diarmait snorted and returned to his drinking horn.

Following the meal, the remainder of the day was spent in rest and recuperation, although the plan for the assault on Dublin continued apace. Diarmait made time to speak with Aoife. Sitting at her side, his shoulder pressing hers, he took her hand. She noticed beads of sweat glistening on his brow and the dark shadows staining his eye sockets. His body seemed less bold and muscular than of old, resembling a sack with some of the contents removed.

'Is all well with you, daughter?' he asked.

She nodded warily. 'Yes, Daidí.'

'It was handsome of your husband to give you lands to yourself. A gesture to warm your tender heart, eh?'

'Indeed, it was generous,' she agreed.

'He contents you?'

She frowned, unsure where he was leading. 'He has been kind to me,' she replied.

'Good, good.' Diarmait patted her hand. 'But you be careful, my girl. Do not allow gifts and fair words to turn your head. Remember where you come from and to whom you owe your allegiance. Be a good wife to the Norman, but do not let him steal your heart and claim your loyalty. If he tells you things you think I should know, come straight to me. I am trusting you to be truthful with me and I am trusting you still to be mine, even though I have set your hand in his.'

Aoife experienced a flash of resentment. She had her own mind and would decide for herself what was best, but she looked at him with wide eyes. 'Yes, Daidí, of course I will come straight to you, you know that.' She reached up to touch his thinning hair and changed the subject. 'How is your leg?'

'Better,' he said with a grunt. 'Your mother has bandaged it with her unguent. I will be back on a horse tomorrow; don't you worry about me. You keep the Norman happy, and remember what I told you. You're a Murchada first and a de Clare second.' He pinched her cheek between forefinger and thumb. 'Now, get to that marriage bed of yours and breed me some fine grandsons for my old age, eh?'

Aoife blushed furiously and he laughed aloud.

That night Richard made love to her and again it was a gentle thing that brought her warm pleasure, but afterwards she moved a little away from him. He rolled onto his side to stroke her hair. 'It is a dark waterfall,' he murmured. 'Beautiful.'

She pretended to be sleepy and did not answer, but her mind was busy pondering the alchemy of what had just happened and the feelings in her body that gave pleasure but left her restless. She remembered the sound he muffled against her throat as he spilled his seed within her and she wondered if she could rule him and what it would be like to bring her own female power to bear. To a degree she could twist her father around her finger and knew that being compliant and gentle was not the way to win him over. Her mother was compliant and gentle and her father ignored her.

She had noticed how Richard treated women of his own rank with civility while placing them in his own idea of what their niche should be. He clearly valued Basilia for her housekeeping and logistical abilities, but her power was constrained within narrow parameters. His word was law, even if clad in a courteous glove. However, as his wife, she was in a unique position to weave her way through the strands of his will and tailor her own design. To succeed in Ireland, he had to keep her satisfied. What she had to do for her part was keep him not just satisfied, but in thrall, on edge and off balance.

In the morning she was awake and dressed again by the time he stirred and looking out of the window. She glanced over her shoulder at him when she heard him move. 'It is raining,' she said. 'You will have to grow accustomed to rain in Ireland.'

'I do not mind,' he said, smiling. 'There are many things to occupy a man even when it is raining, especially when he is newly married.'

'Are there now? But women still have their usual tasks to perform.'

He left the bed and joined her, putting his arms around her and nuzzling the nape of her neck. She made a soft sound, still aroused by her earlier thoughts of having the power of a participant with a capacity to dictate what happened. She pushed him away and pointed to his shirt. 'This, for example, it will need a wash today.'

Without taking his eyes from hers, he removed it and gave it to her, and now she had a full view of his torso in daylight. He was not bulky and powerful like her father; his strength was tensile with defined musculature. This man could leap on and off a galloping horse and dance between crossed swords with nimble agility. She swallowed, her mouth dry and her body liquid. His eyes were sparkling with humour and a desire that held a nuance subtler than lust, although lust was a major part of it. He pulled her into his arms again and kissed her, and she dropped the shirt and followed him to the bed.

He undressed her with haste, but not roughly, parted her legs and entered her. This time she arched to meet him and gripped him inside her and felt her own part in each surge, no longer passive. She used her nails, her tongue, her teeth, the strength of her own taut female body. The feeling was so intense this time that she clung to him for dear life, every part of her clenched as sensation swept through her body and as she felt him gasp and pulse within her.

Replete, a little stunned, Aoife unclasped her legs from his hips and let them flop. Breathing raggedly, he kissed her throat, her jaw, and eyelids. 'Well, wife, that is as good a beginning to a day as I have ever experienced,' he said with a chuckle. She pushed her hands through his hair, feeling lassitude in her limbs and a sense of wellbeing and wonder. If her wedding night had been unsettling because it was not what she had expected, then this was a revelation – like learning to sing a song and then discovering new notes she had never known existed.

'I think I am going to like rainy days in Ireland,' he said as he left the bed and took a clean shirt from his coffer.

'It rains a lot,' she replied mischievously. 'Sometimes for days on end.'

He looked her up and down and gave her an incorrigible grin. 'I'll look forward to it.' Leaning over, he stole another kiss.

When he had gone, Aoife rose languorously from the bed and, picking up the dropped shirt, went to the window. She sniffed the linen, drawing in his scent, and hummed to herself.

'You look like the cat that has licked the cream in the dairy,' Deirdre said with a twinkle when her women arrived for the day. 'So did your lord when I encountered him on the stairs.'

Aoife said nothing, allowing her smile to serve as her reply.

24

Waterford, southern Ireland, September 1170

A few days later, Diarmait departed to muster troops for the Dublin campaign. Robert FitzStephen was summoned from Wexford and Richard was kept busy in Waterford with Aoife, sorting out administration and assigning the defence of the town to men he trusted.

News came that the Dubliners had sought their own help and the massed armies of the High King and Tiernan ua Ruari had arrived at the city and were preparing for battle. The High King had set up his military camp at the tower of Clondalkin and controlled the approaches to the city. All the passes through the Wicklow mountains were being guarded and barriers and defences were rapidly multiplying.

'They wasted no time,' Richard said wryly to Aoife who had been playing her harp to him when the scout arrived. 'I would have done the same in their place though.'

'My father will prevail. They are no match for him — for us.'

He was amused at the fierceness in her eyes and a little wry about her devotion to her father and how the 'us' was a correction. It was one thing to enhance one's prowess by fierce words, but there had to be strategies in place based on scouted intelligence and detailed plans – half the reason his men succeeded despite the valiance of their foes. He gave orders to increase the reconnaissance parties and he sent messengers to Diarmait, urging him to make haste. 'We have to be ready to move the moment your father returns.'

'The men of Dublin have no love for Ruari ua Connor and Tiernan ua Ruari,' Aoife said with a shrug. 'They will see the High King and his allies not as saviours but more as predators come to look them over and decide how easy the pickings are. They will play one off against the other and hope that my father and Ruari come to blows. Whoever wins will have been weakened by the fight and therefore be less of a threat and readier to negotiate.'

Richard pursed his lips, for she had a valid point.

'Trust no one,' she said. 'And you might stay alive.'

He took her hand in his. 'You have learned harsh ways for one of tender years.'

She gave him a bitter smile. 'In order to survive,' she said. 'My father taught me well.'

Perhaps too well, he thought. 'Am I not trustworthy?'

'As much as any man can be trusted,' she answered, and began playing her harp again, with a swift look at him from under her lashes.

Disturbed by her ambiguous answer, he did not pursue it into deeper water.

Diarmait returned two days later, riding into Waterford with axemen, cavalry, spearmen and archers. Every warrior was burning to march on Dublin, and an air of determined, vengeful exultation filled the camp. Reports from the scouts, however, said that all the roads into the port were heavily defended by the High King's men with no way through except by pitched battle.

Sitting in council, Diarmait listened to the intelligence with his lower lip thrust out and his ulcerous leg propped up on a stool. Worried, Aoife had offered to wash and dress the wound, but he had snapped a terse refusal.

'All the passes through the mountains are heavily guarded,' Richard said. 'They are just waiting for us to make our move.'

Diarmait grunted and reached for his drinking horn. 'What about the pass at Glendalough?'

The scout frowned. 'I do not know, sire. It is little used and we did not think—'

'Then you should have done. Go and find out!' Diarmait banged his fist on the table and the man ran out.

'It's a narrow track,' Domnall broke in to explain, 'well out of our way – not a direct route.'

'Passable?'

Domnall nodded. 'In summer the paths can be ridden. Ruari doesn't have the resources to guard every single path, but it won't be easy.'

'He won't expect us to come from that direction because of the increased difficulty,' Diarmait said. 'It's not what he would do. We can bring an army through and send in scouts to deal with any outriders.'

In the golden late September morning Richard paused dressing to look at Aoife. She sat on the end of their bed, naked, her dark hair falling in a tangle to her hips. He admired the sinuous lines of her body and was lured by the sultry expression in her eyes. Now she had conquered her first fear of the marriage bed, she was eager to lie with him. He loved the sounds she made and the way she wrapped herself around him. He loved her wildness, her elemental fire. He was enjoying discovering the quirks and facets of her personality. When she served him his cup in the hall she would take his hand and kiss his cheek, making her desire for him plain to all. Richard was gratified when she acted that way in front of her father, for it revealed to him that her loyalty had been loosened from its fixed abode and now he had his own claim.

'I shall see you again in Dublin, my love,' he said. 'At the victory feast, God willing.'

She rose to embrace him. 'I have prayed to Saint Bridget for your protection. I shall not be far behind you. Be safe and carry the day.'

'With God's help.'

'It means everything to my father. Dublin has dwelt in his heart all of his life.'

He saw fierce sadness in her expression. Diarmait was unwell and this might be his last campaign as an active leader. Since he had sworn Richard as his heir, Richard needed to prove himself too. A victory at Dublin mattered as much if not more than victory at Waterford and would not be easy. 'If I can, I will carry the day for him and for our own future, I promise.' He took her hands and kissed her lips, still warm and soft from earlier kisses, and it was a sweet farewell; a wistful one too, for a parting kiss could be as final as death.

Diarmait's army rode through the narrow pass in the Wicklow mountains with the hardest Norman fighters to the fore. Diarmait's son Domnall led the Irish contingent because Diarmait's leg was troubling him. Then came Raymond le Gros with a strong complement of knights and mounted archers. Richard rode with Diarmait and the main body of his own knights and Diarmait's bodyguard. Hervey had stayed behind at Waterford with a small garrison to protect the women.

Their path brought them in a wide sweep down to Dublin's walls, adding several miles to their journey but swinging them around Ruari's flank. Scouts galloped back and forth, keeping close watch on Ruari and Tiernan's amassed forces, but the assembled army made no effort to attack even though Ruari must have realised by now that Diarmait's troops had found a way through his checks and blocks.

Diarmait's army pitched their camp before the walls and Diarmait summoned Maurice Regan to his tent. 'Well,' he said, as Regan sat down at a table and produced a wax tablet and stylus, 'let us see what the men of Dublin have to say now we are here.' With relish, he began dictating the terms for surrender.

'You intend leaving the Norse in command of Dublin?' Richard asked sharply.

Diarmait took a long pull from his drinking horn. Two furrows of pain sat between his brows. 'I have not yet decided – let us wait and see what happens.'

Richard gave him a dubious look, and Diarmait scowled at him. 'I am thirty years older than half the men out there,' he growled. 'Even those nearer my own age do not have my long experience of warfare. You yourself barely know this land or its people. Aye, you may have clawed the surface and drawn blood, but you are nowhere near the vital organs. You did not know of the pass at Glendalough until I spoke.'

'That is true,' Richard acknowledged. 'We would be lost without your expertise. But you asked for our aid, and it would help to know your mind.' He spoke courteously but had every intention of taking Dublin. His soldiers had risked their lives and were hoping for great reward, and those who paid their wages including the merchants of Bristol were expecting to seize the port of Dublin from the Hiberno-Norse and make it their own.

Diarmait shrugged his shoulders. 'When you have a great enemy against you, you do what you can to divide his forces. Ruari's army is here because I am the enemy. The men of Dublin fear me; they worship strength above all else, and who has the stronger force now?' His hard smile displayed several missing teeth. 'Ruari is holding off because he knows what happened at Wexford, Waterford and Dun Domhnall. He hasn't got the belly to attack unless the Norse attack from the walls first. And he does not trust them. So, we offer the Norse terms and they accept and Ruari rides away.'

A servant set a dish of carved beef down in front of him and he attacked it with gusto, throwing it around his mouth in order to chew with his good teeth. 'Now do you understand?'

Richard nodded thoughtfully. 'Yes,' he said. 'I understand very well indeed – father.'

Diarmait snorted at the address and continued dictating to Maurice in between rotations of his jaw.

* * *

A dew-damp September dusk was falling as Richard returned to his tent, the chevron banner fluttering from the top of the pole. Dropping onto his bed, he looked at Raymond and Robert de Quency. 'Diarmait is playing a cunning game,' he said. 'We have to work with what he has said, what he hasn't and what he expects us to fathom for ourselves.' He gave them the gist of what he had learned in Diarmait's tent.

Raymond bit his thumbnail. 'The men will not be pleased if he agrees a truce. There will be no plunder and it leaves us as little more than his hired mercenaries, when we could have the city for our own and under our rule.'

'I know what you are saying,' Richard acknowledged, 'but the talks are aimed at preventing the Norse from agreeing a pact with the High King. If we can accomplish that, then Dublin is for the taking. Diarmait no more wants the Norse controlling the town than we do, but he has to weaken them first, which means making very sure the High King knows they are negotiating with us and not him.'

Raymond gave a pragmatic nod. 'There is sense in that.'

'We continue with our plans to take the town, but for now we play Diarmait's game and we wait until the time is right. I can tell you for certain there will not be a truce – we cannot afford it.'

A meeting to discuss terms took place the next morning outside the town walls with Maurice Regan representing Diarmait, who sat in the background, having had a chair and footstool brought to the meeting place. Lorcan spoke for the Dubliners, whose archbishop he was, at the same time being Diarmait's brother-in-law, and so with a foot in each camp. Lorcan was vociferous on behalf of the Dublin citizens. They desired to be at peace with Diarmait, he said, and would swear allegiance to him as they had done before. Maurice replied that they must pay the price and provide hostages this time as proof of their goodwill. Now and again he turned to consult with Diarmait, who would nod and gesture and give him instructions, knowing very well that the scouts and spies belonging to Ruari and Tiernan would not mistake what was happening.

The Dublin Norse eventually agreed to Diarmait's demands, requesting a day to round up the hostages who would be brought to the gate at first light, at which time Diarmait would be acknowledged as overlord of Dublin.

The meeting broke up, but Lorcan stayed to speak personally with Diarmait, clutching his staff, and glowering. 'I know what you are about,' he said, and flicked an angry glance at Richard and his men standing behind Diarmait's chair. 'You have no truce planned at all, have you?'

Diarmait lifted his leg off the stool, fever glistening on his brow. 'Have I not?'

'Do not take me for a fool,' Lorcan warned, thumping his staff on the ground.

'I have never done that,' Diarmait said with a grimace of pain. 'Do not challenge me on this and the Church will receive its just due.'

Lorcan wagged his forefinger. 'If they open their gates to you, then how many will survive? You tell me, my brother by marriage.'

Diarmait fixed Lorcan with a forceful stare. 'This reckoning has been coming since I was five years old, when they killed my father, threw the body of a maggot-infested dog on top of him and spat on his grave. They say they need a day to find their hostages. Perhaps they would better use that time in taking to their ships. I know they chose you to speak for them because you are my wife's brother and they think I will heed you and be lenient. But I must also listen to my other kin, the beloved dead. Where were the men of Dublin when I was forced into exile? Do you think I am going to trust them now? Tell them to leave or take the consequences and perish.'

Lorcan tightened his lips. 'The blood is not on my hands.'

Diarmait's lips parted in a sneer. 'It never is – brother.'

Lorcan turned on his heel and stalked away.

Diarmait looked at Richard. 'Do what you must,' he said harshly. 'I promised you Dublin, and I promised the men of Dublin I would have vengeance on them for what they did, and I am a man of my word.'

The smell of smoke loomed over Dublin like a pall after a short, sharp battle to take the city. The warriors defending the walls had been slaughtered and the rest had fled to their ships and rowed away, leaving those unable to flee to their fate.

Clouds had been gathering since midday and the sky over the city was almost purple. The first white veins dazzled the sky and Diarmait stood on the bloodstained walls to watch the storm come in. Lightning before him, fire behind, and blood on the soles of his shoes.

'The scouts report that the High King's army has left. He has refused to give battle,' Richard said, joining Diarmait. A little further along the walk, a banner bearing the six red chevrons of de Clare snapped in the wind.

'Of course he has,' Diarmait said. 'The Dubliners sealed their own fate. They sent for aid and then turned their backs on it, the fools.' The first drops of rain spattered his face like tears.

Richard said nothing. Treachery appeared to be the order of the day and no man's word could be trusted for it was broken as soon as it was given, even when fierce oaths were sworn. Honour was slain in the dirt, and he was a part of it.

'I have avenged my father's bones today,' Diarmait said. 'No longer shall the Norsemen rule my seaboard. But there is much still to do. Ruari may have departed but this is not the end.'

Richard made to take his leave. 'I need to see to the men. When the hounds are unleashed, a keeper still needs to know when to whip them to heel. I would not want Dublin to go up in flames.'

Diarmait nodded brusquely. 'I leave that to you.'

The rain was spotting harder and Richard raised his hood. But Diarmait lifted his head to the sky and embraced the storm.

25

Dublin, Ireland, December 1170

The hall was dark in the winter dusk and the wind howled against the shutters, but inside there was the joy of music and dancing and tale-telling around the fire. The cauldrons bubbled with rich meaty stew, and wine and mead flowed in abundance. Sitting beside Richard and her father at the high table, Aoife looked out on the gathering with a smile on her lips. She loved the convivial atmosphere, the hall packed to the rafters. It brought back the best winters of her childhood when the men were home from war, the harvests safely gathered, and when the bad weather had drawn everyone to the comfort and safety of the hearth. Even the drunken brawls that occasionally erupted had a routine familiarity.

Throughout the autumn she had dwelt at Fearns with the other women of the royal household while Richard and her father were consolidating their victories. Richard had concentrated on Wexford, Waterford and Dublin. Her father had been on campaign with his Irish troops and Norman auxiliaries, determined to stamp his mark not only on Leinster but on his neighbours and bring down Tiernan ua Ruari if he could. He had raided Meath and Clonard, the valleys of Blackwater and the Boyne. He had burned Kells to the ground and had raged over the land like a huge avenging bear, taking down enemies one after another in a frenzy and serving notice to Ruari ua Connor that the name of MacMurchada was once again to be feared.

Aoife had come to know Basilia a little better in the months they had been together while the men were campaigning and had learned much of the art of being a Norman lady, although she treated it as a role to inhabit rather than a change of who she was. She had improved her grasp of the Norman language and was now better equipped to listen to opinions and gossip from that side of the fire.

Her sister by marriage was calm and collected among the other women. Poised and cool. Coming to know her better had not encouraged warmth or familiarity. Aoife did not particularly like Basilia, and sensed the feeling was mutual from the sidelong glances she caught being sent her way – as if Basilia considered Aoife beneath her, some kind of uncouth wild girl her brother had been forced to marry out of necessity. Aoife bore with Basilia's attitude because she was learning from her, while marking every moment.

Aoife noticed how often Basilia's gaze inadvertently wandered to Raymond le Gros whenever he was present, although she would come to herself and swiftly look away, as though she had been eyeing something forbidden. Raymond was always very proper towards her and courteous in conversation, but Aoife did not miss the occasional speculative glance he cast Basilia's way as she walked through the hall.

In the months following her wedding, Aoife had wondered if she might be with child, but her bleeds had come as usual and the sight of the monthly flow had filled her with both anxiety and relief, the latter because she need not yet face the burden of childbirth and motherhood, but she worried too lest Richard's seed was weak. However, he was home now for the winter and they had plenty of opportunity to find out. On their wedding night she had feared her duty, but now the thought of his strong, warm body in the bed with her filled her with anticipation and healthy forthright lust.

He took her hand now and kissed her fingers. 'I have missed your singing,' he said. 'Will you give us the pleasure, my love – while we are still sober enough to take delight in your voice?'

'For sure I will,' she said, and taking up her harp, she sang to the company of trials and battles and homecomings. Looking over the rapt audience she felt the power coiled like a serpent in the pit of her belly. Her father was smiling and Richard, as always, had closed his eyes to savour her voice. Others watched her intently, and some wiped their eyes. The power flexed within her that she could bring these toughened warriors to tears. Men who would stand hard and fight to the death. Men who would cut off heads and burn homesteads, and now they were swallowing their emotion with aching throats. That indeed was satisfying.

Raymond rose abruptly and staggered from the hall, still clutching his cup, the wine sloshing over the rim. Badge trotted at his heels, nimbly avoiding his master's unsteady legs and the splash of the drink. Aoife observed his exit and attached no significance apart from noting that when he was off duty, he drank heavily and the polished veneer was exposed as a mask.

'You sing like an angel,' Richard said later in their chamber, drawing her into his arms. 'I could listen to you for ever.' He kissed her while the wind howled and threw fistfuls of rain against the shutters. He loosened her braids and wound his fingers through the wave-ripple strands. 'And to know you are mine . . .'

Aoife threw back her head and closed her eyes. The need for him rose in her, as powerful as the storm. She wanted this man with an appetite she had not known existed until a few months ago. The Church might disapprove and say it was the sin of lust, but she cared not. She needed him with her and inside her, and from the quiver of his skin under her touch she knew he was similarly bound. 'And you belong to me,' she said, making them equals. 'You are mine, my fine English lord, and I will have you.'

They tumbled onto the bed fully clothed and in seconds he was over her and inside her, his lips on hers, hips surging. She was so ready that within a few thrusts she was climaxing, clutching his shoulders, and feeling his groan of release vibrate in their kiss.

He regained his breath still above her and within her but took his weight on his elbows. 'I might have missed your singing,' he gasped, 'but dear God, I missed this too.'

She did not reciprocate and say how much she had missed him; showering him with endearments would have made her too vulnerable. 'But you are a man,' she said. 'You are a great lord. You can have your pick of women. Surely you have eased yourself along the way – it is what men do in war.'

He pressed his hips forward again. 'Why would I drink water when I can have mead?' He nibbled her throat.

'Because you are thirsty,' she said with asperity.

'Not that thirsty.'

'Do not tell me you have been chaste . . . Men are never chaste.'

He shook his head. 'I am telling you the truth. Some men find release through women, some through drink. For others the fighting and killing itself is an outlet for what is inside them. My desire is a safe home with music and company and good governance with a contented wife and children at my feet. Why would I waste my substance elsewhere, when all my wherewithal is here with you?'

Aoife's bones melted. After the first rush of lust, this was the sweetness. To have him say such words to her and to voice her dearest wish as his own. For family, for safety, for the peace to make music. She drew him down to her and without speaking kissed him again.

Raymond climbed to his own bed loft and flopped down on his pallet. His stomach was sour and heavy with the wine he had consumed. Aoife's singing, rather than soothing his soul, had torn open a patched wound. Throughout the recent battle campaigns he had been at the forefront, bearing the brunt. Sometimes terrified but subsuming it with aggression, leading from the front and turning dire situations into triumphs. The clifftop at Dun Domhnall, the walls of Waterford, and after that Dublin. He had become a talisman to his men. A battle commander who brought them to victory every time. But when the drink broke down the barriers, and when Aoife's voice pierced his heart, he had no shield from the dark places in his soul. All the things he had seen and perpetrated and done. He was exposed, and beyond that exposure dwelt a bitter resentment of Richard who could give the orders but had never faced the extremities as he had. And who now had a beautiful young wife with her ethereal, deadly voice.

Then there was Basilia. Gliding through life, reserved and calm, gown flowing as she walked. Tall, graceful and untouchable. His heart ached when he looked at her and to know she could never be his. Richard would not permit her to wed someone like him. A younger son, a leader of mercenaries.

Turning on his side, he curled his knees towards his chest like a child and wept – great tearing sobs that welled up from deep inside where a small boy huddled in the storm, just wanting someone to hold him. Badge whined and licked his face and Raymond held him and cried until he was empty, sore, and so exhausted that he tumbled into a wine-sodden slumber.

In the sobriety of morning daylight, the men went about their duties in suffering silence and found quiet things to do. Mending harness near the fire, tending to weapons, slowly eating a crust, eyes narrowed against the light. Aoife sat with her father on the dais while he ate some bread and drank a horn of weak ale. Both of them could see down the hall and observe the little knots of affinity between the men and what was happening, and in that way Aoife felt like an extension of her father and her father's power.

'I take it all is well with you and your Norman husband?' Diarmait said.

'Yes, Daidí, very well.' She gave a small, self-satisfied smile.

'Good. Perhaps now he is home you will soon be giving me grandsons, eh?'

She bit her lip. Bearing children was her duty to her family and to Richard, but children made a woman vulnerable. She would have to be constantly vigilant for their welfare and protection as well as her own. It was a rite of passage like her marriage and another hurdle to jump. 'Yes, Daidí,' she said again, not smiling now.

'Let us pray this winter season is a fruitful one for setting seed. I am not going to live for ever, and best for you to have sons of my blood in the cradle.'

She sent him a concerned look; she hated it when he talked of death, of not being there. 'You still have the high kingship to achieve,' she said. 'Look at all the gains we have made. You will live a long time yet.'

He exhaled down his nose. 'But not as long as I had when I was a young man. Time is running short, I can feel it in my bones.'

'It is just the melancholy of last night's drink in you speaking,' she said crossly. 'I will fetch my harp and play for you and we shall play chess.'

'If you want, daughter.' He gave her a weary smile.

Worried, Aoife went to her chamber to fetch her harp. As she was picking it up, Richard arrived and closed the door behind him, dropping the latch. He was white, every freckle standing out, and his jaw was clenched so tightly that his cheeks were grooved. He held a letter in his hand, the seal dangling.

Aoife was immediately alert. 'What's wrong?'

He sat down on their bed and gave her the letter. She looked at the seal and stiffened.

'The King has embargoed all ships from sailing to Ireland,' he said. 'There will be no trade and no supplies. Furthermore, he has seized my other lands and stripped my title.'

Aoife stared at the parchment and then at Richard, the shock a red-hot blade in her chest. 'He cannot do that; he has no right. They are your lands – and mine!' Her dower lands and her children's patrimony. 'You had his permission to come to Ireland and now he betrays his word. How dare he!'

Richard grimaced. 'I did not tell you . . . I kept it to myself, but as I was boarding the ship to Ireland, Henry sent a messenger forbidding me to sail.'

'What?' Aoife was appalled. 'Why did you not say so?'

'If I had not sailed the time would never have come again and I had already deferred twice because of the King's will. Your father's enemies whispered in the King's ear and told him you had been promised to me in marriage together with land and riches. Henry cannot bear to think of me succeeding in a place he has long coveted for himself.'

'You should have warned us!' She stamped her foot. 'It is my father's land, not yours or Henry's. You had a duty to tell me – and my father!'

Richard rose and faced her. 'Yes, in hindsight I should have spoken, but we have all been busy on campaign and until now I had . . . I was . . . The truth is that I put it from my mind. I was intending to write to Henry in the spring and smooth matters over.'

'And just when were you intending to tell me and my father?'

'Would it have made a difference?'

'Of course it would!' she spat. 'How can I trust you when you are not open? How can I rely on your judgement and your promises?'

He reached for her and she batted him away.

'Would you have had me turn back on the shore?' he demanded, his own temper rising. 'Where would you and your father be now if I had obeyed that summons? I made a mistake in not telling you, but I had no choice.'

She curled her lip. 'You will need to do something sooner than the springtime, my fine English lord.' Her fury was still sparking because she could see them being brought to ruin. If they had known, they could have acted. 'There are laden ships waiting in Bristol to sail for Dublin. There are fighting men to bring across, but how will they reach us now? The loss of shipping is hard enough, but the loss of your lands cannot be borne. It is not just your patrimony at stake, it is mine too!' She struck her chest with her fist. 'My dower rights. The rights of my children! All of that is threatened or even destroyed!' She wanted to attack him, to scratch out his eyes. 'How could you let this happen?'

'Aoife . . .' He grabbed her and held her fast, arms banded around her body as she fought to escape. 'Aoife, listen to me . . .'

'Why? What have you got to say that I would want to hear?' She kicked him in the shins and wrestled out of his arms, panting.

'Aoife . . . you are my wife,' he said with exasperation. 'I need your support. Be angry, rage at me for not telling you before, but do not turn away. We must be united in this. I cannot fight back without you by my side.'

She bit her lip and tears filled her eyes as his words probed under her shield.

'I know I have let you down. I know the situation is difficult. But we must fight to win and we cannot do that with recrimination and division. If we go into the hall and you refuse to look at me, the men will wonder what has happened and they will lose their confidence. We must be united and show ourselves ready to take every difficulty in our stride. You need to stand strong for your father's sake too, because this could bring him down.'

Another jolt shot through her. She wanted to blame him all over again, but he was right. Without him they might be in a much worse bind – impoverished, exiled, or even dead. Yes, he should have told her, but Henry was the problem they had to resolve. She exhaled hard, letting her anger calm down, and puffed out on a sigh. 'You are right,' she said. 'We have to decide what to do. You must send someone to Henry – do not go yourself lest he imprison you. My father could go; he will know what to say and he was responsible for asking Henry's permission to recruit in the first place.'

Richard did not think the suggestion was either wise or indeed possible, for Diarmait was a sick man. 'We shall see,' he said. 'Let us all talk together first and decide what to do.'

When everyone had gathered to eat late in the afternoon, Richard rose from his chair at the high table. He wore his wedding tunic and Aoife was resplendent in an embroidered gown with gold ribbons in her dark hair. Richard raised his drinking horn and addressed the men. 'Some of you by now will have heard rumours that King Henry has banned ships from sailing between England and Ireland. Some of you may even have heard that my lands have been sequestered. What I say to you in truthful answer is that I am in negotiation with my liege lord regarding certain matters we did not have time to conclude before I embarked to come to King Diarmait's assistance. There is no cause for concern. We still have everything we have gained and we can look to our achievements with pride. I have brought you here, I have paid your wages and you have profited greatly from the summer and autumn campaigns. That success will continue. I give you my word all is well.'

Diarmait lurched ponderously to his feet. 'What my son-in-law says is true.' He waved his own drinking horn. 'We shall hold fast and continue making our preparations and when the spring grass grows green and lush, we shall be rich with cattle and booty!' He took a swallow from the horn and passed it to Domnall, who drank and passed it in turn, man to man, while fists banged tables and oaths were cried aloud, sworn in the red blood of wine.

When the meal was over, Diarmait convened his own circle of advisers together with Aoife, Richard and Richard's senior knights in a group at the high table to discuss Henry's letter and what they should do.

'It was always possible this would happen, and there is no point wringing our hands,' Richard said. 'We have no choice but to come to an arrangement with Henry – we cannot survive an embargo. Without my lands and title, I have no resources. If we try to placate the King, he will prevaricate and seek more. We must approach him with a strong stance and negotiate with diplomacy but without abasing ourselves. The resolution must satisfy honour on both sides. I would go myself but he may detain me, and then there is no room to negotiate.'

'Would he do that?' Diarmait cocked an eye.

Richard shrugged. 'He is more than likely to keep me at court and procrastinate. We need to probe his mood and find out what he wants without giving everything away ourselves.'

Diarmait snorted. 'I know what he wants. I have known since Aoife was a babe in arms. I have always said he would eat the world if he could.'

Richard sensed Aoife's eagerness in the way she leaned forward, lips a little parted. She wanted her father to go on their behalf, but Diarmait did not have the capacity. He would not fare well travelling to Normandy in winter. All he had done these last few weeks was sit by his hearth and rest his swollen leg. Besides, even if he went, he would act from the Irish side and all to his own advantage.

Raymond cleared his throat. 'I will go,' he said. 'I know how to speak and if you will lend me your authority, I will do my best.'

Everyone looked at the blond knight. Richard wondered if he could trust him. Hervey would have been his first choice, but then again Hervey was useful here: he had more experience of administration and a better rapport with the Irish. It couldn't be Diarmait, and he had no one else more suitable to send. 'Very well,' he said, rubbing his chin. 'You are my man. I trust you to put our case and do what you can. It is my life – all our lives. Do not betray us.' He looked round and received nods of agreement from the others, although Aoife was silent and a little purse-lipped.

'I surely shall not, sire,' Raymond said with sincerity, his complexion flushing. 'I shall bring back success if it is at all possible.' He stood up, but only to kneel to Richard, who clasped his hands between his and gave him the kiss of peace.

'I shall have letters written,' Richard said, 'and you can leave tomorrow at first light.'

'Raymond will do well for us, I think,' Richard said to Aoife as they prepared for bed. 'He is level-headed and firm of purpose. He will stand his ground.'

Aoife frowned. 'He pushed himself forward very quickly.'

'What is wrong with that? He is decisive and confident and I value that in a battle commander. It is better employment for him over the winter than kicking his heels waiting for the campaigning season to start. You have seen how he drinks in the hall of an evening with nothing to occupy him.'

Aoife thought Raymond would bear watching. He was clearly ambitious and would see this mission as a furthering of that ambition and favour. Who knew what he might say to Henry or what his agenda was? 'What if he drinks too much at King Henry's court?' Kneeling, she removed Richard's boots. 'You cannot afford for him to say the wrong thing while in his cups.'

'He won't, because he will be on duty,' Richard replied impatiently. 'His duty is everything to him, and he is loyal to me. He drinks to excess when he is off the leash but I have every faith he will stay sober for this.'

Aoife wrinkled her nose. She also thought Raymond would do his duty, but she was not as sure as Richard about his motives, and he would expect reward. He might be Richard's man, but he was not hers or her family's and her influence over him was tenuous. 'I still think you should have sent my father.'

Richard pulled her against him with amused exasperation.

'Your father is a great man, but it is better if one of mine argues my cause. Besides, the campaigning season has been hard on him and he needs to rest. Better to spend his time in the hall with you looking after him. Let a younger man turn his face into the winter wind while we weave policy at home.'

She gave him a pursed smile. 'You are trying to persuade me of something you have already decided.'

'But your father agrees. Do you think if he had been against Raymond going he would have let it happen?'

He laid his cheek against the top of her head and she leaned against him with a sigh. The matter had not resolved exactly as she wanted, but she could live with it, and she felt secure having him hold her like this while outside the winter wind howled at the shutters.

My lord and king, it was with your consent that I came over to Ireland in order to help your faithful liegeman who had so sworn to you, Diarmait, in the recovery of his rightful lands. Whatever lands therefore I have had the good fortune to acquire in this country either in right of Diarmait's patrimony, or from others, I consider to be owing to your gracious favour and I shall hold them at your free disposal.

Richard read the words with bitterness, but it had to be done. Once the document was sealed, he gave the folded parchment to Raymond together with a pouch of silver for the knight's expenses on the journey. 'God speed your mission. May you return with a fortuitous reply.'

'I shall do my utmost, sire.' Raymond bowed first to Richard and then to Aoife. His squire came forward with Badge on a leash. Raymond briefly fussed the dog's silky ears, before turning to Basilia. 'If it please you, my lady, of your kindness, I ask you to care for Badge while I am gone.'

Basilia blushed, but she took the leash from him, making sure their fingers did not touch. 'Of course, messire,' she said calmly. 'I wish you a successful mission and by God's mercy a swift and safe journey.'

'Thank you, my lady. I am in your debt.'

Aoife eyed the interplay thoughtfully. He might be a valued member of Richard's household, loyal and efficient, but even if Richard was prepared to trust him, she was not.

As Raymond left, Badge strained on his leash, barking, but Basilia fussed him and fondled him, before eventually picking him up, and bearing him like a wriggling child to the back of the hall.

26

Fearns, Leinster, Ireland, February 1171

Aoife lay on the bed amid a pile of winter furs, her hair a dark tangle, her body flushed with the pleasure of recent lovemaking. Gazing at her, Richard's heart filled with tenderness and feelings that were harder to pin down. His relationship with her was so different to the love and companionship he had experienced with Rohese. Aoife was unpredictable and challenging. She was often prickly and her fire was a flash, easily ignited, but that fire was also passion and her heart had an enormous capacity for powerful emotion, and that included love. She amused and entertained him, she filled him with fierce desire, protectiveness and pride.

He began reaching for his braies and she stroked his spine with a languid hand, making him shiver. 'Come back to bed,' she said sleepily.

He turned with a chuckle. 'When we were first wed you refused me when I said that to you,' he teased. 'You have changed your tune since then.'

She wrinkled her nose. 'If I have, it is your fault.'

'Because everything is always my fault, I realise that.' He made a sudden grab and pounced on her and they tussled, laughing amid the bedclothes. He tickled her, and she pinched him and rolled over to straddle his body, her eyes shining.

'My bright and beautiful Aoife,' he said tenderly. 'My wife, my joy, my tumult.'

Pulling her face down to his, he kissed her, and heavy warmth swelled in his groin, even though a short while ago he had thought he was finished. She laughed and moved teasingly upon him.

Outside a hunting horn sounded an arrival at the gates, faint but insistent, and Richard muttered under his breath. Moments later his squire knocked on their door and called through the wood, 'Sire, Raymond le Gros has ridden in.'

'Very well, I will greet him in the hall.'

Suddenly Richard's breath was short and his belly churning. The hard heat subsided. Aoife lifted herself off him, already gathering and braiding her hair while he grabbed for his clothes. He had been on tenterhooks awaiting Raymond's return for several weeks. His first thought was *Thank God*, but it was followed swiftly by a feeling of sick apprehension.

'Do not let him say anything until I arrive,' Aoife ordered as she scrambled into her shift.

'Yes, but make haste.'

She shot him an irritated look, but he was already out of the door.

Raymond was in the hall, crouching on the floor while Badge jumped all over him, licking his face and whimpering with excitement, Basilia looking on with a smile. On seeing Richard, the knight hastily stood up, straightening his cloak. His face was heavy with fatigue, and fine creases fanned from his eye corners.

'Sire,' he said, bowing deeply.

Richard clapped his shoulder in greeting. 'I am right glad to see you. We have been looking for you for several weeks now.'

'The weather has kept me from sailing, sire. I had to wait five days in Bristol before a ship could put to sea, and it was a choppy voyage.' His gaze briefly met Richard's before sliding away, and Richard's heart sank, for Raymond's response told him the news was not good.

'Come to the fire and I will summon everyone,' he said.

*   *   *

Raymond pushed his cup aside and clasped his hands on the crumb-scattered trestle. 'I did what I could,' he said. 'I represented you as well as I was able and I held to the truth. The King wanted to know everything we had accomplished and I told him without compromising your position. However, he delayed his judgement, which is why I have been so long. In truth, my lord, his mood was sour and the negotiations were difficult.'

Raymond's report was not what Richard wanted to hear but he remained impassive. Beside him, unwell and feverish, Diarmait loudly broke wind and the smell wafted across the board, giving the news the odour it deserved.

'There were other Irish at court,' Raymond continued. 'Men from the High King's court. They were dripping their poison into the King's ear all the time I was there, accusing you of blind ambition.'

Aoife gave an indignant splutter and Richard quickly put his hand over hers to silence her. 'Go on.'

'I swore you were loyal and I did not rise to the bait,' Raymond said proudly. 'The King is under great pressure and his decisions have been harsh to many. He said you may send him whatever you wish as proof of your loyalty.'

Richard frowned. 'What does that mean?'

'He is waiting to see what you offer before he goes further in this. He desires tribute and he is not setting a limit on that tribute.' Raymond opened his hands. 'I did what I could, but the King refused to move.'

'You are saying we are no further along than we were before?'

Raymond grimaced, plainly unhappy at being pushed into a corner and having to acknowledge defeat. 'No, sire, but the King wants you to make a worthwhile offer to change his mind. For the moment our situation is trivial to him.'

'Trivial?' Diarmait's voice had developed a dangerous growl.

Raymond looked round the board. 'Archbishop Thomas Becket is dead, murdered at the King's behest, and there is nothing else on his mind just now.'

Basilia gasped and put her hand across her mouth.

'What do you mean "murdered"?' Richard demanded.

Raymond took a long drink and sighed. 'While I was at the Christmas court, three bishops arrived from England – Archbishop Becket had excommunicated them for disobeying his will. The King lost his temper and accused his courtiers of allowing him to be humiliated because the Archbishop was doing just as he pleased.'

Richard raised his brows.

'Four of the King's knights took it upon themselves to cross the sea to England and then murdered the Archbishop on the altar steps of his cathedral. They broke open his skull with their swords and spread his brains abroad. The King stands under suspicion of ordering the death of his own archbishop and is suffering widespread condemnation.'

'He is damned then,' Aoife said flatly.

'Yes, Countess, there is talk of him being excommunicated.'

'The man has lost his mind,' Diarmait opined with a snort of disgust. 'There is nothing wrong with keeping priests in their place – indeed they should be – but choose your priest and choose the place.'

Richard was not surprised. It was just confirmation of a pattern. He did not doubt Henry's hand was behind Becket's murder, even though the man had once been his closest adviser and companion. He agreed with Diarmait. The Church needed to be managed but not by such savage means. 'I take it he has set aside the matter of the embargo and the confiscation of my lands while he deals with what has happened at Canterbury?'

'Yes, sire,' Raymond replied. 'Once we heard about the Archbishop's murder, it became the only business of the court.'

'Then we have no recourse but to wait and send again in a while,' Richard said heavily, wishing that just once the road could be clear and not strewn with thorns.

Richard sat by the fire in his chamber and poked the embers, thinking of the fires of hell. Aoife came to rub his shoulders. 'My love, we must soothe this situation,' she murmured. 'We cannot afford to raise the anger of such a tyrant – a man who would command the murder of his own archbishop.'

Richard hung the poker at the side of the fire and drew her round onto his knee, burying his face in her hair and inhaling the smell of herbs and smoke.

'He shall not get the better of us,' Aoife said.

'Yes, but we cannot fight him blade to blade; he has all the resources.'

'Then we should make him our ally,' she said practically. 'I would go to Henry myself if it were possible.'

Richard smiled grimly. 'You are brave to speak of walking into the lion's den, my love.'

'I have done it before and survived.' She tossed her head. 'He has murdered his archbishop and many will abhor him. It will have weakened his position and he will be looking for allies. We should seize the opportunity to support him.'

He was amusedly proud of her swift ability to see the political advantage in any situation, but he was also wary. She had the capacity to think in all manner of devious and opposing ways. Sometimes they were not entirely honourable, but he could not fault her instinct for survival. 'Ah Aoife, you are ahead of us all,' he said and, kissing her tenderly, took her to bed.

27

Fearns, Leinster, Ireland, March 1171

Aoife stood at her chamber window sniffing the air. It was the middle of March, and the first signs of spring were brightening the days. The new lambs born of the ewes brought over from Striguil before the embargo were springing at their mothers' sides. Trees were swelling with bud and the air smelled green. Although the weather was still often cold and windy, winter was relinquishing its grip. Aoife laid her palm against her belly. Her flux should have come at the feast of St Bridget, but she had not bled. Now another month had passed; she had begun to feel nauseous at odd times of the day and her breasts were tender and swollen.

She knew the signs from observation and listening to the other women. She was pleased to be in tune with the season and to know she was fruitful, but she was afraid too. A baby would take away her present life and bring a very different one in its place with new obligations. She would no longer be the child, but the mother responsible for a child. Well and good if they had peace, but in times of strife, if Richard was absent, or unable to protect her, she would have to fight for that infant's survival as well as her own.

She was keeping her knowledge to herself, although she knew the maids and her mother must be suspicious because she had not bled. It was too soon to make a public announcement. When the child quickened and began to kick inside her, then she would speak. Things did not have to change today.

She turned from the window and left the chamber to join her father in the hall where he was dozing by the fire swathed in furs. An unpleasant smell hung around him composed of sour breath and suppuration from his bandaged leg and she had to swallow her nausea.

Richard was at the far end of the hall, holding his own court, and she was strongly aware of her role as a link between the two sides, Irish and Norman, like a gold chain binding them together as the child would bind them too. When he glanced her way she smiled at him, making a conscious effort not to put her hand to her belly. Trying not to inhale too deeply, she filled her father's horn with mead and sat at his feet to play her harp for him. For a time, he listened, turning now and again to talk to others, but there was nothing worth overhearing.

Presently he leaned down to her as she was adjusting a tuning peg and laid a heavy hand on her shoulder. 'Come,' he said softly in her ear, 'you can tell your old father the truth and I will not spread the news. Are you with child?'

Aoife stifled a gasp and covered her confusion by being even busier with her harp. 'How . . . ?'

'You have spent plenty of time this winter between the sheets with that husband of yours doing more than sleeping! A winter sowing and autumn's harvest, eh?'

'I do not know for sure, but it seems possible,' she answered in a low whisper. 'But you are not to go spreading rumours!' She reached back to tug his beard sharply and he gave a rumbling laugh.

'Does your man know?'

'Not yet, I want to be sure. It is too soon.'

'Ah, so I am the first.' His voice was rich with satisfaction. 'It will be a boy, undoubtedly.'

She scowled at him in warning. 'Keep it to yourself,' she reiterated. 'I shall be angry if you do not.'

'On my oath,' he said, signing his breast, but he was grinning.

Exasperated, she bent to her harp but was distracted by a commotion as two of Diarmait's guards burst into the hall.

'Sire, sire, the High King's men are here – an army!' one panted.

On the instant Diarmait threw off the cloak of sick old man and became a warrior ready to defend his hall. Pushing to his feet, he began yelling commands and brusquely ordered Aoife and the women and children to retire. Richard and his men were already heading for the door, grabbing shields and buckling on swords. Her father joined them, and even if he was limping, he still moved at speed.

Aoife accompanied the women, but she was impatient with them for they were like a huddle of squawking poultry. She felt sick with fear, but pushed herself beyond it, and gathering the children around her she began to tell them a story in song, as much to steady herself as them. Whatever was happening outside, it was too late to run.

When Richard and Diarmait reached the palisade gate, it became clear that the 'army' was either a large raiding party or a reconnaissance force, not big enough to pose a major threat, although of sufficient size to defend itself from attack. Richard's anxiety diminished, but he sent Raymond and a contingent of men to fortify the gate.

The warriors approaching the gate wore fine clothes and the light gleamed on their armour and weapons as though they were part of a parade. They showed no desire to attack. One man carried a large staff resembling a crosier, although he was not a priest. A two-wheeled cart rumbled behind the riders, pulled by a sturdy horse. The group drew rein out of arrow range and the warrior with the staff rode forward, brandishing it on high before striking it on the ground, making his horse turn and dance.

'Diarmait of Leinster, you perfidious traitor!' he bellowed. 'You have broken your word to your lawful king – a law you swore to obey on pain of forfeit. Here now is the harvest of your wickedness. Take back your son! Take back your kinsmen! And may your own head roll if you break your word again!' He gave a peremptory signal and one of the warriors whacked the pied horse on the rump, sending it at a gallop towards the gate. At the same time, several round missiles flew from the enemy lines and thudded into the ditch. The warrior reined around and the party rode away at a fierce gallop.

Richard's gorge rose as he realised that the objects catapulted into the ditch were human heads and that the cart was laden with a grisly cargo of blood-stained, decapitated bodies. The gate was opened and Raymond ran to grab the horse's reins and bring the cart into the compound, patting the animal's sweating neck. Domnall led a party to retrieve the heads from the ditch. Richard quickly ordered his own men to keep a quiet, respectful distance, for the situation was volatile and the Irish might decide their foreign allies were the reason for this tragedy.

'These people . . .' Hervey said, and broke off to palm his face.

Diarmait's warriors lifted the bodies from the cart, still loose and warm, and laid them in a row on the ground. Domnall came, a stained linen ball in his hands, and unfolding the fabric, removed Connor's head. Tears streaming down his face, he gently placed it at the top of his half-brother's body. 'Sixteen years old,' he said in a raw voice. 'He was sixteen.' Leaning over, he kissed the pallid brow.

Diarmait gazed at the row of dead young men, but remained standing for had he knelt he would have been a felled tree. 'This shall not go unavenged.' His voice was strangled on grief and rage. 'I will not stop until they are all dust in my fist, poured out upon the dung heap. Cover his face!' Turning away, he limped back towards the hall. Moments later the wailing began as the news reached the women.

Richard ordered his men to the armoury to sort weapons and

look as if they were busy while staying out of the way, and turned with the intention of intercepting Aoife, but she was already running towards the bodies ahead of everyone else, skirts flying.

'No!' she screamed. 'No!'

'Aoife . . .' He stepped across her path, but she pummelled her way past him, and stopped abruptly before the rowed corpses. When he tried to grab her again, she fought him off. 'No, I don't want you!'

'Leave us,' Môr shouted at him, wild-eyed. 'Go away. This is not your business, Norman!'

Aoife dropped to her knees at Connor's side, and removing the linen cover from his face, stared at him, shaking her head, before letting out a heart-rending wail that flashed through Richard's bones, for never had he heard such pain. It was elemental, savage and wild, and he could do nothing for her but let it run its course. He was sickened, and through that sickness felt smirched and dirty, for with Connor dead, Aoife was now Diarmait's sole legitimate heir.

The bodies were washed in clean water and sewn into linen shrouds. Môr performed her duty to prepare her only son for burial, her howls of grief muting to soft keening. Aoife dealt with Connor's clothes – the saffron shirt, darker-coloured trews, and a fringed, patterned hood. Using a small knife, she split the seams in the hem of the tunic and removed the gems and coins concealed in there. A small fortune, but what was a fortune compared to her brother's life? She looked at his pale body as her mother washed it in rose water. The legs that had run so strongly with hers through the fields. The hands that had pulled her hair and held hers as they swung each other in play. His familiar face now pallid and alien, the light extinguished. A head, like those with which her father had dressed his hall.

Fresh tears spilled from her hot, sore eyes and ran down her face. The wild grief had burned itself out, but a tender spot bled in her soul. She put her hand to her belly, to the baby that was barely conceived, and safe for the moment – for as long as she was safe. To bring a child into a world such as this. To bear a son and have him die like this. What a pointless waste, and yet all of them were forced like prisoners to continue down this road. Anger boiled inside her, churning with a fresh wave of grief.

The bodies were borne in solemn procession to the church and laid before the altar. A cold smell of the slaughterhouse pervaded the atmosphere. Aoife stayed close to her mother, head bowed in prayer, and avoided Richard's gaze because she was too overwhelmed to deal with him at the moment. Her father stood broad and tall in the face of tragedy, shrugging off his sickness to provide example and leadership. Defeat and setback had only ever put fire in her father's soul and it burned there now, harsh and hard. If he suffered remorse for sending Connor to his death, it was without self-pity.

When they left the church to the monks, a sea of candles blazing around the bodies of the sacrificed young men, Diarmait walked at Aoife's side, drawing her close, and she sensed he was doing so for his own comfort as much as hers. 'I shall not let anything happen to you, precious girl,' he said. 'You are my comfort now, and my last resort. You carry our hopes – you have never been dearer to me.'

She wanted to lash out and wound him by asking how dearly he had loved Enna and Connor, but she bit her tongue, saving her wrath for High King Ruari and Tiernan ua Ruari who had brought this torment to their door.

She was setting meal places at the high table when Richard came to speak with her. She had seen him in the chapel, but had ignored him, indeed had even felt a trace of hostility towards him for being some of the reason for Connor's death. It was not rational, but it was part of a melange of pent-up emotion.

She placed the dish of polished elm with a chased silver rim precisely on the white cloth in the position of honour at her father's right-hand side. Then came a knife in a leather sheath with a bone hilt, and an embellished drinking horn. 'These were Connor's,' she said flatly. 'It is the last time they will ever be used.'

'You do him fitting honour,' he said gently.

She lowered her gaze and continued with her arrangement, fiddling with the position beyond need. He set his hand over hers, stopping her motion. 'You are loved dearly, even if you do not know it at this moment or will not accept it.'

Aoife's chest was so tight, she could barely breathe. She put her other hand to her mouth and bit down on the fleshy side of her palm, concentrating on the pain. 'You do not understand.'

'Then tell me.'

She shook her head; she did not understand either, except that it was unbearable.

'I am here,' he said. 'Honour the dead, mourn them, but in God's name, do not cut off the living.'

She nodded jerkily. God had nothing to do with this.

'What is done cannot be undone. We have a future to make that we can mould as we choose and make a difference. If we are to continue, we have to bring good out of bad. We must mourn, but we must go forward.'

He drew her against him. She resisted briefly and then crumpled, clinging to him, digging her fingers into his arms, her body shuddering. He held her and rubbed her back, and at last she drew away, sniffing, and wiping her eyes.

'You are right, we have to go on from this, for Connor's sake,' she said tearfully. Avenging him was one strand but living for him was another. Her brother was dead, but she had a new life to nurture, and she was determined her child would never be sacrificed to the political whim of others.

'You should go,' she said. 'I want to finish this myself.'

He thumbed away her tears. 'When you are ready,' he said, and walked away.

That night, Aoife sat down on the bed beside Richard, took his hand and put it on her womb. She managed to smile at him although she was afraid. Telling him would make it real, but with Connor gone he had to know so he could protect their unborn baby. 'You are to become a father,' she said. 'That is why I was so upset today. I am afraid for our child.' Her voice cracked again.

Richard gazed at his hand on her belly, and then put his other arm around her and drew her close. 'I know you are grieving and worried,' he said, 'but you need not be afraid. We are blessed and I will do everything to protect you and keep you safe. You are mine and I love you, my beautiful, clever wife, and this is the best news you could ever have bestowed on me. When will the child be born?'

His fingers were warm and she liked the feel of them against her skin. 'Near the end of the year, perhaps at the time of Samhain.'

He kissed her softly. 'I care not whether it be a son or daughter, only that it be strong and healthy. Am I the first to know?'

She climbed into bed and he joined her. 'My father asked me today when I was sitting with him before . . .' Her voice stumbled. 'Before Connor came home. Somehow, he knew. He wanted to announce it in the hall but I told him I wanted to be sure first, and that you must know, but Connor's loss changes everything. We should announce it soon because it will give us all hope and a way out of this.'

'I agree. Arrange it as soon as you wish, my love.'

He blew out the bedside candle and drew her against him, holding her close, and she wept again in the dark for Connor and for their unborn child and the uncertainty they faced.

*　　*　　*

A week after Connor's funeral, the hall was bright with a blaze of extra lamps and candles. The days had begun to lengthen and the evening sky was a woven blanket of soft pink and gold, shading to purple on the horizon over the palisades. Diarmait raised his drinking horn to the gathering of kinsmen, knights and vassals, Irish and Norman. 'A toast to my daughter who has brought me the glad news she is with child and will bear me a grandson before this year is out! And to my son-in-law, a man of great prowess wherever he plants his standard!'

Cheers and shouts ensued, and some bawdy laughter. Men hammered the table with their fists and sent around the mead jugs. Aoife looked down modestly as befitted her situation, but she managed to smile, and even found herself enjoying the attention despite the undercurrent of deep grief lingering in the hall. Her father's acknowledgement emphasised to others her importance as his heir and the continuation of his line.

As the spring advanced, Aoife's pregnancy gave Diarmait a new lease of life. The sores continued to weep and ulcerate on his leg, but he still went out to watch the men train and to roar advice. He was busy planning his revenge against Ruari ua Connor and Tiernan ua Ruari, but he needed Richard's men for the task and Richard was hampered by the continuing embargo from England and the lack of revenue and supplies from his earldom.

'I am sending to Henry again,' Richard told Diarmait. 'Hervey is going this time.'

Diarmait snorted with contempt. 'Sure, and your uncle has a silver tongue, but do you think he will succeed where your battle captain did not?'

'What else am I to do?' Richard demanded. 'I shall offer Henry my allegiance as his vassal and pay a fine to allay his ire. Hervey is a courtier with experience of the world, and I can better spare him on the battlefield than I can Raymond.'

Diarmait curled his lip. 'You had best get it sorted then, lad, because the swallows will soon be here and the grass is full green.'

Two days later Hervey departed for the Norman court bearing gifts for Henry of a pair of fine Irish hawks and several illuminated books, and a letter of assurance.

'I am depending on you to find a way forward,' Richard told him.

'Do not worry,' Hervey replied, giving Richard his customary reassuring smile as he mounted his horse. 'All will be well.'

Raymond watched Hervey and his entourage ride away, his flint-grey eyes narrow. 'The King is a hard man to please,' he remarked.

'Indeed, but after what happened at Canterbury, perhaps he has had time to reflect and become more amenable. I am willing to negotiate, but I must know where I stand.' *And hope it is not in the same position as before.* He could see the same thought reflected in Raymond's eyes, although the knight forbore to comment.

Returning to the hall, Richard found Basilia talking to a priest about provision of alms for the poor. Raymond bowed to her and she responded with a slight incline of the head, pink colour filling her cheeks.

'Where is Aoife?' Richard asked.

'Sitting with her father – his leg is troubling him badly this morning,' Basilia answered neutrally. Her relationship with Aoife was managed mostly through lukewarm tolerance and general evasion. No sisterly bonding had developed between them for they were very different in their ideas and behaviours. Richard was the only thing they had in common, but he was a battleground rather than a source of unity.

Richard raised his hand in acknowledgement and continued to his father-in-law's chamber. Diarmait lay on his bed, both legs raised on cushions while Aoife bathed his brow with a herb-soaked cloth.

'Hervey has set out to the King,' Richard said, 'and Raymond is assembling a patrol. I am sorry to see you sick again when you were only on a horse two days ago.'

Diarmait snorted in disgust. 'I would still be on a horse now if I could. Priests and women, they fuss too much. I am only resting this morning to please my daughter now she is with child. I would not indulge her otherwise.'

'Of course not.' Richard colluded with the lie while exchanging a glance with Aoife above Diarmait's head. He could feel the fever-heat emanating from Diarmait's body and he was worried, for without him to manage the Irish faction and retaining their support, governing these lands would be twice as difficult. 'I hope to see you recovered and sitting in the hall tomorrow night.'

Diarmait made a wry face. 'You will be fortunate, my boy.'

'I hope God is bountiful and I will have prayers said for you.'

'As you wish,' Diarmait replied, 'but there are better ways of spending your coin than giving it to a priest.'

'Sons,' Diarmait muttered. 'Where are my sons?'

Aoife had been sitting at her father's bedside, falling asleep in her chair, barely leaving him lest his soul slip its anchor while she was not on guard. The fire of activity that had burned through him after Connor's death had consumed him rapidly and as the days lengthened into full spring, he had grown increasingly weak. For three days he had not risen from his bed; the sores on his leg were angry and suppurating. His skin was hot to the touch and his breathing harsh. He was often delirious, speaking in riddles of fire and blood and battle.

'Domnall is in the hall with Richard,' she said. 'Enna is at prayer in the abbey. Do you wish for them?'

He shook his head. 'No, there will be time for them later. You are the one at my side, Aoife, you are the one who does not leave me.'

'And I shall not, Daidí, I swear.' She took his huge hot paw in hers. 'You rest and get better. I saw a swallow this morning;

they are here just as always. Shall I arrange to have your bed brought to the window?'

'Aye, that would be a fine thing, girl – to die with the light in my eyes.'

'But not yet, Daidí,' she said with anxiety bordering on panic. 'You still have so much to do.'

He gave a rusty laugh. 'No, girl. That is for you and that husband of yours to accomplish as my heirs. I am soon going to be finished with this world. Bring me a drink, the sweetest mead. I would taste it again while I can.'

Going to a small flagon on the coffer, she poured the last of its contents into his drinking horn, the light through the window glinting it to liquid gold.

'You will be all right whatever happens when I am gone,' Diarmait said hoarsely. 'I remember well the day you were born into the world with all the morning light around you. You are mine and you will survive. I will continue in you and your children. Always ask yourself what I would have done, and that way I will always be with you.'

She helped him sip the mead and wiped the drips from his beard. She refused to think of him gone from her life.

'Remember that asking yourself is only the first step after all, but whatever you choose, be certain, and have a whole heart.'

The end of April was soft and green. The grass was lush and the new calves were suckling at the udder. Cheese and butter making had started again, and in between tending to her father, Aoife was busy supervising in the dairy.

She tried to make Diarmait eat and drink; she played her harp and told him stories to lift his spirit and keep him in the world; but although she denied it, her heart knew the truth.

She no longer had him to herself. Everyone gathered in his chamber to pray, to say their farewells and bear witness. Waiting. Playing chess, talking among themselves. Guards stood at the door but they could not prevent death from entering the room and approaching the bed. Lorcan had just received Diarmait's confession and absolved his sins. Abductions and rapes, destruction and carnage. All swept clean away.

Propped up on numerous pillows, Diarmait turned weakly towards Richard. 'Take care of my grandchild,' he said, 'and beget many more with my daughter. I will not be here to see the line pass on but it is my will it goes through her.'

Richard looked Diarmait directly in the eyes. The deep sea-green was muddy and dark. Diarmait's dying would put them in grave danger; their enemies were already circling like wolves. 'Sire, I shall ensure it comes to pass. For your sake and for mine, but mostly for love of Aoife and because it is right and just. Neither your land nor your honour will be lost to your family, I swear. I will defend and protect them with my life.'

'I hold you to that, my boy. Through marriage to Aoife you are my son as verily as a son born of my seed.' He tried to raise his voice, but it was an ashy remnant of its former roar. 'I want all to witness this – that Leinster shall be ruled by my daughter and her husband and their line. So I willed when I was well in my hall, and so I speak now. This is my choice, for Enna is blind and Connor lies slain in his grave. Pledge your oath to my daughter and her man, for he has restored to us our land.'

After a long pause, Domnall stepped decisively forward and knelt at the bedside. 'I do so swear, my father,' he said, then turned and knelt to Aoife and Richard. 'I put my skills, my lands and my life at your disposal.'

Richard embraced him with relief, glad to see sincerity in his eyes, for Domnall was a solid backbone. He was no leader, he needed to be given direction, but within that direction he was staunch.

Aoife resumed her seat at the bedside and clung to the position with tenacity, refusing to move. Her mother remained to one side with the other women in the passive role of observer, counting her prayer beads and signing her breast. Aoife was the one coddling the fading spark of his life.

Watching her grip Diarmait's hand, tears spilling down her face, Richard wanted to draw her away but knew she would refuse – perhaps even turn on him. She was like a feral animal that would only come to his hand of her own will and he understood better now how to deal with her. Diarmait's death would be like an erosion for her, a massive chunk of cliff falling into the sea, and as that part of her life washed away she would need him as a bulwark.

The spring dusk of the last day of April closed in. Servants lit the candles and still Aoife clutched her father's hand, aware only of him despite the room being packed with witnesses. The people gathered beyond the bed were a distant blur.

'Daidí, can you hear me?'

'Aye, girl, I hear you.' His voice was the thinnest thread and he did not open his eyes although she could see their shine through his lowered lids.

She gripped his hand harder and thought she detected a twitch of response. She wanted comfort but he had none to give.

'Don't go, Daidí, I need you here with me,' she whispered. 'I want you to see your grandson.'

Her answer was silence. A breath. Another long silence, and this time it stretched for ever and the glint of the eyes under the sparse lashes was fixed on eternity. The hand in hers was flaccid and the chest was still. A little foam bubbled on his lips.

Panic seared through Aoife's heart. 'Daidí!' Uttering a hair-raising wail, she spread herself over his body.

As Lorcan made the sign of the cross over her father's still form, she understood the finality – that he was gone where she could not follow. She stumbled to her feet, her eyes blinded by tears, uncaring who saw her grief. Richard waited quietly nearby, his own eyes bright and full. Uttering another forlorn cry, she flung herself into his arms because her father's would never again hold her close and she was desperate for the solace, the protection, the love. She sobbed against his chest, and he held her fast as the storm tore through her. Diarmait had named them his heirs, but it did not mean everything was cut and dried, even if the men here had sworn to follow. Many more would be undecided and might renege their allegiance, and with Henry hostile, Richard was under no illusions how much danger they faced.

Diarmait was laid to rest in the grounds of the Abbey of St Mary at Fearns, beside Connor, and Richard prepared for war without resources from England, making do with what he had.

Strife blew in faster than a spring storm. Domnall had sworn for him and a handful of other Irish lords, but he had to quell rebellions in Waterford and Wexford. An attempt to retake Dublin by the displaced Norse under their leader Asculev had been thwarted by Richard's knight Miles Cogan, and Asculev had been beheaded on the riverside, but they were far from safe. The victory at Dublin had been a hard fight. There were few supplies to replenish the losses of equipment and fighting men, and Richard had somehow to reinforce Dublin against another attack. His spies reported that his enemies were conspiring together to make an assault. The King of Man had promised thirty ships to ring the port and prevent aid from arriving via the coast. To compound his troubles, Aoife's uncle Lorcan was sympathetic to the opposition because he feared the encroachment of the Norman Church on Irish territory.

Entering their bedchamber, Richard found Aoife mending a small tear in her chemise. Her belly curved with the gentle swell of mid pregnancy and her hair was a lustrous dark waterfall around her shoulders. Since her father's death, she had been quieter and softer than usual – less fiery and more affectionate. He enjoyed these moments of calm with her, even if people told him it was just the way of a nesting woman and not to take it for granted.

Tonight, he was sore-eyed with tiredness. He had spent most of the day consulting with his men, delegating, deciding what had to be done. Sending messengers. He had weighed up numerous different opinions and evaluated the situation through both Norman and Irish eyes. He was worried about Hervey's mission to King Henry. He needed the embargo lifting and it might already be too late.

Aoife finished her sewing and folded the chemise before facing him, her hand on her belly. 'I am coming with you to Dublin,' she announced.

Richard shook his head. 'I forbid it. We are heading into the teeth of war and facing the combined forces of the High King, Tiernan ua Ruari, and a Manx fleet. I will not place you and my unborn child in such danger.'

Her eyes flashed, and she was certainly not soft now. 'You think I will be in any less danger remaining here? If Dublin falls, they will come to Fearns and destroy us. My place is with you as my father's heir and bearer of his grandchild. It will concentrate the minds of the men and remind them why they are fighting.'

'You should go to England, to my mother, or my cousin.'

Aoife stood tall. 'I am the daughter of a king. This land is mine and this fight is mine even if I cannot wield the sword myself. My father brought you here and our union sealed the pact between the sword and the state. I will not be excluded. Or do you believe we will fail? Is that what you are saying? That you will let me down?'

Richard rubbed his aching temples. 'I need you to be safe and protected,' he snapped. 'I don't want to have my attention distracted worrying about you.'

'But if I am with you, you won't be distracted. My presence will make you concentrate on what you have to do. You will have to imprison me to prevent me from coming to Dublin, and then what will your position be in the eyes of my people?'

Richard inhaled to argue.

'Women are the peace weavers too,' she continued relentlessly. 'You might need me to speak with my uncle Lorcan. If you go without me, you are not taking your full resources. You will not change my mind.'

'You are a stubborn baggage, you know that?' he said with exasperation, all notion of thinking she had mellowed disappearing.

'Would you say that of my father? Would you say that to one of your men?' She curled her lip. 'I am your match. I may be your wife and I owe you my duty, but I am Lady of Leinster and just as surely you owe me your allegiance.'

The air between them sparked with tension, but from somewhere he found the control to draw back from the brink. 'An impasse is no use to anyone,' he said. 'I will bring you to Dublin as you ask, but do not set the blame on me if anything untoward happens – for I shall already have set it upon myself.' He pulled her roughly into his arms and gave her a crushing kiss to which she responded in kind, digging her fingers into his upper arms, telling him without words that whatever the means of communication she was his equal and more, and she would never back down.

28

Dublin, Ireland, summer 1171

Basilia sat down beside Aoife in the chamber where Richard's inner council had gathered to discuss business. 'We have enough resources remaining for two more weeks. After that we shall have to start slaughtering the horses.' She spoke calmly, without emotion. 'Eventually, and sooner than later, they will starve us out.'

Dublin had been under siege for a month; they had been surrounded soon after they arrived. Manx ships blockaded the river, and on the other side they were surrounded by the High King's army, including the host of Tiernan ua Ruari. They were here in their thousands, and vastly outnumbered Richard's troops.

Richard folded his arms. 'But even now they dare not attack,' he said. 'Our reputation keeps them at bay.'

'For how much longer?' Raymond retorted. 'In two weeks' time our situation will have deteriorated and I am not prepared to eat my warhorse. Are you? Whatever our choice, we must make it now.'

Richard rubbed the back of his neck.

'Send for my uncle Lorcan,' Aoife said. 'He will mediate.'

'Your uncle helped to bring this down upon us in the first place.'

'His interest is the Church,' she said impatiently. 'He may not like your presence here, but he will negotiate with the High King if that is what must be done.'

'We are not going to receive succour from King Henry within

the next two weeks, are we?' said Maurice of Prendergast. 'Even if your uncle succeeds in resolving the situation with him, it is too late. We must fend for ourselves.'

Richard grimaced. Their choice was stark and had to be made soon. Negotiate their way out of this or fight. Both bore great risk. He was still annoyed with himself at allowing Aoife to come to Dublin because they had no escape. 'I will fight if I must,' he said, 'but first let us see what negotiation can accomplish. Let us find out what the High King wants. From what I have seen and the reports I hear, he is a cautious man who will not commit unless he must or the odds are greatly in his favour. He is like a miser who collects a hoard of gold but refuses to spend it unless forced.'

'Tell him he can have Dublin in exchange for the head of Tiernan ua Ruari and see what he says,' Aoife said with a cynical curl of her lips.

When her uncle Lorcan arrived, Aoife presented him with a silver chalice of wine as she had done all those years ago as a little girl. Lorcan ignored it but gave her the kiss of peace on either cheek. 'Daughter, you should not be here,' he said with a troubled frown and a censorious look for Richard. 'This is no place for you.'

'It is the only place as my father's heir, and at my husband's side, lending him my authority for me and our offspring,' she responded firmly, folding her hands over her belly, showing him the obvious swell. 'Nothing is more fitting than that.'

He gave her a shrewd but still disapproving look. 'Even so, it is no fit place for you. Be that as it may, I am here to broker peace between yourselves and the High King, and see if it is possible to avoid slaughter, for there has been a surfeit in recent times.' He gazed pointedly at Richard's knights.

Richard said: 'Tell the High King I am willing to do homage to him for the kingdom of Leinster if he will lift his siege and agree peace between us.'

'I will tell him so, but he will want more,' Lorcan replied with a hostile edge to his voice.

Aoife lifted her chin. 'As my father held Leinster of him, so now do I hold it for my family. Would he deny us our right? Why has he come to Dublin to make strife? Does he fear us so much?'

Aoife's charisma raised the hair on Richard's nape as she answered her uncle. His young wife had donned her father's mantle, and watching her grow into it filled him with admiration and misgiving.

'Any head of a household would fear wolves at large,' Lorcan said.

'I desire peace from this,' Richard answered with quiet steel. 'I would rather not it be the peace of the grave and so I am willing to negotiate. My position is as stated and I will know what the High King has to say.'

Lorcan gave him a narrow look but inclined his head. 'I will take your proposal to him and return with his answer.' He rose to his feet and departed, punctuating each stride with a strike of his crosier against the floor.

Lorcan returned near dusk and was ushered into the hall with tense courtesy. He accepted wine and a seat at the high table, where he opened a leather wallet and placed a sheet of parchment on the cloth.

'You may read as you wish,' he said to Richard. 'I can tell you that the High King will accept your allegiance, but he refuses you Leinster. He is willing to cede you Wexford, Waterford and Dublin. You took those towns from the Norse, and you may hold them as they did. That and no more. Accept and have peace or decline and have the King storm the city. He refuses to guarantee the safety of any within these walls, including the non-combatants.' He flicked a glance to his niece and Basilia.

Richard maintained a neutral expression. 'And you, my lord

Archbishop, will you guarantee their safety as a man of the Church?'

'I shall do what I can, but I make no promises when I think of what happened the last time this city was stormed.' Lorcan sent Raymond le Gros a stony look. 'In the face of overwhelming blood lust, the Church has no recourse except to prayer, with the knowledge that the Almighty will judge at his throne. I have spoken of mercy to the High King, but he will do as he sees fit – as is the wont of kings.'

'Then tell him we shall debate his terms among us, and he shall have his answer soon.'

Lorcan finished his wine and eased to his feet. 'It was an evil day when Diarmait brought you to our land and twined his line with yours. But I must care for the souls of all and I will do what I can . . . we are all God's children and in God's name, take his terms.'

A heavy silence followed his departure. Eventually Richard cleared his throat. 'Now we know where we stand.'

'Did you notice the way he was taking stock of everything?' Raymond demanded. 'He will report all he has seen to the High King.'

Richard shrugged. 'He might, although he strikes me as having a will of his own and he knows this place well enough to make a report without having to mark it in this moment. Ruari thinks we have no choice but to submit because we are running out of supplies – he has enough spies without using Lorcan.'

'We should take the fight to them,' Raymond said. 'They will not be expecting it and they will not stand to face us for they know our capabilities on the battlefield. That is why they have hesitated so far. They are waiting for us to weaken further. There are more of them, but it matters not to our warriors. Most of the corpses I see after a battle belong to our enemies – face down in retreat. I say we take on the High King and bring him down.'

'I agree,' Richard said. 'It was my thought also. Tonight, make sure every man has full rations and that the horses are well rested.'

Aoife lay in bed, tired but unable to sleep. The men were busy with the morrow's battle plans, but she had retired because the talking was over. Her survival depended on whether Richard and his men succeeded tomorrow. They had proven themselves against the odds time and again, but at some point, she feared they would fail. Enna had been blinded and sent mad, Connor beheaded. What would Ruari do to her and her unborn child if Richard failed? They had to win this battle, and she was not sure they would.

The baby was awake too; she could feel its limbs fluttering inside her womb. She loathed being vulnerable, and even admitting to it was a weakness. Turning over, she pushed the sheet off her body with her feet and through the open shutters watched a ripe summer moon sail the blue-black sky. There was no breeze to disperse the heat that had accumulated during the day. Airless, sticky, hot.

Outside their chamber she heard Richard murmur to his squire and then open the door, dropping the latch gently behind him. She felt rather than heard him tip-toe to the bed and then the dip in the mattress as he sat down and started to disrobe. Rolling over, she placed her palm against his spine, making him jump

'I thought you were asleep.'

She wanted to ask how he thought she could sleep knowing he was going into battle next day, but she bit her tongue. 'I was waiting for you.'

'Well, I am here now.' He kissed her damp neck and put his hand on her belly. Aoife buried her face against his chest and drew in his scent. 'And I will be here tomorrow night, God willing.'

But what if God was not willing? She pushed it away. 'I hold you to that. Do not dare make me a widow and your child fatherless.'

'I will do my best in God's hands.'

He kissed her again, once on the lips, and once on her womb. Aoife dug her fingers into his hair and squeezed her eyes tightly shut to contain her tears.

Aoife and Basilia stood on the city walls to watch the men ride out at a rapid trot, making haste so that Ruari and Tiernan would not have time to realise what was coming at them. Miles Cogan, a doughty fighter, led the first group out of the gates followed by Raymond le Gros in the centre with Aoife's half-brother Domnall and Maurice of Prendergast. Aoife noticed how Basilia's eyes were fixed on Raymond astride his powerful grey.

Bringing up the rear, Aoife saw Richard upon Ajax, the red and gold chevron banners wafting above his household knights, and her heart turned inside her with pride and fear. Six hundred men facing six thousand. A handful of Normans and Irish remained behind to defend the city, but essentially every capable fighting man was committed to this all-or-nothing gamble.

When the last rider had vanished beyond a falling trail of dust, Aoife left the walls and walked with Basilia to the cathedral, her lips moving in silent entreaty to God and the Holy Virgin.

Richard's small force crossed the river at the shallows of the Finglass ford and rode swiftly through the summer heat, making a wide circle around Ruari's main camp at Castleknock. Scouts rode back and forth, keeping the commanders informed of the state of the enemy's movements.

'Sire,' Philip of Prendergast, Maurice's son, reported, joining Richard, 'the Irish king is bathing and sporting in the river with his bodyguard; no one is armed or ready for a fight. There are perimeter guards, but they are not on alert.'

Richard smiled grimly. Ruari was expecting him to hide behind Dublin's walls and was supremely confident he had the upper hand. It would not have entered his head that so small a number would ride out to take him on. 'All the better to pay them a visit.'

He sent his orders through the line. No delay, no announcement, no hesitation. Just hit them with everything as hard and fast as they could. No ransoms, no quarter.

Gathering the reins in his left hand, he gripped a javelin in his right. His heart was galloping in his chest, but his mind was steady and cold. They would either succeed or they would die, and he wanted this more than Ruari did. That was why Ruari was cooling himself in the river while Richard rode an army straight into the heart of his camp.

Richard's force struck the Irish position like a sudden thunderstorm through a field of wheat, and although greatly outnumbered, so swift and unforeseen was the attack that it caused utter devastation. Robert de Quency planted Richard's battle standard outside the High King's own tent as the rallying point for their troops. Swords slashed, hammers smacked down, and spears rammed into flesh. The Irish fled in panic, most clad in no more than shirts and linen breeches, and were ridden down and trampled as they tried to escape. Richard spurred Ajax to the river where he and his knights were greeted by a small band of Irish warriors, lightly armed with spears and shields. Richard reined about, came in sideways, and hurled his javelin into their midst, followed by a second one, bright point flashing. The Irish fell back before the onslaught, and beyond them Richard saw a white-haired man whipping a dappled grey horse along the bank edge. He wore a red cloak, but beneath it Richard could see his pale buttocks bouncing up and down as his mount galloped away. His bodyguard rode with him, brandishing spears and axes, but focused entirely on escape. Ruari ua Connor, High King of Ireland, was fleeing the field naked, his army scattering in disarray.

'Sound the recall!' Richard roared to de Quency as the Irish survivors fled towards the moors and bogs beyond their camp. It was foolish and profitless to pursue individuals and the Irish knew the terrain better than they did. Ruari's baggage was theirs, stuffed with enough supplies to replenish Dublin's empty undercrofts. Fifteen hundred Irish corpses littered the camp by the riverside – more than twice the number of Richard's army.

Richard's commanders gathered around the chevron banner at Ruari's tent. De Quency's squire had discovered a cask of fine Rouen wine and Raymond, his face blood-freckled, presented Richard with a brimming cup. 'To the victors the spoils!' he cried.

The vessel was decorated with coils of gold interlacing studded with garnets. Richard drank deeply, until the wine ran down his chin. 'Behold, I drink from the High King's cup!' he roared, thrusting it aloft. His men bellowed their approbation. 'They were ten times our number but we have scattered them like chaff! Yet again we have proven our mettle against far greater odds. Men shall speak of our deeds for years to come, as will our children and our grandchildren's children. I am proud of all of you, and we shall go on to even greater renown and glory!' He waited for the roar to subside. 'Let the captains take and sort the plunder and let each man have his fair share in due course!'

Richard entered Ruari's tent and a shiver ran down his spine. Less than two hours since, this had been the preserve of a king; now no more than trampled grass and plunder under canvas. All the regalia was his to bring home to Aoife. How easily the wheel of fortune turned. One wrong decision, one moment of dropped guard, made the difference between having everything and having nothing. Between being alive and being dead.

Hands clasped, head bowed, Aoife prayed in the cathedral, begging God to keep Richard safe and bring him home to her unscathed. Chasing her prayer beads through her fingers, she repeated the same words in a constant litany, imagining them forming a shield around his body. Basilia knelt at her side, her own lips moving, and Aoife wondered for whom she prayed. At least they were united in their common purpose, for if the men did not prevail, their fate was sealed.

A young guard who had been posted outside the cathedral hastened up the nave to the women and, bowing, spoke swiftly in Irish to Aoife. 'My lady, there is news. I am bidden to tell you the Earl has won a great victory. The High King has fled for his life and his entire baggage and supplies are ours.'

'What does he say?' Basilia demanded, her gaze wide with anxiety.

'Richard has prevailed! He's won!' Aoife said, shaking with joy, with pride, with utter relief. She would not usually hug Basilia but she did so now, throwing her arms around her, weeping with relief, and Basilia clung back fiercely.

'Thank God, thank God, He has heard our prayers!'

'The Earl, is he unharmed?' Aoife demanded of the smiling soldier.

'Yes, Countess; we have very few injured and dead, but more than a thousand of the enemy lie on the field.'

For an instant, his words checked Aoife; some of those dead, even if they had intended her ill, were kin and Irish men. But she pushed it aside. What mattered was that they were saved, they had survived, and God had allowed them to carry the day.

The women hurried to the city walls. The sun beat down, the light intense after the soft shadows of the church. Aoife was breathless from the run and the child tumbled inside her belly as though running with her. She felt vindicated, for now she and her baby could have an illustrious future. She was determined to put on the best feast Dublin had ever seen to celebrate.

She sought more news but everyone was full of the victory and had none of the detail she craved but at last the returning army came into sight. Aoife narrowed her eyes, striving to glimpse Richard amid all the glitter and dust. Frantically she sought his banner, worried in case he was wounded. There! Her eyes lit on the red and gold of de Clare wafting in the throng and men cheering, their voices an ocean roar surrounding the standard. And then she saw Richard on Ajax, the stallion's coat dark as liver with exertion and creamed with sweat under the harness. Her heart was full and the baby continued to tumble in her womb, exulting with her.

She descended the battlements to go and stand alone in the castle doorway and wait for Richard. She drew herself to her full height, a small, dignified figure in the midst of the joyous turmoil, expressing her power in her stillness. Amid the milling horses and shouting men, she sent her will out to him to catch his attention. He had removed his helm and his hair clung to his scalp in sweat-soaked tendrils the same hue as his horse. As he dismounted, he met her gaze and their eyes locked. He gave his reins to his squire, strode over to her, and still in his full armour, knelt at her feet and took her hands.

'My wife, my countess, my queen,' he said, and his smile dazzled. 'I have done my duty as has been God's will and I bring my success to give into your keeping for us and for our heirs.'

Aoife swallowed hard. In kneeling to her, he had made her a public focus – the reason why these men had risked their lives. The move was politically astute and deliberately dramatic, but her heart still melted. She wanted to throw herself into his arms and weep her relief and pride on his chest, but she had her own role to play in the arena. She tugged on their clasped hands, indicating him to rise.

'My dear lord and husband, you have fulfilled your vow,' she declared, raising her voice. 'You have done more than your duty and you are honoured here among all who owe you their service and allegiance. And I honour you also.' In turn she knelt to him and kissed his hands to resounding cheers, demonstrating to all that she and Richard were two halves of one whole.

He raised her up, swept her into his arms and carried her inside to an increased roar from the crowd. Briefly alone behind the door, they kissed with passion.

'I knew you would come back,' she said breathlessly, 'but I never dreamed of so great a victory.'

'And I never dreamed I would see the King of Ireland fleeing with not so much as a saddle cloth between his bare arse and his horse. It's more than a defeat, it's a humiliation!' He laughed again and swung her round. 'All his baggage too. We have enough to live on for weeks!'

'We shall hold a great feast tonight and celebrate fittingly!' Her chest swelled with elation. 'If only my father was here to see this, and his father before him. They would be so proud – and vindicated.'

That night men raised brimming horns and goblets to the rafters to toast Richard's victory. The hoarded food and drink was distributed for they no longer had to ration it and was augmented by supplies from King Ruari's baggage train. Aoife played her harp and sang stories of the great Irish heroes, weaving Richard into them, and Richard continued to drink from Ruari's own gilded cup.

At the height of the celebrations, Maurice of Prendergast and Miles Cogan organised a parade of knights up the hall to the high table bearing Richard's chevron banner and fastened to the spear head the green laurel crown of a victorious battle commander.

Richard rose to accept their presentation, his eyes bright with emotion. Aoife took the wreath in her own hands and placed it on his head, and kissed him, overflowing with pride and triumph.

The toasts continued and the cheers and carousing grew more raucous as the men recovered from battle by celebrating the hot, vital life blood still flowing through their veins, while their enemies lay dead in the grass.

Basilia sat at Aoife's other side, clad in rose-coloured silk. She had drunk more wine than usual; her cheeks were flushed and an unguarded sparkle shone in her eyes, especially when she looked at Raymond le Gros. Raymond himself was watching Basilia the way men did when they had been fighting and were on the edge of control, drunk with the euphoria of victory, the memory of slaughter and survival as vivid in their minds as the blood of their last kill.

The dancing began but was too vigorous for Aoife. She trod one measure with Richard and enjoyed it, but he was flushed and his eyes were glittery, even though he was still steady on his feet. She deemed it time to retire, taking Basilia and the other ladies with her. 'Leave the men to their carousing,' she said. 'We want no more regrets in the morning than there have to be.' She sent a pointed look in Basilia's direction.

Basilia returned her glance with surprise. 'Are you saying it is dangerous for us to stay?'

'I am saying it is not wise,' Aoife replied. 'Especially for an unmarried woman. We might all be under Richard's protection, but he cannot be everywhere, and some men in their cups might take liberties if they think they have a chance.'

Basilia drew herself up. 'I hope you do not think I would encourage any man in such behaviour!'

'Of course not, but tensions after battle are wild – best not to set a spark to tinder, even if it is unintentional.'

Flushing, Basilia compressed her lips. Aoife said nothing more. She sat with the other women for a while and played her harp. Basilia went to sit in a corner by herself and by candle light stitched the long seam on a chemise she was making, while the other ladies played chess and dice.

Aoife could not relax for tonight was only a respite. As soon as the men had recovered from the feast, Richard would have to ride to Waterford to relieve Robert FitzStephen. Although they were celebrating a victory, they were not yet safe.

She had retired to her chamber but was still in her chemise when Richard arrived. He was drunk and unsteady, but not stupefied. Maurice of Prendergast and Robert de Quency helped him onto the bed, although they too were swaying and giggling. They bowed to her, lurching into each other, slurred their goodnights and wove from the room.

Richard struggled to sit up and made a clumsy effort to remove a shoe, before falling back with a laugh. Amused and exasperated, Aoife did it for him and unbuckled his belt, wondering what would happen if they were attacked now. He reached for her, but she evaded him, although not unkindly. 'I fear, my lord, you will be no good to yourself or to me tonight, and it will be a waste anyway – either you will not remember in the morning or you will have regrets if you do.'

'No regrets,' he said, and grabbed for her again, but he lacked the coordination and, giving up, flopped back, arms wide. 'Do with me what you will!'

Shaking her head, Aoife finished undressing him. She removed his hose, left his braies, and wrestled off his tunic. He managed to snatch hold of her for a moment and leaned his cheek against her womb.

'I have done what I said I would.' His voice quavered, seeking approval.

'Yes,' she said tenderly, stroking his head. 'You have, and I am proud of you.'

Removing his shirt, she gasped to see the bruises blooming over his arms and chest, and a lower one disappearing into his braies. He had said nothing earlier; had spent the evening acting as if nothing was wrong. She fetched a pot of salve and rubbed the ointment gently into the marks. How hard he had fought for this.

The pungent smell of marigolds filled the air and he groaned. Seeing his bruises made her realise anew how easily she could have lost him, and soon he was riding to Waterford to risk his life all over again.

She climbed into bed and lay down beside him, one hand on her womb, the other holding his hand, meshing it through hers.

* * *

Richard slowly opened his eyes. Someone appeared to have poured a thundercloud into the space between his ears. The light filtering through the shutters assaulted his eyes, and when he raised his hand to cover them he could barely lift his arm it was so stiff and sore. Stifling a groan, he tried to go back to sleep, but his bladder ached with the need to piss. Gingerly he sat up, propping himself against the pillows while he assembled the wherewithal to leave the bed and waited for his rolling stomach to settle. A faint herbal scent emanated from the pillow stuffing and he inhaled its clean astringency. His clothes were neatly folded on the chest at the bedside and his shoes placed underneath them and he knew he had not done that for he could not remember coming to bed.

A pot of salve stood on the coffer. He took it, sniffed the contents, looked at the finger marks in the grease and the bruises on his body, and assembled the evidence. Aoife was sound asleep beside him, her dark hair spilling across the pillow. He smiled and touched a dark strand, a tender pain in his heart. 'Without you, where would I be?' he asked, and thought of each decision in his life that had brought him to this place, and this woman, carrying his child. He leaned over to kiss her brow before quietly leaving the bed to relieve his swollen bladder, and then went in search of a tisane for his throbbing head.

Following a day's respite to recover from the battle and its aftermath, Richard set out to relieve Waterford, leaving Miles Cogan to command Dublin. Once more Aoife stood on the town walls to watch the men leave, and although Richard had won a great victory and rode with a laurel crown on his banner, she was still sick with worry and resentful that it was a woman's lot to wait, desperately thinking of ways to survive if it came to the worst. She watched until he was gone from her sight and then went first to pray and then to visit her uncle.

'The worst thing your father ever did was to bring these

Normans into our land,' Lorcan said grimly when she sat down with him. 'They will not stop until the Irish are trampled underfoot in the way that their ancestors trampled the English.'

Aoife shot her uncle a defensive look. 'What choice did my father have when Ruari ua Connor ran us into the sea? Or when the men of Dublin buried my grandfather with a dog to show their contempt? Like you I want peace – and so does Richard.'

'He has a strange way of showing it,' Lorcan scoffed. 'And even if he does, his soldiers do not, for they are here for land and plunder.' After a moment he sighed and kissed her forehead. 'It behoves you and your mother to set examples to all and encourage thoughts of peace and mercy while we bear our burdens the best we can.' He looked her in the eyes. 'This Norman warlord husband of yours – do you truly have more than duty for him in your heart?'

'Yes,' she said but did not elaborate because she could not explain the complexity to her uncle; he would not understand how Richard made her feel. In truth she did not understand herself at times.

Lorcan smiled rather sadly. 'Then at least he has one saving grace. I will pray for both of you.'

29

Southern Ireland, summer 1171

Guided by his Irish brother-in-law Domnall, Richard and his troop rode to relieve Robert FitzStephen in Waterford. They had to forge their way through the mountains fencing the town's north-west boundary, travelling narrow, difficult paths, constantly on watch for ambush from the remnants of Ruari's army and other hostile Irish lords.

The trees were in full leaf and arched in dark, midge-filled tunnels over the path, reminding Richard of the deep Welsh forests where many English troops had come to grief at the hands of small Welsh warbands. It was perfect ambush territory. Stragglers had been picked off and trails had been sabotaged with trees dragged across the path, or iron caltrops scattered to lame the horses. Richard kept an eye on the line, constantly riding through the men to watch their responses and observing from all angles.

Rolling along on a plain brown gelding was one of the soldiers' chaplains, a forthright English priest from Hereford called Nicholas. Before taking his vows he had been a soldier himself and took a broad view on the ecclesiastical oath not to shed blood. An axe haft poked through his belt and a crossbow was slung at his shoulder. Father Nicholas understood that his charges were sinners who fornicated, blasphemed, got drunk, had hearts full of violence, lust and cruelty, but who would weep like terrified children at the thought of dying unshriven. It would not do to have such a one serve in a cathedral where the prelate's robes glittered with spun gold, and the voices raised to God were cultured and pure, but here in the field, amid the filth and blood, he was in his element and highly valued.

Richard looked at the man's rough brown robes. 'How did you come to be a priest?' he asked curiously.

Father Nicholas gave him a broad grin crenellated by missing teeth. 'Through a long disreputable life, my lord.'

Richard laughed. 'Many would claim the same path.'

The priest shrugged. 'My father was a garrison serjeant at Hereford. I learned to fight and follow in his footsteps, but then I fell from a horse and broke my arm. While I was healing one of the chaplains took me under his wing and gave me some learning.' The chequered smile flashed again. 'Somehow I wound up being ordained, but I always preferred the camp fire and guard room to the interior of a church. Fighting men need a commander to trust and honour, and a priest who will give them absolution and hold their hand when they're in extremis, and not judge too harshly – aye, and one who can say the mass in the time it takes a man to piss a pint. Fighting men want God to be with them, but do not want to spend too long on their knees!'

Richard grinned at the priest's forthrightness and thought he would go far.

They rounded a turn in the path and a scout arrived, warning of more branches dragged across the route. Drawing rein, Richard ordered a deputation forward to clear the obstruction; but as the men moved to the task, a multitude of Irish attacked with spears and axes, swords and bows, sowing mayhem, bringing down horses and men. The knight Meilyr FitzHenry was felled by a stone to his helmet and dragged to safety by his companions under a hail of darts and missiles while Raymond and his soldiers strove to haul the trees clear of the path and force a way through. William Ferrand held off three determined Irishmen armed with daggers and axes, parrying their blows on his shield, striking back, preventing them from attacking the path clearers.

A yelling young Irish lord came at Richard, his high rank displayed in the decorated finery of his armour and weapons. As he pulled back his arm to throw his spear, the chaplain's crossbow bolt struck him in the bare thigh. The young warrior fell, a look of amazed shock on his face as blood spurted from the wound, and then he was screaming and rolling on the ground. His compatriots grabbed him and dragged him away and within moments the attackers had fled into the trees under a final barrage of stones and arrows.

'Do not give chase!' Richard bellowed. 'To me! Stay together!'

His men regrouped and quickly tended to the dead and injured of which there were several, including William Ferrand, who had taken a knife in the chest and was coughing blood. Richard saw the mounts redistributed and the riderless men either doubled up or put on sumpters, and they continued towards Waterford in close formation. Nicholas of Hereford busied himself among the wounded, seeing to those most seriously injured who needed to be confessed and comforted. William Ferrand died smiling within sight of Waterford, gripping a cross in his bloodied hands, his wish to end his life in battle finally granted.

Approaching the town, Richard smelled the smoke and saw the dark smudge rising from behind the walls, boding ill for both the inhabitants and the garrison. Arriving, they found the gates open and the town sacked. The grain and food supplies had all been looted, and the livestock had either been taken or slaughtered. Of the enemy there was no sign.

The garrison had held the fort, but Robert FitzStephen and five other knights had been captured and taken hostage by the Hiberno-Norse who had rowed out to a fortified island in the middle of the river and were holding their hostages there, warning that if Richard attempted a rescue, they would behead FitzStephen and his men and return them to Richard in tribute.

Richard tightened his lips as he received the news from a shivering, terrified cleric. Having seen what had happened at

Fearns, he did not doubt the threat would be carried out. He could do nothing about FitzStephen for now. Springing him from Ceredigion's dungeon was very different to extricating him from the grip of the belligerent Hiberno-Norse of Waterford.

'So narrow a strip of water,' Raymond remarked, gazing speculatively at the river.

'We can starve them out,' Richard said. 'They do not have the men to take us but they will kill FitzStephen if we try to rescue him. Leave the matter for now. We have the town. No matter how much they shout from their island, sooner or later they must come to terms or die of hunger.'

Richard had been in Waterford for six weeks and Aoife had joined him from Dublin when Hervey returned from court well after dusk had fallen. Looking haggard and uncomfortable, Hervey approached the dais table and Richard's heart sank as he saw the look in his uncle's eyes. Bidding Hervey be seated, Richard directed an attendant to pour wine.

'From the look on your face I take it your news is not joyful,' he said flatly.

Hervey took a drink from the goblet. 'It was difficult,' he said. 'I put your case and praised you as a fine warrior and loyal subject. I exhorted the King to be understanding and merciful.' He grimaced. 'He requires you to attend him personally – nothing else will assuage him.'

Anger and disappointment curdled Richard's stomach. 'So, in essence you achieved nothing and we are no closer to a resolution.'

Hervey eyed him reproachfully. 'That is not so, nephew. What I achieved for you is a stay of execution.'

'Execution?' Richard stiffened.

'The King is in an ill humour,' Hervey said. 'He is alarmed by your success and angered that you send your men instead of coming in person – he considers it an insult. I assured him countless times of your loyalty but he says you must go to him and abase yourself and he will decide whether or not to be merciful when he has spoken to your face. He requires your presence immediately.'

Richard looked round at his men, his friends, at Aoife, her belly round with his child. If he went to Henry he might never see them again and they would be left weak and vulnerable. If he stayed, he was trapped and powerless with the embargo continuing and his lands sequestered. A rebel and outcast. He had no option but to obey despite his laurel wreath. He could not defy Henry. Neither Raymond with his soldier's upright stance nor Hervey with his courtier's acumen had been able to secure Henry's goodwill.

'I will have none of it,' he growled with the pain of a trapped animal. 'I will not be beholden to an English king who puts me in the gutter!'

Hervey lowered his head but cast Richard an upward look filled with warning and sadness. 'There is one more thing, and it might affect the way you decide to respond to this.'

'What?' Richard snapped.

'The King . . . he is coming to Ireland, and I do not mean in the distant future, I mean very soon. I have arrived ahead of him, but his summons is on the breath of his intention to embark.'

Richard was close to choking on his emotion. So rightly did the proverb say that when a man sees the head of a wolf, the tail swiftly follows.

'He is making his camp at Pembroke, and commands you meet him there.'

'Why am I suddenly so important to him?' Richard demanded. 'Is he so worried about me that he must abandon all other doings and hunt me across the Hibernian Sea?'

Hervey rubbed his face. 'I think he is more worried about the papal legates chasing him over the death of his archbishop and laying an interdict on him. He needs a bolt hole, and Ireland is it. He can deal with the situation here while he is about it to his satisfaction.'

Unable to bear the picture that Hervey was creating, Richard rose to his feet and without a word stalked off to his chamber, crashing the door open and kicking it shut behind him.

Silence fell at the trestle. Then Hervey said: 'I did my utmost, but the King was not for moving. Nothing will shift his opinion save Richard's presence.'

Aoife patted Hervey's arm in consolation. As she had suspected, he was not up to the task, but perhaps no man was. Her father in his prime, maybe. Richard was an unknown quantity but seemed to rile the King at every turn. Since men had failed, it was time for a woman's approach. Her own feelings towards Henry were of defiance and resentment, but he was the King, and if he was coming here, they needed to be prepared.

'I beg your leave,' she said. 'I must go to my husband.'

In their chamber, Richard was staring at the wall, clenching and unclenching his fists, his eyes watery with furious tears.

'I have done all I said I would in Ireland and against the odds,' he said, looking at her. 'I have sworn my fealty to Henry again and again and done my duty by him. Dear Christ, what more does the man want? My head on a plate?' He dug his hands through his hair. 'If I go I am immediately at his mercy, and if I stay, he will declare me an outlaw and I lose everything. Either way I am trapped.'

Aoife went to him, took his hand and drew him to the bed, making him sit down so she could remove his shoes. 'Do not worry about it tonight. The answer will come. Sleep now and tomorrow we shall see what to do. A night will not change the situation but it will help your thoughts.'

Richard sighed, but she was relieved to see that his gaze had recovered focus. 'I have to go to Henry,' he said bleakly. 'If I do not I shall lose everything – my life, my unborn child. Somehow I have to placate him.'

'Then you have your answer,' she said. 'You have no choice but to go, even if you said in the hall you would not.'

'Yes, and it is a bitter brew to swallow.'

'Perhaps, but not the worst. What do a few words and gestures cost?'

He smiled without humour. 'Honour,' he said. 'And pride.'

Aoife stroked his brow. 'All will be well, you will see.' She knew what she thought about honour and pride.

His expression softened, although the worry remained. 'Ah Aoife, you are my saving grace.'

Lying down, he curled up, and she sat with him, stroking his brow until eventually he slept. Her own mind was busy assessing how she could protect them and their baby. She had to play her own game, she could not rely on men. Her sex was often a constraint, but it also gave her the freedom to make her own rules.

In the morning, Richard apologised to Hervey, who accepted with a wry shrug. 'The King wants you, either alive or dead, it does not matter to him, but he truly desires to resolve the matter. He wants to look into your eyes for the truth, nephew.'

Richard gave him a bleak smile. 'Then let us hope I am good at dissembling,' he said, 'because the truth would probably get us all killed.'

Aoife was packing Richard's court robes into his baggage chest – richly embroidered tunics and a heavy plaid cloak lined with marten fur. He watched her fold one of his shirts. She had insisted on doing it herself, refusing to leave it to the maids. He thought her utterly beautiful with her burnished dark hair, sparkling eyes and delicate features, her pregnancy as round as a full moon, and realised this might be the last time he ever saw her. He grasped her hand and drew her to the bed with him and gently pushed up her chemise to expose her swollen belly and kissed her there before setting his palm over her taut skin. This might be the last time too that he felt the stirring of their child in her womb.

'Be good for me, little one.' He wanted to say he would bring back all manner of victory but knew the odds were not in his favour, and besides, it was tempting fate. 'I will return as swiftly as I can.' Movement throbbed against his hand and he swallowed. 'I shall miss both of you.'

Aoife ran her fingers through his hair. 'I do not want you to go.'

'I must, and set everything to rights. Trust in Hervey, Raymond and Maurice. They will steer the ship. Look after yourself and our child. I will want you when I return – I will always want you. Come now, no tears.'

Aoife wiped them away on the heel of her hand and rose from the bed to continue packing, numbing her feelings so she could cope. 'Be very careful what you say to Henry. My father always said he would eat the world and look round for more. He has a bottomless hunger.'

'I know it well.'

She folded and rolled up a shirt. 'He is coming here because it is a place to lie low while the uproar over Thomas Becket's murder sinks into the silt. He will demand to hold Ireland as its overlord and you will have to cede the coastal towns to him, especially Dublin.' She looked up at him, her green eyes calculating. 'But if we can persuade him to cede them back, then once he leaves, the country will be ours to do as we choose. Give him what he wants, because in the end it is the only way to obtain what we want.'

Richard shook his head and smiled with admiration and slight wariness. 'You never fail to astonish me,' he said. 'I am glad you are in my camp and not another's.'

She shrugged with a touch of impatience. 'It is the only chance we have. We must play the game to win; only then will we survive.'

30

Pembroke Castle, South Wales, October 1171

Arriving at Pembroke, Richard was reminded of an ants' nest as he was immediately engulfed in the commotion and flurry of a court and army on the move. Amid the boil of motion, everything had its place and purpose. He was immediately shown by a marshal where to pitch his tent in the ward and domicile his men, while news of his arrival was taken straight to the King.

Raising his tent in the ward of a castle where he had played as a youngster and that had been his pride and possession in young manhood, Richard was discomforted and banged the pegs into the ground with the strength of resentment.

An usher came to bring him to the King, and Richard followed him to the white-washed timber and stone hall where he had once dwelt with his family, dispensing justice and largesse. Here he had lain abed with Rohese, making plans, none of which had come to fruition as Fortune's wheel turned his life upside down.

The main room was crammed with people and activity. Scribes scratched away at their lecterns. One man leaned back, opening and closing his cramped, ink-stained fingers, and puffed out his cheeks. Bidden to wait, Richard gazed around. Little had changed in the sixteen years since he had lived here. The furnishings were different, but the limewashed walls still bore the same sooty marks around the candle sconces and the dais table stood in the same position.

William FitzGerald of Carew, Pembroke's constable, greeted

him – a broad man with a rolling gait and shrewd grey eyes like Raymond's.

'How is my son?' FitzGerald asked.

'I am well pleased with him,' Richard replied. 'He is a fine soldier and popular with the men. You must know he has won several victories and made a name for himself.'

'Indeed, and I am proud of him.' William looked pleased. 'I knew he would do well at your hearth. He has always had an aptitude for warfare.'

'I have certainly utilised his skills,' Richard replied. 'For now, I have left him guarding my household.'

'Ah yes.' FitzGerald scratched his beard and looked embarrassed.

Richard shrugged. 'I expect everyone knows why I am here. I do not intend to create a difficult situation, but to build bridges if I can.'

'You are wise,' FitzGerald said. 'Are you aware there is already an Irish deputation in the camp? They arrived two days ago.'

Richard shook his head, dismayed. 'I did not know, but we have but recently arrived and we have been pitching tents. In truth I am not surprised.'

'They say they have taken Robert FitzStephen hostage and they are begging the King to intercede and stop your depredations on their lands and livelihood.'

Richard rubbed the back of his neck. 'They do indeed have FitzStephen hostage, and I am not surprised they are supplicating the King, but thank you for telling me.'

'Their complaint involves my son too, and I would rather you were forewarned,' William of Carew said, giving him a meaningful look, and stepped back as the usher arrived to take Richard to Henry.

Richard entered Henry's chamber with determination. He was in a life-or-death situation – it might well be the latter, but it could not continue. He did not know what the Irish had said to Henry specifically, but he could guess the content.

Henry sat near the window with the light behind him the better to read the documents presented by the scribes.

Richard knelt and bowed his head. 'Sire, I have come at your summons to submit myself to you,' he said.

Henry looked up from his reading matter and fixed him with sharp eyes. 'Not without wriggling every way to escape the hook. You did me the insult of sending me your underlings rather than come yourself – until you had no other choice.'

'Sire, I intended no offence. Is it not the way for a man to use negotiators and brokers at the outset?'

'That is a hollow excuse,' Henry said curtly.

Richard maintained a calm façade, although his heart was hammering in his chest. 'Sire, I hope we can find common and amicable ground, for disagreement benefits neither of us.'

Henry studied Richard intently as though assessing an opponent across a chess board. 'Well then, what do you have for me that might create such ground? I have heard of your exploits from several sources, and I know what you have achieved in Ireland.'

Meeting the King's eyes, Richard took the leap, knowing he had to sacrifice in order to gain. 'Sire, whatever I have achieved in Ireland, I acknowledge you my liege lord. I lay before you Dublin, Wexford and Waterford. I kneel to you and renew my oath of fealty – in the hope of your mercy in restoring my lands and castles.'

Henry stroked his chin. 'But can I trust you?'

Richard met Henry's gaze squarely. 'Sire, I have always been loyal.'

A long silence ensued. Richard knew Henry could not accuse him of disloyalty in sailing to Ireland because he had given his permission. Withdrawing consent at the final moment might be interpreted by others as the act of a vacillating and vindictive king and Henry was trying to detach himself from that sort of judgement in the wake of Thomas Becket's violent death. He might consider Richard had been disloyal – he clearly saw him as a threat – but to say so would tilt a delicate balance.

'I hope to prove myself worthy of your trust if you will give me the opportunity,' Richard added. 'All I have ever asked is the opportunity.'

'You are a man who stands his ground, I will give you that,' Henry acknowledged grudgingly.

'I also stand by my word, sire. I do not know any other way. When I give my oath, I keep it.'

'That remains to be seen, for deeds speak louder than words, but since you have come to me personally and promised to swear fealty to me as your lord in Ireland, I will agree to lift the embargo on your ships and restore your estates.' He raised a forefinger. 'Not Pembroke, only Striguil. You will acknowledge my right to Dublin, Wexford and Waterford. Whatever else you gain by conquest, you and your heirs will recognise me and my heirs as your sovereign lords in right of those lands.'

They were tough terms, but Richard set his jaw and bowed his acquiescence. Henry had spoken of heirs and that meant his line would be entitled too, not just for a lifetime but for ever. 'I do so swear,' he said.

Henry nodded curtly. 'Then we have an agreement, and I shall announce it in public later so all may witness your oath to me and know of our accord. You will attend me at court until I cross the sea.'

'Thank you, sire.' Utter relief flooded through Richard, although mingled with trepidation, for trust journeyed both ways and he did not have it for his sovereign whose sole concern was power and acquisition.

An acerbic smile curled Henry's lip. 'I also hear I must congratulate you on your marriage. You owe me the necessary fine for wedding without my permission.'

Richard knew that Henry would extract his pound of flesh

but he seemed to be taking it without rancour and it was in the open now. 'Yes, sire; I request your generosity on the matter and crave your forgiveness, for indeed I am guilty of this sin of omission.'

'Be warned, I shall fine you heavily for something so serious; I shall have to consult with my advisers on the fee. Nevertheless you have my consent.'

Richard concealed a grimace and bowed. At least he had something concrete rather than a nebulous threat hanging over him.

'You are finding your Irish princess a convivial wife?'

Richard wondered why Henry was asking. Perhaps probing for a chink in Richard's armour he could exploit. 'Yes, sire, she pleases me well and she sends you her regards.'

'I shall see her soon no doubt,' Henry said. 'I met with her father five years ago and she was pleasing even then.' He flexed his eyebrows, hinting at untold intimacies.

'I count myself a fortunate man,' Richard replied evenly, not rising to the bait. He omitted to say that Aoife was with child, deciding he had used up all his good fortune for one interview. Let Henry settle into restoring his lands first.

Henry waved one hand in dismissal. 'There is still much to discuss, and my clerks have work to do on the matter, but we shall talk again presently.'

Richard bowed from Henry's presence. Returning to his camp, he fended off the questions of his men, intent only on reaching the haven of the private space behind the canvas partition screen at the back of the tent. He sat down on his bed, put his face in his hands and shuddered with relief, his belly sucked in tight to control his sobs. Later would come the euphoria of having negotiated a path through the dangerous straits and emerging if not unscathed, then at least in one piece. He had succeeded, and once again Striguil was his. He was galled to yield the lucrative coastal towns, but Henry would not have settled for less, and he still had Leinster, and could work towards acquiring concessions and privileges in the fullness of time.

When he was certain of his composure he wiped his eyes, washed his face, and went out to his men. Now at last they could go forward. Now they could build on solid ground.

Aoife pushed her arms into the sleeves of her new over tunic. The garment fastened loosely at the front over her first gown and fell to just above her ankles. The style, borrowed from the Norse, was flattering, enabling her to move with comfortable elegance in the last weeks of pregnancy. Her mother and Basilia wanted her to stay in her chamber because of her size; the midwives opined it would not be long, but news had arrived that the King's fleet had been sighted and its arrival was more imminent than the birth of her child. Nothing would keep her in her chamber. She flatly refused to yield her position as senior lady of the household to either her mother or Basilia.

Anxiety was making her queasy, but she was trying to remain calm. If Richard had been deposed or imprisoned in England, she must be ready to fend for herself.

She had prepared Henry's private chamber and had had trestles set out for a feast in the hall. Another battle had been fought in Richard's absence and Dublin had been attacked again, although the Irish had been driven off with heavy losses and Tiernan ua Ruari's son-in-law, who was his heir, had been killed. The victory had made Aoife's position less precarious but had not alleviated her worry about what was happening at the English court. She might be a widow and not know it.

Attended by a mingling of Irish and Normans, she set a smile on her lips, concealed her fear, and went to the wharf side to greet the King's ship.

By the time she arrived, Henry had already stepped ashore and stood amid a large group of nobles, his cloak lined with squirrel fur and pinned by a huge round brooch. Tall and lean,

Richard stood at Henry's side. He was clearly on his guard, but his expression revealed neither despair nor defeat and when he saw her waiting on the wharf, he smiled. Henry was beaming too, widely, with appreciation.

She advanced to greet him with a sparkle and a smile, but she was modest rather than bold. She knelt at his feet, her pregnancy concealed beneath her full cloak and flowing coat, and behind her, the household members knelt too. 'You are most welcome to Ireland, sire,' she said. 'We are honoured by your presence and trust we can make your stay pleasant and comfortable.'

Henry gazed at her like a predator considering its next meal. 'I am sure you and your lord will excel, my lady of Leinster.' He raised her to her feet and kissed her warmly on either cheek. She inhaled the scent of incense from his clothes, mingled with that of healthy sweat and fresh air.

Richard introduced Henry to the senior lords waiting on the wharf and cast Aoife an approving look over his shoulder. She lowered her gaze and continued in her modest role. She was desperate to know what had happened across the sea. Clearly an agreement had been reached. She glanced at Hervey, who bowed and, under the pretext of giving her an avuncular kiss, murmured in her ear, 'All is well, have no fear. There is much negotiating to be done, but Richard has smoothed the ground.' His reassurance settled her sufficiently to play the role of hospitable hostess and she threw herself into it with renewed commitment.

The cooks had prepared a spiced beef stew, roast fowl, and sea trout with herbs. There was plentiful bread, and honey, and all manner of cheeses. Once everyone was seated at the banquet table and the food blessed, Aoife presented Henry with the first cup of wine, and as she knelt to him, her coat flowed open.

'To your health, sire,' she said.

The smile froze on Henry's lips as for the first time he

noticed the ripe curve of her womb. 'And to yours, Countess,' he replied as he took the cup and directed a sharp look at Richard. 'You did not mention you were about to become a proud father.'

'I beg your pardon, sire,' Richard said. 'We were engaged on other matters, and since my heir is still unborn, I thought it better fortune not to tempt fate.'

Aoife flicked her glance between the men and recognised Henry's annoyance for what it was. Had she not eluded him at Saumur he would have had her virginity. Instead, Richard had succeeded in Ireland, had married her, had enjoyed the first taste and got her with child, thus stealing several marches on his king in sensitive masculine areas.

Henry raised his cup. 'To Richard and his lady and whosoever shall follow after!' he declared, and toasted her womb, graciously acknowledging her condition even while his words were decidedly ambiguous and his eyes hard.

Aoife was quiet and unassuming throughout the meal. She honoured their royal guest by playing her harp and singing, but as soon as she could she withdrew to her chamber, her mind working furiously. They needed Henry's approval; without it they were finished. She had counted up the number of troops Henry had shipped over and clearly he intended to exert his authority. It was vital that she and Richard secured their own position in the regime.

It was late when Richard eventually came to their chamber and she flew to him the moment he shut the door.

'What happened while you were away?' she demanded without preamble. 'How safe are we really?'

'Safe enough.' He pulled her into his arms. 'Henry has restored Striguil and all my estates, so your dower is secure, as are my resources. I had to yield Dublin, Waterford and Wexford to him, but there is every chance of receiving them back providing I swear to him as my overlord.'

She was annoyed that they had taken all the risks and now Henry was here to harvest the fruits for himself, but such was the way of kings, and they had been expecting no less.

'Why did you not tell him I was with child?'

'I was unsure how he would respond and it would have been tempting fate to tell him before we sailed.'

She gave him a considering frown. 'We must bring Henry into our camp and enter his too. That is the only way to survive.'

'It will not be easy.'

Aoife, to the contrary, thought it was very easy indeed. 'Tell him what he wants to hear,' she said impatiently. 'You say you are a player – well then, play the game. We need his goodwill and favour, and we need it for longer than a moment. We must bind him to us by whatever ties if we can.'

He gave her a rueful look. 'What are you planning now?'

Aoife began braiding her hair ready for sleep. 'We should ask him to be godfather to our child,' she said. 'It will ensure his interest in our heir and draw us into his affinity.' Her face grew tight and determined. 'All my life I have had to think of ways and means of being safe, and this will help to achieve it – both for us and the child.'

'I agree.' He took her in his arms. 'You have a bold, courageous heart and I love you dearly for it. You are right. Indeed, I believe the King might be insulted if we did not ask.'

'I am always right,' she said, slanting him a smile. 'You should always listen to me.'

Richard rolled his eyes and laughed. 'I will bear it in mind.'

In the morning, the men of Waterford brought a chained and fettered Robert FitzStephen before Henry. FitzStephen was filthy and unkempt, his face a mapwork of purple and yellow fading bruises.

'Well,' said Henry as the prisoner dropped to his knees before him, 'what do you have to say for yourself, you wretch? You have gone treacherously against me and you know what happens to traitors.'

'Sire, I have always been your loyal servant and honoured you,' FitzStephen said through pain-bared teeth.

Henry snorted. 'So honourable that you defied me and plundered lands for your own gain. You were the first to cross to Ireland and you had no permission. You have seized lands unlawfully and harassed the innocent. You deserve whatever comes to you.' Henry's voice rang out to make his point.

Listening among the witnesses, Richard realised Henry was setting an example and sending out a warning that he could have Richard in chains if he so chose – indeed anyone. He had four hundred ships with him, five hundred knights and four thousand foot soldiers and archers. No one would dare to question his will. Aoife had been right last night: they did need to be in Henry's camp.

FitzStephen reiterated his loyalty. 'I was a prisoner in Wales because I refused to deny you, sire,' he said. 'When I was released, I came here to fight on your behalf – not my own.'

'That is not the story I have been hearing.' Henry looked at the Waterford Irish.

FitzStephen turned to glare at them. 'Who has a glove?' he demanded. Raymond le Gros unfolded a gauntlet from his belt and stepped forward to hand it to FitzStephen, who held it aloft in challenge, his fetters clinking. 'Let any man who dares call me traitor before my king step forward and I shall do battle to prove my innocence here and now! I do not fear the judgement of God!' He bared his teeth in a snarl at the Irish.

'I will stand surety for this man's honour,' Richard said, 'even as I stood surety for him in Wales.'

Robert de Quency followed suit, as did Raymond and Philip of Prendergast. The Waterford men looked at each other uneasily and shuffled their feet.

Henry cupped his chin in his hand and watched impassively.

'Enough,' he said eventually. 'I am impressed that so many would step forward to endorse your character, but since they are your partisans and relatives, it is to be expected. I will ponder the matter further and, in the meantime, you may await my pleasure as I have instructed.' He flicked his hand and two guards removed FitzStephen from the room. The latter walked proudly, the glove still clutched in his fist.

Henry dismissed the Waterford deputation courteously having thanked them for bringing FitzStephen to him and promising to deal with the matter fittingly. Then he looked round at the gathered court. 'Loyalty is commendable,' he said, 'especially to your king. I want you all to remember that.'

'What is going to happen to FitzStephen?' Aoife asked Richard when they were in bed that night. The candles were still lit and Richard was drinking a cup of wine and reading a letter from his mother.

He shrugged. 'It remains to be seen, but today's performance was just that – an act for his captors and a public warning to everyone else. I doubt FitzStephen is going to rot in a dungeon for years as he did in Ceredigion. He's a powerful warrior and loyal to Henry. All his relatives are here and the King won't alienate every one of them just to make an example. Nor will he let a clutch of Irish Norse dictate to him. If you were to take a platter of bread down to FitzStephen now, I hazard you would find him already well fed and curled up in a warm blanket with his chains removed.'

'You hazard or you know?'

'I might just have seen food and raiment being conveyed to the dungeon. The Norse will receive no joy from Henry when it comes to complaints about FitzStephen. He's far too valuable a soldier to let rot. His imprisonment will be neither onerous nor long.' He waved the letter in his hand. 'My mother reminds me I should be taking in hand the matter of husbands for my daughters. If all goes well over winter, I shall summon them to Ireland in the spring and consider the matter. They will have a new mother to greet too, and a half-sister or brother.'

Aoife gave him a sweet smile that was not entirely sincere. She was not keen on being anyone's mother except her own children. Having never met the girls, she knew nothing about them, only that they had the potential to divert Richard's attention from his new family. However, at least if she welcomed them, she could keep the upper hand from the high ground.

31

Waterford, Southern Ireland, autumn 1171

Henry remained in Waterford for several days, taking oaths from the Irish lords who came to surrender to him because they wanted to be under his protection. FitzStephen remained in his dungeon where he dined on choice morsels sent from the high table. He was provided with a bath and fresh clothes but kept from sight.

Henry set off on progress around southern Ireland with his army, taking homage and tribute from those who had not submitted to him at Waterford. Richard accompanied him, and Aoife settled back into a gentler domestic routine. She did not visit FitzStephen, but she sent him her good wishes and continued to provide him with food and wine from the high table as per Henry's instructions.

A fortnight after the men had gone, feeling restless and unsettled, Aoife decided to sort through a chest full of fabric in search of a new project. The child was weighing heavily and her walk had become a waddle, although she still refused the midwives' advice to take to her bed. An intermittent pain in the small of her back had been bothering her for a couple of days but she was ignoring it.

'You should be careful,' Basilia warned as Aoife began dragging a coffer away from the wall the better to throw back the lid and search the contents.

'I can manage,' Aoife snapped as Basilia moved to help her. 'I know I have some saffron cloth somewhere. My father was given a bolt in tribute.' Her mind filled with an image of cloth the colour of the sun, more valuable than gold. 'I have a mind to make some hose for Richard.'

Basilia blinked. 'He will certainly stand out.'

Aoife was irritated by Basilia's obvious distaste. 'He is in Leinster now and he should dress fittingly for a lord of that land.'

Basilia said nothing, her silence eloquent, and Aoife wanted to hit her. She found the cloth, its colour as rich as evening sunshine. Perhaps teamed with a tunic of forest-green and a cloak lined with sables. She dragged the bolt out of the chest and unfolded it to assess the amount of fabric. As she spread her arms, a stronger pain shot across her abdomen and she bit her lip.

Basilia was immediately alert. 'It is the child, I knew it! She looked almost angrily at Aoife, her sense of propriety thoroughly disturbed.

The pain receded, but there was no mistaking that it had been a pain. Aoife tried to shrug it off and couldn't. 'It might be,' she said.

'I will fetch your mother and the midwives.'

Aoife would have denied Basilia, but she could still feel an edge of pain. A little afraid, she buried her face in the folds of the saffron cloth and thought of her father.

The midwives arrived and bore Aoife to her chamber where everything had been made ready a couple of weeks ago, and there was little to do save put the cauldron over the fire. The swaddling bands were warming near the hearth. Fortifying drinks and tisanes had been prepared for the labouring mother and the bed was covered with a layer of straw and fleece, strewn with fragrant herbs.

Aoife set herself to bear her travail with resolution. If a man's trial was battle, then a woman's was childbirth and she was ready to meet the ordeal and prove herself. She had witnessed children being born and had seen all manner of animals giving birth. The event held no mystery. She drank the tisanes, clutched her prayer beads and prayed to St Margaret and St Bridget to succour her.

The pain increased as the contractions strengthened from short cramping surges to powerful, hard squeezes that left her gasping and tearful, but those tears were of grim determination. She forced herself through the pain, working with her body to push the baby into the world, to give it air to breathe and a life to live. She gripped the midwives' hands and pushed, gritting her teeth, wailing with the effort, and the infant slithered from her body. A baby's cry quavered in the space around the bed and Aoife pushed herself onto her elbows to look at the wet, blood-streaked newborn still attached to her by a bluish quivering cord. *Alive*, she thought with triumph. *Alive and strong.*

'A girl, madam, you have a daughter.'

The midwife wrapped the baby in a towel and gave her to Aoife. She stared at the bawling bundle in her arms, the little hands like stars, the legs kicking strongly against the towel, and was astonished that this small being could have grown in her body, from seed sown on a cold winter's night. For her dynasty, she would rather have heard the word 'son' but she was not disappointed. She knew the strength of women. And her daughter was beautiful, whole and robust. An irrevocable part of herself.

The afterbirth arrived without complication. The cord was cut and the baby taken to be washed in warm water by the fire. Aoife lay back, suddenly overcome by exhaustion in the aftermath of battle. The bleeding between her legs, staunched with soft rags, was but a trickle and the labour had only lasted from noon until dusk. She knew she was fortunate and thanked God and the saints with a full heart.

Môr returned the baby to her with a tender look of pride on her face. Behind her Basilia was folding up cloths, her own expression wistful. Aoife took her daughter, parted the blanket and looked again into the little face. Gold light sparkled on top of her head and she had feathery gilded eyebrows. Love washed over Aoife, visceral and intense. Here was something new and pure and clean for herself. 'Nothing shall ever harm you, I swear on my own soul,' she said, stroking the baby's soft skin. 'I shall keep you safe as long as I have breath in my body. Each one I take is for you.'

Richard and Henry returned to Waterford soon after dark, and as Richard dismounted from his tired, mud-spattered palfrey, a servant ran to him with the news of his daughter's birth. Richard handed the reins to a groom. 'And my lady wife?' he asked, striving for normality, but feeling very afraid.

'The lady is well, sire.'

A great welling of relief swept over him and for a moment his knees almost buckled. He felt a huge burst of gratitude to God who had so blessed and sanctioned him.

Beaming, Henry slapped his shoulder. 'A daughter,' he said. 'My congratulations. May she have her mother's beauty. You might have missed the target for a son, but you can try again – that is always a pleasure with a beautiful woman. And you have a continuation of your line.' His expression was slightly smug, because his first child with Alienor had been a boy and thus real proof of virility.

Richard gave Henry a broad smile, for while a daughter was not as solid as a male heir, she was still part of the foundation of his line and he was too relieved to be disappointed.

The men entered the hall, removing cloaks and gauntlets. Richard gazed at the warm glow of firelight and candles and inhaled the smell of meat and onions simmering in the cauldrons. Between his leaving and return everything had changed. The child within Aoife's womb now had its own life, its own path to tread, and he had the joy of a legitimate heir.

Môr entered the hall bearing a bundle in her arms, and coming to Richard she bowed her head. 'Your return is timely to greet your daughter, born less than an hour since.' She hesitated, but Richard took the baby from her with a natural ease.

'Aoife is well?' he repeated, wanting to make sure.

'Yes,' Môr said. 'Of course, she is very tired, it was hard and dangerous work, but she has just taken some nourishing broth.'

Richard looked down at his daughter, and she returned his stare, as if she knew everything about him already, but then she had come from his body, and was part of him. He swallowed, on the edge of tears.

Henry was regarding him with a strange expression on his face, part surprise, part speculation. Richard cleared his throat and wiped his eyes with the hand not cradling the baby. He faced Henry. 'Sire, I beg your indulgence and ask you not only to be my liege lord but also to stand godparent to my new daughter. It is the most I can offer you, my own flesh and blood.'

Henry looked briefly taken aback, but quickly recovered. 'Of course,' he said gruffly, 'I shall be pleased to bless the child in the sight of God for all the people of this land to see, and to take her under my protection.'

'Thank you, sire, I am humbled and honoured – truly.'

The look in Henry's eyes was oddly vulnerable, as if the man had stepped outside the king for a moment and was exposed bare of the shell. But then he shook himself. 'Let it be done,' he said with a brusque nod and turned away to other business.

Richard insisted on returning the baby to Aoife's chamber, Môr walking anxiously at his side.

Basilia opened the door and looked at him askance. 'Aoife is asleep,' she whispered censoriously.

Richard knew this was the sacred space of the birthing chamber, and he should not be here, but he had to see Aoife. The room beyond his sister was dark, lit only by a few lamps, and the air was filled with the scent of incense and herbs. 'I need to see her, just for a moment, I shall not wake her. I just want to look at her. You know why.'

Basilia met his gaze and then stepped back. Môr clucked her tongue in disapproval but neither woman prevented him from tip-toeing to the bed. The curtains were drawn back and a midwife was sitting in vigil beside Aoife. The woman, too, gave him a hard stare and put her finger sternly to her lips.

Aoife was curled on her side, long dark hair plaited in a loose braid, one hand curled against her cheek. His heart lurched at her beauty and filled with tender feelings of gratitude and love. Just looking at her and their daughter he knew that even if nothing went to plan in his life again, in this moment he was utterly blessed. Leaning over, he kissed her very gently on the temple, and then the baby, before giving her back to Môr.

Returning to the hall, stumbling, almost drunk on emotion, he discovered that Robert FitzStephen had been released from his dungeon – as expected – and was sitting with Henry drinking wine and eating pottage.

'I understand congratulations are in order,' FitzStephen said laconically as Richard joined them at the high table.

'Indeed, a fine little girl,' Richard replied. 'I am pleased to see your own condition improved.'

'He is on probation,' Henry said. 'There is no point in wasting good fighting men, and honour has been satisfied.' He lifted his cup. 'A toast,' he said. 'A toast to my new god-daughter, whatever her name may be.'

'Isabelle,' Richard said with a quickening in his heart. 'Her name is Isabelle.' And reached for Diarmait's drinking horn.

In the morning, Henry stood godparent to little Isabelle de Clare at her baptism. She bawled lusty indignation as she was lowered into the font, her yells louder than the priest's voice, but once folded in soft linen swaddling and a warm blanket she lay placidly in Richard's arms, making soft sucking noises against her fist before he returned her to her grandmother.

Henry was preparing to leave for Dublin where more Irish lords were coming to yield to him and Richard was to accompany him, but first he went to bid farewell to Aoife. She was sitting up, fully awake, cradling Isabelle. Her hair gleamed like a sable waterfall against her white linen chemise and she had a smile for him.

Sitting down at her side, he saw the dark shadows under her eyes and felt humbled. 'I am glad you are recovering, and our daughter is truly beautiful,' he said, and kissed her.

'She looks like you,' Aoife said with a smile.

'She is as comely as her mother. Rest and grow strong while I am gone. I wish I could stay but needs must.'

'Be careful when dealing with Henry,' she cautioned. 'He is cunning and he is playing his own game.'

'Do not worry, I will be careful indeed. He is godfather to the little one and it is a fine connection to have.'

When he had gone, Aoife settled back against the pillows to suckle Isabelle. She had refused a wet nurse for the first weeks; she would feed the baby herself with the nourishment of Ireland and the line of Murchada. She was determined that Isabelle's future would be glorious and safe but it could not be left to drift with fate. God helped those who helped themselves. As soon as she was recovered from the birth, she intended seeing to the matter herself and not relying on others.

32

Dublin, Ireland, January 1172

Aoife looked up as Richard entered the chamber. Outside a rainy dusk was settling over the town. The light glinted on his hair, chestnut-dark in the candle light, and her heart jumped with pleasure to see him. She felt a hint of trepidation bordering on shyness, for this was the first time she had seen him since early November and it was like looking at a familiar stranger.

'Aoife.' He spoke her name on a breath, his eyes lighting with pleasure.

She faced him, smiling, but uncertain. 'Since you showed no sign of returning to me, I decided to come to you.'

'When they told me you had arrived . . .' He shook his head. 'You look . . . Dear God you are beautiful!'

Richard took her hands and kissed one then the other before sweeping her into his arms and seeking her lips. She responded with enthusiasm until Isabelle began squawking whereupon she broke the kiss and led him to the cradle. Releasing Aoife, Richard picked up the baby, delight spreading across his face.

Isabelle regarded him solemnly before giving him a gummy grin. 'She has grown!' he said. 'And smiling too!'

'It would be strange if she was not at the end of three months,' Aoife replied. 'She does not know you to miss you, and that is both a good thing and a terrible one.'

Richard gave her a guilty look. 'I would have visited if possible, but the King has kept me close to his side. I see you made good use of that cloth I sent you at Christmas.' He nodded at her gown of dark-green wool, laced tight to her now slim waist.

'It was not the same as having you home.' She lifted her hem to show him the red silk hose she was wearing, which had also been a Christmas gift, and his eyes lit up.

'I am glad you have come,' he said.

She gave him a knowing smile, and taking Isabelle from him jogged her in her arms. 'How is the King?'

'As usual,' Richard answered. 'He is annoyed that the High King refuses to accept his sovereignty although most others have sworn. He is placing men of his own choosing in positions of power as I wrote to you, and he has awarded the Bristol merchants a charter securing their trading rights in Dublin, but he will still confirm Leinster to us.' He paused. 'Tiernan ua Ruari came to bend the knee and give his oath.'

Aoife returned Isabelle to her cradle. 'That is worth nothing,' she said scornfully. 'Tiernan will go back on his oath even while the words are still a taste in his mouth.'

'Perhaps, but he looked old to me and stripped to the bone. His son is dead and he is worn out with fighting.'

'For what he has done to me and mine I count him as dust,' Aoife answered with cold fire. 'Do not spare any pity for him for he would give you none, nor me, nor our daughter. He would slaughter us all if he could.'

'I do not,' Richard said. 'I know what strife he has caused and what he has done. But I admire courage when I see it. He walked up that hall to Henry through the ranks of his enemies with a firm tread and his head high, and that alone deserves respect.'

Aoife tossed her head. 'Why? It takes no courage; for courage you have to have fear, and he is not afraid of any of you. All he has is contempt.'

Richard looked at her with a mingling of amusement and exasperation. 'Oh, I have missed you,' he said tenderly. 'You are the sweetness in my honey jar, but still with the sting of the bee.'

He pulled her to him again and kissed her, and now his fingers were very busy with the red laces at the side of her gown, and Aoife pinched him for his teasing, but then melted against his body, as desirous as he was.

Aoife was leaning over Isabelle's crib about to tuck her in when Henry strolled into the chamber alone and unannounced.

'How is my god-daughter?' he enquired.

Aoife jumped at the sound of his voice but concealed her surprise in a curtsey. 'Thriving, sire,' she said with a smile as she rose.

'I am glad to hear it.'

Aoife's hand was on the side of the cradle and Henry set his own over hers. 'Let me tuck her in,' he said. 'As her godfather I should see to her comfort.' He fussed a moment with the little bedclothes and chucked Isabelle under the chin. 'I think I prefer babies to growing sons with all their demands,' he said ruefully. 'You have produced a fine start to the next generation. She shall be a great marriage prize indeed.' Standing upright, he faced Aoife. 'Now then, let me look at her mother. Are you well?'

The words heightened Aoife's alertness; no question from Henry was ever simple. 'Sire, I am well indeed, but still recovering, of course.'

'Then I hope you will soon return to full health.' His gaze pierced her. 'Look after my god-daughter, and I shall pray that your full recovery will lead you and your lord to yet more happy news of family.'

When he had gone, Aoife sat down on the bed and breathed a sigh of relief even while her eyes were narrowed in calculation. She had to lure him in to keep him interested and allied, without allowing him to catch her and without causing a scandal – she had a difficult task indeed.

Over the following weeks, Aoife often sat with Henry at the high table and spoke of her countrymen in pithy ways that made him laugh but gave him food for thought. She played chess with him, and racier games of dice and hazard. She washed his feet when he had been out hunting while he relaxed and picked at a dish of dried fruit. She listened to him and teased out the nuances of his character. Impatient, vigorous, determined to be the centre of the world, brooking no opposition to his will, and using everyone. He was like her father, but in more subtle ways. A lion, not a bear. She noticed he seldom spoke of his wife and seven children, save as spokes on the wheel serving the hub that was himself.

'Your husband,' Henry said, smiling as she played him at chess one evening in the hall. 'What do you truly think of him? Come, you can tell me.'

'I am a loyal wife and Richard is dear to me.' She flicked him a look from under her lashes. She had no intention of telling him anything intimate for he would use it as leverage. 'I greatly value a man who is a strong protector and keeps his lands and family safe.'

He sent her an amused glance. 'The stronger the better.'

Aoife dropped her gaze to the board. 'So my father taught me.'

'A wise man, your father.'

'Perhaps the wisest I have known. I miss him greatly.'

Later, on her way to her chamber, Henry cornered her in a recess and stood so close that his breath was in hers, and took her hand. 'I have some rings in my jewel box that might suit your fingers. You are welcome to come and see if there are any that please you.'

Aoife fought down a wave of panic at being trapped with a wall at her back. 'That is very generous of you, sire.'

'I am always generous to those who please me.' He raised her hand to his lips and kissed it with slow deliberation.

She felt the moist pressure of his lips, the bristle of his beard, the heat of his body within a fraction of touching hers and could not stop herself from trembling. She wanted Henry's protection, but she would not become one of his meals. She had evaded him before as a young girl; she would do so again. She withdrew her hand from his grasp, pushed him away and ducked under his arm.

'I hope I do please you, sire,' she said, a quiver in her voice, 'but we both know I cannot come to your chamber and accept gifts from you in private. I will be missed and there will be trouble.'

Henry stared at her, breathing heavily, and she stared back. Her heart was pounding, but she held her ground.

Suddenly he laughed and shook his head. 'You are an extraordinary woman-child,' he said. 'So much wisdom, and so much wildfire. I suspect your lord does not know what a fortunate man he is – or what he has on his hands. Go then. I shall send you a ring of my choosing that I think will suit.'

'Thank you, sire.' Aoife curtseyed and made her swift escape, feeling weak with relief. He had not been in full earnest, or he would not have let her go so easily. Testing the ground, she suspected. It had been a salutary lesson.

Richard was already in their chamber, sorting through a coffer. Going to him, she grabbed him and kissed him passionately.

Half laughing, he held her away by the waist. 'What's this?'

'Dear God, Richard, I need you,' she said urgently. 'Don't ask . . .'

She kissed him again, transferring the terrible weight of sexual tension into this moment with him, her lawful husband. She wanted him quickly, desperately, without time to remove their clothes. She clasped her legs high around him as he entered her, needing him deep inside her. 'I love you!' she gasped as he thrust into her. 'No one but you!' And then she cried out, climaxing as swiftly as the men did with their women when they returned from battle and had all their pent-up life force to expend in relief.

Richard had not finished and slowed down, kissing her throat,

322

her mouth again, curving his hands along her naked thighs, deliberately taking his time while she rose on a second, almost unbearable surge and bit down on the collar of his tunic to endure the sensations, until at last she felt him release inside her, strong, hard, like the beat of a swift and steady heart, and it was done; they were one.

He nuzzled her throat, withdrew from her, and tidied himself while she pulled down her skirts, suddenly shy. He drew her back against him and kissed her nose.

'What was all that about?'

'Can a wife not desire her husband and ask him to render the marriage debt?' she asked with a breathless laugh. Sensation still flickered in her loins.

'As often as she likes, but you are not usually so . . .' He frowned, seeking the word. 'Desperate. What is wrong?'

'Nothing,' she said, but the words came anyway, forced out of her by guilt. 'The King will be leaving soon and I am worried about our future.'

He eyed her in surprise. 'Why should you be worried? You have strong protection.'

'Because I have to be worried.' She drew away and sat up. 'If you had any sense you would worry too. Who protects the protector?'

Richard sighed and pillowed his arms behind his head. 'For that we must trust in God.'

She tossed her head. 'And God helps those who help themselves.'

'I have seen the way Henry is with you,' he said after a moment, 'and you with him. He is a king and he thinks he has the right to take what he wants. I watched him with the women of the court when I was in Normandy, some of them barely out of girlhood. He has a reputation and you will acquire your own reputation if you continue to dally with him as you do. Soon he will be gone, and then where will you be?'

Her cheeks started to burn. 'Do not be foolish,' she snapped.

323

'Aoife, my love, I am not a fool, that is the entire point. I will not be made a cuckold in my own household. The King has already damaged me by imposing himself on my land and fencing me in, and there comes a sticking point beyond which I will not be pushed. Do you truly think so little of me and my honour? If I were to ask you where you were five minutes before you came to our chamber, how would you answer me?'

She had not realised he noticed so much. She had seen him looking sour when Henry was in the hall but had thought it because of Henry's political machinations and embracing of favourites. As always, when challenged, she attacked. 'It avails us nothing to be cold towards the King. You sent Raymond le Gros and he returned empty-handed. You sent your uncle and the same thing happened. When you went to negotiate you won some ground, but what you have truly gained remains to be seen because he has not finished carving up the land. Women are the peacemakers and the ones who help to secure accord. I am my father's daughter.'

She lifted her head, proud, but her smile was downturned and bitter. 'I know what Henry is. I was one of those young girls at his court across the Narrow Sea and he would have had me if he could. But I outwitted him and won concessions for my family. Now I am a woman, a wife and mother – my father's heir in Leinster. I will use what I have to keep that rule intact. If it means smiling at the King and flirting a little, I will play the game – and still he shall not have me, ever. I am yours. Do you understand?'

Richard grimaced as if he had vinegar in his mouth.

Aoife laid her hand on his sleeve. 'It is for the good of our family and in your own interest. If I am near him, I can hear everything he says and report back to you and we can make our plans accordingly.'

Richard curled his lip. 'He says everything twice, two different ways, so it makes no difference.'

'Of course it makes a difference!' she said with exasperation. 'At least you know what he has been saying. Did you know he has been taking detailed notes of the lands of every man in your entourage?'

'I still do not have to like it,' he said, and then sighed. 'I agree that sometimes silk triumphs where steel does not, but I want you to be safe, even with my king. If he lays a hand on you . . .' He stopped speaking and shook his head. 'Do you understand?'

Richard was always so controlled that Aoife had not anticipated such fierceness and was glad she had not succumbed to Henry's demands in the recess. She stroked his face, trying to lighten the moment. 'Do not worry about me, my love, I can well look after myself.'

Richard raised his eyebrows at her. 'I hope you can, my young wife.' He pulled her into his lap. 'But if you say "I am yours", then make it so.'

'Have I not just proven it to you?' She put her arms around his neck, hugged him tightly. 'Henry will soon be gone,' she said. 'It won't be for much longer.'

A fortnight later, Henry concluded his business in Dublin and moved to Waterford to prepare for his return to England. Pulling gently at his beard, he gazed over the throng of courtiers, supplicants and soldiers gathered to hear his word, and addressed Richard, who stood waiting before him. 'We must establish a stable, governable land here. We have to discourage factions and strengthen our borders. My lord, you have Leinster to control, and that is a sufficient portion for any man to undertake. I would not give you so big an area that you cannot control it.' His look said he almost considered Richard a faction.

He indicated the nobleman Hugh de Lacy with an open hand. 'I am appointing my lord de Lacy as Constable of Dublin and my effective deputy. He will act in my name. You may all feel secure in the measures I am leaving in place. Every man shall have governance of his own lands and my scribes have so noted those lands. In my lord de Lacy you have a higher authority to ask for aid if you experience incursions on your borders. To uphold his authority, my lord de Lacy shall have the kingdom of Meath and will go there forthwith to negotiate with the High King.'

Richard had an urge to seize Henry by the throat and strangle him. He almost took a step forward but managed to root himself to the spot. After all he had done, after all the sweat and toil he had expended, Henry had gone his own way and put his own man in charge.

Henry's brow rose a fraction higher, revealing his awareness of Richard's anger and that he expected compliance. It was his prerogative to dictate as he chose and Richard's duty to obey. Nothing was said, everything was accomplished with subtle gesture and expression. In giving Meath to de Lacy, Henry had made him as powerful as Richard. He might have won back his title of Earl of Striguil, but he had been declined as Henry's deputy in Ireland in favour of this man. Richard swallowed it down because he had no choice. A glance at Aoife showed him that her spine was stiff and her expression blank.

Business concluded, the scribes prepared the documents for sealing. De Lacy made a point of coming over to Richard.

'I suppose I should bow to you,' Richard said.

'Ah no, none of that.' De Lacy clapped his shoulder. 'There must be no bad blood between us. We have long known each other and we should be compatriots come what may. The King would not have us be enemies.' He leaned towards Richard and lowered his voice. 'We are dealing together on our terms, not Irish ones, and we should never be at each other's throats.'

'I would have peace too,' Richard said, but still felt as though he had been served a cupful of vinegar. At least if de Lacy was his neighbour in Meath he would not be constantly looking over his shoulder for raiders because de Lacy would be a buffer. 'Indeed, we are allies.' It did not prevent him from being furious with Henry.

Aoife curtseyed to de Lacy with demure formality. 'My lord, you must call upon us for whatever assistance you need.'

De Lacy inclined his head. 'I hope we shall be of help to each other, Countess, especially when the King leaves. United we are strong.'

He left to speak with others. Richard looked after him and tried to appear loose and relaxed although he was fuming. 'After all our hospitality,' he said. 'It has all been worth a pot of piss. Does he think I am some kind of lackey?'

'I like it no more than you.' Aoife took his hand and smiled up at him as though they were having a pleasant conversation. 'But had I been in the King's place I would have done the same. You still have Leinster; you still have me. Do not see this as the end of the game, it is just another move on the board, another throw of the dice. Henry will leave and de Lacy will hold the border with Meath for his trouble – and we shall not have to bother. Remember, the King's goodwill is a moveable feast.' She dug her nails into his palm, reminding him that they were under scrutiny.

He looked at her and shook his head with wonder. She often exasperated and baffled him to distraction, but she had such clear insight and wisdom too. She knew precisely where to strike and how to soothe. He turned her hand over and lifted it to kiss her knuckles. 'Put your claws away,' he said with a wry smile and indicated the food being brought out to the trestle tables. 'The feast is about to start, moveable or not. I am not in a mood to eat, but I heed your sage advice. And do not tell me it is only what your father would have done. You are more than him . . . much more.'

Aoife stood at the top of Ragnall's tower and looked out over Waterford. She was panting from the climb but she had wanted to come up here to look out over the land. A brisk March wind tugged her veil and put tears in her eyes as the smell of Ireland came to her, all green with the spring. She had a longing to go to Fearns. Another week and it would be April. She set her hand to her belly. Her monthly flux had not come and she suspected that the long nights spent reassuring and comforting Richard had yielded their result. This time it would be a son to inherit, she knew it in her bones. 'Daidí,' she said softly. 'Daidí, what would you think if you were here now?' Suddenly the wind-stung tears in her eyes were real ones.

Hearing a footfall below, she hastily wiped her eyes. A moment later Henry arrived at the top of the tower, chest heaving. Clutching his side, he joined her. 'A fine view, Countess,' he said as he regained his breath from the hard climb.

'Indeed, sire,' she replied. 'From here you can see all the lands and none of the bloodshed.'

'But it is a good view for a commander.'

'Or a king.'

She was intensely aware of his proximity, and although they were not touching, it was still a feeling of intimate contact. She had muted her flirtation with him having come too close to being burned but still, her spine was tingling. She had so little time to obtain what she needed from him.

'If my father was still alive, I would feel safer,' she said. 'I love and trust my husband but no one can ever take my father's place and I miss him. I wish you did not have to go.'

'You equate me with your father?' he asked neutrally.

'No, sire, only that I shall miss your strength when you are gone, as I miss his.'

'I am sure you will be safe no matter what, my lady, for you have wit and fortitude,' Henry replied. 'Your husband is a fine man and a bold warrior.'

Aoife was surprised for she would not have expected such a generous remark towards Richard given their previous history.

But then Henry was playing his own game. 'He is indeed a good husband,' she replied. 'I love and honour him, but my children are my priority.'

Henry raised his brows, and she put her hand to her belly.

'Yes,' she said. 'You are the first to know. I have told no one else yet.'

'Not even your husband?'

She could see how much satisfaction he was deriving from the knowledge and she was glad to give it to him if it vouchsafed her own desire. 'Not even Richard,' she confirmed, giving him a sidelong look. 'If he were not here, I do not know what I would do. I have few enough people I can lean upon.'

Henry's eyes filled with reluctant amusement and respect. 'You have at least one king to take your part who has a personal interest because of his god-daughter,' he said. 'You know you have my protection.' He set his hand over hers and squeezed.

'Thank you, sire.'

She needed more, but it was a start. Henry's promises needed to be hammered into place to make them secure, but she had a plan.

That evening, Aoife sought Henry in his chamber where he was surrounded by his barons and scribes. His moment of quiet on the battlements had been replaced by a mood of ferocious activity. The wind had changed direction and he was making hasty plans to leave. Richard was at his side, talking to Hugh de Lacy.

'Sire' – she performed a deep curtsey – 'my mother craves a moment of your time. She has a personal gift for you before you leave and begs you to indulge her. It is important. I would not ask your time otherwise.'

Richard shot her an enquiring look which she returned with a slight shake of her head.

Henry chose to humour her, his expression full of curiosity

329

and a hint of wariness. 'By all means, Countess,' he said, and gestured for her to lead the way.

Aoife brought him to the women's quarters and dismissed the maids so that only she and her mother remained. Henry looked at them askance, although he was smiling.

Môr curtseyed and then set a carved ivory box on the table in front of him. Having unlocked it with a key unhooked from her girdle, she opened the lid to reveal a torc of twisted gold with animal-head finials. A royal neck collar gleaming with the regnal power of centuries and of weighty, blood-bought authority. Henry's eyes widened and he could only stare.

'This has belonged to my family through many generations and I brought it to my marriage with Aoife's father, Diarmait of Leinster,' Môr said. 'It would have gone to my son, Connor, but he lies in his grave. I give it to you now in token of the ties between my blood and yours, that they may remain indissoluble.'

Henry lifted the heavy, cool gold and rubbed his thumb over the inter-twining. He knew Aoife was the instigator, not her mother. Aoife amused and entertained him with her scheming. She was a daring young vixen who made him lick his lips but he felt a kindred connection with her that went much deeper than lust. They were two of a kind, running side by side in the forest. He could have her if he chose, one way or the other, but something stayed his hand – not her husband. He was still ambivalent about Richard, although beginning to realise that de Clare was formidable in his own way, and he would rather have him fighting for him than in opposition. He turned the torc and the garnet eyes glinted at him. Sleeping dragons. Gifts were always a means of conducting business. He wondered just what these women wanted and why they were being circumspect about it.

'That is very gracious of you, madam, and generous, for this is a treasure of rare craftsmanship, not lightly given outside your family.'

'Indeed, sire,' Môr said, 'but little enough if it will persuade you to take my daughter and her children into your special care should it ever prove necessary. I have lost one child, and I would not lose my remaining one. It is my mind to retire to my husband's foundation at Kilculliheen, and I would have this settled before I go.' Her gaze beseeched him.

Henry looked at Aoife whose own eyes were clear, steady and ruthless. Whatever it took, she would have his protection as her shield; she must have been driving towards this throughout his visit. He was used to refusing much greater supplication than this. He was accustomed to playing people on his line and only acceding to their requests if it benefited him. But Aoife touched some quick and tender place in his heart. Her smile, her beauty, the juxta-position of innocence and knowing; her courage to dare. He had been deftly manipulated into a corner, and he was wryly amused.

He turned to Môr. 'You need not give me this in order to have my protection, but I accept it nonetheless and I am glad to grant your wish.' He looked at Aoife. 'You shall have a safe conduct to visit me whenever you choose, and a guarantee of my protection.'

When he had gone, Aoife turned and embraced her mother, relief flooding through every fibre of her being. 'Thank you!' She and Môr seldom saw eye to eye, but in this they were one.

'I hope this will be enough to keep you safe,' Môr said, adding grimly, 'Better to buy a future than adorn a corpse.'

'What was all that about earlier?' Richard asked Aoife when they retired to their bedchamber.

She shrugged as if dismissing the matter; she had been arranging insurance for her own safety and masculine pride could be so prickly. He would frown on her making bargains with Henry, and he was already suspicious. 'My mother wanted to give the King a personal gift, a piece of traditional jewellery that has been in our family many years, and she did not want to arouse covetousness in other men's eyes.'

'Why would she want to present it to Henry in the first place?'

'Because it does no harm to keep the goodwill of a powerful man, especially when you are a widow. She herself will have no need of it in a nunnery.' She adroitly changed the subject. 'Never mind my mother, I have some other news for you.' Taking his hand, she placed it against her womb. 'I am with child again – by the next Christmas feast, we shall have a second heir.'

His expression immediately lightened and, pulling her into his arms, he kissed her thoroughly. 'That is great news, my wonderful, clever wife.'

Aoife gave him a smug look. 'We have each other, we have a child in the cradle and another to come. We have castles to build and lands to grow – what else do we need?'

'You remind me how much bounty we have indeed. I shall light a candle and thank God for the grace he has given us.' He sat down on a bench and drew her down beside him. 'Now matters are more settled, I am going to send for my daughters and see them married. I have been thinking that Robert de Quency and Matilda would be well matched – they were friends in England. And William FitzMaurice for Aline. They are good men and will protect their wives, as well as suiting what I have in mind with regards to rewards and lands.'

Aoife nodded. Sooner or later she would have to meet and accept Richard's daughters into the household. It had to be done, and now she was more established herself as Richard's wife and mother to his children, she felt a little more secure in her own position. Some of his men had taken Irish wives, but she had noted that no Irish men had been raised to positions of authority by being offered marriages to Norman women.

'Have you ever thought about finding a husband for Basilia?' she asked.

Richard eyed her in astonishment. 'Why would I? She is settled in the household, and she is a grown woman. Besides, who would she wed?'

'Perhaps you are right,' she said with a shrug. If Basilia was settled in the household it was because Richard needed her expertise with the stores and supplies. Aoife suspected his sister would rather be back in England or else in a bed with Raymond le Gros. Not that Basilia would ever admit to such a thing, and she probably did not understand herself well enough to realise her desire.

'Has she said anything to you?'

'No, of course not,' Aoife answered with a sharp laugh. 'She would never do that; but you should notice her as a woman, and not treat her as a part of the household furniture.'

He looked blank, and she was amazed anew at how he could be so perceptive and so unaware at the same time. He and Basilia were a matching pair.

'I don't treat her like that,' he said. 'She's my sister. She has her role and she has never complained.'

'Indeed,' Aoife said, 'but do you ever wonder what she is keeping to herself?'

He grimaced. 'What goes on within the head of a woman is always a mystery to me. She will have plenty to occupy her when Matilda and Aline arrive.'

Aoife said nothing more. She had given him food for thought. Whether he consumed it was another matter. Men, even the best ones, were often foolish in underestimating their womenfolk.

Henry sailed for England on an April morning with a fresh breeze pushing white clouds eastwards across the Hibernian Sea. Loaded on board his ship among the effects of his personal chamber was a jewelled ivory box containing the gold torc. In exchange, he had presented Aoife with a ring set with pearls and rock crystals in token of his promise to her, and she wore it on the wharf side, as she formally curtseyed to him in farewell. She wondered as he stepped aboard the galley and tugged his short cloak around his stocky body whether she would ever see him again.

33

Fearns, Leinster, Ireland, spring 1172

Aoife was in the hall at Fearns playing her harp for Richard when a man walked towards the dais. Silence trailed in his wake, for he was Irish and nephew to Tiernan ua Ruari. Normally he would have been an enemy at their gates, but the guards had let him through. He came unarmed and alone, walking tall with a straight back and proud expression.

Halting before Richard's chair, he knelt and presented him with a sealed parchment. Filled with apprehension, Aoife watched Richard break the seal and open the message. He read it and passed it to her.

'Tiernan ua Ruari is dead,' he said. 'Slain at a parley.' He looked at the kneeling man. 'Is this true?'

'Yes, my lord. Tiernan ua Ruari has been dispatched to God, however God may deal with him.'

Aoife's ears were ringing. She set her harp aside feeling faint and sick.

'How?' Richard demanded, and called Maurice Regan forward to translate from Irish into French.

The man hesitated, choosing his words carefully. 'The lord Tiernan invited Hugh de Lacy to a parley and they rode out to speak with each other in the space between their warriors. Seven of de Lacy's knights had been pretending to joust for their own amusement and they turned on him and charged. When the lord Tiernan rode for his own lines, his men refused to protect him. The Normans brought him down and struck off his head. Hugh de Lacy has sent it to Dublin on a spear, but Tiernan was finished before that. His own people disposed of him. It is done, and Donall son of Annad rules over us now. It is with him you must now treat.'

Even through the cloud fogging Aoife's mind, his words pierced her, sharp and bright as needles of lightning. Grief welled up in her and she struggled to breathe because an enormous wail of anguish and relief was blocking her chest. She put her hand across her mouth and the sound trickled through her fingers.

Richard turned to her full of concern.

'It should have happened earlier,' she said in a strangled voice, still fighting for breath. 'So much suffering could have been avoided. What has it all been for? Nothing!' She bit into her clenched fist, choking on grief. She had been bracing herself for so long against this man whom she had never seen, who had caused the maiming and deaths of her brothers and sent her father into exile. Now he was dead, she had nothing to withstand and she too was face down. Her reality had vanished.

Richard's arm curved around her shoulder. 'Hush now, hush now, it is over.'

'I know.' She pressed her face into the soft wool of his tunic, her shoulders shaking.

'Go and lie down,' he said gently. 'You do not want to harm yourself or the child.'

She nodded, knowing she could not sustain herself any longer in the hall. Richard gestured, and her women helped her to her chamber, where she threw herself down on the bed and sobbed until her stomach ached and her throat was raw as she released all the grief and fear that had been stored inside her for such a long time, not least her sorrow that her father had not lived long enough to see this day. Eventually she fell asleep, tumbling into dreamless twilight, and when she woke and drew the bed curtains, it was well past noon. She was queasy and weak, but her head was clear.

'My lady, are you feeling better?' asked Deirdre.

She nodded without answering. Ainne brought her a bowl of

broth and some fresh bread on a basket tray. 'Here, my love,' she said. 'Eat some of this and you will feel better.'

Aoife sat up in bed and slowly ate the bread and broth. The physical comfort of nourishment began to revive her and as she looked around, she noticed that the world seemed sharper and more polished. The flames in the small hearth burned more brightly and the carved details on the coffers stood out in stronger relief. The pattern on her quilt, the glint of gold braid on her cloak thrown over the clothing pole. The pain had gone, flushed out on the storm of tears. Tiernan was dead; that particular chess game was over, bitter and bloody though it had been. And she was still here, still surviving.

'I will have this victory for you, Daidí,' she said softly. 'Even if you cannot be here, I will celebrate for you. I shall use what I have been given. I shall weave my net around powerful men and they will be my allies and protectors, not my enemies.' She would write to her mother where now she dwelt among nuns at Kilculliheen, but it could wait until tomorrow.

Leaving the bed, she clapped her hands and called for her gown of white wool with the green and blue braiding, and she had her ladies dress her hair with jewels. She pinched her cheeks to bring up the colour and bit her lips, and then she went back out to Richard.

His gaze kindled when he saw her and he held out his hand. 'Are you feeling better, my love?'

'Yes,' she said, raising her head proudly. 'I needed to weep, and now it is done.'

'Good, for we have a long night of celebration, and you, my dearest love, are the queen of all.'

She laughed, and as her heart lurched upwards she discovered that she was indeed ready to dance.

In late May Richard's daughters arrived on a merchant galley from Bristol to be married, Aline to William FitzMaurice, and

Matilda to Robert de Quency. Standing beside Richard on the wharf side, Aoife saw two vibrant young women, exquisitely dressed, reminding her of younger versions of Basilia in the way they stood, proud and elegant.

Richard's face broke into a broad smile. 'Matilda! Aline!' Leaving Aoife, he ran to the ship and up the gangplank to greet them. Aoife watched him throw his arms around his daughters, and anxiety rippled through her, for she had no history with these young women and could never know them as their father did. Nevertheless, observing his way with them, how they hugged him wholeheartedly and laughed, she tried to reassure herself. For a man's daughters to react to him like this was a positive sign of his character, and anyway, they would soon be married with men of their own to occupy their interest.

He assisted them onto the wharf, single file down the gangplank, and then, with an arm around each daughter, brought them to Aoife. The girls curtseyed demurely and Aoife responded with a strained smile and welcomed them with formal kisses on the cheek. Usually she was not aware of her Irish accent when she spoke Richard's Norman tongue, but she was very conscious of it now.

Matilda and Aline were close to her own age – gently raised young ladies, who had led a gracious existence and never known a day's hardship. All they had in common with her was Richard, and she was worried lest his relationship with them diminish his bond with her.

The girls greeted Basilia with cries of joy. Aoife watched Basilia hug them, her face alight with joy. There was genuine love, pleasure and shared experience, and Aoife felt an uncomfortable prickle of exclusion.

'You did not tell me your daughters were so beautiful,' she said, loudly enough for the girls to hear.

Richard smiled at her. 'I did not know myself, they have grown so much since last I saw them.'

'You must be very proud.'

'I am,' he said with a wistful note in his voice. 'Very proud indeed.'

Matilda and Aline were very taken with their baby half-sister, Matilda especially, and soon she was holding Isabelle in her lap, blowing against her soft little neck, making her squeal with delight. Aoife restrained the urge to snatch Isabelle back telling herself it was a good thing for her daughter to have doting half-sisters. 'I am your stepmother,' she told them with a rueful look, 'but I do not want young women near my own age calling me mother. Madam or Lady Aoife will suffice, and let your memories of your own mother stay intact.'

'I do not remember her,' Matilda said. 'She died when Aline was born.'

'But people must have told you about her.'

'Yes, Papa has always done, and Aunt Basilia of course.' Aline was the more formal of the girls. She wore her rich brown hair tightly drawn back under a wimple and sat with her hands folded in her lap.

Aoife wondered if she was vying with a paragon who could do no wrong because she was dead. She could not compete with that, so she must do her best to cultivate Aline and Matilda while making it clear she was Richard's legitimate wife and mother of his heirs. 'It is good you have the stories and your father to guide you,' she said, and wished a little forlornly that she still had her own father to call her his precious girl.

Richard's daughters were accomplished embroiderers. Sewing was not one of Aoife's favourite pastimes although she was competent and would do so to socialise. To Aline and Matilda it was second nature, and they sat with shoulders touching as their needles flew in and out of their work. Basilia stitched alongside them in a trinity of domestic enjoyment that made Aoife feel excluded.

Work halted when the two prospective bridegrooms arrived to visit the women. Robert de Quency and William FitzMaurice were a little ill at ease and embarrassed to be joining the ladies rather than being occupied with masculine pursuits, but they were eager to have time with their soon-to-be wives.

Aoife took control, pre-empting Basilia. She welcomed the knights, offering them wine, before sending them to sit and play chess in the window seat with the girls, although within full view and earshot of the other women. She knew Richard had chosen the men carefully for their abilities, for their connections, but also taking his daughters' wellbeing into account. There had been no shortage of suitors. Indeed, Richard had passed over Raymond le Gros, who had been a contender for a while.

'You do not know how fortunate you are,' she said to Matilda as the young woman brushed past her, carrying the ivory box containing the chess pieces.

'You are wrong, Lady Aoife – with respect,' Matilda replied with gentle contradiction. 'Indeed, I do know how fortunate I am.' She gave Robert de Quency a dazzling smile.

A month later Richard's daughters were married at Dunamase, a hilltop fortress fifty miles to the north-west of Fearns in a double wedding amid magnificent celebrations with music, entertainment and feasting. Richard wore his laurel crown and a tunic of costly midnight-blue silk. He sat in Diarmait's chair as lord of Leinster, king in all but name, with Aoife enthroned beside him, voluptuous in pregnancy, a jewelled circlet crowning her veil. She perched Isabelle on her knee in a pose that deliberately evoked the Madonna and child and basked in Richard's proud gaze.

Matilda glowed as she danced with Robert de Quency, her gaze only for him. Aline was more circumspect with William FitzMaurice but content and willing to do her duty.

Aoife kept a constant watch on the hall for although everything was good-natured for the moment, high spirits could turn on the instant to drink-fuelled violence and quarrels. Raymond le Gros, she noted, had embarked on one of his drinking bouts. His gaze kept flicking to Richard's daughters and his mouth was downturned. He watched Basilia too, his expression that of a hungry gazehound upon a hare. Basilia was resplendent in a gown of madder-red silk offset by a belt of black and gold embroidery. Her braids showed beneath her veil, thick and fair-gold twined with silk ribbons, and her cheeks were flushed from wine and dancing.

By the end of the evening, Aoife was relieved that the only mishaps had been a couple of easily contained brawls and the usual casualties of any celebration who had had to be carried away to sleep off their excesses. The newlyweds were escorted to their marriage beds and their unions blessed by Richard's chaplain. Attending each bridal chamber in turn, Aoife was placed at the forefront beside the priest, her fruitful womb a powerful symbol of family fecundity. She accepted the role with pride and enjoyed having a central part in the proceedings. She kissed her stepdaughters and wished them well. 'May you have as much joy as I have,' she said, and sincerely hoped they would.

The couples bedded, the men returned to the hall to continue celebrating, and Aoife retired to her own chamber, knowing it would likely be dawn before Richard came to bed. Walking towards her room, she came across a couple groping in the dark at the foot of the stairs. The sight was common after a bedding ceremony. The proceedings and the amount of drink consumed always served to inflame lust. The woman had been responding to the man but had changed her mind and was now trying to push him away.

'No,' she panted. 'We cannot. It is wrong!'

The man gave a soft laugh. 'It's not wrong. You want what I want, don't deny it. You have been denying it for too long already.'

With a jolt, Aoife recognised Raymond and Basilia. 'What is this?' she demanded, and Basilia gasped and tore out of Raymond's arms. She gave Aoife a horrified look, and fled up the stairs, wiping her mouth on the back of her hand. Raymond, chest heaving, shot Aoife a defiant, bloodshot glare.

Aoife's heart was thundering with shock and fear, but she stood firm. 'You dishonour yourself in drink,' she said coldly, 'and you have overstepped all bounds of honourable behaviour. The Earl shall hear of this.'

Raymond curled his lip in a sneer. 'Tell him,' he slurred. 'What do I care for his opinion? I am not his dog to do his bidding.'

'He is your lord and you are sworn to him.' Aoife's voice was ice. 'You will respect all women under this roof. No matter your deeds in battle, if you cannot master yourself between times, you are nothing. There will be a reckoning for this.'

'Yes,' he said bitterly. 'I risk myself again and again and for what? A place at the hearth? Glory? But when it comes to giving true reward I am ignored. My cousin may marry de Clare's daughter, but I am passed over when without me, none of this would have been possible.'

'Drink has run away with your tongue,' she snapped. 'We shall deal with this in the morning. Go to bed and sleep it off, you fool.' Turning on her heel, she followed Basilia up the stairs, half fearing he would drag her back and strike her, and was relieved to hear his footsteps shuffling away, amid a litany of drunken curses.

What she had just witnessed between Raymond and Basilia had been a potential danger for a long time but the way it had erupted now brought them to a dilemma. Could Richard afford to keep Raymond? More tellingly, could he afford to lose him?

Basilia was sitting by the fire in the women's bower, her arms wrapped around her body, rocking to and fro. Aoife poured them each a cup of strong, sweet mead and sat down beside her.

'Drink this,' she said.

Basilia took a small, prim sip, her hands shaking. 'I did not know, I swear it. He was drunk . . . I never realised . . .'

No, you didn't, because you cannot see the nose in front of your face, Aoife thought with irritation. 'Fighting men are not safe when they are in their cups,' she said. 'They need little encouragement.'

'I have not encouraged him,' Basilia said indignantly. 'I have always been safe with him. He is part of the household, and someone I thought would protect me from such as this.'

Aoife was astonished at Basilia's blindness. 'You blush when he looks at you,' she said forthrightly. 'You look for him when the fighting men return and you are always fussing his dog. That is all the encouragement he needs.'

Basilia's face suffused with pink. 'But I have a care to all of my brother's senior officers. Should I ignore and slight them?'

'Of course not, but you know very well what I mean; you were not fighting him at the outset, were you?'

Basilia covered her face and through her fingers made a soft sound that was almost a moan.

'You realise Richard will have to know.'

Basilia raised her head. 'Yes,' she said. 'I understand. It is my mistake as well as Raymond's. It will not happen again. I shall retire now. I am very tired.' She rose to her feet and retreated with dignity.

Aoife finished her mead and sought her own bed, a frown between her brows. Raymond might be a powerful warrior and commander, but he was a dog that could not be trusted without its muzzle. He was becoming a threat, and she was not keen to call him brother-in-law. This had to be stopped before it went further, and indeed, should never have gone this far.

It was a very muted household that stirred from the previous night's ashes, with many a clutched head and eyes narrowed against the harsh morning light. Aoife brought Richard a tisane for his malaise and while she changed Isabelle's swaddling, told him about Raymond and Basilia, slanting the blame in Raymond's direction.

'You need to deal with him,' she said. 'He is a servant who desires to become a master.'

Richard washed his palms over his face and groaned. 'He

drinks too much and then he goes too far,' he said. 'I will speak to him. I know you and Basilia are not close, but I ask you to look out for her and I will have a word with Hervey too.'

'Of course I will,' Aoife said. 'I have already spoken with her. You may leave her to me.'

Washed and dressed but still feeling like death warmed up, Richard summoned Raymond to his chamber with a feeling of sullied distaste for what he had to do. Aoife was right, but he would not have chosen to spend the morning after a wedding chastising one of his household knights for bad behaviour.

Raymond eventually arrived red-eyed and bleary as they all were, but at least his clothes were clean and he had dunked his head in a water barrel on the way, for his hair was sleeked back and his collar was damp.

'I need to speak with you.' Richard folded his arms. 'I think you know why – unless you were so far in your cups that you have no recollection at all.'

Raymond's pallid complexion flushed. 'Yes, I know, sire.'

'Disrespect my sister again and it will be the last thing you do on this earth, is that understood? It is not the behaviour I expect from a senior knight of my household. You set an example to us all in battle. Now set it in my hall also or get out.'

'I crave your pardon, sire,' Raymond said stiffly. 'I was drunk and my behaviour was unacceptable. I should not have done it. I am willing to take whatever punishment you mete out to me and apologise unreservedly to you and to the lady Basilia.'

Richard frowned, trying to assess what was happening behind Raymond's stoical mask. Once he had taken Raymond at face value, but recently he had begun to wonder. 'I cannot keep a man in my entourage who oversteps the bounds in such a way. I ought to cut off your balls and hang them from the battlements.'

Raymond's colour remained high. 'I misjudged my drink, sire. I will make amends and it will never happen again.'

'Indeed, you will make amends. Leave the drink alone, for clearly it unmans you. Go and take a patrol down to Kilkenny and then ride the border. I do not expect to see you back here for a month and I shall expect better of you when you return.'

Raymond's expression was a blank wall. 'Do I have your leave to depart, sire?' he asked woodenly.

'As soon as you may. I expect you and your men to be gone within the hour.'

Raymond bowed, his lips set and tight, and turning on his heel, walked out.

Richard rubbed his forehead and swore under his breath. He was angry with himself for not being sufficiently vigilant and he was furious with Raymond, the more so because he was such a fine soldier and he relied on his expertise. Now he would have to be watched, and Basilia too, for clearly she was vulnerable.

Basilia tensed as Richard entered the women's chamber where she was sitting with her newlywed nieces and the other ladies including Aoife. She had known this moment was coming and she feared the outcome but was determined to face it with courage.

Richard embraced his daughters and asked if they were well, receiving rosy blushes and coy smiles in return. He kissed Aoife, and little Isabelle who was sitting in her lap. And then he turned to Basilia. 'A word if you will, sister.'

She stood up, feeling queasy, and followed him out of earshot.

'Aoife told me what happened last night,' he said. 'I am sorry I was not there to protect you. I never thought you would be at risk from one of my own men.'

Basilia clasped her hands together and raised her chin. 'Have you spoken to Raymond?' She wondered just what Aoife had said to Richard.

'Yes,' he said tightly. 'He is taking out a patrol and I have told him to stay away for a while. When he returns I shall decide what to do with him.'

Guilt washed over her, for she did not want to be responsible for the loss of a good man. 'He is your best battle commander, and when he is not in his cups he is courteous and honourable.'

'Then he had better not be in his cups again while he dwells in my household,' Richard said grimly. 'I have given him time to think on his behaviour away from me and the household.'

She nodded and dropped her gaze, relieved that Richard had not come upon her and Raymond last night for there would have been no return from that. Raymond would have died. She did not want his blood on her hands, for whatever bounds he had overstepped, she had overstepped some too. At least his absence would dampen everything down and she could pretend nothing had happened.

Richard left and Basilia returned to her sewing but she could not concentrate. No one said anything, but she was aware of their circumspect glances. Aoife leaned over to give her hand a reassuring pat and Basilia almost struck her away. Aoife seemed more like an opponent on a chess board who had just made an advantageous move rather than a concerned sister-in-law. Saying she had to check how much wine remained after last night's depredations, Basilia excused herself. But for all she cared the wine could run dry. Indeed, it might be better if it did.

She was crossing the courtyard towards the wine store when Raymond emerged from his chamber, his baggage sack tied to his spear and Badge trotting at his heels. She stopped abruptly, her face growing hot with embarrassment. He stopped too and looked away sheepishly. But then he turned his head and fixed her with a candid flint-grey stare that left her in no doubt as to his thoughts. He bowed to her with formal correctness and continued on his way.

Basilia entered the storage area and gazed at the remaining casks of wine and found herself completely unable to numerate them because the cogs in her mind were no longer connecting and all she wanted to do was weep.

34

Fearns, Leinster, Ireland, winter 1172

'A boy, madam, it's a boy!'

Aoife heard the words through the cramping pain of the final effort to expel the child from her womb. A baby's lusty wail filled the room as the midwife cleaned the mucus and blood off his slippery little body with a towel. Aoife had been standing up, gripping a rope at the side of the bed as she strained to push him out, but now she collapsed onto the mattress and held out her arms. 'Give him to me,' she said.

The midwife passed him over and Aoife examined him minutely to check he was whole and that he truly was a boy while he bawled and thrashed his arms. She had to touch and feel him for herself to make it real. Like Isabelle's, his hair glinted with gold, and his eyes were misty blue. She saw herself in him, and her father, and Richard, all mingled and blended. Tears filled her eyes and she pressed a tender kiss to his brow before handing him to the women to be bathed while she and the midwife dealt with delivering the afterbirth. The blood was sponged away and soft rags placed between Aoife's thighs. She drank a cup of honey in hot water infused with herbs and rested against the pillows while her attendants washed and swaddled her son.

When Môr, who had come from her retirement at Kilculliheen to assist with the birth, prepared to take him to show Richard, Aoife stopped her. 'No,' she said. 'Send for him, I will give him the child myself.'

'That is against all propriety!' Môr said, horrified. 'You cannot rise from your childbed to do such a thing!'

Aoife stared her mother down. 'I have borne a son to inherit Richard's earldom and my father's lands. No other will present him to his sire. I have done the work and I shall have the accolade.'

'You do not know what you are saying!'

'I know exactly what I am saying, mother,' Aoife replied imperiously. 'Ask Richard to come to me. Take Basilia with you.'

Her mother hesitated, but eventually yielded to Aoife's desire. Basilia was shaking her head with an air of 'what did one expect from the uncivilised Irish', but Aoife stared her out until Basilia too dropped her gaze.

When they had gone, Aoife turned her attention to the baby snuffling in her arms, her heart full of love and joyful pride. She so wished her father was here to see him.

Hearing Richard's voice in the ante chamber she gestured for Deirdre to help her out of the bed, silencing the maid with a glare when she started to question. As Aoife stood up her vision blurred for an instant and she felt queasy, but she was determined to have this moment. Lips set in disapproval, Deirdre straightened Aoife's chemise and tucked a soft shawl around her shoulders. Aoife lifted her chin, drew a breath, and stepped through the curtain, the baby in her arms.

The coldness of the floor struck up through her bare feet, but she ignored it, intent on having this moment with Richard. He was staring at her, tension and hunger in his face, his gaze flicking between her and the bundle she held.

'Our son,' she said, and placed the baby carefully in his arms.

His throat worked. He took one of the miniature curled fists in his hand and folded his fingers over it, encasing it like a shell around a nut, completely absorbed. And then, rousing from his wonder, he looked at her, moisture shining in his eyes.

'It seemed like too much to ask God when He has done so much for us already, but now I believe we truly have been granted

His favour,' he said in a choked voice. 'I am doubly blessed to have a wife such as you, and now a son.'

She gave him a wide smile. 'We are both indeed truly blessed.'

He looked at her bare feet. 'You should not be out of bed.'

'I know what I am doing.' She raised her chin. 'I am the one who has borne this baby after all. Take him and announce your heir to your men and celebrate, and I shall return to my rest and be a model of propriety.'

'I doubt that,' he said with a slow smile, and leaned forward to kiss her in farewell. 'Be assured we shall drink many a toast in your honour.'

'I need no assurance on that score,' she replied with a laugh and retired, letting the curtain swish down behind her. Suddenly her eyes were heavy and she was nauseous with exhaustion, but it did not detract from the euphoria. Climbing back into bed, she allowed Deirdre to place a warm stone at her feet. She drank some more of the honey and herb tisane, content now to relax and savour her triumph.

Once again Aoife was enjoying the Christmas feast, this time held in the great hall at Dunamase. She loved the firelit dark, the tales around the hearth, the closeness of family gathered in an intimate circle. The pungent aroma of so many bodies in proximity, rather than being unpleasant, spoke to her of kinship and security. It was the scent of safety and the pack, with everyone in the den and not risking their lives outside. And this year she had a baby son to bring to the feast. She had deliberately chosen to wear a sweeping gown of blue wool to honour the Virgin, loosely gathered around her recovering body, and a gold circlet on her head of regnal gold. She basked in the awed looks people sent her way, and the pride and wonder shining on Richard's face as he gazed at her.

Further along the dining board, Basilia observed the family amid bitter thoughts. She could hold her niece and new nephew in her arms – when Aoife permitted – but her own womb remained barren while Aoife lit up the room with her ethereal beauty and her motherhood. Richard was clearly besotted by his young wife, even more now she had entrenched her position by bearing a son. Basilia sometimes felt she was like a leaf turning sere with the first winds of autumn. Her girlhood was gone and her ripe years were swiftly diminishing. She could see herself dwelling in this household, performing tasks as Richard required, overseeing the duties of the ladies in the bower while Aoife preened in her chair, until eventually Basilia became the bent old woman feeding logs onto the fire and mumbling bread and milk with her toothless gums.

She pushed the thought away with vigour and revulsion and her glance wandered further down the board to Raymond. He was usually absent on patrol duties and when he was in the household he avoided her, treating her with aloof courtesy when they had to be in the same company. She had avoided him too, while still being intensely aware and wary of his presence. Her skin prickled when he was close, and while fear was an element, it was fear of herself as much as of him. He scarcely drank at all in the hall these days – a single cup with his meal and any subsequent cups cut with spring water. She knew he still thirsted after undiluted wine – she could see it in the way he inhaled as the jugs were carried past – but he abstained.

As the dancing began and Matilda and Aline rose to lead the women, Basilia retired to her chamber. Her head was throbbing and she felt dull with weariness. She sent her maid to fetch a hot tisane and removed her headdress because the jewelled head band and the pins tightly securing her wimple were part of the reason for her headache. She was unwinding her braids and combing her fingers through them when she realised that Raymond was standing in the doorway watching her. Stifling a scream, she took a step back.

He swiftly raised his hands. 'I am sober,' he said, 'I mean you no harm. I did not intend to startle you.'

'Do you truly wish to be thrown out of my brother's household?' she demanded, trembling like a leaf. 'Or worse?'

'That is not my intent at all, my lady, but if it happens, so be it. I needed to see you for a moment, to set matters right.'

His gaze was focused avidly on her exposed hair, an intimate thing never revealed in public. Raising her chin, she fixed him with a frigid stare.

'What happened before – it preys on my mind every day. I was in my cups and my head was dark with memories of battle and what we had had to do to survive. You were like a cold, clear well. I want to apologise with every part of my being, and ask your forgiveness, even though I do not deserve it. If it has taken me a long time to speak to you, it is because I have lacked the courage. Fighting a battle is one thing, but facing you is another.'

Basilia bit her lip as he knelt to her and bowed his head. The candle light gleamed on his thick hair, the colour of ripe wheat on the day of harvesting.

'You have my service and loyalty always. In token of my esteem and to make amends, I beg you to accept this gift from me, without obligation, save that we may again speak to each other in passing as friends.' He presented her with a small book, bound in red leather on wooden boards, and secured with a jewelled clasp. 'It is a life of Saint Anne. I wish to honour you and show you my loyalty – and ask you to trust me again.'

She looked down at the exquisite little book, emotions boiling through her when she would far rather have had weary calm. 'I do not know if it is possible,' she said, 'but thank you for the gift – it is beautiful. I can only accept it by way of a peace offering. No more than that.'

'Indeed not,' he said. 'I understand.'

The maid returned with the tisane and looked between them with widening eyes. Raymond bowed to Basilia, gave her a single, intent look, and took his leave. She rubbed her thumb over the book's cover, feeling frightened and excited and knowing this must be an end, not a beginning. She turned to the maid who was putting the tisane on the coffer, her gaze studiously lowered. 'Messire FitzWilliam brought me a gift to celebrate the Christmas season,' she said. 'I shall tell the Earl about it myself, and I expect your discretion.'

'Of course, my lady. I hope I have served you long enough for you to know that I can be trusted.'

Basilia gave a stiff nod. 'I am not asking you to hide anything, for there is nothing to hide. Come,' she added briskly, 'help me with my hair. I wish to retire.'

35

Dunamase, Leinster, Ireland, April 1173

Richard was eating roast beef from the spit, served with a mustard and herb sauce. Fresh bread accompanied the dish and knobbly strands of batter scattered with salt that crunched between the teeth. Isabelle, seventeen months old, perched on Aoife's knee eating morsels of bread and finely chopped meat. Her pale gold hair framed her little face in infant ringlets and her eyes were round blue pools, absorbing everything with curiosity. Richard was holding Gilbert and the baby had wriggled an arm free of his swaddling to reach for his father's slice of beef. 'No, not for you yet, little one,' Richard said with a laugh. 'Wait until you have teeth!'

'He will be a great lord, your son. He will do everything early, for he is a Murchada as well as a Clare,' Aoife said, her eyes sparkling with amusement.

'That explains much!' Richard used his free hand to reach for his wine and paused as he saw his usher escorting a royal messenger up the hall. Richard recognised the man – a tough, wiry individual with dusty brown curls and sharp brown eyes. Exchanging a glance with Aoife, Richard handed Gilbert to Matilda, knowing this must be urgent news.

'My lord.' Bowing, the messenger handed Richard a package closed with the royal seal. 'I am to return with an immediate reply.'

Richard broke the seal, opened the letter, and as he read the lines his heart sank with dismay. He nodded to the messenger.

'I need to draft a reply. Go and take some refreshment and find a bed for the night. You can leave in the morning.'

'Sire.' The man bowed and departed down the hall to a trestle where a place was made for him and bread and pottage doled out.

'What is wrong?' Aoife demanded.

Richard grimaced as he gave her the parchment. 'The King summons me to serve in Normandy,' he said quietly so that the words did not carry beyond her hearing. 'I am to muster my knights and come to him as soon as I can.'

'But you have business here. You cannot leave!'

'I must at his summons. I am obliged to serve him in the field for forty days. He has the right to command my presence.'

'Does he say why?'

Richard shook his head. 'His messenger will have that information. I will speak to him in private when he has eaten.'

'Henry would not summon you from Ireland so swiftly just to perform military service,' Aoife said. 'Something is amiss.'

'I agree.' He glanced round the hall, mentally assigning positions to those he would take and those he would leave behind to govern. He wondered what kind of trouble Henry was in and what it meant for his own security.

'You do not have to go. Send Raymond or Hervey with soldiers.'

He shook his head. 'The King has specifically summoned me as a vassal in chief. It is my duty to go in person.'

She tightened her lips. 'He has no right.'

Richard said nothing, not wanting to become embroiled in a tit-for-tat argument. She knew he had no choice even if she was refusing to accept it.

He retired to his personal chamber and Aoife followed him, leaving the children with the other women. The messenger was summoned together with the senior household officials and knights, and once they had all gathered, Richard sought answers.

Henry's messenger cleared his throat. 'Sire, Queen Alienor

and the King's three oldest sons are in rebellion against him. The King of France is aiding them and has crossed the border into Normandy. The King summons you and your soldiers to help him deal with the situation.'

'His sons and his queen are in rebellion?' Richard was taken aback but not entirely surprised. Henry had spoken little of his wife and sons while in Ireland, but there had been an undercurrent, and letters had arrived towards the end of his stay that had made him frown.

'Sire, the Young King is disputing territories that he says were promised to him and King Louis has taken his part.'

Which he would do with alacrity being the Young King's father-in-law, Richard thought. Anything that threw Henry off balance would be grist to his mill. 'And the Queen?'

'She has agitated her sons against their father, sire. Again, it is concerned with land but I do not know the detail.'

Richard bit his thumbnail. 'What of England?' he asked, thinking of his de Clare kin. 'Is there rebellion there too?'

'I do not know how widespread, sire, but the Earls of Leicester and Norfolk are under suspicion.'

Richard exhaled hard. This was serious.

'What is it?' Aoife's gaze darted between him and the messenger.

He shook his head. 'The Earl of Leicester is my cousin. His father was my mother's brother.'

'So, the King might be watching you for a similar betrayal,' she said.

He looked at her. 'There is no "might" about it. I expect he is.'

The messenger said, 'The Constable of Dublin has already been summoned, my lord. I delivered his letter on my way to you.'

Meaning that Henry was either in dire need to be summoning his lords from Ireland, or perhaps he wanted to keep them under close scrutiny. Was it trust, or lack of trust? Emptying Ireland was not a good idea, but perhaps Henry had no choice. 'Doubtless my lord de Lacy will send me his own messengers in due course,' Richard said. 'I will write to the King immediately. You may tell him verbally that I shall answer his summons and join his service as swiftly as I can.'

Once the messenger had been dismissed, he turned to his gathered men. 'From a lull to a storm in the space of an hour,' he said wryly. 'You have heard what has been said, and also what has not. We must answer the summons as swiftly as we may, but there is no need to spread the news abroad just yet. I shall have to go, I am specifically summoned. Raymond shall come with me. Hervey, you will govern in my absence . . .' Richard deliberated with his counsellors, making arrangements and decisions to be acted upon initially.

'We will talk more in the morning,' he said eventually. 'We must be sure of our ground and a night's sleep will benefit us all.'

The men departed. Alone with Aoife, Richard looked at her – so fine, so slight and beautiful, and when he thought about leaving her here with the children, he was filled with misgiving. 'I have no choice but to answer the King's summons, and quickly. Who knows how much support the rebellion has gathered.'

Aoife bit her lip. She had invested in Henry to keep them safe and could not allow that investment to be destroyed. 'I agree, you must go,' she said. 'We have both grown up in times of strife, not knowing if the ground beneath our feet would still be there the next day or week or month. I do not want that for our children.'

Richard nodded. 'Henry, whatever his faults, is a more stable ruler than a youth of seventeen. We have to ensure he remains King. And if we succeed, Henry will be in our debt.' He took her hands in his. 'I cannot leave you here in Ireland, you and the children must go to Striguil.'

Initially taken aback, she quickly saw the sense in his words, given the factions at work. It would be so easy without his

355

protection in Ireland for someone to end her life and the children's too. 'If we must,' she said.

'I think it a wise precaution. I want to know you are protected and safe.'

'Who else will come? Basilia, I assume, and your daughters?'

'Yes. I will leave as strong a military garrison as possible to protect Leinster, and Hervey and Domnall shall hold it fast. My service is forty days . . . but it may be for longer.'

Aoife pressed her lips together and he pulled her into his arms. 'I do not want to go, and I know you feel the same, but since we have no choice, we must seek the advantage in the situation.'

He was right, and she showed her agreement by stroking his cheek. 'When will you leave?'

'By the end of the week.'

She gave a small, almost bleak smile. She had waited for him for three years while the swallows came and went, and now in the space of a few days he was to leave just as swiftly as a migrating bird.

Aoife had thought to be overjoyed to return to Striguil, but the castle had not been occupied by more than a garrison and constable since Richard had left three years ago. The defences were maintained and strong but the domestic area had a musty, empty smell and the air was cold even though it was early summer.

The first meal on arriving was a greasy lamb pottage. Gilbert was teething and kept up a constant grizzle, his little cheeks bright red. Richard was preoccupied with the troops and Aoife, pursued by her insecurities, grew increasingly agitated that his attention was focused elsewhere because on the morrow he would be gone and she would have to stay here and wait, powerless. As the day progressed she grew more irritable and anxious, snapping at everyone until they avoided her. She cuddled the children and she pushed them away and then cuddled them again, feeling horrible and guilty, but unable to stop herself.

When she and Richard retired that night after he had finished talking with his knights and completing plans for the next day, she was tetchy and shrugged him off.

'Come now.' He pulled her against him. 'You cannot bid me farewell like this. I thought we were agreed.'

'But you are looking outwards and I must sit here and wait. God knows I have waited long enough for you before – too long. If you do not return to me whole by Christmas, I will return to Ireland, I swear I will,' she said, her anxiety making her tone querulous.

'I will be back long before then. You are safer here than anywhere else.' He gave her arm a gentle shake. 'Is this any way to bid your lord farewell? Do you think I want to leave you?'

She shook her head and started to cry. She did not want to lose him; she did not want him to go and she was frightened of her situation. And when she was frightened, her instinctive response was to fight.

'Hush now, I love you and I promise I will return.' He rubbed her spine. 'You are Countess of Striguil and Lady of Leinster and I am counting on you to do your part.'

She pressed her face into his shirt, inhaling his scent, needing the closeness, knowing that in a few hours he would be gone and she would be fending for herself and her children. Forced back on her own resources, she rallied. 'You will be sure to write to me and send messengers – and with the truth. I will know if you do not,' she warned.

He responded wryly, 'I could never keep the truth from you. If I tried I would fail for you always have means of finding out. You shall know everything, my love – as though you were there yourself. I promise you.'

'I doubt it,' she said, but found a smile. 'Very well, but return to me in one piece. I want you whole and strong in my arms and in our bed.'

'I promise.'

She sealed her lips to his and kissed him passionately and he took her to the bed, and they made love until they were satiated with nothing more to give or take.

Rising on her elbow, she looked at his long, lithe frame and strong muscles and the thin stripe of hair running into the auburn bush at his groin, and even though she had reached her limit, she still wanted him all over again just to have the security. She kissed him, and he wound his fingers through her hair.

'Indeed, I shall hurry home – I am going to miss you badly.'

'Not as much as I shall miss you.'

'I would argue, but you always find a way to win.'

'No,' she said, losing her smile. 'Win or lose it is always about survival.' She left the bed to fetch her ivory jewel box and removed a ring set with pearls and rock crystals. 'When you greet the King, I want you to show him this,' she said. 'Promise me.'

He took it and raised his brows at her.

'When he was in Ireland, I asked him to protect us all because Isabelle was his god-daughter and he swore he would. He gave me this ring in token of his word. Tell him that I ask him to honour that vow—'

'You said nothing to me,' Richard interrupted.

She jutted her chin. 'It was none of your concern. I was making provision for the future the same as you, but as women's business.'

'And what did you barter in return? Henry never gives something for nothing. Did he have you? Was that the price?' he demanded, his eyes bright and fierce.

'No, by God he did not!' she said furiously. 'I would rather cut my throat than be one of his whores, and I would rather cut yours than have you believe that of me. For Ireland and for my family, I would make it seem so to him even if I had to lie and lead him on.' She pushed her hair away from her face. 'The danger time is long past anyway. Henry's mistresses and whores are always young women. When they lose their innocence and grow older or get with child, his lust for them wanes. He is fond of me, but not in that kind of way.'

'Then in what kind of way?' Richard asked, narrow-eyed.

'Henry has courtiers aplenty and people who serve him out of loyalty, or admiration, or who have kinship ties, but none whom he can call friend. He quarrelled with and murdered his last true friend. But he counts me in some strange way as such and he takes an interest. He will serve himself first always, but he gave me that ring as a token of his faith, and I trust him to hold true as much as it is within him to do so.' She closed his fingers over the ring. 'Do as I say and give it to him for both our sakes.'

Richard grimaced. 'I spent many years as Henry's enemy but I made a truce with him to save my family. As you say of others, I serve him out of duty and because he is the King. But I would never call him my friend. For you to have this bond with him, to be his golden woman . . .' He shook his head, still a little hostile.

'And I am yours,' she said firmly, 'not his. Remember that. I could have been his, but I chose you. As you are mine, and no one else's.' She put her arms round him and pressed her face to his. 'Remember that when you are in the camp.'

'I don't want anyone else.' He pulled her into his arms and lay down with her, holding her close. 'You are enough and more.'

Basilia knelt in the church of St Mary in Striguil, hands clasped as she prayed at the altar, asking God to look after the men going to Normandy, and those who had to wait upon their safe return. She tried to be a good Christian and pray for her brother and Aoife but was hampered by her anger. She was an important cog in the household, but always taken for granted, like a piece of furniture to sit upon, and her resentment had begun to consume her.

Her stomach churned as she prayed for the men – for one

man in particular. She had consciously avoided singling him out, but the deeper layers would not be denied and she saw his face clearly behind her closed lids. Last night at supper he had reached for some bread, almost but not quite brushing her body with his. She had felt his breath against her cheek and sensed his power. This morning he had held a curtain aside for her and they had passed within each other's space, as close as lovers. In an hour he would be gone and she was going to miss experiencing the disturbing but exciting frisson whenever he entered the room.

Bowing her head, she counted her prayer beads through her fingers.

The chapel door opened and she heard a firm tread up the nave and knew, even before she turned, that it was Raymond. Without speaking, he went to light a candle and to cross himself before the statue of the Virgin, haloed in the flames of supplicant candles. He sang a prayer, his hand upon his breast, and knelt to attend to his devotions. Basilia bit her lip and concentrated on her tightly clasped hands, although her prayers had flown away like startled birds.

When she rose to leave, so did he.

'I wish you success and Godspeed, messire,' she said.

'I hope for His mercy,' he replied. 'I have prayed and it is in His hands.' He hesitated, and then said, 'When I return, things are going to be different.'

'In what way?' Her heart leaped and she could barely meet the intensity of his stare.

'I have made up my mind about certain matters, but they will wait this short while. It is strange, is it not, that a man can excel at something and not be content in his heart and soul.'

Basilia thought of her own experience of being a capable chatelaine, seeing to the logistics with ease. 'Yes,' she said, 'but I do not think it is rare.'

He smiled wryly. 'Perhaps, but I intend to change it.' He bowed to her and left the church.

She stood for a moment, wondering what he had meant, then made her way back to the castle, more unsettled than when she had come to pray.

36

Verneuil, Normandy border, autumn 1173

Tired and sweaty, muscles aching, Richard rode into Verneuil with the late afternoon sun burning on his helm and mail. In the places not gleaming with perspiration, the troop was floured with thick dust. Despite the satisfaction of a task well accomplished, Richard was finding it hard to hold up his head and ride with a straight back.

Blackened buildings and burned timbers told the story of the town's recent sacking by the French, although the damage was sporadic and the donjon was still intact behind its protective defences. The stink of charred wood permeated the air even though the smoke had dissipated. The French had fled as Henry's relief force augmented by Richard's Irish contingent had arrived just in time to prevent the donjon from being overrun and its constable Hugh de Lacy from being taken prisoner.

Henry had remained at Verneuil to secure the town and Richard had cut off to harry the French and push them back over the border. Their efforts had been a success and they had seized much booty along the way. Now, the mop-up complete, they had returned to Verneuil to report to the King.

Richard dismounted at the stables and handed a lathered Ajax to a groom. Leaving Raymond to deal with billeting the men and horses, he went in search of Henry, pausing only to gulp down a cup of spring water and sluice his hot face. Henry was not a man to put appearance above business and Richard knew the value of coming to him grimed from the field.

Henry was in his chamber with de Lacy, and looked up as Richard was announced, his eyes fiercely expectant, but with a glimmer of anxiety. De Lacy was silent and tight-lipped; clearly Richard had interrupted a difficult conversation.

'Well?' Henry gestured Richard to his feet as he started to kneel.

'Sire.' Richard rose and pushed his sweat-soaked hair off his brow. 'We scattered the French and pushed them back over the border. For now, at least, they are in disarray. We captured two siege machines and five wagons of plunder. We have some captives you may want to milk for information. I have sent out scouting parties to report on movements along the border, so we can pre-empt anything else and deflect them.'

Henry's tension visibly eased. 'You have done well.'

Richard shrugged. 'In Ireland you expect this all the time. It becomes a way of thought.'

'Clearly you have to live there for a while to let it sink in,' Henry said with a sharp glance at de Lacy, whose expression remained impassive.

Henry had several maps on the table and he and Richard perused and discussed, Richard pointing out where he had driven the French back and where new attacks might begin, and what could be done to prevent them.

'It is a good thing we have at least one man who knows his business,' Henry said, casting another look at de Lacy.

Richard said nothing, although a small glow of satisfaction kindled at de Lacy's discomfiture. The balance between them had certainly drawn closer to level. De Lacy's expression remained blank if a little stiff.

Henry drew back, tugging on his beard in thought, and then turned purposefully to Richard. 'I know you have had a difficult time in Ireland, but after your work for me on this campaign, I judge you capable of dealing with whatever comes your way. I want you to handle my affairs there and be my regent. Hugh will stay behind with me for now.'

Richard had been expecting Henry to reward him, but was astonished at the turn-around, and even a little shocked. He had been doing his duty in a difficult situation and hoping for recognition in a general way, but Henry was viewing his toil as something extraordinary. He had been living on crumbs and suddenly a full banquet had been thrust under his nose.

'Sire, this is indeed unexpected.' He wanted to feel gratitude towards Henry but having received so many blows from him in the past did not trust him.

'Yes,' Henry said. 'In more ways than one.'

'Sire, I truly thank you, but do I have your permission to remove my armour and wash the grime from my body?' He needed a means of escape; it was difficult to look at de Lacy or to know what to say.

Henry waved assent. 'By all means. We shall discuss the rest later.'

Richard made a hasty exit. In his absence, his men had pitched his tent. He kept the news to himself because he was still trying to grasp the implications.. His squire had filled a barrel with tepid water and, stripping off, he climbed into the tub and used a rough linen cloth to scour off the filth of several days in the field. The cool water refreshed him and sharpened his mind. He drank a cup of watered wine as he dressed in clean garments, including a tunic worked with an interlaced Irish patterning at the hem and cuffs. The embroidery was Aoife's fancy, but appropriate now that Henry had in effect made him Regent of Ireland. A surrogate king. The thought swelled his chest, but filled him with trepidation too, especially in relation to de Lacy. If he was to keep the Irish lands stable, he needed allies, not rivals. He had to make things right between them.

Rummaging through the jewel box in his baggage for a cloak pin he noticed the ring Aoife had given him. He had presented it to Henry on first arriving in Normandy. Henry had taken it, given him a long, considering look, and restored it to his hand.

'Tell your lady I honour the oath made on this ring,' he had said. 'Keep it safe and return it to her with yourself in due course.' Richard still did not know what the oath was, and he did not trust Henry, but he trusted Aoife after their last night together; something had changed between them, like a gem turning a different facet to the light. He pushed a ruby ring of his own onto his middle finger, pinned his cloak and, squaring his shoulders, went to speak with Hugh de Lacy, although he was unsure what he would say.

De Lacy was waiting in the ante chamber outside the great hall and immediately took Richard's arm, pre-empting him. 'I know how awkward this is,' he said. 'I do not blame you or think you pushed yourself forward. God knows the King always makes up his own mind. I made a tactical mistake and Verneuil would have fallen but for your swift arrival. I bear no grudges and I want us to remain allies. We gain nothing if we turn against each other.'

Richard cleared his throat, still feeling embarrassed. 'Indeed, I am not your rival,' he said. 'We must guard each other's backs in Ireland if we are to survive. I honour you and I hope we shall continue to be friends.' He bowed to de Lacy and was relieved when the latter clapped his arm across his shoulder, and they entered the hall side by side.

37

Castle of Striguil, Welsh Marches, autumn 1173

Sitting in the middle of the bed, Isabelle strove to undo her plait with one hand while holding her mother's ivory comb in the other. It was proving difficult and her hair was becoming ever more tangled.

Aoife had been watching her efforts with amusement. 'Come,' she said, 'let me help you.'

Isabelle pulled away, pouting. 'No, I do it!' She had started to string words into sentences and Aoife was proud of her cleverness and the speed at which she was picking up new words.

'But a princess has a maid to dress her hair, and if she does not have a maid then she has her mama. Let me comb it for you and put some jewels in it just like mine.'

Isabelle pursed her soft pink lips, considering, and then handed over the comb. Aoife took it from her and gently began untangling the snarled plait. Isabelle had Richard's temperament. For a child on the edge of two years old, she was strong-willed but seldom threw tantrums and unless she was fractious with tiredness could usually be made to see reason. Gilbert, ten months old, was a little whirlwind, always reaching for things and driving everyone to distraction now that he could crawl everywhere at speed.

Isabelle's hair was of Richard's family too, not red like her father's but fair-gold and thick. Like Basilia's, although Aoife preferred not to think about that. 'Here,' she said. 'Blue jewels for your hair to match your beautiful eyes.'

'Blue,' Isabelle repeated, as Aoife expertly pinned a gem into her braid. Her chubby fingers reached for the pile of hair ornaments Aoife had scattered on the bed. 'Another blue one, Mama.' She poked among them, telling Aoife their different colours. And then she took one of Aoife's veils and draped it over her head.

'No,' Aoife said. 'Like this – you have to fold it a bit further over.'

'Am I pretty?'

'You are beautiful.' A lump came to Aoife's throat at Isabelle's innocence. The jewels and the veil spoke of what was to come. 'In the fullness of time you will come to the marriage bed a woman – too soon yet to be so big, mark my words. Do not hurry to grow up, my love.' She reached for Isabelle and drew her close, rocking her back and forth, reflecting on her own life. 'I will die before I let anyone steal your innocence,' she said.

Her glance flicked to the coffer where Richard's most recent letter lay on top of the pile he had already written. He had fulfilled his promise to keep her informed, and she was still savouring the news and hugging to her heart the detail that Henry was not only sending him back whole and in good health, but as viceroy of Ireland. Their losses had been restored and their star was rising. Richard had done Henry great service and proven the right to the laurel wreath crowning his banner. She had read the words repeatedly until she knew them by heart, and then had re-read them, running her fingers under the lines. Even if written by a scribe they were still at Richard's dictation, and she could hear his voice and see him telling the scribe what to write, with that familiar little frown of concentration between his brows.

'Your grandfather was right to choose him,' she whispered to Isabelle, 'and so was I. I pray God that in your turn you will wed with the right man, my precious girl.' Using that endearment made her think of her own father, and her eyes stung.

A young maidservant entered the chamber and hurried up to

her, flushed from running. 'Countess, the Earl is sighted on the road!' she said.

Aoife's heart jolted. 'How far away?' She set Isabelle down.

'Half a mile. A groom was exercising the horses and saw him and rode back at a gallop with the news.'

Aoife clapped for her women, furious that she had no further warning than this but filled also with joy, anticipation and anxiety. What if he was wounded? What if he was no longer 'her' Richard? Absence did strange things to people. She needed to look her best and she had no time.

'Quickly,' she said, 'the white dress.'

She pulled off her everyday gown of brown wool and the women hurried to bring out the one of fine linen, bleached to the colour of milk, and decorated with braid of blue and green. She grabbed the comb she had been using on Isabelle and quickly worked on her own hair, at the same time giving hasty instructions for food and drink to be prepared. She fastened her belt, her fingers trembling. Things were not as perfect as she desired but she lacked time to make them any better. Matilda and Aline were doing the same, anticipating their husbands and all in a flurry. Basilia was the calm at the centre of the storm but even her colour was high, although she did not change her gown.

Aoife heard the horns winding outside. Whatever the state of the household it would have to do. Leaving her chamber, she ran to the hall, nurses carrying the children behind her. Richard was walking in through the door as she arrived, and she ran to him and flung herself into his arms. He laughed and lifted her up, swinging her round three times before landing her on her feet and kissing her.

'I have returned to you before Christmas, whole and unharmed as I promised you!' His grin was almost as wide as his face and his eyes vividly alight. He seemed taller and broader somehow, vital and handsome. His cloak, lined with blue and white squirrel fur, was fastened by a large gold pin. He was clean, spruced up, and every inch a prince.

'Yes, you have,' she said, laughing, her breath short with excitement, desire and pride. 'Why did you not tell me you were coming? We could have organised a hero's welcome!'

'Hah, we wanted to surprise you. Time enough later for welcomes and feasts and ceremony.'

He looked with amusement at his daughters who were greeting their husbands in a similar wise.

The nurse set Isabelle on her feet and she ran to Richard, holding out her arms. 'Papa!'

'See, she remembers you!' Aoife said as he picked her up, and then laughed at the jewels braided into her hair.

'At least someone has been making ready,' he said. 'What a big girl you are!'

'I'm a princess,' Isabelle said proudly.

'For certain you are, and I am very pleased to see you, and how you have grown!' He put her down and turned his attention to Gilbert, whom Aoife was holding by both hands as he toddled with her support. 'Hah, little man!' Richard crouched to touch his son's ruddy golden hair and kiss his cheek. 'I hope you have been looking after your mother.'

'He has certainly been keeping me busy,' Aoife said wryly. 'The moment I look the other way he is off and up to mischief!'

'Is that not always the way with sons?' Richard answered, chuckling.

Together they turned and walked up the body of the hall. Aoife was longing to have him to herself but it had to wait upon social formality. For now, she was ecstatic to have him home, victorious and unscathed at her side.

In their bedchamber, Aoife put her arms around her husband's neck. 'You will be the greatest lord in Ireland,' she said, 'and I am your countess. By God my father would be proud if he could see us now.'

He held her by the waist. 'Indeed, he would, but the fight is not over yet. If Henry has given me authority in Ireland it is because he wants me to send him more soldiers. There are still barons in rebellion.'

'Not you,' she said with sudden fear. 'He is not keeping you in the field?'

'No, you need not worry, my love, but he wants some of the commanders. Robert FitzStephen and Maurice of Prendergast for certain. We will cross bridges when we come to them as always.' He reached in his pouch and brought out Henry's ring. 'Henry returns this to you with his greeting,' he added neutrally.

She took it from him and swiftly put it away in her coffer out of sight. Leading him to the bed, she cast him an amorous look. 'Never mind Henry for now,' she said. 'It has been a long time.'

Aoife woke to Richard throwing back the shutters, allowing morning light to flood the bedchamber. He was already dressed and looked at her over his shoulder with a gleam in his eyes. 'Are you going to linger abed all day? I should be the one who is exhausted!'

She sat up, her hair spilling over her breasts. 'I do not see why. I am sure the horse is wearier than the rider after a ten-mile gallop.'

He grinned at her. 'Is that what it was, my love?'

She dismissed him with a tilt of her chin.

'Get dressed,' he said. 'I have something to show you. I didn't have a chance yesterday and I wanted to leave it until we had more leisure.'

'What is it?' She was immediately intrigued and excited.

He folded his arms and leaned against the wall. 'You didn't think I would return without a gift for you?'

Warmth blossomed in her heart. 'You have brought me the gift of your success. I never thought further than that.'

'Did you not? I am sure you were wondering.' He unfolded his arms at a knock on the door. 'The thing is that it would not fit in my purse.'

He opened the door to admit a maid bearing bread, cheese and a jug of buttermilk. 'Break your fast, get dressed, and I will show you.'

She felt a swirl of excitement. She had indeed expected him to bring her something from Normandy – a gown or some jewels, or a silver cup – but they had been too busy with other matters yesterday. If it would not fit into his purse, it must be something larger. 'A horse,' she guessed. 'You have brought me a horse.'

His lips twitched. 'A horse might come into it.' He took a piece of bread from the meal. 'Certainly, it is in the stables.'

'You are a tease!'

'Hurry up then and I'll show you.' Chewing, he returned to the window.

Aoife hastily finished eating and donned her clothes, summoning Deirdre to help her. She still could not imagine what the gift was other than a horse.

'Cows. You have brought me some Norman cows for Leinster.'

He shook his head. 'A good idea, but no.'

She secured the last pin in her veil. Taking her hand, he kissed her knuckles. 'Come then, my Irish princess, and I will show you your gift.'

Mystified, she followed him and had to stop herself from dashing ahead of him to the stables.

A soldier stood guard outside one of the fodder barns and made his obeisance as they arrived. Richard dismissed him with a coin and a nod, and then, standing to one side, swept his arm towards the barn's shadowy interior. A covered baggage cart occupied the space within with enough room to walk around it. 'The horse is in the stables,' he told her, 'a fine Norman draught mare. I mated her to Ajax while I was in Normandy and we can expect a foal in the spring. Her value and the foal are yours, but this is your true gift. I thought you might have a use for these items.'

Dust motes turned like minute flakes of gold in the light streaming into the barn. Aoife walked around to the back of the wain and stared at the contents with her mouth open. The wain was packed from base board to canvas top with all manner of textiles folded into bolts. She could see silk and damask, and numerous different hues of woollen cloth. Chests and boxes, coffers and sacks. Richard climbed inside and threw back a chest lid, and her gaze lit on gilt dishes, cups, candlesticks and flagons. She gazed and gazed, and still her eyes could not take it in.

'We captured a French baggage train,' he said, 'and this is my share – our share. Do with it as you choose. It is too cumbersome to unload just to load up again to take to Ireland.'

He jumped down from the cart and took a folded piece of cloth from the top of the pile – a green damask patterned with a shimmer of golden peacocks. 'I can imagine you playing your harp and wearing a gown of this cloth,' he said, 'with green jewels in your hair.'

She took it from him and pressed it to her cheek. 'I am not worthy of all this,' she said in a subdued tone. 'You do me great honour.'

'You are my wife and more than worthy! You gave me the opportunity to change my life. You have given me heirs. Those are things more precious than a thousand cartloads of booty.' He lifted her in his arms and sat her on the cart on top of some of the bales. 'The queen of my heart.' He swept her a deep bow.

His action broke the moment and she laughed at him with a sparkle of tears. 'Get me down, you fool!'

'So now my wife insults me!' He lifted her and set her on her feet, pulling her close.

She raised her arm to touch his hair. 'You are the finest man,' she said softly. 'There is no other for me.'

Arm in arm they walked slowly back towards the keep, content not to rush the moment together. In the distance, they saw Matilda walking similarly with Robert de Quency.

'She has some good news for him,' Aoife said.

Richard raised his brows.

'The child quickened last week. I have told her I have no intention of being called grandmother.'

Richard looked towards the couple and smiled. 'That is excellent news. I am glad to be a grandsire, but then I am older than you and it is good to see generations stretching into the distance like jewels on a necklace.' He stopped and drew a deep breath – a pause to absorb satisfaction and pleasure. For today, everything was whole and perfect. 'I thought we could ride over to Goodrich,' he said. 'I have a mind to build a keep there, and I value your opinion.'

She took his arm. 'I am glad to hear that you do.' It would be pleasant to ride out and have a little time to themselves, and planning a new keep would be interesting. In time she could adorn it with all the plate and silver from France. Indeed, she could make it her own.

'I'll have the horses saddled,' he said.

Basilia was taking stock of the barrels of wine that had recently arrived from Bristol when Raymond came to see her, ostensibly to ask about supplies for his men, but having received the answers in short order, he leaned against the wall and stayed to talk.

'The Earl excelled in Normandy, and the King has rewarded him well,' he said.

'Yes.' She busied herself with her counting so she did not have to look at him.

'We all shared in his success, and it is fitting since we all helped to achieve it.'

Basilia wondered where this was leading and why he was speaking to her. 'My brother values his men,' she replied.

'Perhaps some more than others.'

He spoke pointedly, and she flicked him a quick glance before the intensity of his stare made her look away.

'I have seen the way you labour to keep the household supplied,' he said. 'Even now you are working while others are taking their leisure.'

She moved her shoulders in a gesture of negation. 'What else would I do? I would rather keep myself occupied and know what we have.'

'But does it not bother you?'

She shook her head.

'You could be lady in your own household. You could be cherished and appreciated for what you are instead of being taken for granted.'

She felt her cheeks start to burn. 'You have said enough. I am busy as you can see. I have things to do. Don't you?'

He pushed himself off the wall. 'Yes,' he said. 'But I wanted to give you this from my own share. I want you to see how beautiful you truly are.'

He presented her with two palm-sized ivory discs connected by a brass hinge and carved with a foliate design. A small clasp sprang open to reveal a mirror in which she could see her face reflected – the dry lines and her prim mouth unaccustomed to smiling, her youth all spent. Spoils of war. Who else had owned this trinket and looked into the glass?

She closed it with a click and held it out to him. 'I see nothing in this that pleases me,' she said. 'I cannot accept it and I have told you, I am busy.'

Raymond made no attempt to take the mirror back. 'Very well,' he said tautly. 'I see the lie of the land.' He gave her a formal bow and stalked from the chamber.

Basilia looked down at the little ivory case, feeling queasy.

When the company had ridden in yesterday she had looked for Raymond among the knights and soldiers to reassure herself he was safe, and having seen him, she had made her escape, filled with relief and trepidation. She missed him when he was absent, but she was disturbed by his presence. Her reputation was one of the few things she had for her own, and the attention he paid to her put it at stake. Worried, unsettled, she put the mirror case in the purse hanging at her belt and tried to continue with her counting, but found it impossible.

Richard sat in the great hall with Aoife, enjoying a cup of wine while she played her harp and gave him fond looks, which she had been doing ever since he had given her the wagon in the barn. At Goodrich that afternoon they had spent a golden time planning the future arm in arm and had watched a family of otters playing in the river where it flowed close to the castle enclosure. Something had changed between them, as if his return in triumph had filed off the remaining sharp edges from their relationship, leaving them a smooth and subtle fit for each other.

Isabelle wanted to sit in his lap and he lifted her onto his knee and cuddled her magical lithe weight in his arms. She was holding a soft doll that Aoife had made for her, with fair braids and a blue gown like her own. The way she chattered away to the doll made him chuckle and filled his heart with a deep, contented warmth. Little Gilbert for once was napping in his cradle after an exhausting morning of crawling around pulling himself up against people's knees. Another month and he would be walking.

Aoife suddenly paused her harping and Richard lifted his gaze from his daughter to see Raymond advancing on them, a look of square-jawed determination on his face. Immediately Richard was on his guard.

'I wonder what he wants now,' Aoife murmured, suddenly tense.

'I suppose we are about to find out.'

Raymond halted before them and bowed. 'Sire, if I may have a word in private.' His gaze flicked to Aoife, who gave him a warm smile but with cold eyes.

'Of course.' Richard dismissed the retainers and servants within earshot and gave Isabelle to her half-sister Matilda. Aoife stayed where she was. 'The Countess is a party to everything,' he said as he saw the slight twitch of Raymond's eyelids.

Looking discomforted, Raymond cleared his throat. 'I want to talk to you about a marriage for Basilia.'

Richard's eyebrows shot up.

'She is well beyond the age at which women come to wed,' Raymond said. 'You cannot keep her for ever in your household as she is; it is not fitting, and I have a suggestion to make that will solve the matter.'

Raymond's declaration rendered Richard speechless with astonishment and dawning indignation.

'I think you would agree I would be a worthy husband for Basilia, considering all my achievements on your behalf in Ireland and my service to you in Normandy,' Raymond ploughed on. 'I sit among your advisers every day. Basilia would still be close, and I would be joined to you as your brother by marriage, and only strength would come from such a bond. I have long held the lady Basilia in high regard, and you are my liege lord.'

Richard swallowed down his anger, for although their conversation was quiet, they were in a public place. He was amazed at Raymond's audacity. A landless knight whom he had given a place at his hearth and in whom he had put the utmost trust. This man was brazenly asking for a favour that would bring him right into the heart of the family. It was not to be borne and he was not about to yield to Raymond's over-ambitious dictates.

Controlling himself, he looked Raymond in the eyes and smiled. 'You have certainly sprung this on us,' he said. 'I understand why you came to me without using an intermediary, and I know your directness of manner, but I cannot give you a reply without due consideration. I need to deliberate on this and consult with other members of my family. Is my sister aware you have made this petition?'

Raymond flushed. 'No, sire, she is not.'

So Basilia was not necessarily complicit. Given the incident at Matilda's wedding, he should have been watching out for something like this. 'Well then, give me your pledge.'

Raymond unfastened a sheathed knife from his belt and gave it to Richard hilt-first in the traditional way of oath swearing.

'I shall give you my answer in due course,' Richard said.

Raymond bowed and departed. Richard watched him leave, his chest so tight he could barely breathe. Leaving the hall, he stalked off to his chamber to compose himself, but the more he thought about Raymond's proposal, the angrier he grew.

Aoife covered her harp and, signalling her women to remain where they were, went out after Richard. Raymond's request had certainly set a cat among the pigeons but she was not surprised for she was keenly aware of everything that happened in the court – all the tiny undercurrents and nuances of behaviour and body language that a woman's eye was often swifter to pick up than a man's.

Richard was thrashing about the room, picking things up, throwing them down. 'How dare that man,' he said as she entered. 'How dare he! Who does he think he is to ask for Basilia? He may have done sterling work but it does not entitle him to walk up to me and without intermediaries demand the hand of my sister in marriage!'

Aoife set her hand on his arm in a calming gesture. 'I agree,' she said. 'It will not do to let Raymond have his way in this considering his behaviour. Basilia is your sister and a lady of high degree. If she is to wed, there are more suitable matches to be had. Come, sit down and we shall find the answer.'

'I already know the answer,' Richard snapped. 'It is for him to cut down his ideas altogether.'

Aoife poured him a cup of wine. 'He has always watched Basilia. I think he has had this in mind for a long time – perhaps ever since the occasion when he grabbed her while in his cups. I do not believe his intention has ever gone away, even if he no longer drinks as before.'

'He is going to be sorely disappointed,' Richard muttered. 'Have you noticed Basilia encouraging him?'

'They exchange glances in the hall sometimes and I have seen him look at her like a wolf at a deer, but they are never private together – to my knowledge – if that is what you mean.'

Scowling, he sipped the wine, and then looked up as Hervey entered the room.

'You sent your squire for me,' Hervey said, looking between him and Aoife. 'What is wrong?'

Richard grimaced. 'Raymond seems to think he is a suitable candidate for Basilia's hand in marriage.' He told Hervey what had happened in the hall.

Hervey's eyes widened in astonishment, but then he began to chuckle as he accepted a cup from Aoife. 'Is there no end to that man's hubris?'

'It seems not,' Richard said irritably. 'And it is no laughing matter.'

'What did you say to him?'

'That I could not answer him immediately and I would need to think about it and speak to others, but I know my answer.'

Hervey sobered. 'Then we will meet him as a united family.' He set a supportive hand on Richard's shoulder. 'I will back you up to the hilt on this; I agree with you. It's a challenge to your authority and you must answer it as such.'

'Of a certainty,' Richard replied. The flush had left his complexion and he was determined and steely.

When Hervey had gone, Aoife said, 'You know this will mean losing Raymond. He will not stay if you turn him down.'

He looked at her and sighed heavily. 'He is a valuable man, I agree, but he has overstepped the bounds. What would you do?'

'If Raymond feels the need to marry, there are some fine Irish ladies who would better answer his need and being younger would vouchsafe him heirs,' Aoife said. 'If you wish I will consider who might suit among them.'

Richard nodded. 'That is a good idea. In the meantime, I will speak to Raymond, and to Basilia, and if it comes to the worst, Hervey is capable of replacing Raymond and has as much experience.'

Richard summoned Raymond to his personal chamber the next morning with Hervey in attendance while Aoife sat quietly in the background. Richard wanted to resolve the matter. It was like going into battle, already knowing the outcome, but still anticipating the moment he would have to use his sword.

Raymond arrived in his usual brisk manner, his cloak arranged in smooth folds and pinned at the shoulder by a large round brooch. 'Sire.' He bowed before standing upright, straight and formal.

Richard cleared his throat. 'You made a particular request of me yesterday and I have now had time to consider . . . I am not disposed to grant that request; Basilia is settled in her life and position under my protection. However, I know what it is to desire heirs and have a wife and hearth of one's own and I would not deny you that comfort. I grant you permission to seek elsewhere to marry and beget offspring. Perhaps take an Irish wife as I have done. The Countess is very willing to assist you in that endeavour.'

As Richard spoke, Raymond became as rigid as an effigy. 'In that case, my lord, I accept your decision for I can do no other,' he said stiltedly 'I can see there is no point in arguing with your decision.' His gaze flicked briefly and with venom to Hervey. 'I was coming to visit you even as I received your summons because

I have had news that my father is ailing at Carew and unlikely to recover. I must leave immediately and go to his sick bed.'

It might be the truth but it was also a way of saving face and allowed Raymond to depart with dignity. 'I am sorry to hear that,' Richard said with relief. 'You have my leave to depart. But think upon what I have said about an Irish wife.'

'Sire, I shall.' Tight-lipped, Raymond bowed and strode from the chamber, his cloak flaring behind him.

Hervey put a supportive hand on Richard's shoulder. 'You did the right thing. He was taking his ambition too far. Some time out in the cold will not harm him and no man is irreplaceable.'

Richard nodded agreement, but although he felt a certain triumph in denying Raymond his suit and putting him in his place, he was losing one of his best men. Raymond's behaviour had been inappropriate, but he was aware that this was not one of his own most glorious moments.

Basilia was outside, speaking to the laundresses who were pounding lye-soaked tablecloths with their mallets to beat out the food stains, when she saw Raymond leading his palfrey, Badge nudging his heels. He was packed for a journey and nearby his squire was loading more baggage onto a sumpter beast. Raymond's destrier was there too. Glancing across, he saw her with the laundry wenches and came towards her. Basilia quickly bade the women wait upon her orders and met him halfway, for she did not want them to overhear whatever was said.

'You need not worry,' Raymond said as they met. 'I shall not present you with any more gifts. I know my own worth, and it is not what others have in their mind.' He stood with his hand on his sword hilt, his grey eyes full of bitterness.

Basilia was taken aback. Dear God, what had he done? And what had Richard done? 'Have you quarrelled with my brother?'

His lips twisted. 'No,' he said. 'A difference of opinion is not a quarrel, but I see the lie of the land clearly and what I have to offer, no matter that it has been my life many times over, is not sufficient unto my request.'

She gave him a sharp look. What *he* had to offer? For what?

'My brother has written to say my father is ailing and unlikely to recover. I must return to Carew at once.'

'I am sorry to hear it,' she said automatically. 'I will pray for him – and for you and your family.'

'Thank you, my lady . . . I am sorry too.' He bowed woodenly and returned to his horses.

Basilia went back to the laundresses, giving them instructions, instinctively rather than out of conscious thought, for her mind was preoccupied with what had been happening behind her back. By the time she looked round, Raymond had gone and her heart lurched with a feeling of loss.

Leaving the women, she went to find Richard. He was occupied with administration business, but when he saw her, a guilty expression flitted across his face. Across Hervey's too, she noted, and compressed her lips. Aoife, as usual, was watching with avid intensity, sharp as a vixen.

Richard murmured to his men and, leaving them, crossed the hall to join her.

'I have just seen Raymond making preparations to leave,' she said.

'Yes, his father is ailing.'

'So he said, but that is not the whole reason, is it?'

He folded his arms and she could almost see him wriggling like a fish on a line. 'I take it Raymond has spoken to you of his request for your hand.'

'He came to bid me farewell and hinted that he had approached you on a certain matter – of which I knew nothing.'

'I suspected not.'

'And would you have told me?' She gave him a contemptuous look. 'I think any negotiations that concern me, I am wise enough and old enough to understand. I ask of you the respect and

courtesy of informing me should the matter ever crop up again.'
She turned on her heel and walked away with dignity, but also
shaking with anger and reaction that they should have discussed
her future and decided it without her. It was not to be borne,
but she was powerless to prevent it. Perhaps she should enter a
convent and become an abbess. At least she would only then be
answerable to God – who had made man in His image.

She returned to the laundresses to check on their work. A part
of her was glad that Raymond had gone because now there
would be calm in the household, but another part was desolated
for there would be no more gifts, no more looks, no more attention,
even if she had not solicited such things, and her life would
return to one of mundane service.

38

Waterford, southern Ireland, spring 1174

Aoife cradled the newborn baby in her arms and smiled into its face.

'Let me see,' Isabelle demanded, standing on tip-toe. Aoife stooped to show her the child, born less than an hour since. Matilda was lying in bed recovering with a warm drink after a hard but normal labour. The baby was a beautiful little girl, small but perfect with a quiff of gilt-red hair.

Isabelle touched her cheek with a gentle forefinger, and the baby rooted towards it with a little mew.

'She's hungry,' Aoife said.

'Me, me!' Gilbert wanted to kiss her too, and Aoife stooped to him while guarding against an excess of enthusiasm. 'And now we must return her to her mama,' she said, and carried the precious bundle back to the bed.

Matilda smiled and held out her arms for her daughter. 'I only wish Rob was here to see her.'

The men had been in the field since early spring as the campaigning season brought its usual crop of disputes, uprisings and rebellions. The new castle at Kilkenny had been burned down by one of her father's own kinsmen with cattle and plunder seized. Richard and Hervey had set out to bring the raiders to task yesterday, shortly before Matilda went into labour.

'He will be home soon,' Aoife said, 'and you shall have this beautiful child to show him.'

Matilda smiled down at her daughter, and then looked at Aoife. 'Thank you,' she said.

'For what?'

'For helping me through the birth. For holding my hand and encouraging me. For singing to me and rubbing my feet.'

Aoife felt a surge of true warmth towards Matilda of whom she had grown fond after her initial wariness. Aoife knew the pain and danger of childbirth. Matilda's own mother had died bearing Aline, and Aoife had seen Matilda's fear of the same as she laboured. Aoife had supported her as a woman who had endured the same ordeal. Basilia had only been present on the periphery. She had paced and fretted, too anxious to remain long at the bedside because of what had happened to Matilda's mother.

'We are all women together in this,' Aoife said, 'whatever our differences. I was glad to help you, and now you have this little one to greet your husband's return.'

A week later, Aoife was sitting at Matilda's bedside, talking to her while keeping an eye on Gilbert who was galloping around the chamber on his wooden hobby horse getting under everyone's feet. Even when he tripped and fell, he laughed and got up again; there were no tears. Isabelle had her own hobby horse and was racing with him, although they had been ordered not to make too much noise. Had it not been pouring with rain, they would have been playing outside.

The baby, christened Matilda for her mother, was soundly asleep in her cradle, lips puckering as she suckled in her dreams. She was thriving. Her mother had been out of bed on several occasions, but for now was resting against the pillows listening to Aoife tell her stories of her own childhood.

'So, if your father had not stolen another man's wife, none of us would be here now?' she said.

Aoife laughed. 'Perhaps not, but it might have happened anyway, for the High King and Tiernan ua Ruari and many others were afraid my father would rise above them – as of course he did.'

'What happened to the woman – the lady Derval?'

'She was very clever,' Aoife said. 'She played the men off against each other. She used my father to put her husband in his place and later retired to the nuns at Clonmacnoise as she had always intended. The outcome for others was not so satisfactory, but my father was content before he died.'

'And are you content?' Matilda asked shrewdly.

Aoife made a grab for Gilbert as he galloped past and he squealed, evading her. 'What is content?' Aoife said. 'In small moments like this I find my solace. And in your father too.'

She looked up as Deirdre came from the ante chamber to speak to her. 'My lady, there is a message from the gate – the Earl is here.' Deirdre's expression was anxious, lacking a smile.

Aoife's stomach lurched at the unexpected news, but she rose to her feet and took charge. 'See to it that all is made ready,' she said. 'Find the lady Basilia and ask about the stabling and food for the men. She will know. And have a bath tub prepared for my lord so that he may wash and change.'

Deirdre hurried away. Aoife tidied her appearance and gave Isabelle and Gilbert into the care of a nurse. She strongly suspected Richard's impromptu return was not good news.

'Is there trouble?' Matilda asked, biting her lower lip.

'I do not know, but if your father is here, we have him to protect us,' Aoife said. 'Go to sleep and I will bring you news as soon as I know more.'

The courtyard was heaving with men, horses and baggage carts all gradually dispersing to their billets. Talking to Hervey, Richard entered the hall, stripping his riding gloves as he walked.

Aoife hurried to his side. 'We had not looked for you so soon, has something happened?'

'We had to turn back from Cashel and we have suffered ambushes and attacks all along the way,' Richard answered her grimly. 'The High King brought up his forces to join the rebels. I lost four hundred good men out of Dublin and their officers. We could not sustain ourselves in the field.'

In an instant Aoife was thrown back to the moment she and her family had been forced to flee Fearns, burning it behind them as they went into exile. Sick with shock, she could only stare at him.

Richard rubbed his palm over his face. 'There is more. Let me remove this armour and take a drink and I will tell you.' He looked at Hervey. 'Tell my officers to gather in the hall in an hour and we shall decide what to do.'

Richard swayed as his squire helped him to remove his mail and padded tunic. A pungent aroma of sweat and horse rose from his body as the garments came off. His hair was lank and greasy beneath his arming cap and his face white with exhaustion. Aoife had always viewed him as vigorous, vital and handsome, but just now he looked old and she was frightened.

He clambered into the upright tub, gasping as the hot water lapped around his body.

Aoife moved to perform the services of a bath attendant, waving away the squire. 'What do you mean "there is more"?' She took a cloth and began to scrub his shoulders and back.

He folded his elbows along the top of the tub and rested his head on them. 'We lost Rob,' he said. 'He was killed in a skirmish . . . an axe . . . nothing any of us could do – couldn't reach him in time.'

Aoife stopped scrubbing. 'Rob . . . you are not saying . . . Oh dear God no!'

'We have his body on a cart,' Richard said flatly. 'I must go and keep vigil tonight after the meeting, but as soon as I have bathed I will talk to Matilda. Do you have some wine?'

Aoife dropped the cloth, brought him a cup and watched him drink. 'She bore the baby a week ago – a little girl christened

Matilda too. She talks all the time about what Rob will say when he sees her.'

Richard handed her his empty cup.

'More?'

He shook his head. 'I need to be sober for this.'

Aoife returned to her ministrations. 'How bad is the rest?'

'Aoife . . .'

'Tell me, I need to know,' she said vehemently. 'My father never hid the truth from any of us. If I know the worst, I can plan for the worst.'

He gave a soft groan. 'King Henry's war with his son means our numbers are stretched and our best battle commanders absent. FitzStephen is in England. De Lacy is still in Normandy. FitzAudelin has been recalled. Raymond . . .' He grimaced. 'Raymond is in Wales. The Irish know it and are rebelling in force, and we are in danger of being overwhelmed.' He raised his head. 'I will be all right in a while. I just need a moment to gather myself.'

So, the worst was being overwhelmed, and that meant killed. Aoife refused to entertain the thought for it sent her directly to panic. She had to think around it and push through. 'But you have a plan to deal with the situation?' Part of his success in adversity was that ability to look ahead, but what happened when the plans ran out?

He gave her a weary, humourless smile. 'Yes,' he said. 'You may doubt many things, my love, but never that.' He caught her soapy hand and kissed it. 'But I am heartsick, especially at the news I must give my daughter.'

Wearing clean garments, his hair sleeked back, Richard entered the chamber where Matilda was recovering from her confinement. It was a woman's sanctum, a place where a man would not come unless specifically invited. He had thought about sending his chaplain or passing the duty on to Aoife, but it would have been cowardly and dishonourable. The responsibility was his. All of it. Behind him, Aoife murmured a surreptitious word of encouragement. The other women were eyeing him with surprise and concern.

'Papa?' Matilda was sitting up in bed. She had been playing a game of dice-chess with her sister and the board was set out on the coverlet. 'Have you come to see the baby? Where's Rob?' Her eyes darted. 'Why are you back so soon?'

Richard gently removed the chess board and pieces and, sitting down, took her hands. 'My love, I have difficult news. Robert is not coming home; I am afraid he is dead. He died valiantly in battle, defending my standard. We were set upon and he was brought down. I grieve to bring you such news, but I would ask no one else to do it.'

She stared at him wide-eyed, shaking her head. 'No,' she said. 'No!'

'I am so sorry.' He squeezed her hands. 'I loved him too, like a son.'

Matilda burst into tears of shock, and he took her in his arms. 'I know, my love, I know. Aoife will care for you as a mother would, and the baby. You will not want for anything, I swear to you.'

'I want Rob!' she wept. 'You cannot give me that!' She struck his chest with her clenched fist.

'No, I cannot. I am sorry.' He held her while she sobbed and railed at him, bracing himself against the storm until the first violence had run its course.

Aoife leaned over his shoulder. 'Drink this,' she said gently to Matilda. 'It is for the shock and it will help you.'

Richard took the steaming cup and urged Matilda to drink. She did so, obedient and floppy now, and eventually her eyelids started to droop. The women eased her beneath the bed covers and tucked her in to sleep. Torn by guilt and grief, Richard looked down at her until Aoife gently drew him away to the cradle near the bedside.

'Your granddaughter,' she said.

He had to blink to clear his eyes as he gazed at the child. 'This is not the return I would have wished.' His throat worked. 'I loved Rob and valued him. He has been in my household since he was a squire, and his marriage to Matilda was a true bond of love. They were friends long before they were wed.'

'I know, and I am sorry,' Aoife said, 'but he has a daughter to walk in this world, and she and her mother are safe with us. It is the living who must concern us for now.'

'Yes,' he said, but his expression remained bleak.

'What would you say if I told you I was thinking of asking Raymond to return and help us through our difficulties?' Richard asked.

Aoife had been combing her hair before retiring to bed, but she ceased her toilet and looked at him, feeling taken aback and perturbed. 'I would say that matters must be difficult indeed. Why do you think he would come? What would make it worth his while?'

Richard made a wry face. 'The men are dissatisfied with Hervey's leadership. It is no lack on Hervey's part, he is competent, but they are used to Raymond's ways and when men are not confident in their leader or enthused by him they are not as wholehearted. Hervey acknowledges this and has the manhood and pragmatism to agree we should seek Raymond's aid.'

'But if Hervey steps aside for Raymond, what will Hervey gain from it?'

'I have some land in mind for him; he will not lose income, and I will find him other duties so his status is not diminished. Our situation is precarious and having Raymond here could mean the difference between survival and going down. I do not say this lightly or with pleasure, but our backs are to the wall.'

Aoife frowned. 'You have already made up your mind.'

'Do you counsel me against it?'

She shook her head. 'No. I know what must be done out of necessity, but like you, I am not overjoyed. How will you persuade him? You did not part on good terms and offering him Hervey's place as your commander and some land to go with it may not be enough.' She knelt to remove his boots. 'You know what he wants . . .'

'Yes. It is certainly the one thing that would bring him swiftly to my side even if it is the bitterest draught to swallow.'

She looked up at him. 'My father did what he had to in order to survive. He would say do what you must and cross the bridges as they come. For now, you have no choice, but you can do something about it later.' She did not elaborate on what. Richard was finicky about his honour whereas she was accustomed to thinking her way out of tight corners by any means.

He sighed. 'You confirm what I know in my heart. I will write to him and send a swift ship to South Wales and then I will talk to Basilia.'

'She will consent, I think. It is what she has always wanted even if she has always hidden from it.'

'Yes,' he said, looking relieved.

'Come to bed,' she said. 'Rest for a while at least. I will watch over you while you sleep. You cannot lead men unless you are strong. It is my duty to protect you, even as it is yours to protect me.'

He lay down and she stroked his hair and sang to him softly in Irish – the Song of Fates. 'May nine ranks of angels and my God be ever watchful over thee, from terror, from caverns of white death, protecting and bearing thee company.'

Eventually he slept, but Aoife continued to keep vigil while her mind travelled a labyrinth of paths, plotting and planning, bent upon survival.

Barely had Richard risen in the morning when a desperate plea for aid arrived from Hugh de Lacy's deputy William Tyrell at

Trim Castle where he was under attack from the High King. The messenger begged Richard to come at once bringing as many troops as he could.

Grimly, Richard prepared to ride; without Trim, Dublin was vulnerable, and if one block toppled, another would follow, and another. As the men made ready, he drew Aoife to one side. 'It is not safe to remain in Waterford. I want you and the household to move to the island. It is well fortified and easier to defend.'

Her stomach clenched. 'What do you mean it is not safe in Waterford?'

'The townspeople are on edge and the news about Trim could cause an uprising. I cannot be everywhere at once. It is just a precaution and only until Raymond arrives. I have to be certain you and my household are safe. I am trusting you to look after everyone and stop them from panicking. I need you to be gone even as I leave. Take the *Bridget*. She's moored at the wharf.'

She nodded and pressed down her fear. It was a retreat to the last resort, and perhaps the final plan. 'Have you sent for Raymond?'

'Yes, the messenger has already sailed. I need to speak with Basilia in a moment, but I hope support will be on its way within the week.'

Not the support either of them would have wanted but needs must, she thought.

'I will leave Philip of Prendergast and Walter Bluet with you,' he said. 'I trust you to go gently with Matilda.'

Aoife touched his arm. 'Do not worry, all shall be done to make her comfortable and ease her pain. She has Aline too for her comfort.'

He took her in his arms and gave her a hard, swift kiss. 'Thank you.'

She shrugged, pushing away emotion so she could cope. 'You had better speak to Basilia. I will fetch her for you.'

* * *

'You wanted to see me?' Basilia eyed Richard warily. Aoife had not been forthcoming but she knew they were in difficulty.

'I will come to the point,' he said. 'You see for yourself the problems we face. I am leaving a garrison and supplies in Ragnall's Tower, but Aoife is arranging for the household to go to the island for safety.'

'That seems prudent,' she agreed, and looked at him expectantly.

Richard cleared his throat. 'I have a great favour to ask of you – indeed I would not do so unless I was forced, but it is the difference between life and death. I ask it of you because I know your steadfastness and your honour to those who depend on you.'

Basilia eyed him warily, wondering just what he was setting up.

'I am asking if you would agree to a marriage with Raymond in order to persuade him to return and help us.'

Her chest emptied of breath and she pressed her hand to her heart. She had settled her feelings about Raymond when he left and to have the pathway torn open was like a scythe ripping through a thorn hedge. 'You thought him beneath me,' she said with angry scorn. 'Have you then changed your mind?'

'I have a stark choice to make,' he replied. 'I need him and his men, and you are the only thing that will bring him back here. It is my last throw of the dice.'

Basilia clenched her fists and struggled to find the wherewithal and the breath to answer. She wanted to strike him across his face. She was supporting an edifice in which she wanted no part, but if she refused, she doomed them all, including her nieces and a tiny baby. 'Do what you think you must,' she said stiltedly. 'I can say no more than that.'

'Thank you for that grace,' he said. 'I honour you.'

'I want no thanks,' she said. 'Nor honour from you. Dear God, Richard, get out of my sight.'

He gave her a long look, but thankfully said nothing and did as she asked. He had used the word 'grace' but she thought that perhaps he should have said 'sacrifice'.

Aoife sat spinning with the other women. There was little else to do while they waited for news both from Trim and from Wales as to whether Raymond would accept Richard's proposal and come to their aid. Basilia had become taciturn and reserved, barely speaking. Matilda had withdrawn too and spent most of her time tending to her baby daughter, praying for her husband's soul. Other than the spinning, embroidery and weaving, prayer was their only recourse. They were trapped with no room to step away from each other.

Aoife leaned over to help Isabelle who was taking her first steps in learning to spin and was busy making a piece of clotted rope, but still it was a passable effort for such a small child. She murmured words of encouragement and gave her a cuddle.

'When will Papa be back?' Isabelle asked.

'Soon,' Aoife said, hoping it was true. 'Very soon.'

For most of her life she had lived with the results of bloodshed and warfare. Of men going off to fight, sometimes returning and sometimes not, leaving wives and children to fend for themselves. The constant worry and the threat; trying to find strategies to stay safe and survive. Ireland was in her heart, her soul, her blood, but she was so, so weary of strife.

'I wish he was here now.'

'So do I, my heart, so do I, but we shall just have to be patient.'

It had been a week since they had come upriver to the defences on the Island of Ines and Richard had ridden to relieve Trim, emptying Waterford of all but a skeleton garrison. They had been without news since. All they could do was wait in blindness, and Aoife had never been good at waiting.

Isabelle's concentration span had reached an end and she abandoned her spinning to skip over to Matilda who was changing the baby's swaddling. Isabelle helped, passing a clean napkin, watching intently. The task completed, Matilda rose and, singing softly to her daughter, walked to the tower window, Isabelle at her side. Aoife smiled at the image they made, Matilda rocking the baby in one arm, the other lightly stroking Isabelle's fair hair.

Matilda's hand suddenly stilled on Isabelle's head and she said in a strained voice, 'What's that glow in the sky? I think it's fire.'

Aoife dropped her spinning and hurried to the window. 'It's Waterford,' she said. 'Waterford is burning.'

The others gathered, crowding to gaze at the glow against the twilight, the clots of smoke. If Waterford was in flames, then another of their defences had gone down and all that lay between them and their enemies was the river and these palisades. They were effectively trapped.

News came late that night. Under cover of darkness, Richard and his troop arrived on the island by ship, having returned from their effort to save Trim.

Richard reeked of smoke and sweat and was still clad in his mail, but Aoife flung her arms around him, uncaring of the smell or the hard mesh against her body. She kissed him, tears of relief running down her face. 'Thank God you are here, thank God!'

'Hush, now, hush,' he chided. 'I am here and whole. We drove them off at Trim, although not before King Ruari had fired the castle. Rather than face us he rode away without stopping to plunder. We chased his baggage train and dealt them damage. He knows now I will assist de Lacy and respond at speed, so he will not be as swift to come raiding again for a while. But we have a new dilemma.'

'We saw the flames,' she said.

He rubbed his hand over his face. 'Anyone not Irish or Norse in Waterford has either fled or been slain. The garrison still controls the tower and they have supplies to last them, but all we can do is hold fast and pray for Raymond to come.'

Aoife wiped her eyes and struggled for composure. 'When

will it end? I am sick of it. My father, my brothers, Rob de Quency . . . How many more?' She could not prevent the tremble of exhaustion in her voice.

'Raymond will come,' Richard said, trying to reassure her. 'I have offered him his heart's desire. King Henry has turned the tide on the rebellions against him that have taken so many of our resources. If we can hold out just a little longer, we shall have calmer waters.'

'They cannot be stormier than this,' Aoife said grimly.

'No, but if we weather this, we can weather anything. I am weary of war too. I want to govern in peace and prosperity. I have to hope, for without hope, what is left? Men commend me for my steadiness. Even in the greatest difficulty they say I will hold firm. You have seen me in my chamber in anger or exhaustion with my head in my hands, but never before my men. Only you and Hervey have ever observed me thus and it is the measure of the trust and faith I have in both of you – as I hope you have in me.'

Aoife nodded. She was hollow now, but calm. 'I do,' she said, 'but what happens if Raymond does not come? What do we do then?'

'We have ships. I would get you away before it came to that and send you to Striguil. But Raymond will come, I am certain of it.'

On a warm June morning several galleys filled with fighting men moored under the island palisades, and Raymond stepped onto the wharf. For a month the garrison had held out in Waterford, everything nailed tight and rationed while they waited.

Raymond had lost weight during his absence in Wales, and the hard bones of his face pressed against his flesh like rock. He was solid and tight-lipped, with a triumphant glint in his grey eyes.

'I want to thank you for answering my request,' Richard said when Raymond was announced into his chamber by a relieved-looking usher. 'I hoped you would come. You and your men will swing the balance. I am grateful.'

'Your letter made it a certainty,' Raymond replied. 'Only a fool would decline your terms. You offer me land, advancement and my dearest wish.' His gaze flicked to Basilia who was sitting across the room with the other women.

'Whatever happened before, we must leave it behind us,' Richard said. 'Different times call for different measures and we are both grown men. When we are secure again, on my word, we shall have a wedding. I have had my scribes draw up the land grants and contracts and documents.' He gestured to the parchments set out on a nearby table. 'You can read them at your leisure and we can witness and seal them together. Welcome back, and let us be friends.' He offered his hand and Raymond did not hesitate to clasp it even though his face remained impassive.

Richard brought Raymond to the women and Aoife rose to greet him first, as Countess.

Ever since Richard had sent for him she had been deliberating how to play the game. It behoved her to be pleasant to Raymond rather than aloof, but at the same time he had to be kept in his place.

'Welcome back, messire,' she said. 'We have had our differences, what family does not, but we have missed your company in the hall and in counsel.' She gave him her hand and he bowed over it with hard awareness in his eyes, which she reciprocated. 'We shall make you comfortable and I will see to it that you have a good feather mattress tonight. Hervey has vacated his chamber so you may put your baggage in there.'

His eyebrows rose as she had known they would. Hervey might not be especially happy, but he would cooperate for the common good.

'Thank you, madam,' Raymond said. 'I am sure I shall be comfortable wherever you allocate my chamber.' His humble

396

words belied the smug expression on his face. As though he had been given an enormous joint of beef all to himself.

Raymond then turned to Basilia, and taking her hand, knelt to her, flourishing his cloak to make a performance. 'My lady, I honour you and look forward to becoming your husband in due course.'

Basilia's cheeks were scarlet. 'Sire, I honour you in return,' she said, but her voice was tight and small.

Aoife noted the sparkle in Raymond's eyes, but it was not solely triumph. She saw genuine emotion; indeed he was almost in tears. He looked round with challenge, daring anyone to take this away from him.

'Come.' Richard slapped his shoulder. 'Let us have a drink and talk about what needs to be done.'

Basilia remained rooted to the spot until Aoife took her arm and led her to where servants were pouring cups of wine at a trestle. 'Whatever your thoughts on the matter, you must carry this through for the sake of all,' Aoife said, smiling warmly for the gathering at large. 'I had to do it when I was much younger than you. You helped me then at Striguil, and I will help you now if I can.'

Basilia pressed her lips together.

'We need Raymond's men and expertise. You have everyone's support in this.'

'I do not need your help.' Basilia shrugged away from Aoife and drew herself up. 'I am perfectly able to deal with the matter myself, and you have done more than enough already.' The words were ambiguous.

'Well, if you have need,' Aoife said, and moved on. There would be time enough to bring her round.

Basilia lay beside Raymond, and holding up her hand to the light from the bedside candle, stared at her wedding ring. The place between her legs was tender and burning, although there had been a certain pleasure on the edge of the pain and until the end, when his crisis had come upon him, he had done his best to be gentle. He slept beside her, snoring softly, a mounded bulk under the bedclothes.

She had agreed to marry Raymond because it was their only chance of survival and she was used to sacrifice. She had given herself to save everyone else. With Raymond commanding the troops and with the additional men he had brought over, they would be safe. But this was strange new territory. She was entering a land she had never walked before – the land of a wife and all it entailed.

It was all very well for Aoife to say she had trodden this path herself, but Aoife had been much younger and more flexible. Basilia did not know how she was going to adapt to the demands of being Raymond's wife. Richard and Aoife expected her to remain loyal and focus on the needs of the dynasty, but she had other considerations now. Taking her marriage vows had been the last duty she owed her brother. From now on she would serve herself, and in that way, marriage had not trapped her but set her free. She would use Raymond's resources but she would not be Raymond's chattel. Never again would she be beholden in a household. If she had to undergo the physical union with Raymond every so often, then it was part of her duties as a wife, and it had not been entirely unpleasant.

They would manage well enough together. Her practical way with logistics and his position as a military commander made for many things in common. They saw the world in similar ways. His presence had always churned her emotions and she was still unsure about them, but she had an open road and she would walk it at her own behest from this night forth.

39

Windsor Castle, England, October 1175

Aoife spread the skirts of her scarlet court gown and performed a deep curtsey. Henry immediately raised her to her feet. 'It is good to see you, Countess, indeed, a welcome surprise,' he said before giving her the kiss of peace on the lips, lingering rather more than was necessary. His grey eyes sparkled with pleasure and curiosity.

She sent him a look from under her eyelids and said flirtatiously, 'Welcome surprises are always the best, sire, I find.'

Henry laughed softly. 'Indeed, they are. I look forward to speaking with you later.' His smile was warm before he moved on.

Aoife patted Richard's arm in reassurance. He had already made his own obeisance, and Henry had been affable towards him too. His support during the rebellion had changed their relationship from wary cooperation to cautious but cordial trust.

'He looks careworn,' she murmured.

'It is no easy matter holding the reins of so many dominions,' Richard said. 'I daresay I look careworn too.'

She flicked him an amused glance. 'You weather it better, and your son is not yet three years old, whereas Henry's sons have all rebelled against him except the youngest, and his wife is in prison for the same. You have had to face neither – yet.'

'I hope I never do!'

'I am sure it can be avoided,' she answered sweetly.

'Of course. I am not Henry for a start.'

She heard the slight edge in his tone and took his arm. 'And I am glad. There are many kings in this world, but only you are the king of my heart, and always will be, above any man.' She secretly squeezed his arm. 'Let me handle Henry in my own way. I have told you before, a woman can go where a man may not tread.'

'Just have a care,' Richard said, still looking troubled.

'Hah, you have nothing to worry about. He might enjoy flirting with me, but he has eyes only for that mistress of his.'

Richard followed her gaze across the room to a young woman with long tawny hair half hidden under a white veil. 'She was with him when I was last at court,' he said. 'His women do not usually last that long. Perhaps she would be queen.'

Aoife snorted. 'She might think so, but why would Henry marry her? There is no advantage in it, and everything Henry does has to have some benefit to Henry.'

'Yes,' Richard said wryly.

Henry had summoned Richard to court to settle matters in Ireland now that he had quelled rebellion in his other dominions. His sons had been brought to heel and his wife locked away at Sarum. Richard had said to Aoife that Henry was trying to nail everything down and keep it tidy. The difficulty was that every time he turned his back, the nails popped out again. But still he was determined, and this gathering at Windsor was his latest effort. Aoife had accompanied Richard, for she was Countess of Leinster and Richard her consort. Richard had left Hervey in Ireland to deal with the administration, and Raymond had been put in charge of the military side, and for now matters seemed to be working well. King Ruari had not come to the negotiations but had sent ambassadors to deal on his behalf with authority to use his seal. The agreement was that Ruari would take the high kingship of all Ireland, apart from the areas ceded to Henry including Dublin, Wexford, Waterford, Leinster and Meath. In the areas not allocated to Henry, Ruari would claim tribute from the other Irish lords, and if they refused to submit to him, he had the right to call upon Henry's representative to help him impose that rule.

Whether the treaty would work in practice was debatable but for now all parties were in agreement and apart from minor matters of detail the documents were ready to be sealed.

That evening, Henry was in a jocular mood and was holding an informal banquet with entertainment and dancing to augment the negotiations. Aoife was thoroughly enjoying herself. She was lithe and nimble on her feet and basked in the admiring and curious glances sent her way by the barons and nobles of Henry's court where Hibernian lords were regular visitors but not so high-born Irish women.

The current dance was a progressive circle, and as it ended she swirled her skirts and turned to Henry who had contrived to stand at her side. He was breathless and perspiring but smiled broadly as he offered his arm and led her out of the circle.

'Now then, Countess,' he said, 'I have not spoken to you properly yet. I trust you are well? You are looking beautiful. Your husband is a most fortunate man.'

'Yes, sire, indeed he is.' She slanted him a mischievous look.

Henry laughed. He looked down at her hand. 'I see you are wearing the ring.'

'It is always there as a memento of your visit to Ireland and your friendship, sire.'

The dancing had resumed and Richard was caught up in it, with Henry's young mistress Rosamund de Clifford on one side, and Henry's half-brother Hamelin on the other. Aoife met Richard's gaze and gave him a meaningful look, which he acknowledged with a raised brow. Rosamund was watching them too and frowning.

Henry drew Aoife away from the hall to a private chamber beyond, with cushioned benches set before the hearth. 'That is better.' He gestured for her to sit. 'I can hear myself think.'

Going to a nearby table, he poured two cups of wine and dismissed the waiting attendant, before joining her.

'To Ireland.' He raised a toast. 'To her green grass and fine cattle, her bountiful granaries, her fierce hawks and fast horses. I wish I was hunting there now.'

'We would certainly welcome you.' Aoife sipped the wine, which was rather sour and with a thickening of sediment. 'I am pleased you remember your visit so fondly.'

He gave her a long, appreciative look. 'I certainly remember the beauty of her women.' Removing her wine, he set it at the side of the bench and took her hands. His gaze dropped to the outline of her breasts and he kissed her.

Aoife felt the pressure of his lips, but she was older and wiser now and within her own power. Gently pushing him away, she regarded him with candour. 'Sire, I appreciate your attention and the salute of a friend – I am sure you did not mean more than that.'

He returned her look and then pulled back too, and his eyes were filled with wry amusement. 'Perhaps I did, but you remind me it would not be prudent and that the time is past. If I was going to have you, it would have been long ago.'

'I was too fast for you even then,' she said with a mischievous smile.

'Swift as a young deer,' he conceded.

'But we may still be friends.' She remained relaxed and smiling. 'We may enjoy each other's company and discuss business and share concerns.'

'You are wise, my dear,' he replied with a sardonic glint in his eyes. 'You are a greater player than that husband of yours realises.'

'You leave my husband to me.' She gave him a knowing look. 'It is about survival, we both realise that.' She retrieved her drink and sipped it.

Understanding each other perfectly without need for words or treading on territory best left alone, they drank their wine.

He asked about his god-daughter and Aoife replied that both Isabelle and her little brother were thriving, although she knew his query was a matter of form.

He turned swiftly to the business of Ireland. 'As soon as this treaty is sealed your high king will be seeking aid from me to put down his opponents. It behoves you to lend him that aid and keep the peace with him.'

Aoife inclined her head. 'Of course. I would have peace above all.' But she would fight for every inch of what was hers and her children's.

'Henry?' A young woman entered the chamber. His mistress, Rosamund de Clifford. Her gaze darted between the two of them. 'I am sorry,' she said. 'I did not realise you had a guest.' She curtseyed to Aoife, tension in every line of her body.

Of course the young woman had realised, Aoife thought cynically. She had seen them leave the room. But then a mistress had to protect her territory. She even felt a little sorry for Rosamund. Riding a lion was a dangerous occupation.

Aoife rose to her feet and swept her own deep curtsey to Henry. 'By your leave I shall return to my husband,' she said. 'He will be wondering where I am.'

Henry's lips twitched. 'We would not wish to give him cause for concern.' He took her hand and kissed the ring.

Aoife made her exit and dipped her head in passing to Rosamund, who reciprocated, suspicion rife in her eyes.

In the great hall, the dancing continued but Richard had left the circles and was talking to John FitzJohn, one of Henry's marshals. Another knight stood with them, tall and broad-shouldered with intelligent dark eyes and a ready smile.

The men bowed to Aoife as Richard introduced her. The knight was FitzJohn's younger brother, William, and he was also a marshal but in the Young King's retinue and his tutor in the military arts. The brothers had similar features and both had been blessed with good looks. However, clean, handsome and personable did not always mean trustworthy. The Young King had gone to war against his father, and his marshal had been part of that entourage and was therefore to be treated with caution, even if the rebellion was over and everything reconciled.

A new dance was beginning and he asked her to do him the honour of partnering him. Aoife wondered if he was being too familiar, but he had made his request with a courtier's fine manners and a slightly playful air. Obliging him, she discovered he was an excellent dancer. He had presence and charisma, and kept his focus fully on her, as though she was all that mattered.

'If you visit Ireland, I shall show you the dances of our country,' she said as he escorted her back to Richard. 'And the songs.'

'I would enjoy seeing them, madam,' he replied, with a genuine smile.

She thought he might make something of himself one day if he was not undone by the fierce rivalries, politics and favouritisms of the court.

She retired with Richard soon after that. They had pitched a large tent in the ward for the numbers at the gathering were too great for everyone to be accommodated within the keep.

They prepared for bed, washing their hands and faces and undressing as far as their chemises. Before she loosened her hair, Aoife went to the tent flap and peeped out to check that no one was within earshot beyond Richard's trusted guards. Returning, she sat down on a stool and gave Richard her comb, asking him to groom her hair.

'Well then,' he said, as he started to work. 'What did Henry want?'

'To catch up on old times and ensure we would adhere to his treaty,' she said. 'He is keen to settle his affairs with his neighbours.' She gave a small shrug. 'He wanted to talk too. He has few friends, and I have a view from further afield. Doubtless he will speak with you in due course.'

'Doubtless,' Richard said wryly.

'Of course he will, and while we are here we must obtain what we can from him and make our alliance with him solid.'

'It is usually Henry wringing what he can from us.'

'That is his nature, but he needs his supporters to uphold his dignity and standing, and remind his son of how powerful he is, and that he can deal with him whenever he chooses. If we stand firm at his side, it can only be to our benefit.'

Richard put down the comb and, raising her to her feet, pulled her to him. 'I do love you,' he said. 'You are a ruthless woman and my dearest treasure.'

She touched his cheek. 'I am not ruthless at all, save to protect my own dearest treasures. I think Henry has more in store for Ireland than this treaty, but as it suits him for now, so shall it suit us.'

40

Palace of Westminster, London, March 1176

'Sombre thoughts, my love?'

Aoife looked round at Richard. She was sitting on the bed, sorting through her jewels, and was holding a brooch with the two hounds chasing their tails. She ran her thumb over the gold interlacing. 'This was my christening gift from Derval, wife of Tiernan ua Ruari,' she said. 'I do not know how she came by it, but it has always felt ancient to me – like the tales of the old heroes passed down through the generations. One day it shall be Isabelle's for it was given from a woman to a woman.'

'It is a beautiful piece.'

'It makes me think of Ireland, and of who I am.' They were returning to Leinster in the morning. After spending the Christmas feast at Windsor, they had visited Striguil and the new keep at Goodrich and attended the Feast of the Purification at Tintern before returning to Westminster. 'I need to set foot on my own soil, but I have also grown used to living here. After what happened in Waterford, after all the bloodshed and fear in my life, this is a different world for me.' She touched her heart. 'Ireland is here inside me, in my very marrow, but my blood is mingled with yours in our children, and now England and Ireland are inseparably woven within me too.'

'I do understand,' he said. 'Ireland has threaded into my own soul, through and in spite of all.' Sometimes stitched with a very sharp needle, but the pattern had a savage beauty. He looked at the jewels spread on the bed. 'What are you doing?'

'Henry will want a parting gift,' she said. 'You know what he is like. What do you have in the strongbox?'

Sighing, Richard fetched the casket containing his own jewels and rings and sitting down at her side tipped the contents on the coverlet beside hers. She pointed to a thick gold chain set with a ruby.

He shook his head. 'It was my father's and Henry has often seen me wear it. What about this one?' He indicated a collar set with green stones and rock crystals.

Aoife frowned. 'It would not suit Henry.' She had already given him the gold torc in exchange for his promise of protection and was not inclined to sacrifice any more special pieces just to purchase his general goodwill.

'But if you gave it to him as a gift for Mistress de Clifford, I think it would please him greatly.'

Aoife reared back in indignation. 'It would not please me greatly! I think I ought to keep it. My father gave it to me, and I will not have it worn by some concubine, no matter the store he sets by her.'

Their boundaries delineated, they finally settled on a ring set with a jasper intaglio that had no emotional ties for either of them, a pendant of Norse gold from booty taken at Dublin, and an enamelled, jewelled cross from Constantinople. Richard puffed out his cheeks. 'We shall have nothing left,' he said ruefully. 'I always feel poorer after we have been with Henry.' He returned the casket to the strongbox but left out the garnet and gold chain to wear over his tunic.

As he was straightening up, his scribe Nicolas arrived clutching a letter.

'Sire, Countess, this letter has just come from my lord de Montmorency, you need to read it.'

Richard looked at him sharply as he took the letter. Nicolas was authorised to read all the routine correspondence from Ireland

and his agitation raised instant alarm. As he read what was written, Richard swore under his breath.

'Does the King know yet?'

The scribe shook his head. 'No, sire, I came straight to you.'

'What is it?' Aoife grabbed the letter from him and walked to the window, and as she read, anger flared up, hot and bright. 'Raymond!' she spat. 'I might have known!' She flung round to Richard. 'We have to go home – now!' She felt sick.

The treaty to which they had agreed in October had entitled High King Ruari to call upon the Constable of Ireland to aid him if he had need. Ruari needed help to defeat a rebellion in Limerick and Raymond had taken up the cause with a vengeance and extended his brief to plunder and raid at will, acting not as a deputy but as a ruler in his own right, demanding tribute and laying down the law as he saw fit. And using Leinster's funds to pay his Brabançon mercenaries.

'He has married your sister and now he thinks he has the right to sit in your chair – in my father's chair!' Her stomach knotted at the betrayal. Raymond did not just need putting in his place, he needed nailing into it; so did Basilia, for she knew they would be acting in tandem.

'It is a good thing we are returning to Ireland,' Richard said grimly. 'We should have gone sooner, but we will deal with it now.'

She gave a sharp nod and told herself that Raymond's action was just another turn in the game, neither a beginning nor an end, and they must play to win.

Henry had also received a copy of Hervey's letter and was not best pleased. 'Trouble in Ireland already and the treaty barely sealed,' he said with exasperation. 'Your brother by marriage is supposed to be holding the land stable, not mauling it like a lion and taking advantage!' He shot a furious look at Richard. 'I want this man leashed!'

'Sire, I am as disturbed by these tidings as you are,' Richard replied. 'I entrusted him with the defence of Leinster while I was conducting business here in England but he has overstepped the bounds of his remit. This has come with no permission of mine, I swear to you. I will deal with it.'

'I will curb him,' Henry said tersely. 'I will not have such disruption in my kingdom. He shall come and answer to me at court, either in peace or by force, I care not, and I will deal with him myself. You will return to Ireland with four of my officers. Two of them will bring him to me to answer in my court and two will stay to investigate his dealings. I expect your full cooperation in this. We cannot have factions. Do I make myself clear?'

'Yes, sire,' Richard said, understanding very well that his own position was under threat on two fronts now. This was what happened when you had to ask a man for help when you had no other option. Raymond had infiltrated his family, and his ambition was causing strife and untold damage. 'I shall make sure all is done to bring this back under control.'

Henry nodded brusquely. 'See that you do,' he said, 'or find yourself replaced.'

Arriving in Dublin, Richard found the situation on the surface much as he had left it. Raymond himself was a hundred and twenty miles away with the majority of his troops in Limerick.

Basilia greeted him and Aoife with a courteous smile on her lips and a question in her eyes as she looked at the four officials Henry had sent to assess the situation and bring Raymond to Henry. Aoife returned Basilia's smile with equal courtesy while noting the tension in Basilia's clasped hands. On the journey home, Richard had expressed his concern for Basilia's wellbeing and had pondered the feasibility of having her marriage with Raymond annulled, but Aoife suspected Basilia would not thank him for it. She was Raymond's wife now, and probably every bit as ambitious as her husband.

Henry's four officials afforded Basilia courtesy but remained aloof.

'These officers have come from the King,' Richard told her, 'to check all is functioning as he intended from the treaty we agreed at Windsor. There is no need to worry. Aoife will take care of you. I am sure you have had a difficult time – Hervey told me as much.'

Basilia's gaze flew to Hervey like a thrown dagger. He returned the look blandly.

'I do not know what has been said, but I am well and nothing is wrong,' she said coldly.

Aoife raised her brows. 'If you say so,' she replied. 'But these lords have business with Raymond – the King's business.'

White-faced, Basilia bit her lip.

'Raymond is to accompany Master de Genermes and Master de Bendignes to report to the King,' Richard said. 'Master de Horlotera and Master le Poer will look over the accounts and expenditure in the meantime.'

Basilia shook her head. 'I do not know what this is about. Raymond has done nothing wrong.'

'I am sure it will all become clear very quickly,' Aoife replied. 'We are here now and all is in hand.'

41

Dublin, Ireland, spring 1176

Richard was busy in the stable yard where several horses were awaiting the attention of the farrier. Isabelle had followed him and he had put her up on the back of a placid sorrel pack pony while he talked to a groom.

'I'm riding, Daidí, I'm riding!' she shouted.

He looked over his shoulder and chuckled. 'All the way to Canterbury, you've a long way to go yet!'

Her liveliness and her imagination amused him. The spring sun shone on her blonde plaits and her blue eyes were bright with joy. Her brother was napping, watched over by his nurse, but Isabelle was as busy as a little grasshopper.

He turned back to the groom. 'So, the grey mare is lame?'

'Yes, my lord. We're not sure – might have picked up a stone or cut her frog.'

'Bring her out and I'll have a look.'

'My lord.'

While Richard waited, his mind, free to idle, returned to the matter of Raymond like a tongue to a sore tooth. This morning two of Henry's men had set out for Limerick with a contingent of knights and serjeants, the summons in a saddle bag. But taking Raymond in hand did not solve the military problem, indeed it exacerbated it, for Raymond was highly skilled at what he did and there were few to match him. But even if Henry let Raymond go with a warning, Richard could not trust him again. He needed him and wanted rid of him at the same time – an untenable situation.

'I need you to ride with me!' Isabelle squealed, pulling him out of his troubled thoughts. 'There's a wheel in the road. Look out!'

The sumpter horse, placid though it was, flickered its ears at Isabelle's high-pitched voice and her kicking legs. Going to her, Richard lifted her off. 'Rescued in the nick of time,' he said, kissing her temple and hugging her. 'We need to go to your mama now; I have to examine a horse's hoof and it is dangerous for you to stay.'

He whirled her round, making her giggle, then tucked her under his arm and carried her back to Aoife who was trying on a new gown cut from a bolt of cloth Richard had brought from Normandy. He set Isabelle down and watched her run off to pick up her doll.

'I have to check the grey mare,' he said. 'She's lame on the left fore.' He looked Aoife up and down. The deep red colour of the gown enhanced Aoife's pale skin. Green jewels adorned the neckline and the side laces were green too. A garment of the court, establishing her position as the highest lady in the household. 'You are beautiful,' he said, because she was, but he thought her true beauty shone when she was lying in bed beside him, clothed only in her hair.

She smiled and posed a little. 'Now you will have to host a feast.'

'Indeed, if you organise it.'

Her smile deepened and he suspected she probably already had plans afoot and was deciding who to invite to obtain the best political result.

Richard approached the mare, stroked her soft muzzle and rubbed her ears which were furry inside, almost like a donkey's. 'Whoa, lass, whoa,' he soothed. She was usually a placid, stoical creature, but she had been lame for several days. The groom was worried she might have hoof rot or an abscess but wanted Richard's opinion.

She whickered and tossed her head but settled under his gentle voice. Richard ran his hand down her leg and lifted the affected hoof. Taking a cleaning knife from the groom, he probed gently at the frog until a sudden spurt of pus and blood made the mare plunge. Richard stepped back swiftly but she danced, bringing the full weight of the shod forehoof down across the end of Richard's foot. There was a moment of nothing and then blinding white pain. Richard doubled up, teeth clenched, but when people hurried to help him, he waved them away. 'It is nothing,' he said. 'I will be all right in a moment. See that the hoof is dressed and packed with sage.' He straightened and limped away from the horse, but he was in agony. He could not afford to be injured but knew from the weight that had crushed down across his toes that there might be serious damage for he was only wearing a light leather boot and a thin sock – no protection against the stamp of a powerful horse.

His boot was growing heavy and blood was seeping through the leather. Cursing, he hobbled into the kitchens, calling for Mark, the butcher, who was their chirurgeon when they were on campaign and accustomed to dealing with battle injuries.

He eased himself down on a bench and waved away the goggling servants. Mark arrived, wiping his hands on a towel, and shook his head at the sight of the bloody leather. 'I will have to cut it off,' he said. 'It's going to hurt.'

'Never mind that,' Richard gasped. 'It hurts enough as it is. I can stand the pain. Just do it.'

Richard was white and sweating by the time Mark had finished cutting the mangled boot off his foot. The flesh across his toes was bloody, pulped and swollen in an arc corresponding to the shape of the mare's shoe. Clucking his tongue and shaking his head, Mark cleaned the wound with salt water and a rag. Richard clenched his jaw, but the pain still broke through and made him cry out. 'For God's love do not stop!' he wheezed as Mark hesitated. 'Get it done, damn you!'

'Shall I fetch the Countess?' Mark asked, swallowing.

'No! Just pack and bind it. She must not see this.' He did not want to see it either; it was more than just a broken toe that would heal of its own accord while being a minor inconvenience.

'Sire, you cannot walk on this. You must rest with your leg propped up.'

Richard waved his hand irritably. 'Yes, yes.' Perhaps for the rest of the day, but he could not afford to be incapacitated. Broken bones took weeks to heal, and given the situation with Raymond, he did not have that sort of time.

Mark packed the wound with a layer of linen smeared with honey and padded it with fleece and more layers of bandage tightly wound around the foot and ankle. 'You should have this looked at by a physician, not just a soldier's knit-bone,' he said unhappily.

Richard gave an impatient nod. The pain and the shock had exhausted him and a vile headache was pounding at his temples.

'Shall I help you to your chamber, sire?'

'Yes. I repeat, do not tell the Countess. It will worry her to no avail to hear it from others. I will tell her myself.'

His arm over Mark's shoulder on one side and his squire on the other, Richard hopped his way to his chamber but refused to lie on the bed. 'I have work to do,' he said. 'Sit me at the trestle with a footstool and bring me a drink. If my mind is busy, I won't think on the pain.'

The men exchanged glances but did as he asked. Richard winced as they eased his foot onto the stool. The pain throbbed and burned in his toes. Osbert de Horlotera arrived to talk to him about the accounts and he forced himself to concentrate on what he was saying, pushing his mind through the pain, insisting it was nothing when Osbert voiced his concern.

Isabelle had been enjoying a story and a cuddle on Aoife's knee and was now asking about fathers. 'Where is your papa?' she asked.

'He is with God,' Aoife replied. 'He went to God before you were born, when you were still a seed growing in my womb.'

Isabelle frowned, and Aoife could see the question forming about how seeds grew into people.

'My Daidí was big and growly like a bear, but he was kind and soft like a dog. And he was hunted and hunter like a bird. And he was brave and daring like a wolf. That was my Daidí, your grandfather.'

Isabelle gazed at her, round-eyed, drawn in by the words and the magical, sing-song language.

'He was a king,' Aoife continued, 'and I am his daughter, a princess, and you are his granddaughter. You are precious to me and more than me. You are precious to everyone, and the world will lie at your feet.' She rocked Isabelle in her arms, filled with love for her small daughter.

When Richard did not return from the stable, Aoife left the children with Deirdre and went to look for him, finding him in his chamber with his foot heavily bandaged and propped on a stool. A wine jug stood at his elbow and he had been drinking for his face was flushed and his eyes glassy.

'What has happened to you?' She came to sit on the bench and looked at the bandage with concern, for he had clearly suffered more than a scratch.

'It's nothing.' He shrugged. 'The mare trod on me while I was examining her. It wasn't deliberate but she was in pain and I wasn't fast enough to leap out of the way. It will be all right – it's just a nuisance at the moment. I won't be able to sit a horse for several weeks and depending on what I hear about Raymond, I may need to.'

'You should have let me look at it,' she said. 'Who treated you?'

'Mark, he's a good man. Don't fuss, it will be all right.'

'I will make you a tisane to help the pain and you should go to bed.'

An expression crossed his face exactly like Gilbert's when he was preparing to refuse something out of sheer stubbornness, but then he capitulated with a gesture that told her the extent of his discomfort. 'Just to please you,' he said, but he waited, plainly wanting her to leave before he got up. Indeed, she wondered if he could get up, and panic knotted her stomach.

Leaning over him, she put her hand to his forehead and felt the heat coming off him. 'Dear God, you are boiling up. Let's get you to lie down and I will open the window.' She summoned a couple of attendants.

Richard was sweating with pain and whining behind his clenched teeth by the time the men deposited him on his bed. Aoife flung open the shutters to let cool air blow over him and went to fetch her herbs and nostrums. His auburn hair meant that he was already of a hot, choleric nature so ideally he needed to be bled, but a physician would have to do that. At least the cool air would help. She made him drink the tisane and bathed his brow and face with tepid rose water.

He managed the semblance of a smile and squeezed her hand. 'I will be all right in the morning, I promise – I always keep my promises, you know that.'

She kissed his cheek. 'Yes, you do,' she said, but she was worried, and after she had settled him she went to find Mark to ask him just what was under Richard's bandages. 'The truth,' she said. 'Whatever it is, I would know. Look at me when you speak.'

He raised his eyes to hers and she saw the fear in them. 'The mare brought her full weight down and she was shod,' he said. 'It will not heal easily; many small bones were broken and the flesh is crushed into them. I washed and bound it as best I could, but the Earl will have to rest for several weeks. Even when he is back on his feet, he will be lame for some time.' He looked away.

'I see,' she said. 'Thank you for telling me.' Her stomach was hollow with dread at what he was not saying. 'Lame for some time' was probably a euphemism for 'the rest of his life'.

She returned to Richard, who had fallen into a feverish doze, his face twitching as he muttered to himself, made restless by the pain. It was ironic that he had come through so much war unscathed only to be brought low by a stupid, mundane incident.

She watched over him, barely sleeping herself for worrying about him while he continued to toss and mutter.

In the morning, he was cooler and the pain was less intense. Aoife made him drink more of the tisane. The physician arrived and bled him from the vein in his arm and examined both his blood and his urine. Richard refused stubbornly to let him look at the injury. 'It was dressed yesterday,' he snapped, 'and well bandaged. No good will come of poking about. I have things to do.'

'Then perhaps tomorrow, sire,' the physician said.

'Yes, perhaps.' Richard dismissed him and looked at Aoife, who stood with arms folded and lips compressed. 'I cannot afford to be stuck here in bed,' he said irritably. 'I need to ride out to—'

'You will not be riding anywhere for some time,' she interrupted. 'That much should be obvious to you even half out of your wits. I spoke to Mark yesterday. I know what that bandage conceals. You should let the physician at least look.'

'Whatever he has told you, he is exaggerating. Leave me to do my work. Send in Hervey and Nicolas.'

Aoife clucked her tongue and stalked away to her duties. The cheese making had started again in earnest as the spring advanced. There were letters to answer – pleas from abbeys for alms. The pressing matter of Raymond's indictment. She made herself busy but she was desperately worried. Richard whole and strong was a powerful lord and protector, but the moment the predators knew he was weak, they would start circling, and she knew how vulnerable she and the children were.

42

Dublin, Ireland, spring 1176

Over the next few days Richard grew ever more irritable over the state of his foot. He had a crutch made so he could get about the castle at least and preside at the high table in the halls at mealtimes, but he was never hungry and his fever persisted despite drinking Aoife's tisanes and being bled again. The pain exhausted him, but he refused to give in to it, becoming increasingly febrile and querulous. He pretended the injury was minimal and that beneath the thick bandages it was healing.

On the fourth day, Aoife insisted that the physician remove the bandage to look at the wound and clean and redress it. Stains had leached through the layers and she could smell something faintly unpleasant like the taint of old meat. When the wrappings were eventually taken off, Aoife stared in horror and bit the side of her hand so she would not cry out.

Richard stared too in shock, feeling as though his heart had stopped and his breath with it, like death before death. He had seen this sort of thing before when men had been wounded, and the only cure he had ever seen to work was amputation. He could not visualise himself as a one-legged man. It was untenable.

The physician suggested lancing the injury to release the putrid matter and Aoife sent for her uncle Lorcan. 'You should have it washed in holy water and blessed by the Archbishop,' she said, and then pressed her lips together, silently raging at Richard for being such a fool. His body was anchoring him into a grave but it couldn't be, because his son was not yet four years old and they were surrounded by enemies. He had sworn to protect them and now his oath was rendered useless by a single stamp of a horse's hoof.

The physician applied hot poultices to the wound to draw the poison, and Richard arched on the bed in agony. Aoife bathed his brow with a cool cloth and murmured to him in a mingling of Irish and French, telling him everything was all right, that he would be well by and by. That Lorcan was coming to bless the wound and God would have mercy. And not believing a word.

Richard came to awareness to find Lorcan at his bedside, incanting a blessing and sprinkling both him and his foot with holy water. He had an uneasy relationship with Lorcan; he knew well that the Archbishop viewed him as an interloper. One of the devil Normans who had inflicted themselves upon the Irish like a plague. But he also knew Lorcan would do his best by Aoife. 'Stay awhile,' he requested. 'I want to talk to you.'

Lorcan gave him a meaningful look and inclined his head.

Once the wound had been redressed and the inner layer smeared with honey, Aoife saw the physician out and left Lorcan and Richard alone.

'God works great miracles and I am praying for one,' Richard said in a low voice, 'but if it is not to be I want my family kept safe from harm and provided for. Promise me you will do all in your power to protect them.'

'Of course, my boy, that goes without saying.' Lorcan patted his arm.

Richard stared into the priest's dark blue eyes, searching for sincerity beyond the platitude. 'Do not let Aoife be disparaged or sold off in marriage against her will. Many will try to pressure her and trade her, not least the King for all his friendship.'

Lorcan's brows pushed together in a frown. 'I shall keep her as safe as I can, I give you my solemn word. Both she and your children will remain safe by the Church, and in the hand of Mary, mother in heaven.'

Richard swallowed. 'Thank you.'

'But your wife is strong and adept. Take heart and comfort from what she is. Do not underestimate her ability.'

'I do not,' Richard whispered. 'She is the best of me.'

Lorcan removed a jewelled cross from around his neck and pressed it into Richard's hand for comfort. 'I shall return later and read to you if you wish, and we can talk some more.'

'Thank you.'

Richard closed his eyes and slept. When he woke up again the sun was streaming through the window and Isabelle was sitting on the counterpane looking at him. Her eyes were filled with light that turned them to the blue of sea-shallows on a summer morning. She was playing with the jewelled cross Lorcan had given to him, tilting it to make the colours in the gems dance on the walls in translucent shards.

'Is your leg feeling better now, Daidí?'

'A little.' It wasn't true. He felt hot, sick and parched. 'Improved for seeing you, my love.'

'If you could take yourself out of your poorly foot, you would be better, Daidí.'

'Yes, I would.' She was right, and it would come down to that in the end, but he had too much to do and no time left. Whatever strength remained to him must be used to deal with the essentials. 'You see all those colours flashing on the wall?'

'Yes, Daidí.'

'You can only see them in sunlight, but they are still there even when the sun goes in, only your eyes do not realise. I will always be here.'

She gave him a puzzled look.

'I want you to be a big girl and help your mama if I am not here,' he said. 'She will need you and your brother in more ways than you know.'

She looked at him wide-eyed. 'Yes, Daidí.'

'One day you will be a fine young woman, I can see it in you even now.' Although he would not live to see it – and the thought was more painful than his wound.

Aoife arrived bearing a bowl of fresh tepid rose water and a cool cloth. 'Your father has to rest,' she said. 'Go and find Ainne, there's a good girl.'

'But Daidí said I had to help you.'

'And you shall, but later. Give your father a kiss and do as I say.'

Isabelle pressed a petal kiss on Richard's cheek and skipped off to find her brother and their nurse.

Richard felt the cool touch of the cloth on his brow. 'That's good.' He closed his eyes.

'Oh, you are such a fool,' she said softly.

'So my womenfolk have always told me,' he answered with a weak smile. 'And some have loved me for it, and some have not.'

He could not stay awake and wandered in feverish dreams. People came and went. Aoife, Lorcan, Hervey, Nicolas. Sometimes he thought he spoke to them but could not be sure because the words he wanted to say kept spinning out of sequence and vanishing before he could speak. Sometimes he was aware of Basilia's presence, and he would recoil because he had much to atone for, but at the same time he knew how dangerous she was. He heard her murmuring solicitously to Aoife, not to worry, that she would take care of everything, and he wanted to shout a warning, but he was fighting for every breath in a choking sea of dark red and knew he was drowning. He felt Aoife at his side, bathing him, talking to him, and tried to reach for her, but his arms refused to obey his will, and as he thrashed about, he could hear her weeping. 'Do not leave me, husband,' she whispered. 'Do not leave us, I beg of you.'

He felt the tug of the undertow and resisted it. There were things he had to say before he was swept out to sea. Things to lock in place to protect Aoife and the children, and time was short. 'I will always be here for you whether in this world or the next,' he said, struggling to the surface. 'Whenever you call me, if God is willing, I will come. I hope I have been a good husband to you.' He wanted her to say he had, but knew he had often failed to measure up, and that in dying he was letting her down beyond forgiveness.

'Do not weep for me,' he said as her eyes started to brim. 'You must be the rock, my love, not the water eroding the rock. You must hold steady.' His throat was dry and it took so much energy to speak. She tilted a cup to his lips and he sipped, moistening his mouth, struggling to swallow, almost choking.

Aoife wiped his chin with a napkin. 'Do not worry,' she murmured, 'try to rest.'

'I need to . . . I have to speak now, lest I never speak again.' He gripped her hand, cool and dry in his own fevered one. 'I have spoken to your uncle; he will protect you – as will Hervey. You and the children must go to England. Who knows what will happen here when I am gone with so many ambitious men fighting for their share. Hervey will accompany you. You will have to shoulder a heavy load, but I am relying on you as I cannot rely on myself. I saw how strong you were the first time I laid eyes on you at Striguil.'

'I was afraid beyond measure,' she replied with a tremulous smile.

'Yes, but fierce and determined to stand firm, and I know what courage it took.'

He gripped her fingers and she squeezed his in return.

'Yes,' she said. 'I am my father's daughter after all.'

He managed the semblance of a smile, and looking into her eyes, saw the resourcefulness there. He suspected she had plans in progress far beyond his realisation and was a little comforted.

'You must have everything you need to maintain your status as a countess and daughter of a king. Even should you be a widow I want you to look magnificent and to honour me by doing so.'

'Of course.'

'Do not let Basilia dominate you, for she will if she can. This is your estate and our children's, and no other's.'

'It is all in hand,' she soothed. 'Neither Raymond nor Basilia shall scrape our children's inheritance into their own coffers, I will see to it. Do not let it trouble you. Just worry about yourself and come back to me.'

He gave her a tired smile. 'I will never go beyond the love I have for you,' he said.

She made a soft sound and turned her head away. When she looked back her eyes were shiny with tears but they did not spill. 'I would rather you than any man, my husband,' she said. 'Go to sleep now. I will stay.'

Aoife watched the rapid rise and fall of his chest and wondered how she was going to be a rock in the face of the storm. She was going to lose him, and when he died, so too died her power and security. It would be easy to fall into despair, but for the sake of the earldom and her children's inheritance she had to endure and survive. Watching him reminded her of her father's last days and it was like looking at an overlay of the two men. It was for ever. It was beyond death.

Basilia arrived and stood at the bedside. 'How is he?'

'Sleeping,' Aoife answered, tight-lipped and immediately on edge. Basilia had been solicitous and concerned since Richard's injury, organising the household, keeping everything orderly, so that Aoife could concentrate on the sick room, but Aoife did not trust her, for Basilia had no reason to be kind to her or Richard.

'Go and rest and I shall sit with him awhile.'

Aoife shook her head. 'No. I want to be here when he wakes; I will not yield that duty to anyone.'

'But you must sleep, my dear,' Basilia said, expression concerned.

'And so I shall, but not now.' And when she could stay awake no longer, she would ensure that either Hervey or Lorcan sat with him, not Basilia.

Basilia perched on a stool at the bedside. 'Raymond will be here soon.'

'Yes, I know.' There had been no particular inflection in Basilia's voice, but Aoife knew a battle line had been drawn.

She resumed bathing Richard's brow. The fever had melted the flesh from his bones and there were livid shadows in his eye sockets.

Basilia said nothing more; she did not have to. She stayed to pray for a while, running her prayer beads through her fingers, and eventually rose, lightly touching Aoife's shoulder. 'I will bring you some broth.'

When she had gone, Aoife exhaled with relief. She could not bear to have Basilia near her – that touch had been of dominance masked as compassion for the afflicted.

Richard stirred again and he was agitated, demanding to know what would become of certain fields that needed ploughing and who would care for the sheep because soon it would be time for shearing. 'It is not your responsibility,' Aoife said gently. 'Someone will see to it.' She knew it was part of a wider anxiety concerning his duties and responsibilities and his guilt that he could not fulfil them.

She gave him a sip of water and he swallowed clumsily.

'Henry,' he said. 'Do not let him take advantage of you. You are his golden child, but he can still devour you. Do what you can to secure the lands and do not become embroiled.'

Aoife nodded seriously. Standing up to Henry was always daunting, but she knew herself capable. 'I have no intention of being anyone's meal,' she said.

Hearing a footfall, she looked round and was relieved to see Hervey. Had it been Basilia with soup, she might have thrown it over her.

'Come,' he said, 'I shall keep vigil. Go and take some rest and I will call you if there is need.'

'Thank you,' she said with gratitude for his compassion. 'I have letters to write.'

Standing up, she swayed, suddenly dizzy. Hervey caught her. 'When did you last eat or sleep?'

Aoife shook her head. 'I have dozed when I can. Basilia is bringing me some broth, but I would rather receive it from another's hand.'

'I will see it brought to your chamber,' he said, 'and it will not be Basilia.'

She pressed his arm gratefully and her eyes began to fill; but then, remembering what Richard had said about water wearing away rock, she lifted her chin. 'I will return in a while.'

Once in her chamber, she called for warm water and clean linen. Her shift needed laundering and all her garments were sweaty and stale. She wanted to look her best for Richard, out of love, respect and seemliness. She had seen women and men become draggled and apathetic in the face of the griefs and troubles piled upon them, but to do so as a leader was to lose authority and esteem in public.

Once washed, tidied, and wearing clean, fresh garments, she sought the children and gathered them in her arms. 'Your father cannot see you for the moment,' she said, 'but he loves you dearly and he sends you that love and asks you to pray for him.'

Isabelle nodded solemnly and pressed her hands together. Gilbert followed suit, but at a year younger was aping his sister rather than having any awareness.

'And I thank God for both of you.' Aoife hugged them close.

'Why can't Papa see us?' Isabelle asked.

'He is resting. You know a horse stepped on his foot? He has to lie quietly to let it heal.'

Isabelle nodded, apparently satisfied, and Aoife told her and Gilbert an embellished story about a fierce dragon that swallowed St Margaret so that she had to force her way out of its body. Stories about dragons were a favourite, and the children loved them and relished the frisson of fear. A servant arrived with the broth and bread, the latter warm from the oven, and she ate with Isabelle and Gilbert, forcing herself to chew and swallow, even though she was queasy. She needed her strength and she needed her wits about her.

She curled up with Isabelle and Gilbert on her bed and, pulling the coverlet over all of them, closed her eyes. Outside she could hear the sweet song of a thrush warbling on a branch of April green and the sound wounded her heart. 'Richard,' she whispered. 'Don't go.' But she knew it was breath vanishing into the wind.

While Aoife slept, Basilia came again to sit with Richard; even now she would do her duty. The stench from the wound curled her stomach. Aoife might not want her here and guarded him jealously, but she had been part of him long before Aoife arrived with her sharp little claws. Soon Aoife would be nothing, soon she would be powerless, yet Basilia still feared her and the violence lurking at the centre of all the Irish kinship ties. It had to be kept in check. She wished Raymond was here; she would feel safe then. She had no faith or trust in Hervey, who, anyway, was Raymond's rival.

Hervey looked up from bathing Richard's burning brow.

'Will you dismiss me?' Basilia challenged.

Hervey shook his head. 'No,' he said quietly. 'You are my niece and Richard's sister.' He smiled sadly. 'I remember you when you were a small girl with braids no thicker than my little finger. I remember you and Richard playing together the same way that Isabelle and Gilbert do. Just children, full of laughter.'

Basilia avoided his gaze. 'It was a long time ago and it is gone.' She lifted the sheet to look at Richard's leg and recoiled, suppressing a retch. 'He should have had a hot knife on this days ago. He does not have long, does he?'

Hervey shook his head.

'All bodies come to this corruption,' she said with distaste. When he died he would be free of this, she thought. He was probably unaware of it even now. She felt a barren emptiness.

He had never appreciated her and she had always done her duty, if not for him, then for the sake of the family. Now it had all come to this. Perhaps he was so corrupt he was rotting even before his death. 'God will have his way with him,' she said.

'As he will with us all,' Hervey replied, speaking gently, but with warning in his voice.

She sent her uncle a steady look, not yielding an inch. The vitality had been sapped from him. He looked tired. Indeed, they were all tired. This land had drained them, but she was a daughter of warriors and she would fight. When Richard died, as surely he would, Aoife would be focused on her grieving and vulnerable and she would seize the moment. Hervey did not have the strength to stand in her way, and she had Raymond. He was her life now.

'Be kind to Aoife,' Hervey warned, giving her a hard look as if he could read her thoughts.

'Of course, uncle, do not doubt it,' Basilia replied. *As kind as she has ever been to me.*

The household gathered around Richard's bed in the April morning. Aoife had been with him throughout the night. Richard still breathed but long gaps stretched between each inhalation, and she was only glad he was still here as the sun cleared the horizon. She had stopped pleading with him not to go for it was inevitable. Her prayers now were for his soul.

She took his hand in hers and his fingers were cold. 'It is all right,' she said. 'I am here and I release you.'

Richard's eyelids flickered and he opened them fully and looked at her. He was beyond speech, but he met her gaze in an unspoken contract and the look held between them until he ceased to see her and stared past her into eternity.

She leaned over him, feeling for his breath on her skin, still holding his hands, listening for a final whisper, but his soul had flown. There was just the open window and the sunlight, and the weighty silence of the gathered household at the bedside.

Aoife was prepared; she had diverted all numbness and grief to a place deep within; she had to keep her wits about her if she was to survive. She kissed his eyes and then his lips for the last time, breathing her breath into his mouth. 'That you shall know me in spirit,' she whispered. 'Goodbye my fond, fair husband.'

Standing up, she clapped her hands and called for water to be brought to wash his body. Lorcan anointed Richard on the forehead, heart, and the soles of his feet, although he was perfunctory when it came to the remnants of the injured one. Behind her, Aoife heard sobs and snuffles. The shuffling of feet and cleared throats. A rising wail like a storm surrounding an island with impervious cliffs, and she was that island, battered on all sides.

Basilia solicitously folded a cloak around her shoulders. 'The priests will do what is necessary for the vigil,' she murmured. 'You should take some rest and the children should not be here. This is no place for them.'

Aoife controlled the urge to push her away, because she did need a short while alone. And perhaps Basilia was being kind; surely, she must be grieving too somewhere in her soul. 'Where else should my children be but at their father's side to pay their respects?' she said. 'I will have them know everything for they are his lawful heirs.'

Basilia recoiled at the rebuff and withdrew into her own dignity. 'As you wish,' she said stiffly. 'You know best.'

Aoife ignored the remark. She embraced Richard's weeping daughters, and then retired, ushering Isabelle and Gilbert before her. Isabelle was sucking her thumb which she had not done in over a year, and Gilbert was wide-eyed and bewildered.

Once in her chamber, she sat down with them on the bed, her arms around them. 'I want you to listen to me,' she said, kissing them. 'Your father has left us for a little while, like when he had to go and serve the King in Normandy and we did not see him for a long time, only now he is serving God.'

'When is he coming back?' Isabelle unplugged her thumb to ask.

The words struck Aoife like a slap and she drew a steadying breath. 'His body can no longer serve him, but he will always be here in spirit and never desert you. You can always call on him in your prayers and he will answer.' Her throat ached with the effort of controlling her voice. 'We will continue as we are and our lives will be good. We will shoulder our responsibilities with eagerness and courage, and always serve our father who art in heaven. Amen.' The sermon was for herself rather than the children who were gazing at her barely comprehending.

'You are not going to leave us, are you, Mama?' Isabelle's eyes were bright with tears of worry.

'Oh, bless you, of course not, child!' And now she could control her own tears no longer and they spilled down her cheeks. 'I would never leave you, and your father has not left you either. He is still here in spirit and always will be.' She seized Gilbert and Isabelle fiercely to her bosom and rocked them in her arms back and forth, praying for God's support, for they had stepped off a cliff edge into a different world.

Taking the letter from the scribe's hand, Basilia read it in the light from the window. This would bring Raymond to her side faster than anything else, and she needed him here, now.

To her dearest lord, Raymond FitzWilliam, greetings.

His wife Basilia desires for her most loving lord and husband Raymond the same health and happiness as for herself. Dearest, let it be known to you, my true and loving husband, that the large molar tooth that caused me so much pain has now fallen out. I beg of you, if you have any thought for your own future safety or mine, return quickly and without delay.

'Yes,' she said to the scribe. 'That will do.'

Once the wax had been melted, she pressed Richard's own seal into it, and the counterseal from her personal signet ring. She paid the scribe generously for his discretion and took the letter to the messenger herself. 'See that this reaches my lord husband swiftly,' she said. 'Use the fastest horses and do not tarry. Haste is all.'

Now was their time, she thought as she turned away, her step purposeful. She had the keys to Richard's strongbox and she had Richard's seal. It would be broken up of course once news of his death was commonplace, but for now it still had authority. If she kept Aoife well attended to and sequestered in her grief, then she and Raymond could rule the roost. Indeed, they must, she reasoned, for otherwise there would be mayhem and chaos. She knew the Irish and her ambitious countrymen all too well. Someone had to be in control or else everyone would suffer. Aoife would have no need to deal with the harsh details of government. Besides, as a widow, her influence was weakened and the men loyal to the house of de Clare would certainly not look to Aoife to rule them.

The messenger departed and Basilia prepared to eat in the hall, presiding at the head of the table as Richard's sister and closest kin. She had donned her best gown of rich, rose-coloured silk and had adorned her fingers with gold rings, commanding Aline and Matilda to do the same to honour their father.

The two envoys from Henry's court she graciously seated at the high table too, presenting them with the choicest morsels and best wine. Osbert de Horlotera was a royal chamberlain possessing intimate knowledge of the Exchequer and Basilia courted him with particular focus.

'I wonder if it is wise to take my husband to the King when Raymond is such a strong and respected soldier. He is the most able should it come to preventing uprisings from the Irish in the aftermath of my brother's unforeseen demise.' She looked down at her hands. 'I fear what might happen without a strong military presence to protect us.'

Osbert ate his beef stew while he considered his answer, and Basilia waited, reining back her impatience. 'I agree,' he said eventually. 'We shall certainly need new instructions from the King to deal with this.'

Basilia gestured for the servant to refill his cup. 'I hope you will convey to the King that all is in hand. My husband is unswervingly loyal and you can see for yourself how matters are being run.'

Osbert lifted his cup. 'Indeed,' he said, but politely, rather than committing himself. 'Is the Countess not joining us?'

'The Countess needs calm to grieve,' Basilia said firmly. 'She has the comfort of her children and all her needs are being met. She is in no condition to be disturbed by matters of government, as you will appreciate. My brother was dear to me, but I have a different perspective, and I can be more practical in trying circumstances.'

Aoife summoned Deirdre to watch over Gilbert and Isabelle, donned her dark red court gown and went to the hall because life went on and she had to exert her authority. She would rather a thousand times have stayed in her bed, curled around her offspring, nursing her wounds, but this had to be done.

On arriving, her skin started to prickle for already it was like entering a foreign land. There were few friendly faces and she was aware of being regarded with speculation, bordering on predatory intent. Her stomach made a slow somersault as she realised the extent of her peril and how many greedy fingers were reaching to control herself, her children and their lands. A glance at the high table showed her Basilia presiding with full authority, and she immediately knew where the greatest danger lay.

Drawing herself up, she walked proudly to the dais table. Osbert de Horlotera immediately vacated his seat for her, casting a glance at Basilia, who remained firmly where she was. Aoife thanked him with modest decorum and exerted her precedence by ordering the servants to bring her father's drinking horn and his dish.

'Are you sure you should be here?' Basilia said, as though to an invalid. 'I can have food brought to your chamber. You should be resting. Everything is being done to keep the household in order.'

'So I see,' Aoife replied pointedly. 'I am perfectly well and I do not need your coddling. I am the Countess of Leinster and the daughter of a king who taught me well what it is to rule, especially in my own hall.'

An attendant poured wine into the horn. Resisting the urge to gulp it down, Aoife took a measured sip, having first raised a toast to the gathering. She half turned her shoulder, ignoring Basilia, making her an irrelevance, keeping the attention on herself.

Basilia narrowed her eyes but continued to smile. 'Even so, it is a time of great difficulty for everyone. Raymond will be here soon from Limerick, and then we will be well protected.'

The veiled threat churned Aoife's stomach, but outwardly she remained calm. Having Raymond in control would be like letting a wolf guard the sheep fold. She shot a glance towards Henry's two officials. They might or might not be her allies. They were royal servants with their first loyalty to their king, and with Richard dead, the game had changed. 'I expect we will,' she said, her own voice filled with insinuation.

Basilia rose and inclined her head. 'I will bid you goodnight,' she said.

'You have my leave to go,' Aoife replied, and when Basilia sent her a look that was like throwing a spear, she returned it full measure.

Aline and Matilda followed their aunt, but Matilda paused to stoop and kiss Aoife's cheek. 'I know you loved my father,' she said. 'And I know what it is like.'

Tears pricked Aoife's eyes as she squeezed Matilda's arm. 'Bless you,' she said, her voice catching.

She toyed with the bread in her dish and realised that Osbert de Horlotera was watching her with a sympathetic albeit speculative gaze.

'Tell the King when you report to him that I am well,' she said. 'And that I trust in his goodwill and succour.'

'Indeed, madam, he shall have a full report of everything,' Osbert said, gravely.

Aoife forced herself to eat the bread and some cheese, before retiring with dignity. On her way to her chamber she bade a servant summon Maurice Regan. She could not rely on Osbert and his associates to deliver her message to Henry with the correct nuance. Who knew what Basilia had told them, and what their own agendas were.

Maurice arrived with his inks, quills and parchment. Tonight, she noticed how much older he looked, as though her vision had developed a harsher perspective on reality. His beard was more silver than gold and his scalp shone pinkly through his thinning hair. She could have summoned Richard's scribe Nicolas to write the letter, but he might be interrogated by Basilia or inadvertently play into her hands. The last thing she wanted was Basilia knowing her business. The children danced around Maurice, clamouring for his attention, and he joked with them, pulling a silver coin from behind Gilbert's ear and doing the same with a red hair ribbon for Isabelle. Aoife let them play for a moment before sending them to their nurse so she could concentrate on her business.

'You wish me to write letters for you, madam?' Going to the lectern in the window embrasure, Maurice set out his tools.

'Yes. I want you to write to the King, and I wish the correspondence to be private and unknown to all here.'

'You are wise, Countess.'

Lips pursed, Maurice secured his sheet of parchment and

swiftly pricked out the guidelines, and then, dipping his quill in the ink horn, waited.

Aoife dictated her request to Henry, reminding him of his promise to protect her and her children. Maurice crafted her words in fluent Latin and read them back to her in both Latin and Irish. Another letter went to the FitzHarding family in Bristol, telling them that whatever they might hear to the contrary, Basilia and Raymond had no authority to speak for the earldom and any agreement so made was null and void. A final set of letters went out to Richard's relations in England.

When she came to use Richard's seal on the documents and give Maurice money for the messenger, she discovered the keys to the strongbox were missing as was the seal itself. The boxes could not be opened without forcing them which would compromise Richard's exchequer. A cold lump of fear lodged in Aoife's belly. She knew Basilia must be in possession of the keys and the seal, and all done behind her back while she was caring for Richard. What else had she done? Aoife knew she was not strong enough to confront Basilia, who had the Norman garrison behind her. If she approached the Irish, she would bring war and mayhem down on her children's inheritance. The Irish themselves had no reason to keep her and the children alive anyway and were as likely to murder them as give succour.

She still had her father's seal, the one for Leinster with its wheatsheaf emblem, and she fetched it from her coffer. Slipping it from its silk pouch, she gave it to Maurice, together with a purse of silver that she had kept separate for her personal use. She had jewels she could sell if necessary, and gold coins stitched into the hem of her cloak. 'Send the letters now,' she said. 'Henry's officers will not leave until Raymond's return and this must go sooner. I trust you to find someone to do this swiftly and secretly.'

Maurice bowed. 'Leave this with me and I shall see it done.'

'Thank you.' She gave him a swift kiss on the cheek. 'You

were always my father's good friend and adviser, and now mine – I value your loyalty.'

Maurice smiled at her with a sad, sympathetic light in his eye. 'I am a bard and a poet. I spin words to influence men's minds and deeds, or to glorify them for posterity. Even if I am not always loyal to the absolute truth, I am loyal to you as I was to your father.'

'Go now, before you make me cry,' Aoife said, and made a shooing motion. 'Make haste; I want the deed done.'

When he had gone, she wiped her eyes and donned the cloak with the gold coins stitched in the hem. Seeking out Hervey, she asked him to accompany her to the cathedral to pray with her and keep vigil with Richard.

Kneeling before his bier, surrounded by a blaze of candles, she could feel his presence as strongly as if he stood beside her, with his hand on her shoulder. What lay on the bier, shielded by honey-scented flame, was but a shell. Silently she told him what had happened and prayed for his help, and then she prayed to her father the same, for surely they must both be together in heaven watching over her.

Next day she asked Henry's representatives to attend her. When they arrived, she greeted them wearing a simple but elegant gown and wimple, her children sheltered within her arms like chicks protected by a mother hen. Bidding the men be seated, she kept her eyes modestly lowered, and focused on Gilbert and Isabelle, the epitome of a grieving widow.

'You wanted to see us, madam?' said Osbert de Horlotera.

'Yes,' she said. 'I do not wish to trouble you but there is something you should know.' She paused for effect, enhancing the tension. 'I asked my scribe to write a letter to Richard's relations informing them of his death. But when I went to seal the letter and pay the scribe, I discovered the keys to the strongboxes were missing, as was the Earl's seal. As far as I can tell the strongboxes have not been compromised but since the children are in the King's wardship, he should know this, and I ask you to tell him. My sister by marriage may have the seal and keys in her keeping. She has been very thoughtful and has taken much upon herself in the last few days, as I am sure you know.' She looked at them individually, making her point, then dropped her gaze, biting her lip. 'It is just that if the King requires me to surrender my husband's seal that no others may use it, it is not in my possession.'

The men exchanged glances. Osbert cleared his throat. 'Thank you for bringing this to our attention, Countess. We shall report the matter to the King and he will decide what is to be done – and I shall speak to Madam Basilia.'

Aoife inclined her head. 'Of course. I bow to the King's wishes and hope to bring him the tidings to England myself soon, especially since Isabelle is his god-daughter by whom he sets great store.'

The men finished their wine and departed with renewed murmurs of condolence. She saw them taking in the hangings on the walls, the silver gilt jugs on the sideboard that had come from Normandy, and knew they were assessing her wealth and what everything was worth – including herself.

Three days later, Richard was buried in the cathedral in Dublin, the service, like Aoife's marriage, conducted by her uncle Lorcan. Aoife wore her silks and jewels to honour Richard; the children too were splendidly attired and walked beside her in solemn procession. Aoife paced with her head erect, exuding confidence, making herself a focal point. She was steady within her role, because that role was everything, and every part of her was involved in making it an impenetrable shield.

Receiving a blessing from Lorcan, she met his gaze proudly, every inch the dignified widow and countess. She was determined to prevent Basilia from doing anything more to usurp her authority, and thus far she was holding her own. Basilia had been giving her worried glances – an indicator that she still had influence. Osbert de Horlotera had no authority to destroy Richard's seal – that had to come from the King – but Basilia had been put on fair warning that if it was used, he would know the source.

Richard's body was borne down to the crypt beneath the church and Aoife accompanied it, leaving the children with their nurses. Pools of grainy golden candle light illuminated the low barrel arches, the flames painting tall shadows on the walls as she passed. Richard would rest here while a fitting stone tomb was carved for him. Gazing at the sealed lead coffin, knowing what lay within, her chest tightened and she had to choke back her tears. This was the finality. She had to leave him here in the candle light, and eventually in darkness. Kneeling before the coffin, she touched its side, knowing his mortal shell was a fraction from her fingertips. His soul, she hoped and prayed, was soaring above.

'I will do my best for you, my love,' she whispered. 'Your children's inheritance is safe with me, but why couldn't you have stayed? Dear God, Richard, why couldn't you have stayed?'

Abruptly she rose to her feet before the circling anger and grief surged in to overwhelm her. *Stay strong. Do not let the water wear away the rock.* She crossed herself. 'I will see you again,' she said, and turned away. Gripping her prayer beads so hard that they left circular imprints in her palm, she walked through a vaulted avenue of shadows and light and returned to the church where her children waited, sheltered in the wings of Lorcan's cloak.

43

Dublin, Ireland, spring 1176

Basilia was in the hall overseeing the servants when Raymond returned. Watching him stride towards her, his cloak flaring behind him, a surge of utter relief swept over her. She had held out in increasingly fraught and difficult circumstances, but now all would be well.

She ran to him as she had never run to him in public before and flung herself into his arms. 'You received my message!' She gripped his hard biceps and felt safe.

'Yes,' he said, his expression intent. 'All of it.'

Tears of relief filled her eyes that she no longer had to shoulder the burden alone. 'I have been so worried for you. You have no idea what has been happening.'

He rubbed her back. 'I am here now.' He cast an assessing glance around the hall as his men filled it, their mail sparking in the window light. 'You have stood firm and resolute, and that is all you needed to do. Go and take some rest.'

She shook her head. 'I cannot.'

'I mean it. Leave everything to me. I will come to you in a while, I promise.' He kissed her in reassurance.

Basilia was still reluctant, but did as he asked; in truth she was exhausted and to have a moment of respite was more precious than gold. She went to her chamber, but instead of lying down, sank to her knees before her small prayer table, and clasping her hands together before the little statue of the Virgin she exhorted God to hear her plea. Raymond deserved to rule in

Richard's stead, not to be passed over as no more than a useful soldier and underling. He would be the perfect guardian of Leinster for her little niece and nephew rather than their scheming Irish mother.

Her love for Raymond, battled against for so long, was like a garden coming to full bloom from long dormant seeds. She tended it diligently, and a part of her nurture was ambition. She would have the world know what a great man Raymond truly was and they would both have their just dues. She fell asleep in mid-prayer, on the floor, and only roused when Raymond arrived from his business.

'I don't know why you want to sleep there when there's a perfectly good bed behind you,' he said with amusement as he threw off his cloak and sat down on a bench.

She sat up, dry-mouthed, bleary-eyed. 'I was praying.' She rose to her feet, self-consciously smoothing her gown. 'For you.'

'Then let us hope God is listening to you and not our sister by marriage.'

'What did the King's men say?'

'They are leaving tomorrow for England. The wind is set fair.'

'But you are not going with them?' She tried to keep the anxiety from her voice.

He shook his head. 'They need me here. I am charged with keeping everything stable until the King decides what is to be done. I hope I have persuaded them that the accusations against me were caused by rivalry and envy.'

'As indeed they were,' Basilia said indignantly. 'We must impress on them that you are the only one who can provide stability – the military backbone.'

He gave a humourless smile. 'Indeed. My Brabançons were a problem a week ago. Now it appears they are a necessity. Richard himself taught me that men and especially kings are fickle and ungrateful.'

Awake now, she joined him on the bench.

'It is our duty to take care of Aoife,' he said.

Basilia stiffened. As far as she was concerned, Aoife was a viper. But then she wondered just what he meant by 'take care of' and gave him a sharp look.

'We must preserve the lands intact if we are to have authority over them,' he said. 'They could easily splinter and disintegrate. Aoife and those children are the glue holding them together.'

'She is like a serpent feeding young serpents,' Basilia said with revulsion. 'She causes disruption in the hall and she is dangerous. Let her go to England and live on her dower lands. Who knows what she might incite if she remains.'

'Perhaps,' he said, shrugging. 'But we have her under our control while she stays, and she may prove useful.'

'We did not miss her when she was gone before,' Basilia argued. 'She must go to England anyway, to do homage for her estates. We should be the caretakers here in her absence and mould Leinster as we see fit.'

Raymond looked at her keenly.

'It is my due,' she said, 'for all the years I toiled on Richard's behalf without acknowledgement. It is my due for being undermined and insulted by that conniving child wife of his. It is my due for—'

'For being forced to marry beneath you to a man you did not want.'

Basilia gasped, feeling a lurch of physical pain. 'Duty,' she said. 'Yes, I am sick of being a pawn. I was a pawn when I married you, but I have fought to the end of the chess board and I have changed my form and become a queen. And that is because of you. Aoife now is the pawn who was a queen and all is still to play for.'

'I wanted you from the day I first came to Striguil,' Raymond said, brushing her cheek. 'And I waited for a long, long time. You are my queen. I always saw that in you and thought they were fools to take you for granted. You rejected me, but I persevered. I see things through to the end, whatever that end may be, bitter or sweet, life or death. Always.'

She took his face in her hands and kissed him fiercely, and he picked her up. Joined as one, they moved from bench to bed. Basilia allowed the storm to seize her and it was a blissful relief to let go with him and be so overwhelmed that she was absorbed in the tumult and taken to oblivion.

She returned to herself by gradual degrees, becoming aware of his weight on her, and his harsh breathing. She pushed at him and he rolled onto his side, and she filled her lungs. 'Aoife,' she said after a moment, and leaned over to pluck at his chest hair.

'I will speak to her,' Raymond replied sleepily, drugged with satiation.

'Do not let her run rings round you. I know her ways with men. She besotted my foolish brother.'

'Do not worry, my love,' he said, tugging a strand of her hair. 'She has no power over anything now. I will decide what is to be done and she will do as I say.'

Aoife was reading a letter that had arrived from Ralf Bluet, Constable of Striguil, when Basilia swept into her chamber unannounced. 'You are wanted in the hall if you would come for a moment to greet our guests,' she said.

Aoife eyed her in sudden unease. Henry's advisers had left at dawn and she had been tense ever since bidding them farewell.

'Guests?' she said. 'I did not know there were guests.'

'You will want to see them I think.'

Aoife shook her head. 'I am not ready to greet anyone. I am not dressed for such an occasion. Who are they?'

Basilia sidestepped a direct reply, and said in a cajoling voice, 'They will understand you are in mourning. Come, they are waiting for you.'

Feeling disconcerted, Aoife adjusted her veil and smoothed her gown. When the children started to follow her, she bade them stay behind with Deirdre. 'I shall not be long,' she said and gave Deirdre a meaningful look before following Basilia from the room. Basilia walked so swiftly, Aoife had to almost run to keep up with her.

Arriving at the hall, Aoife stopped abruptly for every bench was occupied by Raymond's Brabançons. As she entered with Basilia, a rousing cheer echoed to the rafters and their fierce eyes burned into her. She could smell them, a meaty aroma of blood and battle and ferocity. It was like the time her father had staked the heads of his enemies around the hall and called them his guests. The air held the same savagery and she knew she was among predators not allies.

Basilia grasped Aoife's hand in hers and yanked their arms into the air, responding to the cheers, before dragging her to the dais, where Raymond was waiting, clad in a fur-lined robe of blue silk. He raised one hand, calling for silence, but it was Basilia who turned and spoke as she reached her seat.

'We are gathered to celebrate and honour the bravery of your former leader, my brother, and the Countess's lord and husband Richard de Clare, Earl of Striguil. You are our strength; you keep us whole, and as women of the family we rely on your valour to protect us. We honour you with our food and drink and our hospitality.' She turned to Raymond with shining eyes.

He rose to his feet and the men pounded the tables. Raymond raised his cup to them and called for silence. 'As my lady wife says, we are indebted to you for your service, for which you will be amply rewarded. My lord's untimely passing means we must stay vigilant and keep our sword arms strong. I know I can rely on your loyalty and goodwill, just as you know you can rely on me as your commander to provide for you always with generosity and largesse. Let the feast commence!'

Aoife stared round as servants began bringing in mounded dishes of meat, fish, bread and delicacies. She knew Richard would never have sanctioned all this. It was a profligate waste of supplies. No one had sought her authorisation; this was Basilia's doing. Aoife wondered where this was leading and what was happening behind her back. These men were being shown who to support and who had the authority, and it was like sitting at a feast of wolves.

The food was blessed by a chaplain with whom she was unfamiliar and she could not stomach any of it. As the men settled to eating with gusto, she drank a cup of wine and picked at the fish portion on her trencher.

'I must return to my children,' she said to Basilia, feeling nauseous and afraid.

'Oh, that is a pity,' Basilia said. 'I had hoped you would stay longer since this feast is in your honour too.'

Aoife numbly shook her head thinking it was a travesty of honour. 'I cannot. I am sure you understand.'

'Of course,' Basilia said with smiling sympathy.

As Aoife rose, a signal from Raymond brought the soldiers to their feet as one, almost terrifying her out of her skin. They roared and banged their knife hilts on the tables as she left the hall, and she was intimidated by the salute for it expressed their power and of what they were capable given the slightest order.

Basilia smiled at Raymond who set his hand over hers and squeezed. No one could say they had not acknowledged Aoife.

Once in her chamber, Aoife shot the draw bar and leaned against the door, panting with fear. So many of her family had died in ambitious power struggles, and she was terrified that she and her children were going to be the next victims. She could do nothing to protect them if the knife came in the dark. This was what it was to be powerless. Basilia had established herself as lady of the castle and with Raymond's return, Aoife was at her mercy, just as Basilia had once been at hers.

When her trembling had lessened, she went to sit before the embers in the hearth, rubbing her thumb back and forth over her wedding ring. She hoped desperately that the letter she had written to Henry had reached him, but even so, she did not know what effect it would have. Her vision filled with an image of Raymond's Brabançon mercenaries sitting at the trestles in her hall. Hard-eyed predators. Kites picking at the corpse. Perhaps it was already too late. There were so many factions out for what they could gain. She was walking a knife edge and one slip could be the end for her and her children.

Going to Richard's coffer, she removed his hunting knife, unsheathed it, stared at the mirror-bright edge and then bit her lip, for what use was a single blade against so many? Or she could use it on the few and end it here and now. Another image filled her mind – the mercenary woman Alice of Abergavenny and her mad, wild eyes. God forbid she became like her.

A knock on the door made her start and catch her breath. She sheathed the knife but pushed the scabbard through her belt, and making sure the bed curtains were closed on the children, she went to the door.

'Who is it?'

The knock came again. 'It is Raymond. I need to speak with you.'

Aoife swallowed and touched the dagger sheath. She could turn him away but he could easily have the door broken down. The knock was just paying lip service to courtesy. Taking a deep breath, she drew the bar.

He walked confidently into her chamber, still in his blue silk robe from the feast, silvered at the cuffs with Basilia's embroidery. He was handsome, broad-shouldered and swaggering. His breath smelled of wine, and while not drunk, neither was he sober, and she knew what happened when he was in his cups.

'I wanted to pay my respects in private and have a talk with you, sister,' he said, wrapping his big hands around his belt. Tonight, they were adorned by rings. 'I am sorry for your grief. It was indeed terrible news to receive – so unexpected.'

But fortunate for Raymond, she thought, making a noncommittal sound.

He cleared his throat. 'You have done so well in the midst of tragedy. Now I am here with my men, you will be wanting to go on progress around Richard's estates. I can assure you Leinster will be secure in my hands during your absence.'

She pressed her fingernails into her palms at his patronising words. He was addressing her like a child, but for her survival she had to play to his expectation instead of slapping him down. He could easily arrange to have her murdered. If he wanted her to leave, it was not as bad as she thought. Unless this was a ruse and he intended to have her killed somewhere beyond his jurisdiction where his hands would show no blood.

'Basilia will help you prepare. Whatever you desire, name it, and it shall be yours.'

But it all belonged to her anyway and Basilia had no right. She bit back excoriating words. He thought he was controlling the situation and she must let him continue in that belief until she was free and clear.

'Indeed, I was intending to go on progress to Richard's lands imminently. Be assured I will ask Basilia if I have need.' Hell would freeze over first.

He sat down on the hearth bench, spreading his arms along the back and crossing his legs, showing every sign of settling in. She saw his glance flick with hard amusement to the knife through her belt.

'You are a fine woman, Aoife,' he said affably. 'What will you do with your life now? As your brother by marriage I can find you a lusty man in my entourage or one of your own Irish lords who would do you justice if you decide to wed again.'

Horror and disgust sparked inside her, but she kept it from showing on her face even though she wanted to retch. A latent air of violence hung about him. He cared nothing for her. If she left Ireland he would have a free hand to be a warlord as he

445

chose. If she stayed, he would wed her to one of his allies to further his cause. Either way, his benefit would be her detriment.

'I could not think about marrying again just now,' she said, and dabbed her sleeve at her eyes. 'For sure it is too soon, but I will see when I come back to Ireland later.'

Raymond pursed his lips. 'You could do far worse you know.' He gave her a meaningful look. 'You will be safer inside the family than outside. Who knows what might happen?'

Her stomach felt as if it was full of stones. 'I am sure you are right, and I will wait on your wise judgement when that time comes,' she said demurely, 'but I need to grieve in my own way and you have to be man enough to allow me to do that, Raymond. I count you a dear brother-in-law and I know your thoughts are for my welfare but for now I must have time to heal my wounds, and so must the children. I have to take charge of my dower lands and accede to the King's wishes.' She gave him a drenched look and with a tingle of relief saw his expression change and soften.

He rose to his feet, and taking her hand, patted it. 'We will look after you, I promise.'

She smiled gratefully, putting on him the onus of honourable brother-in-law, encouraging him to inhabit that role. 'That is comforting to know.'

He cleared his throat and his complexion reddened beyond the wine flush. 'I shall leave you then. Think on what I have said.'

Once he had lumbered from the room, Aoife collapsed on the bench, weak with relief at having successfully negotiated the knife edge. She was still not safe even now but she had done her best, appealing to Raymond's higher nature. However, there was no one to hold him in that state. Basilia would egg him on, not leash him, and he was an executioner by trade. She was playing for her life, for her children's lives, and the game was not yet won.

*　　*　　*

'I am going to England,' Aoife said to Lorcan, who was sitting in the window embrasure of his chamber at the cathedral, reading a letter. 'It was Richard's dying wish I do so and I must swear to the King for my dower lands and arrange their wardship.'

Lorcan set the letter aside and regarded her shrewdly. 'Richard spoke of this to me before he died,' he said. 'Even if we did not always see eye to eye, we were agreed on the matter. I can only shield you so far and there will be contention between the Irish and the newcomers. If you stay, you will become a morsel to be torn apart between them and devoured.'

'Raymond has already hinted strongly about that,' Aoife said grimly. 'He seems to think he has the right to marry me off at his will.'

Lorcan's nostrils flared with disgust. 'I am not surprised. He would try and use you for his own ends, although he would never succeed. I would excommunicate him first.'

'Thank you,' she said. 'I know I can rely on you, but I intend to avoid him if I can.'

'You are wise to do so, my dear. I shall do everything in my power to help you.' His eyes softened. 'This has been hard on you,' he added with compassion.

She shivered. To go within herself was too painful. 'I will do well enough. I dare not stay here for the moment. I know the fickle ways of kings but King Henry is my succour and the best chance my children have.'

Lorcan nodded, but his expression was sombre. 'Do not become so enamoured by England that you forget your home, Aoife. Always remember where you were born; you are a princess of Ireland, forged by your father's hand. Your children are of this land. Do not become so blinded by your English wealth that you forget your country. It will always be waiting for you.' He gave her a tender, sad smile. 'Go with my blessing, niece.'

'You advise me well, uncle. I swear I will keep my links to my ancestors strong wherever I may be.' She kissed his ring and impulsively flung her arms around his neck, hugging him fiercely as she had done when she was a child.

'Peace be with you, niece.' He returned her embrace with a gentle squeeze. 'May God go with you and guide your path.'

Three days later, Aoife stood on the wharf side ready to embark. A Bristol galley rode at anchor, all her goods and baggage stowed aboard. She wore her court gown again, and her cloak was fastened with the gold hound brooch. She was every inch a countess and Irish royalty.

Taking a deep breath, Aoife raised her voice and addressed the gathering. 'It grieves me to leave you, my kinfolk, but you dwell in my heart. I have duties to my husband's estate and I must fulfil them in England. I will think of you often while I am gone and I will return to you, as will my children, bearing gifts which you shall deserve for your loyalty. Your love and honour will be a flame in my heart and give me courage in what I must do. Until I return, may that day be not too long in coming, I bid you farewell.'

'Think well on what I have said, sister,' Raymond said, stepping forward to give her the kiss of peace and hand her onto the ship.

'And I shall pray for you,' Basilia said. 'And for my brother's soul.'

Aoife suppressed a shudder and thought that Richard must be turning in his grave, but she smiled and murmured platitudes in reply. Yesterday she had visited Richard's sealed lead coffin in the crypt at Holy Trinity; had put her hand on it and promised him she would preserve their lands for their children and their children's children whatever she must do. Leaving him behind made her heart bleed, but she bore the wound in hope for the future – for their children's future. It was an end, but it was a beginning too.

As the ship cast its moorings and the wind filled the sails, the water, reflecting the sky, was harebell-blue. Setting her arms around Isabelle and Gilbert, Aoife watched Dublin and the coast of Ireland recede before turning her gaze to the open sea. Above her head the first swallows of spring were darting over the shoreline.

44

Clarendon Palace near Salisbury, Wiltshire, June 1176

Arriving at Henry's palace at Clarendon with her entourage, Aoife was admitted through the gates into a large compound of timbered buildings gleaming with limewash. She encountered Henry immediately for he was standing in the courtyard newly returned from the hunt. He was mud-spattered, blood-flecked, and wearing the cheerful expression that indicated a successful day churning through the woods on a fast courser in pursuit of prey.

Hands on hips, he observed her arrival, while an ear-to-ear grin spread across his freckled face. He waded clear of the morass of hunting dogs and helped her dismount. 'Here is a sight to gladden my eyes!' he cried. 'Welcome, Countess, welcome indeed!'

She knelt to him, still holding his hand, feeling his sweat and the calluses on his palms like rough bark. He raised her to her feet and kissed her cheeks and she inhaled the salty smell of his hard-worked body.

'Thank you, sire, you gladden my eyes also.'

She had only travelled a short distance today riding side-seat and wearing fine clothes. A countess worthy of respect and recognition. She would not arrive at Henry's door looking like a downtrodden widow. She had sent word ahead yesterday that she was visiting in person, not sending a representative.

'I doubt that.' He gestured at his hunt-smirched tunic and,

stepping back, turned to speak to an attendant to ensure that a chamber had been made ready for Aoife.

'I have brought you gifts from Ireland.' She indicated a pair of large wire-haired hounds with red leather collars, and four fierce birds of prey in cages. 'My father's dogs and hawks from my forests.' She put slight emphasis on the words of personal possession. 'I was going to present them to you formally, but you can see them in the open here first – and you are fittingly garbed,' she added with a mischievous smile.

'Hah!' Exclaiming with delight, he went to examine her gifts, stroking the dogs, peering in the cages. 'You have an eye for a fine animal, Countess!'

'Yes, I do. Always the finest of the fine.' The comment was light, but it held shadows too, and Henry felt them, for he straightened from patting a dog's flank.

'I am sorry,' he said. 'Deeply sorry. The Earl of Striguil's loss has caused me great concern and sadness.'

'Yes,' she said, holding herself regally, her expression smooth. 'And his loss is why I am here.'

'Then I shall speak with you later at an appropriate moment.' He held her gaze for an instant before looking over his shoulder and signalling to a waiting courtier that he was coming.

They parted company, and the dogs and hawks were taken to the kennels and mews. Aoife was escorted to her prepared chamber, and as she entered the room was poignantly reminded of her first visit to the court at Saumur. How much had changed since then, although deep inside, the same frightened child peered out from behind the curtains.

The white walls filled the space with airy light, enhanced by a delicate frieze of flowers and scrolled greenery. Red tiles with gold designs of deer and hare adorned the floor and ripples of heat flowed from a brazier in the centre of the room, curled with trails of resinous perfume.

While her servants set up her bed and unpacked her baggage,

Aoife washed in a bowl of warm scented rose water and changed her fine travelling gown for the one of jewelled red silk she had worn as a statement when she left Dublin. Fastening Richard's ruby and gold chain around her neck, she went to look out of the window, marvelling at the size of the Clarendon complex, built for pleasure, for entertainment, for gatherings, and realised anew just how much wealth and power Henry had at his command.

She had not entirely let down her guard in England, but she was much less tense, no longer constantly looking over her shoulder, waiting for the knife to strike. From Bristol she had taken the children to Striguil and immersed herself in thoughts of Richard dwelling there as a boy, a youth and young man, and she had envisaged herself as part of it; his wife, not his widow. It had cut her open, scarred her, healed her. She had visited the abbey at Tintern and standing before the tombs of his ancestors had prayed for his soul. He should have lain with them, but Ireland had claimed his mortal remains. She had vowed that Tintern would have hers in exchange should she die here instead of Ireland.

After Striguil, she had gone to Goodrich and enjoyed the smaller keep overlooking the Wye. Indeed, she was considering returning there when she had completed her tasks. She still had to visit Richard's manors in Kent and Essex, but first she had to deal with Henry and submit to him while holding him to his responsibilities.

Henry's chamber bustled with servants, scribes, officials and barons going about their business, but the room had quieter areas and Henry, still full of vigour after a day's hunting, led Aoife to an embrasure with instructions they were not to be disturbed. A servant brought wine and a dish of dried fruit before bowing out of earshot, and their meeting became a private moment in the midst of a public space.

Henry took Aoife's hand. 'Ah, the ring,' he said almost wryly.

She smiled at him. 'I am very fond of it, sire, and the friendship it represents.'

He gave her a shrewd look. 'I will say again that I was grieved to hear of Richard's death. We had our differences, but I came to trust him – he will not easily be replaced.'

'He can never be replaced,' Aoife said, looking down.

Henry patted her hand. 'It would be a disaster for us both if that were the case.'

Immediately she lifted her head.

'That is the Aoife I know,' Henry said with a smile in his voice. 'You must grieve, and I must have regret, but someone has to administer your son's inheritance until he comes of age and your dower estates must be managed to give you security.'

'Richard and I talked about it before the wound fever grew too great,' she said.

Henry arched his brows. 'Indeed?' He looked amused but his eyes were hard.

She clasped her hands together, ensuring the ring was prominent. They were like players locked in a game of chess, save this particular game was for her children's future. She had to walk a fine line between the grieving widow and the proud countess. Obedient to Henry's will but standing her ground and not subservient.

'You received my letter?' she said.

He indicated a sheaf of parchments piled near the flagon. 'Yes. William FitzAudelin is on his way to take charge of the Leinster estates under my instruction.'

Aoife regarded him with an uncomfortable mingling of relief and tension. 'Thank you,' she said. 'I did not know which way to turn – except to you and hope you would heed my petition.' It could be much worse, she thought. FitzAudelin was an honourable royal servant who would follow Henry's bidding to the letter.

Henry snorted. 'Why would I not? I am your overlord, and your daughter is my daughter too, and your son my vassal.'

'But words are not always deeds.'

He said nothing, and she saw the tension in him, the need to rise and begin pacing. But he mastered the impulse and leaned back, crossing his legs. 'Tell me to my face and beyond the words of your scribe what has been happening.'

She looked him in the eyes. 'Richard valued Raymond le Gros for his military skills. I do not deny he is a fine soldier whom Richard and I trusted perhaps more than we should. As my brother by marriage and with the support of Richard's sister he has taken self-appointed responsibility for Leinster – which of course he will now have to relinquish to FitzAudelin.'

Henry pursed his lips and narrowed his eyes. Someone approached to ask him a question and he waved them away.

'Raymond said he would find me a new husband from among his men, or the Irish, but I am in deep mourning for Richard and he had no right or standing to moot such a thing. My children are grieving the loss of their father. They have no need of a stepfather, especially one forced on them by Raymond le Gros.' A note of contempt entered her voice. 'I am sensible of his "kind" offer but I cannot comply with his wishes, and I am sure you will agree.'

Henry's complexion darkened with anger. 'He has overstepped his bounds considerably. You are right that a firm hand is needed, but it will be at my command and no other's. Your husband was my viceroy in Ireland and I shall say who follows him.' He gave her a pointed look. 'Your children are now my wards – you know I must appoint a guardian.'

She returned his stare with fierce intent. 'They have lost their father. I hope you are not going to separate them from their mother too.'

'I would not do that to you or them, but they have to be kept safe.'

'Of course, and that is my first priority. When I was a little girl, I remember my father returning from war with the heads of his enemies tied to his horse's harness by their hair. I saw captured women abused and raped. I saw my brothers blinded and butchered. I have observed men wild with battle rage, their hands red to the elbows. I helped my father burn down our home as we fled our enemies and I thought I would die at any moment.' Her voice shook. 'For God's love, I do not want my children to endure what I endured. I want them raised in peace and safety without worrying that each dawn will be their last. I never had that. I want my son and my daughter to grow up in peace – to know what peace is. If it means having a guardian for all of us, so be it. But let it be someone with balance and wisdom, not a man whose sword is red to the hilt with blood.' Thinking of Raymond, she shivered.

'You speak eloquently, Aoife,' he said, and his voice was husky.

'I want to stay with my children and teach them their heritage. I want them to know who they are and to value themselves as I value myself as the Countess of Hibernia and dowager Countess of the Earl of Striguil. I am asking you not to sell me in marriage to reward one of your lords for political gain. I will grieve long for Richard and my time will be taken up in the stewardship of my dower lands and caring for Gilbert and Isabelle – even with a protector.' She gave him a supplicating look, but it was not soft, for she knew Henry well.

He smiled wryly. 'I had forgotten how passionate and strong-willed you are – and determined to have your own way.'

'But for the good of all. I will raise my children to be your loyal supporters if you in turn support us. If the lands are well managed, it will profit everyone. I only ask you to honour our bargain.'

He gestured. 'Let us come to it then. What is it you want of me, Aoife? Tell me and let us see what might be accommodated.' He took a drink of his wine and when she hesitated said, 'It is good, I promise you.'

'Then I must hope in all things you keep your promises.' Her memories of Henry's wine were less than positive. However, taking a cautious sip, she found it acceptable for once, and hoped it was an auspicious omen. 'I ask for three things as a vassal, and a friend, and to honour that which I gave you in Ireland.'

He lifted his brows to show he was listening, but his expression gave nothing away.

'Your law says a woman should not have the custody of her children because she will remarry and bear other offspring who will then fight over the land, but I beg you not to take my children from me. I am their mother, and they are still little more than babies. They need me. I do not ever want to remarry and I ask you to honour that wish. Even should I finish grieving, I shall never take a husband for I would not imperil my children's inheritance. If I must have a protector, let it be you. You are Isabelle's godfather after all. I need people of military and administrative ability to deal with the estates as Richard would have done, but I am requesting you not to appoint Raymond le Gros and to leave the children with me as a right of nurture.'

Henry gave her a calculating look. 'Very well,' he said. 'I agree that you shall not be separated from your children – at least for now, although subject to change as they grow. We are indeed friends. As you have worked on my behalf, so I will work on yours. In the fullness of time should a marriage come along that is beneficial to all parties, we can and will discuss the terms again – that is not negotiable.'

'And Raymond le Gros and my sister by marriage?'

Henry rubbed his chin. 'They shall not be granted custody of you or your children, nor of Leinster, I promise you, but he is a useful soldier and if I have need of him I will use him in that capacity. I will muzzle his jaws and keep him leashed. I promise.'

Aoife nodded her head as if accepting. She would do battle again and again if necessary. 'I am grateful, sire, and relieved.'

Henry had taken the time to give her a private audience and he need not have done. He had not ridden roughshod over her concerns but had accommodated them – for now. He knew she was not going to bite the hand that fed her, and therefore he trusted her – more than she trusted him.

'Where will you go now?'

'To Richard's estates in England and Normandy, and then perhaps to Goodrich or Striguil, or one of the English manors. As long as we have peace.'

'Then I wish you well.'

She stood to leave, and Henry kissed her on either cheek and then warmly and lingeringly on the lips. 'What could have been,' he said.

She returned him a dazzling smile but with sadness at the edges. 'Yes,' she said. 'What could have been.' But she was thinking beyond Henry, to all the hopes and dreams sealed in a coffin in Holy Trinity Dublin. That was the past, she reminded herself firmly, and tomorrow was the future.

The Wye valley was steeped in the golden haze of a late September morning as Aoife returned to Striguil from a summer spent visiting the manors and holdings of the vast de Clare estates. The woods were tressed in auburn and gold with the last glimmerings of green like a hazel eye. The air smelled of woodsmoke and beech-mast but was still warm enough to be pleasant.

It had been good to hear her children's chatter, to watch them play without fear, and to have time for reflection. Ireland with all its bloody strife seemed a world away. Henry had done as he promised. Raymond's ambitions had been checked and William FitzAudelin and John de Courcy were administering the estates in Gilbert's minority. Aoife knew they would skim the cream off the top for Henry's coffers, but there were far worse men Henry might have appointed. She had custody of her children and her various estates to support her. Henry being Henry, he would try to inveigle her into a new marriage, but she knew she could easily persuade him otherwise.

Gazing at Striguil, perched on its high cliffs above the river, she was coming home to Richard; to the place where it had begun. It still felt like a beginning even now. Against the sharp blue sky, she watched a peregrine falcon fly out from the rugged silver-grey cliffs and her heart soared with the bird. She would survive as she had always done.

Author's Note

My novel projects are always chosen from my curiosity to find out more about my subject. I will encounter an interesting person or a detail from someone's life, and I will want to know more about them. What stories do they have to tell me? What can they tell me that they have never told anyone before? Usually all of this happens while I am working on the previous novel, so I file away those sparks of interest and leave them burning in a quiet hearth at the back of my mind until it is time to begin thinking about my next set of protagonists, and then I will visit my little firesides and watch for pictures in the flames.

I first came across Aoife MacMurchada when I was writing *The Scarlet Lion*, and to me, then, she was very much William Marshal's cantankerous and difficult mother-in-law. However, as I continued to write other novels, I began to wonder how her personality had come to be so impatient and sharp, especially at the interfaces of power between men and women. I had also begun to wonder about her husband. Aoife and Richard were married for just six years, but that marriage was part of one of the great pivot points of history, bringing massive, often brutal change to Ireland, and reshaping boundaries and peoples, creating ripples of effect that continue today.

Usually when I begin trawling through historical details to research my story, I find that what we see on the surface is not always the same as what lies beneath and that there are numerous twists and tangles occurring within the supposedly known history.

It's like having a beach full of pebbles. All the pebbles combine to make a single story (the beach) but each pebble is unique and has its own part to play, and each tide will alter the shape of the beach and create a different story out of the same materials.

My aim in *The Irish Princess* has been to keep the lens on the emotional tale – the thoughts, feelings and coping mechanisms of people who were both very different from and very similar to ourselves.

No one knows Aoife MacMurchada's date of birth, but from the various histories I have read, the most reliable seem to suggest a date of 1151–2 and present Aoife as one of two children born to Diarmait MacMurchada's last wife Môr Ní Tuathail. Aoife had a full brother, Conchobar (Connor), who was indeed beheaded by the High King Ruari ua Conchobar because Diarmait had broken his oath once too often.

We do not know Aoife's death date. The traditional view is that it was somewhere around the time her daughter Isabelle married William Marshal in 1189. This is based on last known charter evidence, but even that is fluid and may date to several years later. Further digging by historian Paul Martin Remfry in his superb work on Goodrich Castle suggests that Aoife may have been alive as late as 1204, living some of the time on her dower manors in Essex and Kent, and some of the time at Goodrich Castle in the interestingly named 'Mac-Mac' Tower – thought to be a corruption of MacMurchada. It is believed from sixteenth-century evidence of a visual of her tomb (now lost following the dissolution of the monasteries) that she is buried at Tintern Abbey, five miles from the de Clare stronghold at Striguil (Chepstow) and sixteen miles from Goodrich. Her daughter Isabelle and several of her grandchildren are buried here too. It is ironic that Richard de Clare lies at rest in Dublin, and Aoife on the Welsh Borders.

Aoife is often confused with a different, shadowy figure from Irish history known as Red Aoife, but the two have nothing in common beyond their Christian names. There is a story too that Aoife's life ended when she was shot through the throat by a crossbow bolt aimed at her by one of the Quinn clan, and was buried at Kilkenny, but the tale is erroneous and easily disproven.

Richard de Clare, born circa 1130, is reported by chronicler Gerald of Wales to have been tall, red-haired, light-eyed and of a pragmatic and steady disposition. In public he was never emotionally extreme, but always a steady rallying point for his men whatever the circumstances. Having fallen on difficult political times and not being on the best of terms with King Henry, he was open to Diarmait MacMurchada's offer of a portion of new territory in Ireland and the hand of Diarmait's daughter in marriage. He has come down to us in history with the nickname of 'Strongbow', a title also borne by his father. Historians have traditionally said this is either because he and his father had a great war bow that only father and son could draw, or because they relied on archers from South Wales to provide their military fire power. However, while researching the novel and again via Paul Martin Remfry, it seems that the title 'Strongbow' is actually a clerical mangling of 'Striguil', the old name for Chepstow. Richard de Clare was never known by that title in his lifetime and neither was his father. I still liked the idea of the bow, so I've given a nod to it in the novel, but I have left the nickname out of the story.

Diarmait himself is an extremely colourful character. Appalling, brutal, ruthless, yet tragic and even heroic. He founded abbeys including St Mary's at Fearns, Baltinglas in Wicklow and Kilculliheen in Waterford. He kept a bard fluent in Anglo-Norman at his side and he appreciated literature and the arts. Often vilified for being the man who brought Norman warlords across the Hibernian Sea, he himself had witnessed the violent death of his father by the men of Dublin when he was just five years old. To add insult to injury, Diarmait's father was buried with a dog as a sign of contempt. I suspect he nursed a lifelong grudge for that. The story of him biting the nose and lips off the head of a defeated enemy comes from his own time. A broken, decorated stump standing in the graveyard of St Mary's Abbey at Fearns is claimed as his grave marker. Much may be made of Diarmait being responsible for the Norman invasion of Ireland – which he was – but at the same time historians point out that in marrying his daughter to Richard de Clare, his bloodline gained vast lands in South and mid Wales, England and Normandy.

At the time that Diarmait was exiled and sought help from Richard de Clare, Aoife was probably about fourteen or fifteen years old, and eighteen or nineteen when she married Richard de Clare. Widowed six years later, she never remarried. This in itself is interesting because she was only in her twenties and would have been a great prize. King Henry II seems to have taken a particular interest in Aoife and I received the impression during my research that they saw eye to eye and were perhaps even friends. Aoife may first have met him as a girl in her mid-teens. Historian Marie Therese Flanagan points out that 'There was little compulsion on Henry to honour the succession to the lordship of Leinster of Strongbow's heirs; yet he chose to recognise Strongbow's wife Aoife, and her two children, Gilbert and Isabelle, as the beneficiaries and heirs of Strongbow.' We do not know if Henry was Isabelle's godfather, but he was in Ireland around the time she was born and I think it very likely given the circumstances. Whatever the situation, Aoife, from her side of the bargain, held everything together for the benefit of future generations.

Aoife's maternal uncle Lorcan, Archbishop of Dublin, is also known as St Laurence O'Toole and his embalmed heart is kept at Christchurch Cathedral in Dublin. As an aside, the relic was stolen in 2012, but has recently been recovered and restored to its rightful place.

The character known as Alice of Abergavenny may or may not have existed. She turns up in an Anglo-Norman poem titled

'The Song of Dermot and the Earl' which tells the story of the invasion of Ireland by the men Diarmait invited over to help him regain his lands. She supposedly killed all seventy of the Hiberno-Norse prisoners at Dun Domhnall with an axe while in mad grief for the death of her own man. I thought that while not true in its entirety, there might be a kernel of truth in the story.

We know very little about Basilia, Richard de Clare's sister, but the moments that do emerge show her as both a pawn and a woman of strong will. Raymond le Gros did indeed request her hand in marriage and having been refused in no uncertain terms, absented himself from Richard's household. When Richard found himself in desperate straits, he asked Raymond to return and offered him Basilia's hand in marriage as an inducement. As soon as Richard was dead, Basilia sent a coded message to Raymond – reported in translation in the novel – which makes it very clear that she considered the death of her brother to be good news but was concerned that there was danger ahead. It interested me, the novelist, to look at the path that led to Basilia's actions and the dynamic between her and Aoife.

Raymond had been summoned to answer to the King for throwing his weight around and acting beyond his authority in Ireland during Richard's absence in England. However, that summons was dropped when Richard died. For a brief period, Raymond took on the authority for Richard's lands in Ireland, but it was swiftly removed from him once Henry's agents William FitzAudelin and John de Courcy arrived to take over the administration. Raymond, although deprived of the top ranking power, was retained in a military capacity, like a ferocious guard dog, and continued to work under the leash and muzzle for Henry's regime. He died some time in the mid to late 1180s and is possibly buried at the Abbey of Molana. Basilia, his widow, was to marry again, to one of William Marshal's knights, Geoffrey FitzRobert – probably to give the latter prestige and family affinity.

She was certainly well beyond child-bearing age at this stage and much older than her bridegroom. What Basilia thought about it is not recorded. The decision, however, must have had the sanction of Isabelle de Clare, and if Aoife was still alive, as Paul Martin Remfry suggests, then perhaps she had a say in it too.

Hervey de Montmorency retired into monastic life at Canterbury within three years of Richard's death and it is thought that chronicler Gervase of Canterbury gleaned some of his information on Ireland from Hervey's eyewitness accounts.

Bibliography

Here is a list of research works I found useful. Some, even while being excellent in places, needed large pinches of salt in others and the accuracy was not always spot on. The biography of Diarmait MacMurchada, for example, cites Richard de Clare as being twenty years older than he actually was and emphasises the detail several times, but on its core subject, Diarmait, is generally good. Gerald of Wales is very pro members of his own family and less enthusiastic about the de Clares but gives a colourful overview. He should also be regarded as biased in his treatment of the native Irish.

Barnard, Francis Pierrepont, *Strongbow's Conquest of Ireland* (G. P. Putnam's Sons, 1888)

Davies, R. R., *Domination and Conquest: The experience of Ireland, Scotland and Wales 1100-1300* (Cambridge University Press, 1990)

Davis, Paul R., *Three Chevrons Red: The Clares: A Marcher Dynasty in Wales, England and Ireland* (Logaston Press, 2013), ISBN 9781906663803

Dooley, Ann and Roe, Harry, *Tales of the Elders of Ireland: A new translation of Acallam na Senórach* (Oxford World's Classics)

Eyton, the Rev. R.W., *Court, Household and Itinerary of King Henry II* (Taylor & Co., 1878)

Flanagan, Marie Therese, *Irish Society, Anglo Norman Settlers, Angevin Kingship: Interactions in Ireland in the late 12th century* (Clarendon Press, Oxford, 1989), ISBN 9780198221548

Furlong, Nicholas, *Diarmait King of Leinster* (Mercier, 2006), ISBN 9781856355056

Gerald of Wales, *The History and Topography of Ireland* (Penguin History, 1982), ISBN 9780140444230

Kostick, Conor, *Strongbow: The Norman Invasion of Ireland* (O'Brien, 2013), ISBN 9781847172006

Orpen, Goddard Henry, *The Song of Dermot and the Earl: from the Carew Manuscript number 596 in the Archiepiscopal library at Lambeth Palace* (Clarendon Press, Oxford, 1892)

Remfry, Paul Martin, *Goodrich Castle and the families of Godric Mapson, Monmouth, Clare, Marshall, Montchesney, Valence, Despenser and Talbot* (Castle Studies Research and Publishing, 2015), ISBN 9781899376926

Roche, Richard, *The Norman Invasion of Ireland* (Anvil, 1995), ISBN 9780947962814.

Acknowledgements

While I am solely responsible for what emerges in print, I have a wonderful life raft of support and friendship that keeps me afloat and writing, and enriches my life.

I would like to thank my terrific agent Isobel Dixon and all the team at the Blake Friedmann agency, whose hard work keeps me solvent in often precarious times and who are always there for me. I couldn't ask for better. On the publishing front I also want to thank my fantastic, perceptive editor Viola Hayden whose comments during the writing process were a great help. Thank you also to Cath Burke for putting us together, and thank you also to the whole team at Sphere for their input in the process, especially Thalia Proctor for her unsung role behind the scenes in moving thing forward. My gratitude must also be paid (fervently) to Dan Balado-Lopez for his keen editorial eye at the interim stage and his ability to spot loose ends from earlier drafts that have flown under my own radar. Any mistakes that remain are totally mine.

I owe a big thank you to my dear friend Alison King. Without her extraordinary talent to time travel, *The Irish Princess* would have been a very different work indeed. May we set the world to rights over coffee for many more years to come.

My thanks to the members of my online community, many of whom have become dear friends and who keep life 'normal' during coffee and tea breaks. It would take several pages to name you all, and I'd be sure to leave someone out – but you know who you are, and that I appreciate and thank you. Xx

Thank you to my husband, Roger, for his continuing support. For readers who follow my acknowledgement notes, it should be noted that he no longer irons – but that is because we have now installed a tumble drier. However, he is still bringing me mugs of tea, essential for writerly survival, and he keeps me sane and grounded, so he's definitely my hero!

Publishing in August 2020

THE COMING OF THE WOLF

the long-awaited prequel to
Elizabeth Chadwick's
bestselling and beloved first novel,

The Wild Hunt

'An author who makes history come
gloriously alive'
The Times